YOU KNOW YOU ARE *DYING FOR IT*, WHEN . . .

You mainline the ashes of the girl you loved
Your multiple personalities treat you to an orgy
Your lover "lives" in a formaldehyde tank
Medieval torture turns you on
You marry a ghost
You have a love affair with your own dead twin
You buy a haunted house for the bedroom
You can only get it up on a ship that's going down
You build your own mermaid from a corpse

A gourmet collection of necromantic erotica
by today's most compelling authors

Edited by Gardner Dozois

Killing Me Softly: Erotic Tales of Unearthly Love
Dying For It: More Erotic Tales of Unearthly Love

Published by HarperPrism

DYING FOR IT

More Erotic Tales of Unearthly Love

Edited by

Gardner Dozois

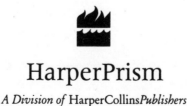

HarperPrism

A Division of HarperCollins*Publishers*

HarperPrism
A Division of HarperCollins*Publishers*
10 East 53rd Street, New York, N.Y. 10022-5299

This is a work of fiction. The characters, incidents, and dialogues are products of the authors' imagination and are not to be construed as real. Any resemblance to actual events or persons, living or dead, is entirely coincidental.

Cover photographs: Jake Rajs\Photonica and Tatsuya Morita\Photonica

Printed in the United States of America

ISBN 1-56865-585-1

Acknowledgments

The editor would like to thank the following people for their help and support:

Susan Casper, who provided technical support and computer expertise; Virginia Kidd; Vaughn Hensen; Sharah Thomas; Ellen Datlow; George Scithers; Darrell Schweitzer; Jack Dann; Janeen Webb; Pati Nagle; Mary Rosenblum; Michael Swanwick; Andy Duncan; Tony Daniel; L. Timmel Duchamp; Pat Cadigan; Chris Fowler; Michael Bishop; Ian R. MacLeod; Mike Resnick; Kristine Kathryn Rusch; Robert Reed; Nancy Kress; Steven Utley; Tanith Lee; Madeleine E. Robins; Esther M. Friesner; M. Shayne Bell; K. D. Wentworth; Robert Silverberg; and special thanks to my own editor, John Silbersack.

Contents

DYING FOR IT

More Erotic Tales of Unearthly Love

ONCE MORE, WITH FEELING

Steven Utley

Here's a chilling little close encounter with Unearthly Love that demonstrates that sometimes the problem is not so much letting go of the past as persuading the past to let go of *you* . . .

Steven Utley's fiction has appeared in *The Magazine of Fantasy and Science Fiction, Universe, Galaxy, Amazing, Vertex, Stellar, Shayol,* and elsewhere. He was one of the best-known new writers of the seventies, both for his solo work and for some strong work in collaboration with fellow Texan Howard Waldrop, but fell silent at the end of the decade and wasn't seen in print again for more than ten years. In the last few years he's made a strong comeback, though, becoming a frequent contributor to *Asimov's Science Fiction* magazine, as well as selling again to *The Magazine of Fantasy and Science Fiction* and others. Utley is the coeditor, with Geo. W. Proctor, of the anthology *Lone Star Universe*, the first—and possibly the only—anthology of SF stories by Texans. His first collection will be coming up soon. He lives in Austin, Texas.

ONCE MORE, WITH FEELING

Wanda called to say, "Let's go to Mars for lunch." Jack made a puzzled sound into the telephone. Wanda said, "Lunch with Eldean. His birthday. Remember?"

"Of course I remember. But I thought we were going to—"

"Mars is his new favorite place. It's closer, so you won't have to take your car."

Jack, who did not like disruptions or deviations, looked down at the paper he had been grading and satisfied himself that the tip of his red pencil still marked his place. He said, "What've they got?"

"Eldean says he's partial to the skirt steak with garlic mashed potatoes."

"Sounds heavy."

"He says they've got all kinds of lunch specials. Gyros. Fish wrapped in rice paper. All kinds of Mediterranean, Indian, and Sino-Japanese things. They've got grilled Pacific salmon." Wanda waited. Then: "It's just *lunch*, dear."

"Sorry." Jack made a check mark next to a mistake on the paper and set his pencil aside. He said, "I hate leaps into the unknown."

Wanda laughed. "Don't I know. You two come on, I'll meet you there."

It was a September day, humid but cool, and Jack paused on the steps of the mathematics department to don his jacket. He automatically looked to make sure his Subaru still occupied its reserved parking space across the street. Then he set off down the long hill. His brother-in-law Eldean met him in front of the English department. They crossed the commons at the bottom of the hill, with Eldean, small and bird-quick, setting a brisk pace. When a student called out, "Great class today!" Eldean accepted the compliment as his due and said to Jack, "Today in Tragedies of Shakespeare, I taught *Titus Andronicus* as if it were one of those godawful psycho-splatter movies."

"Did it work?"

"Well, it obviously did for at least one person. I may try it in Nineteenth-Century British Authors next."

They walked two blocks and entered an oak-shaded street lined with well-kept Victorian houses, now occupied by law firms and other businesses. When Jack saw the Mars logo adorning one façade, he said, "This used to be—"

"Yes," said Eldean, "and before *that*—everything's changing faster than I can keep up with it. The city's growing out of control."

"When I was a student, the population here was a hundred thousand people or so." Jack shook his head disbelievingly. "Now they say, in another twenty-five years, it'll be a round million."

Wanda was waiting inside Mars, where the walls were painted a vivid pink and embellished with gold stars, crescent moons, and comets. The decor somehow avoided garishness. Jack and Wanda quickly exchanged kisses. He asked about her day so far, and she said, "The usual." He did not press for details. She was a psychologist at the county jail, specializing in juvenile offenders. While he spent his days with young people who did not know how to work the most obvious problems in geometry, she dealt with young people who did not know how to live their lives. The hostess showed Jack, Wanda, and Eldean to a corner table and handed out menus. "Your waitperson will be right with you."

They scanned the menus. "Everything sounds so good," Wanda said. "I don't know what to order."

Eldean put his menu down and slapped his hands against his own narrow torso. "I haven't been disappointed with anything I've had here."

Jack glared at him. "Not all of us are blessed with efficient metabolisms. Wanda makes me walk miles every day to keep the weight off."

The waitress arrived, and Jack, still studying the menu, heard her ask what they would care to drink. Her voice was a warm Southern purr.

"Iced tea, please," said Wanda.

"Make it two," said Eldean.

Jack looked up. The waitress was in her early twenties, trimly built, with honey-colored hair, light skin, and an abundance of freckles. She had alert brown eyes and a good smile. "Same here," Jack croaked, and she thanked them and glided away.

Jack felt heat creep up his neck and across his cheeks. He was helpless to stop it. He forced himself to look down at the tabletop directly before him.

"Now," Wanda said, "It's time to attend to business. Happy birthday, Eldean!" and she handed him a birthday card. Jack, after some confusion involving the pockets of his jacket, handed over a flat, rectangular gift wrapped in shiny foil.

Eldean laughed and gave his sister a hug. Then he read the message on the card and unwrapped the gift—a double-disc collection of old jazz standards sung by Anita O'Day. He excitedly turned it in his hands and looked at Jack. "Tunes from the tone-deaf?"

"Wanda said you like her."

"I do. I guess I owe one of you an extra hug."

The waitress returned with their beverages and asked to take their orders. Jack tried to stare at her without seeming to stare at her. There was just a hint of reproach in her expression when he admitted that he still had no idea what to order. He fumbled with the menu, ordered the first thing that caught his eye. The waitress seemed to regard him with amused tolerance for a moment before she turned and left.

Wanda aimed a finger and a mildly reproachful look across the table toward Jack. "Close your mouth, dear."

"What?"

"You're gaping."

"I—what? No, I'm not."

"Yes, you are. Bulging eyes, slack mouth—in my book, that's gaping. Or are you just window-shopping?"

"What?"

She inclined her head in the general direction taken by the waitress. "I have to admit, she *is* pretty."

"No. Of course I'm not—"

"Oh, leave him alone, Sis," Eldean said. "You know he's in your thrall." He leaned low over the table with an exaggerated air of confidentiality. "Before he took you to wife, the only figures Jack looked at for forty years were in math books."

"Don't listen to anything he tells you about me," Jack said.

Wanda said to Eldean, "I *like* a man who can balance a checkbook."

Jack had always enjoyed Wanda and Eldean's banter when it was not directed at him. He said, "If you're *through* discussing me—discuss Eldean instead."

"Let's," said Eldean. "*I* have the soul of a poet, not an adding machine. Yet all I've ended up with is ex-wives."

"Maybe," Wanda told him, "you shouldn't have waited until you were married not to have sex."

He laughed loudly enough to draw glances from the far end of the room.

Jack saw, over Eldean's shoulder, the waitress returning with their food. He looked away hurriedly, too hurriedly, he felt, but Wanda appeared not to notice. He kept his eyes on the table as the waitress placed his order before him. He ate mechanically, hardly tasting the food, and had no idea what it was. When the waitress paused at their table again to ask if everything was okay, he made some comment, slightly off the beat of the conversation and instantly forgotten. When Eldean suddenly spoke directly to him, he started.

"What?"

"I said, Mars to Jack, come in, Jack. Enjoy your flight?"

As they were leaving Mars, Wanda said, "This was good. We'll have to meet here again sometime."

"If it's still here," Eldean said. "Restaurants come and go in this town faster than anything."

Wanda offered to drop them off on campus. They got into her Nissan and had traveled a block when she said, "Jack, there's that noise again."

"I hear it," he said distractedly. "Better give Jimmy at Apex another call."

In front of the English department, Jack and Wanda again wished Eldean a happy birthday, and he thanked them again and went inside. The car ascended the hill, dodging jaywalking students and still making the noise. The mathematics department occupied a red-brick building located near the crest; below, in descending order, were the buildings that housed the music, English, and art departments. On the crest above the mathematics department was the science and engineering complex. The order of ascent, the rightness of it, had always appealed strongly to Jack's sense of orderliness; now it soothed and reassured him. Art *belonged* at the bottom: any nitwit could slop paint on canvas and call it art. English was only relatively more orderly, and music meant nothing to him. But mathematics— in mathematics you were right or you were wrong. There was no dissembling in mathematics. And in life, as on campus, to get to science and engineering, you had to pass mathematics.

"I'll see you later," said Wanda as she pulled the Nissan toward the curb in front of the mathematics building." He started to get out, but her thoughtful expression made him wait. She said, "Tell me now, what's bothering you?"

"Nothing's bothering me."

"I can tell something's bothering you." The thoughtful expression yielded to a smile. "It's oh-kay. I'm a trained expert. *And* your wife. You can tell me things."

"You're going to think I'm being ridiculous."

"You are the last man in the world who's capable of being ridiculous. Now what is it?"

"That waitress." He barely managed to get the word out. Something had come up out of his heart and lodged itself in his throat. He was mortified, blushing as uncontrollably as he had in the restaurant.

"A cutie, for sure," Wanda said evenly, "but young enough to be your daughter."

"That's just it. She *is* young enough to be my daughter. She *could* be—she's the image of my first girlfriend. I mean, my first serious girlfriend. My freshman year of college. The waitress looks just like her. It's uncanny. Same hair, eyes, face, everything. Even the freckles."

"Why didn't you ask her about her mom when she came back to the table?"

"I—I haven't seen her—the girlfriend—or heard from or about her in almost thirty years. I haven't even—" He let that sentence go, he had been at the point of saying that he had scarcely thought about her during all those years. "But I remember exactly how she looked."

"Well, that girl at Mars was nowhere close to thirty. Eighteen or nineteen is more like it. She's someone else's daughter. I know we promised never to ask questions like this, but since you've brought it up—what was her name? The girlfriend."

"Jonesy. Catherine Jones."

"Jonesy," Wanda said, "not Cathy. Interesting. So what happened between you and—" she hesitated for a fraction of a second, long enough for Jack to feel, first, the beginnings of embarrassment, then, a flicker of resentment at being made to feel embarrassment "—Jonesy?"

She was watching him closely. Jack nodded past her, past the faculty parking lot. Trees grew thickly on the far side, where the hill sloped away, and, visible above their tops, were the upper levels of a parking garage. He said, "The math and music buildings weren't here back then, and that hillside was all wooded. It was a real thicket and it grew all the way down on the other side to a blacktopped parking lot. The garage wasn't there, either."

Wanda considered the hillside. Then she said, uncertainly, as though she knew she was expected to respond but did not know exactly what that response ought to be, "Well, that's progress," and looked as though she knew that she had somewhat missed the mark.

Jack said, "In the evenings, before we had to be back in our dorms, Jonesy and I used to, you know, *do it* on that hillside."

"What? You're kidding!"

"No. Down the opposite slope, among the trees. We discovered a treehouse someone'd built. We never found out who or why. Maybe bird-watchers, maybe someone from the engineering department. It was a good solid treehouse. When I came back here to teach and saw that the trees'd been cut down on the other side and the hillside bulldozed—" Jack thumped his breast with the side of his fist. "And now, all day every day—" he jerked his head toward the mathematics building "—I can look at what's left from my window."

He studied her expression. "I can't believe I just told you that. You look absolutely amazed."

"Actually, I *am* amazed. The thought of you, of all people, getting it on in the great outdoors—"

"Well, it was the sixties. Later, we got a place together, in an old house that'd been cut up into apartments. It's gone, too. Torn down to make room for condos. Progress, eh?"

Wanda looked at her watch. "Jack, this *is* fascinating, but I've got to get back to the jail."

"Sure. Thanks."

"For what?"

"Listening to me babble like an idiot."

He kissed her, got out of the car, and watched as she drove away.

Jack's afternoon classes went unsatisfyingly. He finally conceded to himself that he was off his stride and dismissed his last class as early as he felt he decently could. He cloistered himself in his office and tried to do other work until it was time to change clothes and go meet Wanda.

She had changed at work, too, and was waiting for him at the entrance to the hike-and-bike trail. "I called Apex," she said after a kiss, "and they said to bring the Nissan in first thing tomorrow. They said they'd try, repeat, try and have it fixed by five tomorrow. So you have to follow me to Apex and take me to work in the morning and pick me up and take me to Apex in the evening." She widened her eyes, widened her smile. "And how was *your* day, dear?"

Traffic on the trail was as heavy in its own way as that on the street. Jack let Wanda set the pace and managed to stay abreast of her, though she ran more often than she walked and he hated running. They did not talk. He was grateful for that, his attention fixed on something within himself, and when at one point he abruptly became aware of his surroundings, it struck him that he must have completed the first two miles on autopilot. At the halfway mark, he followed her to one side of the trail and watched as she knelt to adjust her shoe. His eye followed the line of her body from her hand up her arm, over her shoulder and along her flank, around the curve of her hip, down along her smooth strong leg, back to her hand. It was as though he were seeing her for the first time. She is so, he thought—and then he could not think of a single word or any group of words that might do her justice, but, looking down at her, he experienced a rush of feeling for her so intense that his throat slightly constricted and his eyes stung.

At home, when he emerged from the shower, he found her brushing out her hair at her vanity table. Jack stepped close behind her and gently began to massage her shoulders, near the base of her neck. She said, "Ah," and let her head loll forward. "Can't tell you," she said after half a minute, "how good that feels."

"Lie down on the bed. I'll give you the full treatment."

"Don't have to ask me twice." She slipped out of her robe and lay prone on the bed. He sat on the edge and went to work on her.

After a while, she told him, "You missed your calling. You could do this for a living."

"The secret of giving a good back rub is just to listen. Whatever you do that elicits grunts of pleasure, do more of it."

"Whatever. Mm." After several more minutes, he stopped massaging her but lightly stroked her lower back with one hand, and she said "Mm" again, and then, "Thanks." He ran his hand over her buttock. "Buns of steel," she murmured into the crook of her arm. "Just another way of saying I'm a hard-ass."

Wanda rolled suddenly under his hand, onto her back, and drew a corner of the robe over her pubic area. He found her modesty endearing. She lay looking up at him with one arm across her breasts and the other arm cradling her head. His hand rested on her smooth firm stomach. She moved a hand down, placed it upon his, squeezed gently. He saw after a moment that she was trying to keep a straight face. She grinned suddenly and said, "Making love in a treehouse!" and laughed. She rolled her head from side to side and said, "I'm sorry!" and laughed again.

He wanted to laugh with her; he managed a grin. He bent forward and kissed her shoulder. "Didn't think I had it in me?"

Wanda put her hand upon his forearm, her expression was mock solemn again. "I've always thought you're a good egg, but I've never quite figured you out."

"You promised to love, honor, and not try to analyze me."

"Well, sometimes I regret that third part."

He kissed her again, softly, on the cheek, leaned closer, slid his arms around and under her, held her. Her arms pulled him tight against her. "Ah, Jack," she murmured. They lay quietly holding each other for at least two full minutes.

Then he pulled back slightly and said, "Are you hungry?"

"Starving."

"Me, too. Want to go out? My treat."

"Back to Mars? Not twice in one day. I'm just too tired." She kissed him. "Check out cute young waitresses on your own time." Jack felt guilty and relieved at the same time. "Maybe we can do something this weekend," she went on, "if there ever is a weekend," and groaned elaborately. "Meanwhile, I'm still starving."

"Why don't you lie here and relax while I fix dinner? If you *can* relax, knowing I'm fixing dinner."

"That was a joke!"

"Not much of one."

"True." She put her arm around his neck, drew him to her again, pressed her cheek to his, nuzzled his ear. "But enough of one."

"I'll call you when dinner's ready. Dinner or a reasonable facsimile thereof."

"Don't try to be funny twice in one night."

He kissed her and went and made a respectable dinner. The effort relaxed him. Afterward, they briefly watched television, then made respectable love.

The following afternoon, after dismissing his last class, he called Wanda at her office. She sounded tired and unhappy as she told him that the Nissan would be spending the night at the repair shop. He suggested the hike-and-bike trail. She said, "I don't think I'm up for it today. Just pick me up and take me home, okay?"

"Sure. I'll see you soon."

He left the mathematics building swinging the tote bag containing his sweatshirt, shorts, and walking shoes. He stepped off the curb to cross to the faculty parking lot and immediately jumped back at the sound of a car horn. A black Volkswagen Beetle muttered by. Affixed to its rear bumper were two stickers. One was a circle containing a peace symbol. The other read VIETNAM: LOVE IT OR LEAVE IT.

He stared after the Volkswagen, thought of an imprecation but did not unleash it, then got into his Subaru and went down the hill, straight into rush-hour traffic. It took him an eternity to drive the ten blocks to the county courthouse. Wanda stood waiting on the steps; she looked as she had sounded over the telephone. She accepted his kiss, however, and gave him a wan smile. The corners of her mouth turned up slightly, but the muscles in her forehead remained contracted. "Bad day," he said; he was not asking a question.

"Tell you later. Maybe." She exhaled harshly, then tried another smile, but still the effect was not reassuring. "You?"

"The usual," he said.

He drove, and she sat with her head tilted back and her eyes closed.

Finally, she said, "I lost my temper today and yelled at somebody from the sheriff's office."

"*Bad* day."

"The worst. The kind of day that makes me seriously think I'm not cut out for the work. The kind that's hard on my professional objectivity. That makes me think I'm not dealing with disturbed people, but plain old *stupid* ones, stupid and *evil* ones, and some who're just purely evil. I may have met one of the purely evil ones today. Ah, Jack." She looked sadder than he had ever seen her. "I'm preparing a psychological profile of a sixteen-year-old monster at the jail. He stabbed another kid last week, then hid out until his own grandmother turned him in. He already had a history of—but, anyway—today, while he was being processed, some idiot put another boy, a fourteen year old, into the cell with him and left them unattended. The sixteen year old talked the fourteen year old into hanging himself. Later, when I asked the sixteen year old about it—why he'd done it—he said because he'd always known he *could* do it, and he'd waited long enough. The devil in him was ready to show itself."

Her eyes glistened, she smeared at them with her hands, clutched her head between her forearms, and exhaled a heartbroken and heartbreaking sound. The thought darted through Jack's mind that this could not be his own reassuringly calm and collected wife sitting next to him, looking tireder than tired, looking exhausted, used-up, fighting back tears, speaking nonsense. Her talk of monsters and devils disturbed him—he thought that he could not have been much more disturbed if she had spouted obscenities—and yet, as he had on the trail the day before, he experienced a rush of feeling for her that was almost painful in its intensity.

"I'm sorry." He did not know what else to say. He let go of the gearshift knob and touched her arm. He did not know what else to do.

"No, I'm sorry," she said in an occluded voice. "I promised I'd never take my work home with me. And listen to me. I'm talking about devils and monsters."

"It's okay. If you want to talk about it, who else are you going to talk about it with?"

After a few seconds, she said, "Would that sentence stand Eldean's scrutiny?" and essayed a fresh smile, more or less successfully, and he touched her arm again. Then she said, "Do you mind if we stop somewhere for a drink?"

"Anywhere special?"

"Somewhere with wine and ferns and no local news on the TV."

Soon, Wanda sat lost in her own thoughts and nursing a glass of white wine. Jack sipped from his own glass and waited patiently. He started when he noticed the black Volkswagen parked across the street; even as he jarred the table and wine slopped from his glass, he saw a young woman with honey blond hair walk around the car from the curbside and unlock the door on the driver side.

"Jack!" Wanda said, like a harried mother, as she grabbed a napkin.

"See that girl across the street?"

Wanda, occupied with sopping up wine, scarcely bothered to look. "Not without my glasses."

"Put them on! Quickly! I want you to see her. The one in the—the sixties clothes—getting into the VW—"

As Wanda dug through her purse for her glasses, she said, "Jack, sixties fashions have been back for some time now. Retro-retro-retro, and I may even be leaving out a retro. Don't you pay attention to what your students are wearing?"

"Look at her."

As she fumbled her glasses into position, the Volkswagen pulled into traffic and was gone.

"It was—" He could not bring himself to finish the sentence. Instead, he said, "Just as I was leaving the department to come get you—I almost stepped out in front of that same car."

Wanda wagged a finger at him. "Always look both ways before you cross the street."

"It was *her*."

"Who?"

"The waitress from Mars," he said. *Jonesy*, he thought.

Wanda leaned back in her chair. She said, "Tell me what finally happened between you and your college girlfriend."

Jack meant to say, We broke up, or simply, I don't know. Instead, he said, "I treated her very badly."

"Ah. Remorse. You are just full of surprises." She took a careful sip of wine. "Remorse can be a bad thing or a good thing. Hell is truth seen too late. Then again, remorse comes out of remembrance and may lead to redemption."

"I hardly remembered her at all until I saw that waitress. Could I almost've forgotten someone if she really ever meant anything to me?"

"It depends on what you mean by *meant anything*. How badly, exactly, did you treat her?"

"I don't—can we change the subject?"

"You brought it up. So, tell me—"

"I don't feel like being analyzed right now."

"I'm not trying to analyze you, I just want to find out—"

"Wanda, I'm not one of your juvenile offenders!"

Wanda set her wineglass down with a sharp click. "No, you're not. Let's get the hell out of here."

They went home and ate dinner in excruciating silence and did not speak to each other for the rest of the evening. Jack could not occupy himself with homework papers or television, and the house itself seemed to contract around him. Then, at bedtime, as he sat in his pajamas on the edge of the bed, he looked around at Wanda, who lay on her side with her back to him. He stretched out beside her. He said, "I'm sorry," and touched her shoulder. "I'm so sorry. I never want us to be mad at each other. I'm sorry."

He could feel her hesitate. Then she reached back with her hand and patted his arm. "I'm sorry, too. Sorrier. I'm the psychologist."

"Bad day."

"Yes. Bad day."

"Wanda."

The moment seemed to stretch to infinity. Jack did not want to talk anymore, did not want to speak the things he thought, and Wanda, evidently sensing this, said, "We don't have to talk about anything." But it was as though a hole had suddenly been punched in him and words came pouring out.

"She said she wanted to be with me always. I wanted to be with her, too—but it wasn't safe. So our pattern for the year we were together was start up, stop, start over. I kept cutting her off. Whenever I'd cut her off, she'd call me up in tears, send me anguished notes by mail, *What's wrong, what have I done, what can I do*?"

Wanda turned toward him, propped her head up on one hand, and let the other rest on his sternum. "It was always you who cut her off? And she was always the one who wanted to get back together with you?"

"Yes. She—it was almost masochistic."

"In those days, girls were raised to be masochists."

"Maybe it was something worse. Maybe, the more vulnerable she became, the crueler *I* became."

"Why, Jack?"

He started to say, I have no idea, for he had suddenly recognized the greater extent of the minefield that lay ahead. He had not let himself tread upon that ground for many years; he did not want to do so now. He also knew that he had no choice but to go on. He said, "I knew if I let myself feel something for Jonesy, I'd have to feel other things as well."

"All of this happened around the time your mother died, didn't it?"

Jack took a long slow breath. "She'd died in the spring while I was still a senior in high school. When she was diagnosed with cancer—I didn't really realize until near the end how serious her illness was. She and my father didn't prepare me for what was going to happen. I think it was because they never stopped believing that their prayers would save her, even after the doctors couldn't. When my mother went into the hospital for the last time, I wasn't all that worried. She'd been in the hospital before—I thought she'd be coming home again. She always had before. When she died, it shattered my father. Just shattered him. That shook me as badly as her death. Worse, really. What her death made me feel was shame and horror because I—I didn't feel anything *else*. Just cold and empty."

"You were in shock," Wanda said gently.

"*I* didn't know *that*. Nobody told me I was in shock. And I saw my father, who'd always been the strong, silent type, reduced to—till then, I'd always believed that adults were *in control* of their lives and their feelings. That they took things in stride. I saw how my father fell apart, and I thought, Well, maybe being all cold and numb inside isn't such a bad thing after all. Maybe I'm better *off* never feeling anything. So I stayed in shock. That fall, when I left for college, I didn't just leave for college, I—left. *Left*."

"And met Jonesy."

"We started dating soon after I started college. She was a year older than me, a sophomore. It was casual at first, but we finally did the deed. Deflowered each other. After that, it was like she was determined to make things work on almost any terms. I think she tried so hard because she just couldn't believe she'd made a horrible mistake."

"Losing one's virginity means more to girls than it does to boys. In those days, a girl was still strongly encouraged to save herself for one special person."

"Then Jonesy's one special person was supposed to be *me*. And I wouldn't cooperate. I'd cut her off, I'd relent, we'd get back together for a while. I guess even that finally paled, because, finally, I betrayed her. With other girls. She moved out, and I never saw her again. That was near the end of my freshman year. She wasn't at school the next fall."

"What about those other girls?"

"I betrayed them, too. I got better at betrayal as I went along. Finally, all that—crying and—it started to sicken me. I stopped bothering. I found more worthwhile interests. And then I finally met you. And—and it was like—like when Beauty transforms the Beast and redeems him."

Wanda lay her head on his breast. She said, with such tenderness that his eyes watered, "Why, Jack!"

Jack stroked her hair. "I've spent too much time around your brother."

"He does go on."

He looked at the clock on the nightstand. "It's late. We really should go to sleep."

They kissed lingeringly, turned out the light, and settled beside each other, holding hands.

In the darkness, Wanda cleared her throat softly and said, "If you could see Jonesy now—what would you do?"

"I don't know. Yes, I do."

"What?"

"Ask her forgiveness. Tell her—tell her how sorry I am. Tell her how much I wanted to—return her—feelings. Back then, I mean."

Wanda squeezed his hand. "Jack," she said, "would it kill you to ever say the word *love*?"

A long time after he knew she was asleep, the black Volkswagen passed fleetingly through his mind, trailing a montage of images, incredibly condensed and yet incredibly vivid, of another time and almost another place. He suddenly became aware of his own moist heavy breathing, and of his own skin, bare and hot, and of the touch of even hotter, burning-hot fingertips. He raised his head slightly and looked, and now he saw and felt the girl, the waitress, kissing his belly just below the navel, tracing designs with her tongue and moving her head in a lazy back-and-forth motion so that her cheek repeatedly brushed against the swollen head of his penis. But how—

She turned her face toward him and whispered, "Ssh," and turned her face away and made him groan, half in ecstasy, half in complaint. *It feels so good. Don't make me wait.* But—how—

He could not remember how she had managed to come to him, how things had gotten this far. On finding oneself in bed with a woman, he thought, one ought to remember how one got there. After all, it was supposed to be such a momentous thing. Who had kissed whom, this time or the first time or any time? And how had the kissing gone beyond lip contact to tongues, and what then? And from that to fumbling with buttons and zippers, running the whole obstacle course of feminine underthings—?

He suddenly wondered, Why am I naked, where are my pajamas?

He awoke with a start and a cry. Wanda slept beside him, breathing quietly. At some point after falling asleep, he had released her hand. He turned away from her, onto his side, stared at the dimly moonlit rectangles of the bedroom windows. He lay clutching the edge of the mattress until he saw gray light through the windows.

He was groggy throughout the morning, and his nine and ten o'clock classes and his undergraduate-advisor session were unmitigated disasters. Helpless to stop himself, Jack left his office early and returned alone to Mars. He asked for, and was shown to, the table he and Wanda and Eldean had shared. His waitress had pale skin, reddish blond hair, and heavy eye makeup. He asked what had become of the waitress who had served him before. "Could you please tell me her name? I may have known her mother, years ago."

The waitress regarded him frankly, appraisingly. "This is my table," she said, "and I'm the only blonde."

"Are you sure?"

She made an effort to humor him, there was only the merest edge of impatience in her voice. "Look around."

This is crazy, Jack told himself. He tried to maintain his composure, to will himself not to blush. He had a horror of scenes.

"Now," she said, after waiting several seconds more, "may I get you something to drink?"

He left without ordering, strode back to campus with arms swinging and fists clenched, feeling foolish and humiliated and vowing to
himself never to return to Mars. On the steps of the mathematics
building, he hesitated, turned, looked across the parking lot. A student said hello as he went by, and Jack muttered a reply but did not
see who it was. He stood with his hands thrust into his trousers
pockets and his head pulled down between his shoulders, as though
against a cold wind, and he watched the trees. At last, he crossed the
street and walked past his Subaru, sitting in its reserved parking
space, and entered the trees. The woods closed around him, swallowed him. He knew that he should at least have been able to
glimpse the rear wall of the parking garage through the trees ahead,
but he could not, and when he looked back he could not see the
parking lot or the mathematics building. The woods seemed to
stretch away forever in every direction. Day had somehow become
night, yet he saw perfectly well, as though the air itself were suffused
with light. He saw the treehouse and said or thought *No!* and looked
up through a gap in the leaf canopy and imagined for an instant that
he saw not the familiar and dependable moon and stars but a jagged
rent in the sky, beyond which was true engulfing darkness. He felt
the ground tilt and crack beneath his feet, and he lurched toward the
treehouse with outstretched arms. The treehouse was substantial.
The treehouse was real. It consisted of a wooden platform with low
sides and a partial roof. A ladder afforded access. He put his foot on
the first rung. After a moment, he heard a sound from within the
treehouse, perhaps a voice, perhaps calling to him.

He fled blindly. The ground turned treacherous underfoot. He
slipped, fell, rolled against the base of a medium-sized tree. He lay
there breathing heavily, with earth-smells in his nostrils and the
taste of dirt and blood on his tongue. He wondered if he would ever
get back to where he belonged, but the matter no longer seemed
particularly urgent. This is good, where I am.

From somewhere close by came the sound of approaching footsteps.

Get up, he told himself. Get up. Run.

He got his feet beneath him and used the tree to pull himself
erect. He glimpsed movement among the trees close by and ran
clumsily in the opposite direction. Something whipped his cheek.
His toe connected solidly with an exposed root, and he went
sprawling, cried out, clawed at the ground. When he pushed himself up on his forearms, he found himself at the edge of the trees,
looking across the faculty parking lot at the mathematics building.
The sun was farther down the sky than seemed right.

Jack got up, pulled a twig from his hair, tried to brush the dirt and
bits of plant detritus from his clothes. He discovered a welt on his left

cheek. He limped halfway across the parking lot and then looked back over his shoulder. The parking garage loomed above the trees.

He turned away from the mathematics building and made his way down to the English department. The door to Eldean's office was ajar. Jack knocked on the door frame and leaned into the room. Eldean looked up from behind his untidy desk. His mouth fell open, and his eyebrows rose.

"Jack! My God! What happened? Did you get mugged?"

Eldean had started to rise from his seat, but Jack motioned him back down onto it.

"I fell down."

"Fe—? After you blew off two classes in a row, your office practically put out an APB on you. They called Wanda, she called me. Where've you been all afternoon?"

Jack looked first at the electric clock on Eldean's wall, then at his wristwatch. There was discrepancy of almost three hours. Jack closed the door and sagged into a chair across from Eldean. "I'm not sure where I've been," he said. "In the woods." Eldean picked up the telephone and dialed. "Who're you calling?"

"Who else?" Eldean spoke into the mouthpiece. "Sis, Jack's here in my office." He held the telephone out to Jack.

"I don't know what to say her."

"Try *hello*."

Jack accepted the telephone. "Wanda . . ."

"Jack! Are you all right? Where've you been?"

"I'm fine. I'm okay."

"What's going on?"

He did not answer immediately. Then: "I think I'm being haunted."

"Haunted." Her voice was inflectionless. Two seconds ticked by. "By whom or what?"

"Jonesy."

"Ah, God! Jonesy! Listen to me, Jack, you stay right there with Eldean. I'll be there as soon as I can get a cab."

Jack handed the telephone back to Eldean, who said, "Don't you want to call your office?"

"No. I'm going to stay right here with you till Wanda gets here."

"Oh. Well." Eldean looked concerned. "Can I get you anything?"

"Professional help." Jack grinned as Eldean blinked at him over the tops of wire-rimmed glasses. "That's a joke. Or maybe it isn't. Either I need professional help, or I'm—look, you know me well enough. You know I'm not the type to dwell on the past and not the type to have panic attacks. But it's like I've been brushing up against moments from my own past. From my first love affair."

"People forget years," Eldean murmured, "and remember moments. I forget who said that. Somebody—"

"I wandered into the trees at the top of the hill. Suddenly, it was night, and everything was the way it used to be, thirty years ago—the same but different. The sky became different, everything was different. I think I heard Jonesy—my old girlfriend, the one who looked like the waitress at Mars. The treehouse was there, just like it used to be, and she was waiting for me there."

"The waitress?"

"No! Jonesy! But I got scared. I ran and fell and found myself—back here. Back now." Jack considered the expression on his brother-in-law's face. Neither of them spoke for several seconds. Finally, Jack said, "So you tell me, do I need professional help?"

"Well, if you do, surely Wanda can help you get it."

"I don't *want* professional help! I want a reasonable, rational, *real* explanation for this!"

"Does, um, that mean you *want* this thing to be real?"

"I don't want it to be a hallucination! I don't want it to be *me*. I know it isn't!"

The concern in Eldean's expression had transformed itself gradually into some keener type of interest; now he brushed his palms together and sat forward in his chair. "But if this thing is real, Jack—by which I mean, if it isn't a hallucination—then what've you got?"

"I don't know. What have I got?"

"Ghosts?"

"Eldean, I don't *believe* in ghosts."

Eldean looked exasperated in his own right. "So *then* what've you got? Time travel? If we *must* rule out the unreasonable and irrational possibility that you're imagining weird stuff, it follows that it's got to be one of those other three things. Now, which one sounds most reasonable and rational to you—" he counted them off on his fingers "—ghosts, time travel, *or* you need professional help?" Jack said nothing, only glowered at him. Eldean held up his hands with his right index finger hooked on his left middle finger. "Right—number three!"

"No! I'm going to solve this. If Jonesy's back—"

"How hard can it be to find out if she's back? One call, and Wanda can have one of her buddies in the sheriff's office run a driver's-license check for you. Or you can start conducting an investigation yourself, right here, right now." Eldean pulled out his city telephone directory. "What's her name?"

"Catherine Jones."

"Jones." Eldean thumbed through the directory, then handed the opened book to Jack.

There were three and a half pages of Joneses, but only six C. Joneses and no Catherines or Cathys.

"What should I do?" Jack asked bitterly. "Call? Ask each one of them,

Are you the girl I used to meet in a treehouse, thirty years ago? What're the odds she's married and changed her name and moved away?"

"You're the mathematician."

Jack threw the book to the floor and sat with his head in his hands. Ghosts, he thought glumly. Time travel. Madness.

Wanda entered without knocking. She uttered a little cry of alarm when she saw Jack, bent over him, took his face in her hands. "What *happened* to you?" She scarcely blinked while he repeated the story he had told Eldean. She lowered herself onto her calves in front of him and put her face close to his.

He said, "I'm not drunk."

She said, "Let's get you home."

"I'm not nuts, either."

"I know you're not nuts. No one says you're nuts."

"You never say anybody's nuts. They're always disturbed. I'm not *disturbed*, Wanda. My *mind* is working perfectly. It's trying to figure this thing out. I want a rational explanation!"

"Okay. Okay." Wanda rose and leaned against the edge of Eldean's desk. She held up a hand, palm out, fingers spread, and moved it back and forth as though she were testing the resiliency of some invisible membrane. She said, "Try tearing this whole thing apart, Jack, starting from the top. The girl at Mars reminded you of your old flame. But she wasn't your old flame."

"And she wasn't at Mars today. I checked."

"Oh, you *did*, did you?"

"If I took you there now, you'd see she's not the same girl. And that in itself means something. You saw her, too—you both did. I didn't imagine her."

"We saw *a* girl. Maybe she just looked different when you went back. Maybe, in the interim, she had a complete makeover."

"No. I can't have been mistaken."

"No, not you," Eldean muttered from behind his desk.

Jack said, "What about the old VW?"

Wanda started to answer, hesitated, looked at a loss.

Eldean came to her rescue. "You saw an old black VW," he said to Jack. "How could you tell it was old? The whole time they built those things, they never looked any different from one year to the next. I don't remember when they stopped building them, but I'm sure those things are classics now. Maybe they're making a comeback. Maybe they've started building them again, too. I don't know about cars. Maybe all you saw was a new one."

"With the same bumper stickers my girlfriend put on *her* car thirty years ago? Wanda, what about the hillside and the treehouse?"

Wanda lowered her head and shook it wearily. "I don't know, I don't know. I don't know."

"Eldean says ghosts, or time travel." He looked sharply at his brother-in-law. "What do we know about ghosts, Eldean?"

"Ghosts are the spirits of the dead. Sometimes, they appear to the living for the purpose of delivering warnings or other messages, or they come bent on making trouble for their killers."

"Eldean," Wanda said, "you're not helping matters."

"Well," Jack said, "after all this time, she *could* be dead, but even if she *is*—why would her ghost be appearing to me *now*?" Before either of them could reply, he remembered, with an unpleasant shiver, Wanda's words the day before . . . *He'd always known he could do it, and he'd waited long enough. The devil in him was ready to show itself.* He rallied by reminding himself, I do not believe in ghosts. Even if I *did*, I couldn't believe they wait tables or drive Volkswagens. Or engage in foreplay. He said, "Even if I believed in ghosts, what could this ghost be trying to *tell* me?"

"Maybe," Wanda said, "it's not trying to tell you anything. Maybe *you're* trying to tell yourself something."

"Like, maybe I'm trying to tell myself I need professional help? Funny how it keeps coming back to that." He slumped in his chair. "I don't even want to think about time travel."

"Jack . . . let me take you home."

"I should call the department."

"We'll do it when we get you home. Where's the car?"

"Parked in front of the math building."

"I'll go get it. You stay here, and, Eldean, don't you *encourage* him."

She left. Jack and Eldean regarded each other across the desktop. At length, Eldean said, "Are you sure you don't actually *want* this thing to be a mystery? Because if you do, watch out! Mysteries force a man to think and so injure his health. Poe said that, and look how *his* life turned out."

"I intend to solve this mystery."

"You solve *puzzles*. Puzzles are sterile, they're safe. A mystery's something you have to *fathom*—stick your arm in up to the elbow. Sometimes you have to dive in headfirst. You can drown in a mystery."

Jack stood up. "I don't give a damn about Poe."

They spoke no more. Wanda returned for Jack, and when they walked outside together, he saw the Subaru illegally parked in front of the English building.

"Let me drive," he said, producing his own keys.

"Better let me."

"I haven't been declared incompetent *yet*."

"Will you stop?" She threw up her hands in resignation as he slid into the driver seat. Through a series of abrupt, angry motions, she got in on the other side, closed the door, and buckled her safety belt.

As Jack pulled the car away from the curb, he spotted the black

Volkswagen at the bottom of the hill. He started to speed up, then had to step on the brake as two students jaywalked in front of the Subaru. Wanda yelped a warning. Jack snapped, "I *see* them." As the Subaru entered traffic and turned after the Volkswagen, a minivan abruptly moved in from the left-hand lane to fill the gap between the two vehicles. Jack found himself boxed in by another vehicle in the left-hand lane; he could see around the minivan but could not get around it. The Volkswagen, the minivan, and the Subaru turned at the intersection as though threaded together on a string.

Wanda said, "Jack, where we going?"

"See it? The black VW?"

"Ja—"

"Do you *see* it?"

"Yes!"

Jack gripped the steering wheel so tightly that his knuckle bones looked and felt as though they were about to pop through the skin. "She's in that car! She wants me to follow her!"

"Who?"

"Jonesy! She's come back!"

"Jack, this *is* crazy!"

He laughed wildly when the minivan turned right, then cursed when he saw that the Volkswagen had managed somehow to put another vehicle between itself and the Subaru. The Volkswagen turned onto a narrow street leading into a neighborhood full of big old houses and huge old trees. At the far end of the block, the Volkswagen turned onto a gravel driveway. Jack turned after it and found it sitting parked and empty in the shade of a tallow tree that grew next to a peeling Victorian house. There were no other cars and no one in sight. He pulled the Subaru in so close behind the Volkswagen that he could no longer see its brand-new-looking ancient bumper stickers. He turned off the motor and sat back in his seat; it almost hurt when he unwrapped his fingers from the steering wheel. Wanda looked around perplexedly. He heard her ask, "Where are we?" but he did not answer her. He gazed up at the house. It had been built sometime before the First World War and cut up into apartments sometime after the Second. A venerable oak shaded it. The apartments were cheap and reasonably easy to keep clean and had private entrances. A brass letter C adorned the door on this side of the house, and paisley-print bed linen had been pressed into service as curtains for the two windows. What luxury, Jack thought, after that treehouse . . .

He listened to the sound of the cooling engine and of his own excited breathing and marveled that he was not astonished to find the house intact, though he knew that it had not survived a building boom during the 1980s.

"Jack," Wanda said.

"What do you see?"

"Jack—"

"Tell me what you see!"

"That car. An old house." She clutched his arm as he opened his door. "What are you going to do?"

"Find out."

"Find out *what*?"

"*I don't know*," he said. "But I hate enigmas. And if this is what I think it is—whatever it *is* I think it is—after all this time, I have to seek forgiveness."

"What if her reason for coming back *isn't* to forgive you?"

He hesitated, with the door half opened and his left foot on the ground, and, after a long moment had passed, he thought, I also hate leaps into the unknown. He got out of the car and walked up to the door of apartment C. He inclined his head toward it, listened, felt a chill between his shoulder blades when he heard movement within. He looked back at the Subaru. It was still parked behind the Volkswagen, but it suddenly seemed a lot farther away than it ought to have been. The street was a million miles away. The sky was all roiling incandescence, illuminating Wanda's face as she peered through the Subaru's windshield. Jack saw, across that great distance, that she appeared distressed, appeared to be calling to him, but she was too far away for him to see or hear her very clearly. He made a fist and knocked on the door and thought he heard another, different sound, a voice, perhaps, saying, perhaps, *I'm coming*.

CAIN

Tanith Lee

Tanith Lee is one of the most acclaimed and most prolific of modern fantasists, with over forty books to her credit, including (among many others) *The Birth Grave, Drinking Sapphire Wine, Don't Bite the Sun, Night's Master, The Storm Lord, Sung in Shadow, Volkhavaar, Anackire, Night Sorceries,* and *The Black Unicorn,* and the collections *Tamastara, The Gorgon, Dreams of Dark and Light,* and *The Forests of the Night.* Her short story "Elle Est Trois (La Mort)" won a World Fantasy Award in 1984; and her brilliant collection of retold folk tales, *Red as Blood,* was also a finalist that year, in the "Best Collection" category. Her most recent books are the collection *Nightshades* and the novels *Vivia* and *The Blood of Roses.*

In the intense, brutally erotic, and uncompromisingly graphic story that follows, one definitely not for the squeamish (you've been warned!), she shows us that the closest and most intimate of relationships may sometimes begin even *before* you are born . . .

CAIN

He was born seven minutes before me, and lived for two. By the time I had begun to breathe, he was dead. We were identical, so alike that if he'd lived, no one could have told us apart. Miranda revealed all this many years later, one night when she was unusually, spectacularly drunk. But by then, of course, I knew him well.

One of my earliest memories is that I thought my name was Hill Town. Actually it's Hilton, like the old hotels. I can remember asking my mother why I had this name, and had we lived on a hill? She laughed and dismissed me; I was still at the entertaining but relatively unobtrusive stage. The Girl—always there was a Girl to look after me—took me away, down to the edge of the blue creaming sea. "Look, fishes!" said the Girl. And we watched dolphin, which sometimes came in so near the shore, leaping like gray silk balloons from the water.

The sea house was a large one, with white columns. In the garden were palms and enormous orange trees. But at other times we were in the city. I was taught at home by a succession of tutors. My remote father didn't believe in my mixing in the rough-and-tumble of real life before I had to. I was, needless to say, a lonely child. The Girls were pretty, and mostly tried, I think, to be kind. But in a way they resented me, this dark cute little kid who was swathed in so much money, when they and theirs had had to struggle. Always a problem with servants, I suppose, however well-treated or well-paid. And frankly, I'd imagine the Girls weren't that well-treated or paid. My father gave some of them special attentions, and then they left. I recall my mother, white as marshmallow, shouting in a lofty room. "Since the baby, you don't want me, do you?" "Oh, Miranda," said my father, solid as granite to her sweet wobbling softness, "you're so impossibly self-centered. Why does it have to be you? Couldn't *I* just fancy a change?"

I remember too Miranda's tall morning glasses of fruit juice and gin, which, as the day went on, altered to glasses of pure gin, with only an orange or lemon slice swimming there like a fish.

As the years passed, her marshmallow softness became spread on her more lavishly. But she was a beautiful woman, even large, a fat, white, pampered seal, with yearning coal-dark eyes. Do you sense I loved her? I don't know. I simply watched her. She was a glamorous being hung with jewels and glasses of alcohol, who normally inhabited the same buildings with me.

As I grew older, she became more interested in me—once she saw I was a male, that is, not simply a boy child. She would rub me down with a towel when I came out of the sea or the pool. She would brush my hair, take my face between her hands, and stare into my eyes. She called me her "handsome hound." "So streamlined and slender," she would say. "And such lovely heartless eyes!" At first I think I didn't dislike this. Then it embarrassed me. I can't recollect quite when my self-consciousness began. Around puberty I would think. There was nothing sexual in her actions, though sensual perhaps. But fondling had for me an amorous quality from the very first.

I said I was a lonely child, but that was in the day. I knew instinctively that my questions and conversations bored everyone. What to me was so new and odd was to them merely routine, beyond discussion. Yet also by day I was generally in the company of adults, my mother, sometimes my father, the tutors, the Girls. At night, bathed and combed and put to bed in silk pajamas, the mosquito net drawn like a film of mist about the bed, the window showing in its long frame the indigo star-daubed vista of sea and sky, or the light-hives of a city without other stars—at night, I was alone. More alone than most. My father frowned on any toys that were not instructional, in some way intellectual; I was taught chess at seven. And so no furry, floppy companion shared my bed from the age of five. I'd cried when they took my bear and rabbit away. My father explained that I was too old for them, and that in the children's home to which they went, they were needed far more. He had always this habit, of abruptly seeing necessary benefits for others when he wanted to deprive his own family of something. (For example, the three Girls who were sent away would thereby lose their essential wages, bringing their kin to poverty—how was it my mother was oblivious of this? But she had obstinately continued oblivious.) However, my own horror was mitigated by the knowledge that my friends would be loved and housed.

I think six months elapsed before I replaced them.

How did it start? I had, when alone, talked to myself all that while, because I didn't interrupt myself, or criticize—or very little, something had come off on me from the adult world—and because I found my own voice not repellent or annoying as, very evidently, now and then others did. Somewhere in the preslumbering dark, lit by the blue sea window or the honeycomb of city lights, my talk began to be not to myself, but to another.

Children generally fall asleep quickly. Some nights I spoke for ten or fifteen minutes, on some for one or two. The sense that I was listened to was very definite. And presently, also the sense that this was a secret thing, which should be mentioned to no one else. But then, I wasn't a confessing child, had never been encouraged to be. *Tell mother. Your father wants to know.* These were the phrases attendant on transgression, not invitations to confide.

Even had I confided, of course, my nocturnal chats, though doubtless disapproved, would have been safely enough categorized. I had, like so many lonely infants, an Imaginary Friend.

The Girl had slapped me during my bath. It was a hard slap, across my legs. I'd been splashing a lot. I don't know why. I was never a very boisterous child. The point, which I didn't then—I was eight— understand, was that she had on a gold lamé dress. She had fallen in love with my father and wanted to catch his eye, and to do this, pretending it was for some date she had after my bath, she had had to dress up first—he only came into my room for a few minutes before dinner. Inevitably, I'd splashed the dress. There was a wet patch on the inferior lamé, over her breast, which she'd wanted to sparkle. It looked like the map of Italy.

The slap hurt quite badly, perhaps because I was wet. She looked at its reddening formation on my thighs in terror. She said she was sorry, so sorry, but her boyfriend was so particular. "If señor ask," she said, "tell you slipped, yes?"

"Yes, all right."

"You are good little boy."

In fact, my father never noticed, either the red slap or the map of Italy, or her gaudy clothing.

When they were all gone, I lay in bed, and rubbed my thighs where the sting had been. I told my Imaginary Friend what had happened. And it was then, then for the very first time, I felt him. Because he *touched* me. He touched the place where I'd been slapped. He caressed it, as soothingly as a mother, over and over, stroking me until I tingled. In the end, consoled, curiously excited, yet calm, I fell asleep, and as I did, I felt his arms holding me.

Why didn't I marvel at this? Why wasn't I alarmed? Everything is strange to a child. Very little makes any sense. Why is the sky blue? Why must I eat now when I'm not hungry, and not *now*, when I am? Why are you angry with me simply because I'm here? None of these inquiries, mostly unvoiced, gets a proper answer.

And this—this was very nice. It was comforting, and I'd had no comfort at all. Even falling down in the sand on the beach, cutting my knee on a shell, a great fuss, painful antiseptic, a stitch put in by a scowling doctor—but no *comfort*. Be a brave boy.

Yes, this was nice. And half waking once, the sense that he was still there. Not seen, but warmly touching, holding me, coiled about me, and I about him, the way I had seen cats asleep on sunny walls.

Every night after that, he stroked me, and, leading my hands, led me to stroke him. He felt just like myself. Smooth and thin, almost snakelike, sleek. His hair was exactly the same longish length as mine, and smelled like mine, as his body did, of expensive soap and some child's cologne, of shampoo and sea and salt. Of flesh too, of the warmth of hidden valves, extrusions, and crevices, with their tang of meat and spice.

I don't remember when he kissed me first. It was a gentle brushing thing. I think I must have been ten or so. His closed mouth had a whisper-scent of toothpaste, just like my own.

I'd call him by a name—I haven't said, have I? I left off using it later—which was a makeshift of my own, a childish anagram, *Holtni.* (Hold Me?) But even then I never used this name to him, only when I thought about him by day, which now I often did. *I'll tell Holtni about that big car I saw. I'll tell Holtni Momma was sick and had to lie down.* Or, *Holtni will cuddle me*, because I hadn't done my mathematics very well, and my tutor shouted, saying I was a brainless little rich boy, as if *rich* were an obscenity—as, of course, it was.

But I recall the next events, when everything changed, perfectly well.

Puberty had commenced, but I didn't know. No one had really warned me. There had been a book, which had diagrams, telling, it seemed—I was bored and didn't try hard with it, there were so many dull books they made me read—only things I knew. That I had a penis, and two nipples, all three of which, like soldiers, might suddenly stand to attention. This was funny. I waited, but they didn't. Probably all a mistake, just the same as the idea I would be good at sport, while, aside from swimming, I could do nothing sporting at all. One of the tutors had attempted to give me a sex lesson, but for his own ends, I would guess, judging from his overnight dismissal—something to do with the younger gardener.

I was twelve. I was in my mother's room. Sometimes I went there when she was absent. I had liked to feel her dresses and sniff them, to pry into cupboards, drawers. I found curious things. A box like a shell with a rubber thing in it like something out of the sea—appropriate enough, given the box. And once a carton of things like large cigarettes, but these were, once extracted, too white, and ultimately bendy, and I couldn't see how you would light them. Luckily I never confided anything about these discoveries either. The notion of her preadolescent son routing among her diaphram and tampons would have sent Miranda hysterical.

Her jewels intrigued me too. As a child I loved to see her in them.

She was, for a second, like something from the Arabian nights (doubt-less the expurgated version), leaning to kiss me good night, smelling of *Les Yeux du Noir*, her neck and ears lambent with cool, flashing emeralds, inflamed rubies, or the gold cross set with three diamonds between her breasts. The jewel boxes were sometimes locked, but she was forgetful. It was not until I was fifteen that I learned that these were all copies. The real gems were worn only once or twice a year.

One can say that I had a sexual craving that stemmed from my mother, from her attributes—garments, ornaments—more than her body, her *self*.

This must be so, because that day in her room I was moved to strip, and look at myself in her pier glass, where I could see all of me.

My theory then for doing it was that my own mirrors were either not full length, or in difficult places. My body seemed to me much larger and broader, and I wanted an overview.

Whatever, my clothes came off and I stepped naked to her glass, standing there on the deep carpet in the shining sunlight of the sea house. And here I was, Hilton.

I knew I was handsome. People remarked on it, and I had come to recognize what they pointed out. The large dark eyes and long lashes, the thin straight nose, the thick straight brows and thick straight hair. A long and narrow physique, long-legged, the shoul-ders widening. Clear skin mildly tanned from the days at the beach, the whiter band only about my loins, where, in a black thicket, the snake lay like a little velvet trunk. As I looked, I thought, Holtni's like me, so he too looks just like this. Even though I've never seen him. I'll tell him how I've looked at me. I'll ask him.

As as I said it, a blush went up my face, dark red. And my entire body quickened. I felt a wonderful, shameful, underearth pressure. My blood was full of spangles and darts and up it rose, that velvet trunk, thickening and pushing, straight up, as the diagram in the awful book had foretold.

I put my hand on it in astonishment, and a shudder of the dark-est, most intense feeling went through me. I shut my eyes and played with myself, opened them and stopped. I could feel some-thing building in me, from the base of my spine to the crown of my head, the soles of my feet. It scared me. It was like running along a corridor, and knowing at the end there must come an opening and a colossal leap—but into what?

I turned my back on my image that was also the image of Holtni-Hold Me. I put on my clothes, forcing my deflating erection inside like a naughty animal.

Then I went for a long walk along the beach, drank a Coke at a café I was forbidden, watched other boys, the kind I'd never met, throwing a ball in the paint-blue water.

Very carefully, I didn't think one thought about bed, nighttime, anything like that.

In any case, there was a dinner party that evening, and I was expected to be there for the first part of it. My father, utterly indifferent to me as a person, liked to show me off as a valuable possession. I was well-trained, polite, and, if not witty or skillful, at least graceful in my reticence. I said very little but listened attentively. Guests tended to exclaim that I was a model son.

The evening passed. Miranda wore a green Lavinché gown, and, as ever, got enormously drunk, showing not too many signs of it, she and her body being so accustomed to the state of drunkenness. My father moved among his friends and business acquaintances. Two daughters of some politician, thirteen and fifteen, seemed both quite interested in me. Flattered and uneasy, I sat between them at dinner, eating decorously the iced soup and squab, the skulls of white meringues. One girl, the fifteen year old, told me quietly I was beautiful enough to kiss. If I could find an excuse to leave the party and come on to the balcony, where night-blooming jasmine made a canopy, she'd show me how.

I didn't want to go, and therefore felt I must. My father had always insisted I behave impeccably with his guests.

Outside, the night was full of perfumes and murmurs, the sea, distant music from the little orchestra, laughter and talk.

The girl drew me in under the jasmine. She was one inch taller than I, but this was no problem. She pressed her lipsticked mouth to mine, and slid her tongue among my teeth. Presently we clung together; I, because she clung to me.

At last she drew back. "Not bad. You're a wicked boy. You've been with a woman, I bet."

I said nothing. I had gathered, from literature alone, that to go with a woman was my destiny and function, a cause for congratulation, as with successful schoolwork.

She reapplied her lipstick, pinched my bottom, and went back in to the party.

Soon after, at about eleven, it was suggested to me surreptitiously by the current Girl that I should go to bed.

As I climbed the stairs, nothing about the politician's daughter stayed with me. Although I knew the rising of my flesh was directly connected with what she had done and said, I had *felt* no connection as it occurred. I had not come erect, and, indeed, had known enough to ease back from her, as if to stop her feeling what in fact had not happened.

Even so, I was now disturbed. For in my bed waited my intimate companion.

By now, I'd decided that my own powers of the imagination had made him seem so real for me. Beginning to reason, having been made to do it by my various teachers, I'd awarded him at last the license of My Fantasy. That I was homosexual, oddly, did not occur to me. Until this particular night, I hadn't once equated his caresses and my own with anything other than true companionship.

In my bedroom, however, I began to know differently.

No sooner was the door shut than my penis started to move independently. I'd already bathed before dinner. Now I went into the shower and ran it chill. But this did nothing, save to tone me up, and so excite me more.

I climbed into bed naked, in the dark, trembling with a terror old as life, already hot again, my lips parted.

He met me at once, my Imaginary Friend, My Fantasy, Hold Me. He coiled his arms about me and dragged me down, fierce as a lion, his nails scraping and plowing my shoulders and my lower back. He rubbed himself against me, and I found we dueled, for he, invisible as night, tangible as flesh, was as erect as I. But he knew things I did not. He was tickling my balls, running a finger up and down my spine, kissing me not as the sticky lipstick girl did, but sucking my tongue and my breath right out of me. He exquisitely tortured my penis until I thought I'd choke and lose consciousness, but instead finally I came, exploding in his phantom hand, a shower of silver needles, a gush of syrup and wine.

No sooner did it happen than I began to cry. Then, getting up, I ran to the bathroom and puked out all the exotic dinner.

When I returned, I expected him to be there, to comfort me as in the past. But now, for the very first time, my friend was gone.

He returned. I'm sure you worked that out. He was there the next night, and the next. Initially, I tried to find excuses not to go to bed. I'd sit reading in the rocker by the window. Or I'd watch my TV. Sometimes, seeing the light on, or hearing the television at one o'clock, the Girl would knock and come in, dressed in her skimpy kimono. "Bad boy—you go to sleep now. What will señor say if I tell?"

So in the end I had to sit there in the dark. And once, when she knocked and opened the door, had to pretend I'd been visiting the bathroom.

I took to locking my door. When she knocked then, and rattled, which once or twice she did, I didn't answer. In the morning, she chided me, and I said, "Yes, you woke me up. Father isn't going to like that, is he?"

In any case, whatever I did, unless I slept all night in the chair, I must eventually go to bed. And then, after a few moments, or even immediately, My Fantasy would catch hold of me. He was only sometimes insidious. Usually he overwhelmed me at once, his arms round me, his hands on me, his tongue at my lips. But I was ready anyway. I'd sat in the chair for two hours, nursing my engorgement. Sometimes within a minute of his irresistible strokes, I erupted, whimpering into his unseen yet smothering body. Two or three times, he surprised me, was not there. Then I would thrash about, my face a furnace, the bursting sausage of desire twitching in my own unpracticed grip. And then he would steal over me, shivering fingers along my buttocks, under my ear. He would draw me against his body, massaging my belly, licking my neck, his other hand riding me forward over the edge into the scarlet abyss of orgasm.

I stopped resisting. I simply got into bed without delay and put out the light, and gave myself up, gasping with uncontrollable eagerness.

Once he had had me, I slept. He let me, holding me close. I never ran away again and he never again deserted me. Now and then, generally between three and four in the morning, the window lightening like a pearl, he would wake me . . . That is, I thought, I would wake myself, stiff again, and sometimes then he would take me in his mouth. The bliss of this caused me the first time to scream. Nobody arrived to investigate. I would have said it was a nightmare. I knew, switching on a lamp, they would see no one but me, my nudity safe under the wet sheet and through the mist of the net.

Not until I was almost fifteen did he ease me on to my stomach, and with glorious, melting intrusions, culminating in cannon thrusts, bugger me. I thought I would die of that. I bit my pillows, my saliva mingling with tears and sweat. The orgasm was like death, and, in the morning, I expected to be crippled, disfigured, but everything was apparently the same, save for one tiny drop of blood, my virginity, that I blamed on a bite.

You would probably ask me if I truly still thought by now that I did all this myself, merely through an overactive imagination, and some unlikely contortions of my own body? What can I say? I'd given up. Reason had never been much use in my life. The rules of my daytime world were set, irksome, and unimportant. I longed for and expected nothing. And, by then, I had read of the incubus, the male demon that fastens on hapless sleepers, drawing out their life. I had the attentions of an incubus, then. The fashionable pious religion my parents had once tried to introduce left me unmoved, and I doubted all the messages of the Church. Anyway, they were wrong. I felt no weakness. And he was my friend of long standing. He asked nothing, only my random caresses, my blind pleasure. And the *pleasure*—it was so incredible, it was now my drug. As easy to wean Miranda from her tumblers of gin.

*   *   *

In fact, Miranda was easier. A few days after my fifteenth birthday, following a particularly brilliant public fiasco in an opulent shop of the city, Miranda collapsed. Soon she was in a detoxification clinic, the alcohol all sucked out of her, having to face reality head-on and alone.

She looked, no pun intended, like a mummy, when I saw her a month later. She'd lost too much weight too quickly. Without drink she had no appetite, as she told me, and in detail, constant stomach cramps, flatulence, sensations of asphyxia, headaches, joint pains, nausea, and spots in her vision. The doctors insisted all this was doing her good, but, she petulantly and pathetically mumbled, weeping strengthless tears, she felt so ill.

What could I do? My father looked at her grim-faced, told her she was paying the price for her foolishness, then took me away. A month after that, she was returned to us, walking with a stick on shaking white pumps, in an awful bright cheerful mauve dress that made her look ninety.

She began after this to take an interest in charity work. Someone, perhaps a priest, had told her to have more care of others than herself, and that this would help her. Possibly it did. She ate little, but constantly drank juices, sodas, bottled water. Sometimes she would binge on chocolate, but this brought on agonizing migraines. She'd never smoked, but now talked about taking it up. My father warned her that he detested nicotine on the hands and breath of women. Which must have been a lie, because his latest mistress, the daughter of a tobacco magnate, smoked thirty to fifty cigarettes a day.

Miranda kept away from strong drink for five years. I don't know how she managed this feat. Every day she seemed thinner and more brittle. She had developed, despite the thinness, a large stomach, a light cough, and some strange type of eczema, always hidden in bandages that now and then showed under her sleeves. None of these ailments ever responded to any treatment. She did more and more charity work, then less and less. Sometimes she'd say, "Thank God I gave up drinking. I'm so much better now." The doctors seemed to have taught her to repeat this, like a magical mantra. But it didn't work.

Meanwhile, I was brought steadily into my father's world—dinners, concerts, receptions. He seemed to want me to make up my mind what I wished to do. But I wished to do nothing in particular. In a curious rush, I can't describe it any other way, and can't linger over it, all at once I was twenty. He made a decision for me. I was to go into a junior partnership in the firm of some friend. It had to do with travel and imports—I couldn't have cared less. But as always, my façade of polite attention, my good looks, my apparently superior education—this last a complete myth, for I'd learned practically nothing, and had no application or ambition—saw me well-received in the spurious job. It was all right, in its way. The pretty secretaries ogled me, and a couple of men. But I was suitably aloof. There was nothing unprepossessing in the work, which consisted actually of nothing. And, I had my nights to look forward to, as I'd greedily looked forward to them now for years.

Soon I was sent on a series of missions to wine and dine eminent clients. This, evidently, I was excellent at.

Returning from one of these jaunts, rather drunk, ironically, I found the city house in turmoil. Miranda had been taken seriously ill and rushed to hospital.

She was in a large white room, surrounded by banks of flowers, and bulbous, undersea-looking tubs of oxygen. She sat bolt upright on her pillows, and she was smiling as I hadn't seen her smile for five years. The cause was obvious. On the bedside table stood two magnum bottles of the most expensive and cloudy gin. She'd bribed one of the nurses, and, the times being what they were, the nurse had obliged.

No one else was there.

"Hallo, handsome," she said to me. "Pull up a chair. Have a drink."

"I've been drinking all evening. Should you—"

"It doesn't matter now," she said. "I'm going to die in a couple of weeks."

I was, despite everything, despite my own utter self-centered callousness, shocked. At fifteen, when she was in the clinic, I can't recall being very concerned. I thought her collapse was a plea for my father's notice. But to *die* to get it would be, even for Miranda, a bit extreme.

"Surely that's not so."

"It is so. Have this." She passed me another toothglass of the gin. It was sweet and poisonous. I almost gagged, but got some down. "You're pale, Hilton. Does that mean you care?"

"Of course I care."

"I'm your mother . . ." she said. "Well. There we are. I've got something else in there now. As big as a melon, he said. Did he? Was it a peach? Something appetizing. Absolutely no symptoms, except all the other foul things I've had for years. I just thought it was that. One more pain to put up with. Do you know, he said my liver was quite good. My kidneys too. It's *this* that's going to do it. So. Here's *to Life!*"

I wanted, being me, to run away at once. But how could I? My father was untraceably with one of his women. And no one else had bothered to come, or she hadn't wanted them. The flowers were all they could manage, a call to a top-class florist. They'd do the same for her funeral.

She was very, very drunk. The alcohol, after the space of abstinence, had hit her like a tidal wave. Maybe she'd also been given morphine. She looked happy, almost radiant, her thin face flushed and her eyes limpid with the gin. She didn't seem afraid.

"I want to tell you something, Hilton," she said. "Your father'd never speak about it. I had no one to tell—oh, except I had a counselor, but he kept insisting to me what I felt: Now, señora, you feel *this*, don't you? Or, you must experience the hurt, it mustn't go in but come *out*. And I said, But I don't feel hurt. I feel dirty. There's been a murder inside me. Dirty? he said, Murder? As if I'd confused him. And when I tried to explain, I couldn't get to it, and he corrected me, No, no, it was *hurt* I felt. And then later I thought, So what? I've got a child. I managed that."

"Mother, I'm sorry. I don't understand."

That was when she told me.

She did so in vast, almost technical detail. How the labor pains began when she was in the bath, and she had to be lifted out. And then the private plane, the flight to the hospital, and how she'd given birth, and then given birth again.

"They hadn't known, Hilton. It wasn't the way it is now. And—this is a primitive place, Hilton. *Two* babies. Two little sons. You—and *him*."

I was the second of a pair of twins. Younger by seven minutes. Even as she was screaming and ejecting me, they were slapping him and trying to keep him alive.

"But they couldn't, Hilton. He just folded up like a gray flower and died. There was no proper reason. They said I should just never have had two babies. One had overcome the other. One was too weak, the other too strong." She drank more gin. She said. "You were so like each other to look at. Identical. No one could have told you apart, except *you* were alive. And if he'd lived . . . I used to think you would have played jokes on all of us. You know, the way it is in Shakespeare—" (she pronounced it, drunk, *Shazpure*. For some reason, I remember that very well. Shazpure) "—he'd pretend to be *you*, and you'd pretend to be *him*, and be somewhere else. Or you'd play terrible games with girls. And you'd be inseparable."

We are, Mother, I thought. I drank all the gin in the glass, retched uncontrollably, got a grip. I said, "Why didn't you tell me this before?"

"What was the point? I mean. What was the *point*?"

She leaned back, and her face drooped. "I think I'll have a little sleep, Hilton. Be a good boy and run along. Your father'll be here in half an hour. The nurse said."

Her glass fell from her hand, but it didn't matter, it was empty. She snored softly, and I thought of the cancer in her womb, where we had been, he and I, and I'd crushed the life out of him.

When I stood up, the room spun, and I went into her bathroom and splashed cold water on my face. The nurse, I could tell, seeing me come out, thought that the drops were tears.

That night, I didn't go to bed. I went to a nightclub and drank and smoked dope. In the morning, I was so sick I didn't notice, and fell asleep on the bathroom floor.

It was always in a bed he had me. Always there. Why? Did he only remember the labor-ward bed, or was the coffin, the little tiny white coffin he must have had, like a bed? And nighttime. Darkness.

I kept out of bed, all beds, even a hammock. Slept in chairs, mostly at the hospital, surrounded by harsh lights and muttering people. She went quicker than they said, as if she ran away. She died after three days.

In the mêlée of the next two weeks, the calls, the letters, the servants running to and fro, the ghastly arrangements for a death, it was simple to evade. Even to stop thinking.

The funeral was a classy affair. My father wore his blackest suit and threw a rose into her grave. He abstained from his mistress for a week. God knows why. She certainly didn't, and called him twice, pretending to the servant she was a "friend of the señora's."

In the end, I went and lay on my bed. It was afternoon, and I felt safe. I'd wake again before the darkness came. But I didn't wake, not until the city window of my adult bedroom was patched by black sky and bee-gold lights, and then he was there, beside me.

"I didn't know," I said. "You *know* I didn't know." Talking to him, as I always had when a child. I'd talked to him far less in recent years, only gasps and demands, begging him to go on, do more. "Do you hate me? This isn't hate, is it?"

He put his long formed finger inside me, and moved there. My back arched at once, well taught. His weight was on me, and he tongued my nipples while the other hand cupped my genitals and I swelled. His breath burned my chest, my face. He probed my mouth hungrily. I couldn't speak. The mounting sensation, the unavoidable, was rushing up my spine. On my side, his hand rubbing me even as he edged, twitched, became enormous inside my body.

"Wait—was it my fault—*wait*—"

But he wouldn't wait. Now he clove me in long pounding drumbeats and his fingers skidded on the engine of my seed. The world was going to blow up and I couldn't stop. I gripped the bed and spasmed, my bowels, my belly, my penis, my lungs. I heard my howl, half disembodied. I thought the rollers of it would never stop.

He's killing me, I thought, even as I bucked and grunted in ecstasy. Killing me, as I killed him.

I felt empty when it was over. I lay half off the bed. His weight, his body, were gone.

"Don't go. Listen to me. Can you hear me? *Do* you hear? What are you? *What?* Are you—the one she said—"

But there was nothing in the dark.

He woke me between three and four, tickling the entrance to my body. I had lain awake petrified for three hours, slept for one. Now I tried to fight him off. He paid no attention. He took me in his mouth and all my fear and rage slipped from me as constellations shot through that tiny orifice that knows so much.

And then he was gone once more. He wouldn't stay—to listen. Probably he had never heard me, was deaf and dumb. He was *dead*, after all. He only wanted to do this.

Did it matter? Christ, I'd come to like it so, to rely on it. In all my idiotic life, this was all that was of any real use. It asked nothing but my delight. A lovely present for me at the end of every oh-so-trying day.

And it hadn't hurt me. My last medical showed me fit and strong, as they always did.

What then? Was it revenge? What was it? A demon, a ghost? Should I attempt an exorcism?

I slept, exhausted. I think I felt him in the dark, holding me. Maybe I only dreamed it.

Months followed. I did my nothing work. I slept rather a lot in chairs. I wondered if a hotel room would free me. In the past, he'd come to me in the houses of my—*our*—father. What was his name? They must have had him posthumously christened or blessed—

I began to feel I might be going mad, and my couth, controlled exterior only proved this all the more to me. No one could get inside me (but for my sodomous ghost-lover). I was a dummy from a shop window. Hollow within.

(Now and then I went into my bed. There he always found me. I dreaded it, *wanted* it. I had, after all, nothing else of any interest in my life.)

I had more sense than to confront my father on the matter of my dead twin. But I went finally to the priest who had, haphazardly, received Miranda.

He tried at first to be kind to me, but I, logically, was suspicious. Did he see me as reconverting back into the Faith?

I said, "My mother told me, just before her death, that when I was born—"

"Yes?" he said. His face was bland.

"That there was another child, who died, after only two minutes."

"She told you this?"

"Yes. I think she felt guilty, for some reason."

"She'd used contraception in the past," said the priest. "It weighs heavily on some women, to break the commandments of the Church."

I growled at him, but not outwardly. I said, "Was he named?"

"My dear son, I don't know. You seem troubled." How could he see what no other could? "Why not tell me the real root of your problem?"

I intended to get up and walk out. The slums of the city seethed with diseased and ruined girls who did not break the Church's commandments, and filled the world with unwanted, ill-treated brats.

But I heard myself blurt, "I dream about it. About *him*. He won't leave me alone. Since I was a child—"

What on earth was wrong with me? I hadn't minded, had I, until just now? Until she let me know, twenty years too late, that I was preyed on by an undead brother?

Then I saw my panic, clear as a picture rising up in developing fluid. I saw how everything had changed.

The priest rose as I, belatedly, did. He put a restraining hand on my arm.

"Hilton, my son. I have something to say. God made us, and we have duties to God. To ignore them is unwise."

"What—"

"Please listen a moment. You're of an age, my son, when I'd expect you either to have sought the priesthood—or a woman."

I stood there and gaped at him. I was cold with horror at what I'd suddenly seen to be my existence. That nothing mattered save my nights in the arms of death. To be sucked off and wanked and buggered by death. Disgust, *despair*—both, doubtless, sins.

Then, out of sync, I heard what he'd said.

"You mean I should be involved with a woman?"

"With your father's consent, of course. And with the idea of a true union, a marriage. At your age, what could be more natural? Let me assure you, Hilton, it will get rid of any such nightmares as you've described."

I almost laughed. I stopped myself. I *hadn't* described them. In ancient times, I'd have gone to him, confessed all, been laid out naked before an altar, and flogged to get the devil out of me. Now, this.

Into his hand, I put the money I'd brought (for the orphans), and went away. My head was buzzing. I had an incoherent memory of that lipstick-girl on the balcony, and of the Girls my father had seduced.

Was it so simple? Was it even possible now? I'd never felt anything for a woman. But then, I'd felt nothing for a man either, or for any human thing, save myself. And him.

The evening was gathering in golden polluted clouds on the city. I stood on the steps of the church, staring at the lines of hooting traffic, the flying birds, the glassy towers that touched the sky.

I was frightened, wasn't I? Even ecstasy had become fearful to me. I was in thrall to an incestuous ghost. And going to a priest, had I been given a solution?

Standing there, I felt helpless. And I laughed out loud at the hopeless mathematical equation which, as always, I couldn't solve at all.

Two days later, I saw Meraida. Her name has a structure like my mother's, but I only became aware of that much later. I'd left my smart office, ignoring the fact of my errand-boy assistant, and gone out personally for aspirin. Then walked into a café to swallow them with coffee.

She was sitting at a table, alone. She wore a white short sleeveless dress, that revealed a flawless, almost Martian, tan. Her hair was blue-black and gleamed like silk, falling to her waist, but so thick it was combed straight back without a parting. When she leaned forward to drink her cordial through a straw, I saw the honey tops of her breasts. Maybe I was looking for it, but I had a reaction. Very slight, but definite. I put down my cup and imagined cupping instead one of those full high girl breasts, naked in my hand. The response was immediate. It was as if I'd only been holding it back all these years, the way the celibate is supposed to.

Presently I got up, went over, and sat down at her table. She looked up without affront or dismay. I was used to women gazing at me. She had a triangular, small-boned face, slanting eyes of a hazel that matched her tan. She'd used no makeup, needed none, only a crimson lip gloss that looked as if she'd wet her mouth with strawberries.

"You're wonderful," I said. I'd never bothered to learn any technique for women. What they wanted, after all, seemed fairly obvious.

She blinked. Her lashes were black and silky as little wings. "So are you."

"That's a very good start," I said. "Can I buy you a drink?"

"Yes, all right. I like these."

We sat and talked all afternoon. (Mostly about her, I made sure of that.) She was an art student, but she didn't mind missing her classes for me. I let her know, without quite saying, the walk of life I came from. She could see for herself the suit and shirt and shoes and watch, the Escurier gold ring. I had money all over me. But I think she'd have settled for me anyway, even if I'd come in off a road gang.

I could tell she thought we'd go somewhere almost at once, and she was willing. Young women are now so free. But naturally that wasn't what I required. So we walked in the public gardens, and sat by the fountain. About five, I called in to my partners, and stressed I was laid low by a migraine. Then I took Meraida for drinks and an early dinner.

She ate a lot, but very nicely, and drank a reasonable amount. I told her she should have topaz and amber in her ears, to match her eyes, and she laughed and said she'd never had a man talk to her the way I did, I was too accomplished, and she ought to go at once. So then I took her hand and said I was falling in love with her.

For a moment she looked quite frightened, and then her face turned into a child's at birthday time. She couldn't believe her luck. This handsome, if slightly unbalanced, rich young man, besotted with her as no doubt others more humble had been, trustingly telling her so.

"But you don't know me," she said.

"I've always known you," I said. (Dialogue is easy, if one keeps one's head and has read a few novels.)

"No, but I mean, I mean, my father's a truck driver."

"So what?" All the better. In this city, he'd consent quicker to almost anything.

"You seem so serious about this."

"I am."

"If we make love," she observed, skeptical, "then you'll cool off."

"You don't understand. I think I want to spend my life with you."

"There's no need to lie."

"I'm not lying, Meraida." And I almost wasn't.

When we left the restaurant, again she expected I would take her at once to a hotel. But I stood her on a darkened avenue, and put my hand behind her head and felt her silky hair, and kissed her slowly, the way *he* had taught me. And again, that shivering burning upsurge. But I let her go.

"Don't you want—"

"Not yet. You see, I'm sure. But how could you be? We'll wait a little. Get to know each other better."

She was so disappointed, she glared at me, then smoothed her face. "I think you're playing a game."

"I'll call you tomorrow at eight, before you leave for college."

She shrugged, trying to be brave. "I won't expect it. It was a lovely evening."

I caught her to me again, swept her literally off her feet, and kissed her, tasting wine and brandy and her own clean mouth. Of course, she let me touch her breasts, fleetingly. Unlike the politician's daughter, Meraida could feel me hard as a stone, pressing into her belly.

She refused a taxi, and I could sense her looking back at me as we walked away from each other. *I* did not look back.

In the morning, at eight, I called her. She picked up the receiver after half a second. She was breathless.

"Is it you, Hilton?"

For a week, I courted her. I myself wanted to be sure, and I wanted her to be desperate. By the second outing, under the night-black trees of the gardens, I had my hand inside her low-cut black dress. My urgency reassured me, as did hers. He had taught me such a great deal, that she writhed and nearly reached a climax in my arms. She begged me, almost tearful, Couldn't we go somewhere? But I denied her. Not yet. Oh no.

It was more than cunning. (And cowardice too, let's not forget that; I was, with human beings, a virgin.) I'd thought long and searchingly about some luxurious hotel. Champagne, orchids, possessing Meraida on a milk-white bed, her screams piercing the golden chandelier fitment in the ceiling. I'd thought about it as I shifted in the upright chair, the armchair, striving for a little sleep. For I never now used my bed. (And imagined him invisibly coiled there, imagined what he'd do to me if he got hold of me, until, once or twice, between the memory of my ghost-brother and the new fantasies of a living girl, I haphazardly came anyway.) I'd decided, the hotel test wasn't a fair one. It was true, he might not be able to attempt me in some other place . . . or he might. But in the family houses, the city house, the pillared house by the sea, there he was certain, and there he must be driven off by my woman's presence.

What he would do, what would occur, I had no idea. But he had never been with me when others were. And he had never had any competition, saving that one time on the balcony when I was twelve, which hadn't counted.

My father was going to New York. He would be gone a month. I'd take Meraida to the sea house. She'd love it. We'd swim and eat exotic meals. In the afternoons, we'd walk the hills and the town or lie on the beach. At night—*only at night*—we'd go into my bedroom, spread ourselves out on my bed, and commence the athletics of desire.

Obviously, once I'd told her we were going there, once she'd said

yes—it took her three seconds, this time—I began to suffer a little
gnawing worry. I was totally inexperienced with women, and no
amount of antics elsewhere, or even those clever novels, could
teach me everything. I was partly afraid of proving myself to be a
fool. But then she was so primed, so willing, she'd do half the work
for me. My body was fine, I was fit. She wanted me, and I, to my
continued, amazed, smug reassurance wanted *her*.

It might happen she'd pall, or we'd tire of each other, or she
might fret for the marriage I'd never be allowed to offer. But then I
could wave, or buy, her off. My father, the veteran, would know
exactly how to handle it. Conversely, if I wanted to be safe from
him, I would continue with Meraida until another, better, proposi-
tion came my way. And maybe, seeing how gorgeous she was, this
would last forever. Some women didn't mind the role of mistress,
especially not when cared for. It wasn't that I loved her. And yet I
felt, if she were to save me, I might come to. I wanted to be saved.
I was afraid of him, by now. Afraid of all the feverish joys I'd had
with him. It wasn't that I believed in the soul, or in Hell, or divine
punishment—nothing like that. It seemed to me he'd taken something from me, not only normal *live* sex, but a normal life of any
kind. God knew what I might have been if I hadn't been possessed
by my dead and deathly twin. He'd had no life, he'd pushed and
pulled me away from my own. In the chairs now I had nightmares.
He was looming over me, seen in dream as never before, a gray
mass like a colossal amoeba. He was poking bits of himself into
every crack and hole, and laughing in a soundless, seething way as
I submerged, not in ecstasy, but drowning.

It was filthy, what had been. It wasn't what I should have had.
Who *was* I? What had I lost? Only Meraida and her body could
reveal the state of my potential for rescue or abandonment.

And it might be, it might be, despite everything—I might not be
able. From this concluding possibility, I recoiled in an icy sweat. And
every sexual spasm that took me unawares, I cursed, because I
needed to save up my ardor. I needed to be bursting with it, like a
ripe gourd.

The sky was a hot velvety blue as we were driven to the coast. She
liked the chauffeur, the car, the picnic hamper, and the wine. She
liked the changing landscape as the city fell away, and talked about
wanting to paint it, with that one white cloud there, just posing on
that stand of eucalyptus . . .

Inevitably, too, the house impressed her. We had a ritual tea on
the terrace overlooking the palms and orange trees of the garden. It
still surprised me slightly, all she could eat. I made up the balance

by picking at the food. I was well and truly nervous by now. I
needed a drink, but must watch that too.

We walked on the beach in the evening rosiness, and the glassy
pink sea came in and laved her bare feet. She laughed and skipped
like a child. But I, looking at her beauty in the gold-brown dress I'd
bought her, felt old as her grandfather. What lay in store for me?

The painted dining room set her off again, and dinner—she still
eating heartily, I still leaving almost everything, reaching for the
wine and cognac, tasting, putting them carefully aside—passed in a
sort of whirl of fuss and excitement.

It came to me finally she too might be a little nervous. After all,
I'd built it up so, kept her frustrated, all on edge. And I might, for
all she knew, have strange tastes. Well I *had*, hadn't I?

I showered in one of the guest bathrooms while she lay in a tub
of bubbles en suite to my bedroom. I looked at myself in the mirror,
and saw only what I knew. Most heterosexual women would like
me. There was nothing I needed to hide—physically . . .

Trembling with sudden fear, I sat down on the chair, and took a
swig from the whiskey bottle I'd brought in. Not too big a swig, cau-
tion, for God's sake! So much rested on this. *Everything* rested on it.

When I went into the bedroom, she was lying on my bed. I think
some magazine or book (shades of myself), had told her to arrange
herself in a provocative way. She wore a semitransparent black slip
reaching to her ankles, yet slit along one thigh. It had wired-up lace
cups that lifted and nearly spilled her breasts. Her hair spread everywhere. She smelled of roses and cinnamon, and, through the black
silk and lace, I could see the blacker nest of her center.

The surge came. I rose, as they say, to the occasion. The relief of
it almost made me yell aloud. Instead, I told her she was lovely, and
crossed the floor quickly, dropping my robe as I did so. It seemed I
was to be saved.

An hour later, after she had gone away into the bathroom and
come back, I think after crying a little, she said, "Is it something—
have I done anything—?" She was very young. Younger even than
I was, in many ways, by a thousand years.

"No, I'm sorry. It's my bloody fault. I must have drunk too much
at dinner. Or I'm tired."

We sat at either end of my bed, mulling these inanities over.

Because, of course, you guessed, didn't you, that despite my
flood of arousal, once in contact with her, once called upon to perform the supreme conjunction, my confidence and will left me, my
tower fell. Flaccid and humiliated, I rolled around with her for
twenty, forty minutes, allowing her to try to stimulate me back to
size, kissing her with an increasingly dry unwilling mouth. Until at
last we fell apart, worn out by the hopelessness of it.

No, it wasn't nerves or booze. It was initially the bed, you see. This was so obvious, and I'd never thought . . . the bed, the very bed where I *had* to have her, in order to dismiss my haunting. In that bed, in *my* bed, my body came alert *only for him*. For the feeling of his hands and his fleshly surfaces, that were identical to my own. I mean, *identical*. He'd taught me impeccably. I was *trained*. No other man, let alone a woman, could provide what I needed. And Meraida was—useless.

By the time I let her go, and she me, both of us sweating, pale, sickened, I wanted only to throw myself, or her, from the window. But it wasn't *her* fault.

Even without the bed . . . safe from the ultimate performance, in a park, on an avenue, I'd been able to deceive us both. Oh, I might say I'd try to take her on the floor, against a wall, *tomorrow morning*—but even there and then, even in the much-mooted hotel, it would eventually come down to this. Even without the bed. For *he*—he was my bed, and I was his. And without that, only so far could I go.

She and no one—but he—was my twin. She and no one—but he—was the ghost of my brother. My incubus. Death. Darkness.

In the end, we put out the lights, and she had modestly drawn the curtains and the window was black, the room black, as pitch. We stretched out, not touching, and she fell asleep before I did. It was a big bed.

I thought, at least she would keep him away for this one night. But I knew then it wasn't true, and I lay sodden and still, waiting, until I felt him put his first light finger on my spine.

Then everything came back. Everything I'd tried to build with her. I resisted. I resisted for my very life. But, of course, it was as useless to fight him as it had been to attempt anyone *but* him.

His hands were on all of me, as it seemed, at once. Under my ears, my armpits, my groin. Stroking at my balls, and coaxing my penis, licking my lips, teasing my nipples, unbearably tickling at every sensitive juncture and plain, invading me, filling me up. I'd never gone without him so long—and also I had never known him to be so powerful, so devastating, and he bent my back like a bow, rocking me toward oblivion. As the cosmos disintegrated in my brain and I stifled my own screaming with my fists, I vaguely heard Meraida, four feet away, whimpering shrilly in her sleep.

In the morning, when I woke, dazed, debilitated as if after some fit, I heard her singing in the shower. Dismal, I lay planning how to evict her from my life. At least she was in a happy mood, absurdly had "got over it." Maybe she expected me to be better now and that we should try again, and I'd have to be angry, make up some crime or theatrical idiocy or illness, in order to shunt her off. I was dreading it.

But when she came in, she simply stood, naked and very, very pretty, glowing in the muffled curtained morning sunlight.

I heard her say to me then, that which I heard after, several times (several times, before I truly learned and ended all such times, and went back alone into the dark), from the old and the young, the ugly and the sublime, from a couple more women, and from a few men too:

"Oh, Hilton. It was so amazing! I was half asleep, but what you *did* to me . . . I never knew it could be—like *that*. And the things you did! My God, oh my God! I couldn't even see you in the dark, but you felt so good. Oh God, Hilton, I never came like that before. *Never*. Oh God, Hilton, you're the most wonderful lover in all the world!"

OLDERS
Ursula K. Le Guin

Ursula K. Le Guin is probably one of the most universally respected writers in the world today. Her famous novel *The Left Hand of Darkness* may have been the most influential science fiction novel of its decade, and it shows every sign of becoming one of the enduring classics of the genre—even ignoring the rest of Le Guin's work, the impact of this novel alone on future SF writers would be incalculably strong. (Her 1968 fantasy novel, *A Wizard of Earthsea*, would be almost as influential on future generations of High Fantasy writers.) *The Left Hand of Darkness* won both the Hugo and Nebula Awards, as did Le Guin's monumental novel *The Dispossessed* a few years later. Her novel *Tehanu* won her another Nebula in 1990, and she has also won three other Hugo Awards and a Nebula Award for her short fiction, as well as the National Book Award for children's literature for her novel *The Farthest Shore*, part of her acclaimed Earthsea trilogy. Her other novels include *Planet of Exile, The Lathe of Heaven, City of Illusions, Rocannon's World, The Beginning Place, The Tombs of Atuan, Always Coming Home,* and *Searoad.* She has also published five collections: *The Wind's Twelve Quarters, Orsinian Tales, The Compass Rose, Buffalo Gals and Other Animal Presences,* and *A Fisherman of the Inland Sea.* Her most recent book is a collection of four interconnected novellas, *Four Ways to Forgiveness.*

In the subtle and bittersweet story that follows, she demonstrates once again that love can transform us—sometimes in very surprising ways.

OLDERS

The moon slips and shines in the wrinkled mirror before the prow, and from the northern sky the Bright Companions shoot glancing arrows of light along the water. In the stern of the boat the poles-man stands in the watchful solemnity of his task. His movements as he poles and steers the boat are slow, certain, august. The long, low channelboat slides on the black water as silently as the reflection it pursues. A few dark figures huddle in it. One dark figure lies full length on the halfdeck, arms at his sides, closed eyes unseeing that other moon slipping and shining through wisps of fog in the luminous blue night sky. The Husbandman of Sandry is coming home from war.

They had been waiting for him on Sandry Island ever since last spring, when he went with seven men following the messengers who came to raise the Queen's army. In midsummer four of the men of Sandry brought back the news that he was wounded and was lying in the care of the Queen's own physician. They told of his great valor in battle, and told of their own prowess too, and how they had won the war. Since then there had been no news.

With him now in the channelboat were the three companions who had stayed with him, and a physician sent by the Queen, an assistant to her own doctor. This man, an active, slender person in his forties, cramped by the long night's travel, was quick to leap ashore when the boat slid silently up along the stone quay of Sandry Farm.

While the boatmen and the others busied themselves making the boat fast and lifting the stretcher and its burden up from the boat to the quay, the doctor went on up to the house. Approaching the island, as the sky imperceptibly lightened from night-blue to color-less pallor, he had seen the spires of windmills, the crowns of trees, and the roofs of the house, all in black silhouette, standing very high after the miles of endlessly level reed-beds and water-channels. "Hello, the people!" he called out as he entered the courtyard. "Wake up! Sandry has come home!"

The kitchen was astir already. Lights sprang up elsewhere in the big house. The doctor heard voices, doors. A stableboy came vault-ing out of the loft where he had slept, a dog barked and barked its tardy warning, people began to come out of the housedoor. As the stretcher was borne into the courtyard, the Farmwife came hurrying out, wrapped in a green cloak that hid her nightdress, her hair loose, her feet bare on the stones. She ran to the stretcher as they set it down. "Farre, Farre," she said, kneeling, bending over the still figure. No one spoke or moved in that moment. "He is dead," she said in a whisper, drawing back.

"He is alive," the doctor said. And the oldest of the litterbearers, Pask the saddler, said in his rumbling bass, "He lives, Makali-dem. But the wound was deep."

The doctor looked with pity and respect at the Farmwife, at her bare feet and her clear, bewildered eyes. "Dema," he said, "let us bring him in to the warmth."

"Yes, yes," she said, rising and running ahead to prepare.

When the stretcherbearers came out again, half the people of Sandry were in the courtyard waiting to hear their news. Most of all they looked to old Pask when he came out, and he looked at them all. He was a big, slow man, girthed like an oak, with a stiff face set in deep lines. "Will he live?" a woman ventured. Pask continued looking them all over until he chose to speak. "We'll plant him," he said.

"Ah, ah!" the woman cried, and a groan and sigh went among them all.

"And our grandchildren's children will know his name," said Dyadi, Pask's wife, bosoming through the crowd to her husband. "Hello, old man."

"Hello, old woman," Pask said. They eyed each other from an equal height.

"Still walking, are you?" she said.

"How else get back where I belong?" Pask said. His mouth was too set in a straight line to smile, but his eyes glinted a little.

"Took your time doing it. Come on, old man. You must be perishing." They strode off side by side toward the lane that led to the saddlery and paddocks. The courtyard buzzed on, all in low-voiced groups around the other two returned men, getting and giving the news of the wars, the city, the marsh isles, the farm.

Indoors, in the beautiful high shadowy room where Farre now lay in the bed still warm from his wife's sleep, the physician stood by the bedside, as grave, intent, careful as the polesman had stood in the stern of the channelboat. He watched the wounded man, his fingers on the pulse. The room was perfectly still.

The woman stood at the foot of the bed, and presently he turned to her and gave a quiet nod that said, *Very well, as well as can be expected.*

"He seems scarcely to breathe," she whispered. Her eyes looked large in her face knotted and clenched with anxiety.

"He's breathing," the escort assured her. "Slow and deep. Dema, my name is Hamid, assistant to the Queen's physician, Dr. Saker. Her majesty and the Doctor, who had your husband in his care, desired me to come with him and stay here as long as I am needed, to give what care I can. Her majesty charged me to tell you that she is grateful for his sacrifice, that she honors his courage in her service. She will do what may be done to prove that gratitude and to show that honor. And still she bade me tell you that whatever may be done will fall short of his due."

"Thank you," said the Farmwife, perhaps only partly understanding, gazing only at the set, still face on the pillow. She was trembling a little.

"You're cold, dema," Hamid said gently and respectfully. "You should get dressed."

"Is he warm enough? Was he chilled, in the boat? I can have the fire laid—"

"No. He's warm enough. It's you I speak of, dema."

She glanced at him a little wildly, as if seeing him that moment. "Yes," she said. "Thank you."

"I'll come back in a little while," he said, laid his hand on his heart, and quietly went out, closing the massive door behind him.

He went across to the kitchen wing and demanded food and drink for a starving man, a thirsty man leg-cramped from crouching in a damned boat all night. He was not shy, and was used to the authority of his calling. It had been a long journey overland from the city, and then poling through the marshes, with Broad Isle the only hospitable place to stop among the endless channels, and the sun beating down all day, and then the long dreamlike discomfort of the night. He made much of his hunger and travail to amuse his hosts and to divert them, too, from asking questions about how the Husbandman did and would do. He did not want to tell them more than the man's wife knew.

But they, discreet or knowing or respectful, asked no direct questions of him. Though their concern for Farre was plain, they asked only, by various indirections, if he was sure to live, and seemed satisfied by that assurance. In some faces Hamid thought he saw a glimpse of something beyond satisfaction: a brooding acceptance in one; an almost conniving intelligence in another. One young fellow blurted out, "Then will he be—" and shut his mouth, under the joined stares of five or six older people.

They were a trapmouthed lot, the Sandry Islanders. All that were not actively young looked old: seamed, weatherbeaten, brown skin wrinkled and silvery, hands gnarled, hair thick, coarse, and dry. Only their eyes were quick, observant. And some of them had eyes of an unusual color, like amber; Pask, his wife, Dyadi, and several others,

as well as Farre himself. The first time Hamid had seen Farre, before
the coma deepened, he had been struck by the strong features and
those light, clear eyes. They all spoke dialect, but Hamid had grown up
not far inland from the marshes, and anyhow had an ear for dialects.
By the end of his large and satisfying breakfast he was glottal-stopping
with the best of them.

He returned to the great bedroom with a well-loaded tray. As he
had expected, the Farmwife, dressed and shod, was sitting close
beside the bed, her hand lying lightly on her husband's hand. She
looked up at Hamid politely but as an intruder: please be quiet, don't
interrupt us, make him be well and go away. . . . Hamid had no particular eye for beauty in women, perhaps having seen beauty too
often at too short a distance, where it dissolves; but he responded to
a woman's health, to the firm sweet flesh, the quiver and vigor of
full life. And she was fully alive. She was as tender and powerful as
a red-deer doe, as unconsciously splendid. He wondered if there
were fawns, and then saw the child standing behind her chair. The
room, its shutters closed, was all shadow with a spatter and dappling
of broken light across the islands of heavy furniture, the footboard of
the bed, the folds of the coverlet, the child's face and dark eyes.

"Hamid-dem," the Farmwife said—despite her absorption in her
husband she had caught his name, then, with the desperate keen
hearing of the sickroom, where every word carries hope or doom—
"I still cannot see him breathe."

"Lay your ear against his chest," he said, in a tone deliberately
louder than her whisper. "You'll hear the heart beat, and feel the
lungs expand. Though slowly, as I said. Dema, I brought this for
you. Now you'll sit here, see, at this table. A little more light, a shut-
ter open, so. It won't disturb him, not at all. Light is good. You are
to sit here and eat breakfast. Along with your daughter, who must
be hungry too."

She introduced the child, Idi, a girl of five or six, who clapped her
hand on her heart and whispered "Give-you-good-day-dema" all in
one glottal-stopped word before she shrank back behind her mother.

It is pleasant to be a physician and be obeyed, Hamid reflected,
as the Farmwife and her child, large and little images of each other
in their shirts and full trousers and silken braided hair, sat at the
table where he had put the tray down and meekly ate the breakfast
he had brought. He was charmed to see that between them they left
not a crumb.

When Makali rose, her face had lost the knotted look and her
dark eyes, though still large and still concerned, were tranquil. She
has a peaceful heart, he thought. At the same moment his physician's eye caught the signs; she was pregnant, probably about three
months along. She whispered to the child, who trotted away. She

came back to the chair at the bedside, which he had already relin-
quished.

"I am going to examine and dress his wound," Hamid said. "Will
you watch, dema, or come back?"

"Watch," she said.

"Good," he said. Taking off his coat, he asked her to have hot
water sent in from the kitchen.

"We have it piped," she said, and went to a door in the farthest
shadowy corner. He had not expected such an amenity. Yet he knew
that some of these island farms were very ancient places of civiliza-
tion, drawing for their comfort and provision on inexhaustible sun,
wind, and tide, settled in a way of life as immemorial as that of their
plowlands and pastures, as full and secure. Not the show-wealth of
the city, but the deep richness of the land, was in the steaming
pitcher she brought him, and in the woman who brought it.

"You don't need it boiling?" she asked, and he said, "This is what
I want."

She was quick and steady, relieved to have a duty, to be of use. When
he bared the great sword-wound across her husband's abdomen he
glanced up at her to see how she took it. Compressed lips, a steady gaze.

"This," he said, his fingers above the long, dark, unhealed gash,
"looks the worst; but this, here, is the worst. That is superficial, a
mere slash as the sword withdrew. But here, it went in, and deep."
He probed the wound. There was no shrinking or quiver in the
man's body; he lay insensible. "The sword withdrew," Hamid went
on, "as the swordsman died. Your husband killed him even as he
struck. And took the sword from him. When his men came around
him he was holding it in his left hand and his own sword in his right,
though he could not rise from his knees. . . . Both those swords came
here with us. . . . There, you see? That was a deep thrust. And a wide
blade. That was nearly a deathblow. But not quite, not quite. Though
to be sure, it took its toll."

He looked up at her openly, hoping she would meet his eyes, hoping to receive from her the glance of acceptance, intelligence, recognition that he had seen in this face and that among Sandry's people.
But her eyes were on the purple and livid wound, and her face was
simply intent.

"Was it wise to move him, carry him so far?" she asked, not questioning his judgment, but in wonder.

"The Doctor said it would do him no harm," Hamid said. "And it
has done none. The fever is gone, as it has been for nine days now."
She nodded, for she had felt how cool Farre's skin was. "The inflam-
mation of the wound is if anything less than it was two days ago.
The pulse and breath are strong and steady. This was the place for
him to be, dema."

"Yes," she said. "Thank you. Thank you, Hamid-dem." Her clear eyes looked into his for a moment before returning to the wound, the motionless, muscular body, the silent face, the closed eyelids.

Surely, Hamid thought, surely if it were true she'd know it! She couldn't have married the man not knowing! But she says nothing. So it's not true, it's only a story. . . . But this thought, which gave him a tremendous relief for a moment, gave way to another: She knows and is hiding from the knowledge. Shutting the shadow into the locked room. Closing her ears in case the word is spoken.

He found he had taken a deep breath and was holding it.

He wished the Farmwife were older, tougher, that she loved her farmer less. He wished he knew what the truth was, and that he need not be the one to speak it.

But on an utterly unexpected impulse, he spoke: "It is not death," he said, very low, almost pleading.

She merely nodded, watching. When he reached for a clean cloth, she had it ready to his hand.

As a physician, he asked her of her pregnancy. She was well, all was well. He ordered her to walk daily, to be two hours out of the sickroom in the open air. He wished he might go with her, for he liked her and it would have been a pleasure to walk beside her, watching her go along tall and lithe and robust. But if she was to leave Farre's side for two hours, he was to replace her there: that was simply understood. He obeyed her implicit orders as she obeyed his explicit ones.

His own freedom was considerable, for she spent most of the day in the sickroom, and there was no use his being there too, little use his being there at all, in fact. Farre needed nothing from him or her or anyone, aside from the little nourishment he took. Twice a day, with infinite patience, she contrived to feed him ten or a dozen sips of Dr. Saker's rich brew of meat and herbs and medicines, which Hamid concocted and strained daily in the kitchen with the cooks' interested aid. Aside from those two half hours, and once a day the bed-jar for a few drops of urine, there was nothing to be done. No chafing or sores developed on Farre's skin. He lay moveless, showing no discomfort. His eyes never opened. Once or twice, she said, in the night, he had moved a little, shuddered. Hamid had not seen him make any movement for days.

Surely, if there was any truth in the old book Dr. Saker had shown him and in Pask's unwilling and enigmatic hints of confirmation, his wife would know? But she said never a word, and it was too late now for him to ask. He had lost his chance. And if he could not speak to her, he would not go behind her back, asking the others if there was any truth in the tale.

Of course there isn't, he told his conscience. A myth, a rumor, a folktale of the "Old Islanders" . . . and the word of an ignorant man, a saddler . . . Superstition! What do I see when I look at my patient? A deep coma. A deep, restorative coma. Unusual, yes, but not abnormal, not uncanny. Perhaps such a coma, a very long vegetative period of recovery, common to these islanders, an inbred people, would be the origin of the myth, much exaggerated, made fanciful . . .

They were a healthy lot, and though he offered his services he had little to do once he had reset a boy's badly splinted arm and scraped out an old fellow's leg-abscesses. Sometimes little Idi tagged after him. Clearly she adored her father and missed his company. She never asked, "Will he get well," but Hamid had seen her crouched at the bedside, quite still, her cheek against Farre's unresponding hand. Touched by the child's dignity, Hamid asked her what games she and her father had played. She thought a long time before she said, "He would tell me what he was doing and some- times I could help." Evidently she had simply followed Farre in his daily round of farmwork and management. Hamid provided only an unsatisfactory, frivolous substitute. She would listen to his tales of the court and city for a while, not very interested, and soon would run off to her own small, serious duties. Hamid grew restive under the burden of being useless.

He found walking soothed him, and went almost daily on a favorite circuit: down to the quay first, and along the dunes to the southeast end of the island, from which he first saw the open sea, free at last of the whispering green levels of the reedbeds. Then up the steepest slope on Sandry, a low hill of worn granite and sparse earth, for the view of sea and tidal dams, island fields and green marshes from its summit, where a cluster of windmills caught the sea-wind with slender vanes. Then down the slope past the trees, the Old Grove, to the farmhouse. There were a couple of dozen houses in sight from Sandry Hill, but "the farmhouse" was the only one so called, as its owner was called the Husbandman, or Farmer Sandry, or simply Sandry if he was away from the island. And nothing would keep an islander away from his island but his duty to the crown. Rooted folk, Hamid thought wryly, standing in the lane near the Old Grove to look at the trees.

Elsewhere on the island, indeed on all the islands, there were no trees to speak of. Scrub willows down along the streams, a few orchards of wind-dwarfed, straggling apples. But here in the grove were great trees, some with mighty trunks, surely hundreds of years old, and none of them less than eight or ten times a man's height. They did not crowd together but grew widely spaced, each spreading its limbs and crown broadly. In the spacious aisles under them grew a few shrubs and ferns and a thin, soft, pleasant grass. Their shade was beautiful on these hot summer days when the sun glared off the sea and the channels and the sea-wind scarcely stirred the fiery air. But Hamid did not go under the trees. He stood in the lane, looking at that shade under the heavy foliage.

Not far from the lane he could see in the grove a sunny gap where an old tree had come down, perishing in a winter gale, maybe a century ago, for nothing was left of the fallen trunk but a grassy hummock a few yards long. No sapling had sprung up or been planted to replace the old tree; only a wild rose, rejoicing in the light, flowered thornily over the ruin of its stump.

Hamid walked on, gazing ahead at the house he now knew so well, the massive slate roofs, the shuttered window of the room where Makali was sitting now beside her husband, waiting for him to wake.

"Makali, Makali," he said under his breath, grieving for her, angry with her, angry with himself, sorry for himself, listening to the sound of her name.

The room was dark to his still sun-bedazzled eyes, but he went to his patient with a certain decisiveness, almost abruptness, and turned back the sheet. He palpated, ausculted, took the pulse.

"His breathing has been harsh," Makali murmured.

"He's dehydrated. Needs water."

She rose to fetch the little silver bowl and spoon she used to feed him his soup and water, but Hamid shook his head. The picture in Dr. Saker's ancient book was vivid in his mind, a woodcut, showing exactly what must be done—what must be done, that is, if one believed this myth, which he did not, nor did Makali, or she would surely have said something by now! And yet, there was nothing else to be done. Farre's face was sunken, his hair came loose at a touch. He was dying, very slowly, of thirst.

"The bed must be tipped, so that his head is high, his feet low," Hamid said authoritatively. "The easiest way will be to take off the footboard. Tebra will give me a hand." She went out and returned with the yardman, Tebra, and with him Hamid briskly set about the business. They got the bed fixed at such a slant that he put a webbing strap round Farre's chest to keep him from sliding quite down. He asked Makali for a waterproof sheet or cape. Then, fetching a deep copper basin from the kitchen, he filled it with cold water. He spread the sheet of oilskin she had brought under Farre's legs and feet, and propped the basin in an overturned footstool so that it held steady as he laid Farre's feet in the water.

"It must be kept full enough that his soles touch the water," he said to Makali.

"It will keep him cool," she said, asking, uncertain. Hamid did not answer.

Her troubled, frightened look enraged him. He left the room without saying more.

When he returned in the evening she said, "His breathing is much easier."

No doubt, Hamid thought, ausculting, now that he breathes once a minute.

"Hamid-dem," she said, "there is . . . something I noticed. . . ."

"Yes."

She heard his ironic, hostile tone, as he did. Both winced. But she was started, had begun to speak, could only go on.

"His . . . " She started again. "It seemed . . . " She drew the sheet down farther, exposing Farre's genitals.

The penis lay almost indistinguishable from the testicles and the brown, grained skin of the inner groin, as if it had sunk into them, as if all were returning to an indistinguishable unity, a featureless solidity.

"Yes," Hamid said, expressionless, shocked in spite of himself. "The . . . the process is following . . . what is said to be its course."

She looked at him across her husband's body. "But— Can't you—?"

He stood silent a while. "It seems that— My information is that in these cases—a very grave shock to the system, to the body—" He paused, trying to find words, "—such as an injury or a great loss, a grief—but in this case, an injury, an almost fatal wound— A wound that almost certainly would have been fatal, had not it inaugurated the . . . the process in question, the inherited capacity . . . propensity . . ."

She stood still, still gazing straight at him, so that all the big words shrank to nothing in his mouth.

He stooped and with his deft, professional gentleness opened Farre's closed eyelid. "Look!" he said.

She too stooped to look, to see the blind eye exposed, without pupil, iris, or white, a polished, featureless, brown bead.

When her indrawn breath was repeated and again repeated in a dragging sob, Hamid burst out at last, "But you knew, surely! You knew when you married him."

"Knew," said her dreadful indrawn voice.

The hair stood up on Hamid's arms and scalp. He could not look at her. He lowered the eyelid, thin and stiff as a dry leaf.

She turned away and walked slowly across the long room into the shadows.

"They laugh about it," said the deep, dry voice he had never heard, out of the shadows. "On the land, in the city, people laugh about it, don't they. They talk about the wooden men, the block-heads, the Old Islanders. They don't laugh about it, here. When he married me—" She turned to face Hamid, stepping into the shaft of warm twilight from the one unshuttered window so that her clothing glimmered white. "When Farre of Sandry, Farre Older courted me and married me, on the Broad Isle where I lived, the people there said *don't do it* to me, and the people here said *don't do it* to him. Marry your own kind, marry in your own kind. But what did we care for that? He didn't care and I didn't care. I didn't believe! I wouldn't believe! But I came here— Those trees, the grove, the older trees—you've been there, you've seen them. Do you know they have names?" She stopped, and the dragging, gasping, indrawn sob began again. She took hold of a chairback and stood rocking it back and forth. "He took me there. 'That is my grandfather,'" she said in a hoarse, jeering gasp. "'That's Aita, my mother's grandmother. Doran-dem has stood four hundred years.'"

Her voice failed.

"We don't laugh about it," Hamid said. "It is a tale—something that might be true—a mystery. Who they are, the . . . the olders, what makes them change . . . how it happens . . . Dr. Saker sent me here not only to be of use but to learn. To verify . . . the process."

"The process," Makali said.

She came back to the bedside, facing him across it, across the stiff body, the log in the bed.

"What am I carrying here?" she asked, soft and hoarse, her hands on her belly.

"A child," Hamid said, without hesitating and clearly.

"What kind of child?"

"Does it matter?"

She said nothing.

"His child, your child, as your daughter is. Do you know what kind of child Idi is?"

After a while Makali said softly, "Like me. She does not have the amber eyes."

"Would you care less for her if she did?"

"No," she said.

She stood silent. She looked down at her husband, then toward the windows, then straight at Hamid.

"You came to learn," she said.

"Yes. And to give what help I can give."

She nodded. "Thank you," she said.

He laid his hand a moment on his heart.

She sat down in her usual place beside the bed with a deep, very quiet breath, too quiet to be a sigh.

Hamid opened his mouth. "He's blind, deaf, without feeling. He doesn't know if you're there or not there. He's a log, a block, you need not keep this vigil!" All these words said themselves aloud in his mind, but he did not speak one of them. He closed his mouth and stood silent.

"How long?" she asked in her usual soft voice.

"I don't know. That change . . . came quickly. Maybe not long now."

She nodded. She laid her hand on her husband's hand, her light warm touch on the hard bones under hard skin, the long, strong, motionless fingers.

"Once," she said, "he showed me the stump of one of the olders, one that fell down a long time ago."

Hamid nodded, thinking of the sunny clearing in the grove, the wild rose.

"It had broken right across in a great storm, the trunk had been rotten. It was old, ancient, they weren't sure even who . . . the name . . . hundreds of years old. The roots were still in the ground but the trunk was rotten. So it broke right across in the gale. But the stump was still there in the ground. And you could see. He showed me." After a pause she said, "You could see the bones. The leg bones. In the trunk of the tree. Like pieces of ivory. Inside it. Broken off with it." After another silence, she said, "So they do die. Finally."

Hamid nodded.

Silence again. Though he listened and watched almost automatically, Hamid did not see Farre's chest rise or fall.

"You may go whenever you like, Hamid-dem," she said gently. "I'm all right now. Thank you."

He went to his room. On the table, under the lamp when he lighted it, lay some leaves. He had picked them up from the border of the lane that went by the grove, the grove of the older trees. A few dry leaves, a twig. What their blossom was, their fruit, he did not know. It was summer, between the flower and the seed. And he dared not take a branch, a twig, a leaf from the living tree.

When he joined the people of the farm for supper, old Pask was there.

"Doctor-dem," the saddler said in his rumbling bass, "is he turning?"

"Yes," Hamid said.

"So you're giving him water?"

"Yes."

"You must give him water, dema," the old man said, relentless. "She doesn't know. She's not his kind. She doesn't know his needs."

"But she bears his seed," said Hamid, grinning suddenly, fiercely, at the old man.

Pask did not smile or make any sign, his stiff face impassive. He said, "Yes. The girl's not, but the other may be older." And he turned away.

Next morning after he had sent Makali out for her walk, Hamid studied Farre's feet. They were extended fully into the water, as if he had stretched downward to it, and the skin looked softer. The long brown toes stretched apart a little. And his hands, still motionless, seemed longer, the fingers knotted as with arthritis yet powerful, lying spread on the coverlet at his sides.

Makali came back ruddy and sweaty from her walk in the summer morning. Her vitality, her vulnerability were infinitely moving and pathetic to Hamid after his long contemplation of a slow, inexorable toughening, hardening, withdrawal. He said, "Makali-dem, there is no need for you to be here all day. There is nothing to do for him but keep the water-basin full."

"So it means nothing to him that I sit by him," she said, half questioning, half stating.

"I think it does not. Not any more."

She nodded.

Her gallantry touched him. He longed to help her. "Dema, did he, did anyone ever speak to you about—if this should happen— There may be ways we can ease the change, things that are traditionally done— I don't know them. Are there people here whom I might ask—Pask and Dyadi—?"

"Oh, they'll know what to do when the time comes," she said, with an edge in her voice. "They'll see to it that it's done right. The right way, the old way. You don't have to worry about that. The doctor doesn't have to bury his patient, after all. The gravediggers do that."

"He is not dead."

"No. Only blind and deaf and dumb and doesn't know if I'm in the room or a hundred miles away." She looked up at Hamid, a gaze which for some reason embarrassed him. "If I stuck a knife in his hand would he feel it?" she asked.

He chose to take the question as one of curiosity, desire to know. "The response to any stimulus has grown steadily less," he said, "and in the last few days it has disappeared. That is, response to any stimulus I've offered." He took up Farre's wrist and pinched it as hard as he could, though the skin was so tough now and the flesh so dry that he had difficulty doing so.

She watched. "He was ticklish," she said.

Hamid shook his head. He touched the sole of the long brown foot that rested in the basin of water; there was no withdrawal, no response at all.

"So he feels nothing. Nothing hurts him," she said.

"I think not."

"Lucky him."

Embarrassed again, Hamid bent down to study the wound. He

had left off the bandages, for the slash had closed, leaving a clean seam, and the deep gash had developed a tough lip all round it, a barky ring that was well on the way to sealing it shut.

"I could carve my name on him," Makali said, leaning close to Hamid, and then she bent down over the inert body, kissing and stroking and holding it, her tears running down.

When she had wept a while, Hamid went to call the women of the household, and they came gathering round her full of solace and took her off to another room. Left alone, Hamid drew the sheet back up over Farre's chest; he felt a satisfaction in her having wept at last, having broken down. Tears were the natural reaction, and the necessary one. A woman clears her mind by weeping, a woman had told him once.

He flicked his thumbnail hard against Farre's shoulder. It was like flicking the headboard, the night-table—his nail stung for a moment. He felt a surge of anger against his patient, no patient, no man at all, not any more.

Was his own mind clear? What was he angry with Farre for? Could the man help being what he was, or what he was becoming?

Hamid went out of the house and walked his circuit, went to his own room to read. Late in the afternoon he went to the sickroom. No one was there with Farre. He pulled out the chair she had sat in so many days and nights and sat down. The shadowy silence of the room soothed his mind. A healing was occurring here: a strange healing, a mystery, frightening, but real. Farre had traveled from mortal injury and pain to this quietness; had turned from death to this different, this other life, this older life. Was there any wrong in that? Only that he wronged her in leaving her behind, and he must have done that, and more cruelly, if he had died.

Or was the cruelty in his not dying?

Hamid was still there pondering, half-asleep in the twilit serenity of the room, when Makali came in quietly and lighted a dim lamp. She wore a loose, light shirt that showed the movement of her full breasts, and her gauze trousers were gathered at the ankle above her bare feet; it was a hot night, sultry, the air stagnant on the salt marshes and the sandy fields of the island. She came around the bedstead. Hamid started to get up.

"No, no, stay. I'm sorry, Hamid-dem. Forgive me. Don't get up. I only wanted to apologize for behaving like a child."

"Grief must find its way out," he said.

"I hate to cry. Tears empty me. And pregnancy makes one cry over nothing."

"This is a grief worth crying for, dema."

"Oh, yes," she said. "If we had loved each other. Then I might have cried that basin full." She spoke with a hard lightness. "But

that was over years ago. He went off to the war to get away from
me. This child I carry, it isn't his. He was always cold, always slow.
Always what he is now."

She looked down at the figure in the bed with a quick, strange,
challenging glance.

"They were right," she said, "half-alive shouldn't marry the living.
If your wife was a stick, was a stump, a lump of wood, wouldn't you
seek some friend of flesh and blood? Wouldn't you seek the love of
your own kind?"

As she spoke she came nearer to Hamid, very near, stooping over
him. Her closeness, the movement of her clothing, the warmth and
smell of her body, filled his world suddenly and entirely, and when
she laid her hands on his shoulders he reached up to her, sinking
upward into her, pulling her down onto him to drink her body with
his mouth, to impale her heavy softness on the aching point of his
desire, so lost in her that she had pulled away from him before he
knew it. She was turning from him, turning to the bed, where with
a long, creaking groan the stiff body trembled and shook, trying to
bend, to rise, and the round blank balls of the eyes stared out under
lifted eyelids.

"There!" Makali cried, breaking free of Hamid's hold, standing
triumphant. "Farre!"

The stiff half-lifted arms, the outspread fingers trembled like
branches in the wind. No more than that. Again the deep, cracking,
creaking groan from within the rigid body. She huddled up against
it on the tilted bed, stroking the face and kissing the unblinking
eyes, the lips, the breast, the scarred belly, the lump between the
joined, grown-together legs. "Go back now," she murmured, "go
back to sleep. Go back, my dear, my own, my love, go back now,
now I know, now I know. . . ."

Hamid broke from his paralysis and left the room, the house,
striding blindly out into the luminous midsummer night. He was
very angry with her, for using him; presently with himself, for being
usable. His outrage began to die away as he walked. Stopping, seeing where he was, he gave a short, rueful, startled laugh. He had
gone astray off the lane, following a path that led right into the Old
Grove, a path he had never taken before.

All around him, near and far, the huge trunks of the trees were
almost invisible under the massive darkness of their crowns. Here
and there the moonlight struck through the foliage, making the
edges of the leaves silver, pooling like quicksilver in the grass. It was
cool under the older trees, windless, perfectly silent.

Hamid shivered.

"He'll be with you soon," he said to the thick-bodied, huge-armed,
deep-rooted, dark presences. "Pask and the others know what to do.

He'll be here soon. And she'll come here with the baby, summer afternoons, and sit in his shade. Maybe she'll be buried here. At his roots. But I am not staying here." He was walking as he spoke, back toward the farmhouse and the quay and the channels through the reeds and the roads that led inland, north, away. "If you don't mind, I'm on my way, right away. . . ."

The olders stood unmoved as he hurried out from under them and strode down the lane, a dwindling figure, too slight, too quick to be noticed.

SAVED

Andy Duncan

New writer Andy Duncan is a recent graduate of the Clarion West Writers Workshop in Seattle. He's made fiction and poetry sales to *Asimov's Science Fiction, Starlight, Negative Capability,* and elsewhere and has published critical articles with *The New York Review of Science Fiction* and *The Journal of the Fantastic in the Arts.* A native of Batesberg, South Carolina, he lived for many years in Raleigh, North Carolina, and has recently moved to Tuscaloosa, Alabama.

In the moving and spooky story of love and loss that follows, he shows us that although the camera may lie, it sometimes does so with the best of *intentions* . . .

SAVED

She will not go below. She will watch. She will see all of it, all. She hugs the rail as the *Carpathia* steams into a harbor, into a city, gone mad.

Thousands of people. Millions. Every bridge, pier, and jetty, every visible street and rooftop, aswarm and howling. Every light ablaze in every building. Stars gone, night banished. Along the shoreline, great popping powder bursts and blinding flashes, as the ship's image is burned into the plates of three dozen front pages. It is like a bombardment. The drifting magnesium clouds sear her nostrils, score her throat. She refuses to cough. The cameras remind her of Noel, a vile and ratlike thought she chases shrieking from her mind. A great plume of water, spouted by a fireboat, arcs across the glaring skyline: Why? The din is unendurable. The sirens wail. The liner's foghorn continuously blares, as swarms of smaller craft steam back and forth across the bow, jostle one another alongside, are nearly swamped in the big ship's wake. Ferries, yachts, tugboats, dinghies, barges, each one low in the water, leaden with people. "For God's sake, get clear!" roars the officer with the muttonchops. He leans over the rail, two feet away, slashes the air with his cap. "You damned chowderheads," he bellows, "get back, get *back* I say, you'll wreck us yet, damn you to a man!" The veins stand out on his forehead; the cords of his neck bulge. Right below her, a tug scrapes a ferryboat, and the passengers jamming the decks of each craft are jolted to their knees. The shouting men and women atop the wheelhouse somehow hold on, keep waving their crude signs. The cheap paper furls at half-staff; the placards droop. SEEK CLAIRE ADAMS OF PHILADELPHIA. NEWS OF STEVENSON FAMILY—CHICAGO. WHERE MR. COLLINGS AND SON AGE SIX. "He's a tall man!" wails a woman clawing at one end of a banner that says BILL I'M HERE BILL. "You can't miss him! You must have seen him! He's a very tall man!" This is the end; she can bear no more. Clapping her hands over her ears, screwing shut her eyes, Miss Dorothy Gibson, who has stood silent vigil at the rail of the *Carpathia* for hours, her silence remarked on by dozens of people, finally now begins to scream, scream what she thinks is a string of words—a man's name, over and over—but really is just a scream. She collapses, screaming, onto the muttonchop man, who grapples her to check her slide to the cold gleaming slime of the deck, and who interrupts his roaring to whisper, as urgently as a lover: "Christ almighty, woman, not *you*, too!" Still she screams. And the ship has yet to dock.

Darkness. Piano (merry). Lights up.

Skirts billowing in the silent breeze, a little girl waves to the people back home, her hand flailing as if tied only loosely to her forearm. With her other hand she pushes up her sailor's cap, but instantly it slips down again, leaving her one-eyed and shy. Around her neck is a child's-size life preserver bearing the ship's name.

Cut to:

Three distant people stand at the base of a great funnel six times their height. Steam billows from the flat summit of the funnel. The people wave their tiny arms. The one in the middle is shorter. A family, perhaps? Gulls wheel overhead, register as bobbing flecks, imperfections in the film.

Cut to:

A beaming, slick-haired man in white flannel pants and an undershirt shows off his biceps to an admiring crowd. The man bends forward at the waist, places his palms flat on the deck, kicks his feet into the air, straightens his legs, stands on his hands. The onlookers make clapping motions as he lifts one hand, teeters, recovers. Behind, a lighthouse glides past.

Cut to:

The waving child again. For some reason, she turns and runs, not looking back. A white-jacketed man holding aloft a tray of drinks springs out of her path. Dowagers in deck chairs point and laugh; one can imagine them saying, Look at the little missy, isn't she the cute one. The child grows smaller and smaller as she runs the length of the ship, passes the glaring distant spot where sunlight and deck merge, outruns the limitations of the camera, and vanishes forever.

Dorothy Gibson and Noel Malachard first met after dinner on the fourth night of the voyage, at a long littered table in the first-class lounge, when a dozen drunken strangers, inflamed by ragtime and seized by a simultaneous primal urge, deserted them, rushed as one chortling, giggling mass for the dance floor, chairs tipping and drinks spilling and hems ripping, men and women arm in arm, nearly trampling one another in their lust to perform the fox trot, the horse trot, the chicken scratch, the kangaroo dip, the turkey trot, the bunny hug. They left only three people behind in the ruins, blinking at each other in surprise, like neighbors revealed when an intervening building comes down.

Noel raised his glass and winked at the couple at the far end of the table. "Thank God," he said. "I thought they would *never* leave."

"Better join us down here, I suppose," said the man with the waxed mustache. "Safety in numbers, what? Don't want to make the table uneven, do we? Heh."

He was a hearty British businessman whose name, though lost to history, was one to be reckoned with on two continents whenever talk turned to shoebrushes, as he invariably made sure it did. A self-made millionaire who would leave his widow an enviable estate, he had attached himself to Dorothy several hours before. Throughout the evening, he had struggled against vanishingly small odds, and so his appearance in this story at all is a testament to the tenacity of his hopes.

After brief introductions all around, and more drinks all around, and a brief comparison of travel notes, the conversation took its inevitable plunge, and, after holding forth for a couple of minutes on the infinite subtleties of pig's bristles, the man with the waxed mustache politely asked:

"What business did you say you were in, Mister Malachard?"

"*Monsieur* Malachard," murmured Dorothy, bookended by admirers. She cast a languid look from left to right, from dreary past to promising future.

"Nothing so important as shoebrushes, I am afraid," Noel said. "No, I am in the motion picture business."

"Oh, really?" Dorothy trilled.

"I am a camera operator—a cameraman?—for *Pathe Journal*. The weekly newsreel."

"Oh, really?"

"Hum. Fancy that. Newsreels, eh? Must make good money, I daresay, to be sailing first class and all."

"Alas, it is the Pathe brothers who make the good money, and it is they who pay my expenses. You see, I am on assignment."

"Oh, *really*?"

"Yes, I am to film the entire voyage. The crew, the passengers, the ship. 'As much film as your cabin can hold,' my supervisors said. 'We will edit it later.' So all day today I carried my camera about the ship, and how my neck and shoulders ache! By night, I am a man of leisure on my first Atlantic crossing, but by day I work harder than the captain, harder than the man in the furnace room. Well, perhaps not as hard as *that*! But I am boring the beautiful lady with my troubles."

"Oh, no, no, no, not at all. Claude?"

"Yes, Miss Gibson?"

"Would you be a dear and run down to my cabin and ask Mother to give you some aspirin for poor Monsieur Malachard's backache?"

"Why, nothing would give me more pleasure, Miss Gibson, but . . . perhaps the pharmacy would be somewhat quicker?"

"The pharmacy? Yes, the pharmacy. How clever of you to think of it. Claude, would you please go to the pharmacy and get me a whole new bottle of aspirin, because Mother and I are almost out, and she is prone to headaches in the night, and we wouldn't want her to suffer unduly, would we?"

"Of course not. All right, then. I'm off to the pharmacy. Be back in two shakes—"

"And would you be a lamb while you're gone and go by my cabin, too, and get my silver hatpin, the one that's shaped like a swan? Mother can find it for you. I think I must have left it on the dressing table, or perhaps the writing desk, and without it, I just know that the moment I step outside, my hat will blow straight to Newfoundland, and how could I ever look Monsieur Malachard in the eyes again?"

"Right. Very well, Miss Gibson. The aspirin *and* the hatpin."

"You're an angel, Claude, an absolute angel."

"Uh, Miss Gibson . . . Your cabin number would be . . . ?"

"Oh, I have no head for numbers, Claude, one of the stewards can tell you which one. I get so terribly turned around on this big ship. Do *you* ever have that problem, Monsieur Malachard, blundering into other people's rooms?"

"Miss Gibson. *Mister* Malachard."

"Good-bye, Claude. Now, where *were* we, Monsieur—?"

"Please. Noel."

"Noel, of course. Noel. We were having a fascinating conversation, Noel, but I'm not sure we'll be able to find our way back to where we left off. It'll be like retracing our path in the sea. We'll have to start all over again, as if we were utter strangers, isn't that sad?"

"The sad stories are the most beautiful. So your story, Miss Gibson, must be a very sad one indeed."

"Not yet, Noel, but do please give me time, I'm working on it. Correct me if I'm wrong, but I believe you were telling me about the newsreel business."

"It is not very interesting. Parades and speeches, and sometimes a fire."

"How vivid! I can almost feel it. *Pathe Journal*—the words sound lovely, quite aside from their meaning, of course."

"Yes, but in your country it is called, let me see, *Pathe Gazette*."

"How funny you are. Say it again."

"*Pathe Gazette.*"

"How funny. I never really heard those t's before. And you bare your teeth when you say it. It's delicious."

"Shall I say it a third time?"

"Perhaps later. Tell me more."

"I would prefer to hear about you. What has your voyage been like thus far, Miss Gibson? And remember: you can hide nothing from a cameraman."

"Oh, Noel, that's not true. No one is more easily fooled than a cameraman."

"You speak from experience?"

"I certainly do. I'm a professional fooler. I'm an actress."

"No."

"Yes. A motion picture actress. On contract with the Eclair Moving Picture Company of Fort Lee, New Jersey. In fact, it's part of a French company. Not as big as Pathe, but every bit as French."

"Then we have much in common."

"There is that potential, Noel. Perhaps you've seen some of my pictures."

"Perhaps so."

"*A Woman and Her Past. The Woman Inside. The Bowery Princess*?"

"I do not think so."

"*The Merry Makers*? *Small Town Sally*? *A Modern Helen*?"

"You must forgive me. I am sure the titles are different in my country."

"Oh, *everything's* different in your country, I'm sure. I had *wanted* to get over to Paris and do some shopping, but Mother said the exchange rate wasn't good and I found some of the most lovely things at Selfridge's and just kept going back and back and back and—*A Modern Rapunzel*? No? How about *A Daughter of the West*? I got killed in that one. Indians. Actually they were Italians with feathers, stevedores I think, hired for the day. Terribly noisy. Not even *The Heart of a Woman*?"

"When I am in New York, I will see them all."

"Oh, don't bother, they aren't very good, none of them. I mean, they're hardly Pathe. But sometimes I *myself* am quite good despite them, quite good indeed. Do you believe me?"

"Of course."

"You're just saying you believe me, but you're sweet to say it, you really are."

"I do believe you. To disbelieve you—why, it would be to disbelieve life itself!"

"Are you *sure* this is your first crossing? You're most awfully good at it."

"I am getting better all the time."

"Well, don't get too good too quick, it's only Saturday. Now where were we?"

"*The Heart of a Woman*."

"Yes, well, in *that* one, there's a scene where I get to do this look—this particular sort of look that I do."

"I would like very much to see that look."

"Hell, Noel, I just *did* it. Where were you?"

"Oh, I am terribly sorry. Without my camera, I am a blind man, a horse's tail. Again, please."

"All right. There. Do you see?"

"I see, yes."

"I purse my lips just a little, and tilt my head like so, and tilt my shoulders in counterpoint, and I raise one eyebrow the tiniest fraction—not a full lift, mind you, like *this*, then I would look like mad Doctor Crippen, wouldn't I? And not halfway, like this, either, but just the subtlest . . . push . . . upward, see? Just a hint, but in a close-up on a theater screen, why that's practically a foot! Think about it. Do you know I raise and lower my eyebrows thirty times every morning before the mirror? You'd be surprised how few moving picture actresses have good eyebrow control."

"I am sure I would be."

"But it's hard to find a director who wants close-ups at all, who wants anything but snarling and fainting and gyrations like the Wild Man of Borneo. There's a director over at Biograph who's awfully good, but then we'd all like to work for Biograph, wouldn't we?"

"Or Pathe."

"Or Pathe. Yes, you've done quite well, haven't you? Working at a major picture company, and you so young."

"A major company, but a minor job. I am just a workman, like the man who paints the forests for the fake carriage to ride through."

"I think you're exaggerating, Noel," she said, sliding her hand up his thigh. "I think you have more authority at the studio than you claim."

They looked at each other with absolute recognition of their precarious duet, their breathless perfect balance between thought and act, real and possible. Beneath them and above them and around them, the great ship shivered, a teardrop on the surface of the sea.

Moving slowly, and using the extraordinarily sure and gentle touch of a craftsman, he lifted her hand, and returned it to her.

"I cannot lie to you, Miss Gibson," he said. "I have no authority at the studio whatsoever."

She smiled a small, lopsided smile and sighed through her nose, three audible hisses in a rhythm like laughter. She drew a deep breath and said, "All right, Noel. I believe you. Damn it. You're no more powerful than I am." She touched him even higher on his thigh, gripped him and held him this time, and leaned forward and murmured: "But even in a bad picture, I'm good enough to bring tears to the eyes of some drummer in Dubuque, and make him forget that he's broke and tired and sitting in a dark narrow sweltering room staring at a sheet on the wall. Everything he thinks and feels, it's up on screen where he can see it, it's pouring out of *me*. That's my job. I'm good at it. And even in your lowly job, you're good enough to do . . . what, Noel? What makes you good at what you do?"

He drew a breath, closed his eyes for a few seconds, opened them, and said: "I will tell you. I have never told anyone, but . . . I will tell you."

"Do," she said.

"For Pathe, I go to fairs, markets, races. I go to the seaside. I ask people, may I film you with my camera? Everyone says, No, get someone else, people don't want to look at me, I am not interesting, I am dull, I am ugly, I am not fit for a moving picture, go away. But I do not go away, and I can talk many people into it. And in front of my camera, these people are like people transformed. Before, they merely swam, or danced, or argued, or loved; now, they act as if the world were cheering them on, as if this moving picture will forever set the model of how others should swim, or dance, or argue—"

"Or make love."

"—or make love. Yes. And when I see the picture later, I cannot breathe, for joy. They are *alive*, these moving pictures. They contain life. They *are* life. Such a thing was never captured before, never in the history of the world. Yet *I*, with my camera, I have captured it. I have captured *life*. And I feel that life. I feel it as part of me."

"And you are good at this?"

"Madame, I am very good at this. I am better at this than anybody."

"And you said you were powerless! My goodness. My goodness me. Look, children, look, my dears, beware, beware, here comes Professor Malachard, the stooped and hooded figure who captures people in his camera and carries them away to his laboratory, where he makes them pale and flat and oh so big and forces them to do the same delightful things over and over. And over. Why, I'm a little frightened of the powerless, helpless, pitiful Professor Malachard!"

"Are you so very frightened then?"

"No. Of some things, yes. Not of this. What frightens you?"

"May I show you?"

"Please do."

"It is outside."

"Good."

"Your hat, I fear, will blow to Newfoundland."

"My hatpin is in my bag."

"The silver swan?"

"Yes."

"Not long ago, it was in your cabin."

"I summoned it. I summon *you*."

         *   *   *

They strolled onto the promenade into a steady but pleasant salt-flavored breeze, typical of the perfect weather since Southampton. They walked aft along the rail, away from the babble of the lounge and toward the glow and murmur of the glass-roofed smoking room, but with no real destination, sliding their hands down the unbroken stretch of gleaming brass that separated them from the stars and the great darkness beneath. A hand held in one place too long on that vibrating rail would tingle and go numb, as if frozen. There was practically no moon left, only the ship's lights and, here and there in the distance, patches of floating plants that made their own feeble shimmer, more noticeable from the corner of the eye than when looked at directly. The ship, heedless, mindless, ploughed through these delicate colonies, its keel tearing them apart and its wake tumbling them together again, so that seventy feet below the rail, the foam rushing alongside was flecked with bits of fire. But to look straight down was too dizzying; better to look out at the black promise of nothingness, and to huddle, more closely together than warranted by such a warm night, in the shadow of a great upended lifeboat permanently perched on the brink. The breeze caressed, consoled, tugged gently at clothing, was sweet, was salt.

"You were going to show me," she said, "what frightens you."

"This."

"The night?"

"The *ocean*. Look. There, and there. Look."

"Mmm. Drowning, you mean?"

"You embarrass me. No, no, not drowning. Please. My uncle in Nantes drowned in a bathtub. I once read of a woman who drowned in her own spit. No, drowning is a commonplace, not worth worrying about. But this—look. Even alive, we are nothing, compared to *this*."

"It's beautiful."

"The frightening is always beautiful."

"You're getting these things out of a book, aren't you? Time-honored French aphorisms for the tourist trade. Balzac, I bet."

"I suppose I talk like an old man."

"No. No. Do you know, you're frighteningly beautiful, Professor Malachard, you are. Look at you. Why, you're practically a fifth ocean yourself!"

Faces brushed together, testing contours, textures, smoothness, and scent. Lips first sought cheeks, chin, neck, anything but the other's lips; but then, once mated, they fused. Tongues danced, awkward, vigorous, determined. More fervor, then less, then more. Soft wordless cries and handfuls of hair and the sudden awareness of clothing, layers and layers of it, too much to be tolerated but concealing nothing. Slower, slower. Eyes closed, breathing in each other's breaths, they traced the boundaries of the fabric with their fingers; she his collar, and his shirt buttons, and the pleats of his trousers, he her shoulders, her neck, and the small of her back.

She pushed away, laughing. "You have the advantage, sir. I should have dressed more warmly." She pulled him to her again, and fumbled with his clothing, tugged, ripped. A button dropped, bounced, and went over the side, unnoticed.

Darkness. Piano (very fast). Lights up.

Dancers jam the floor in front of the bandstand, each a frenzy of motion. Pearls swing, dresses shimmer, feathers sway. People throw their heads back and laugh. A woman in the foreground makes a great show of swooning and is dragged away by her partner, legs stiff, feet splayed out. One shoe is left behind.

Cut to:

A man and a woman embrace at the rail.

Cut to:

A man in a bib rips apart a lobster.

Cut to:

Two fencers duel on the grand staircase.

Cut to:

Confetti cascades from the ceiling onto the dancers' heads, pours off their shoulders.

Cut to:

The promenade, deserted, at dawn.

She cried out, and he held her.

"I am here. I am here. What is wrong?"

She twisted, burrowed, drew him closer. Their reflections writhed in the paneling. The cord of the bedside lamp shivered, proof of the engines.

"Nothing. Nothing. I'm just stupid, that's all." Her voice was muffled against his chest. "I woke up and thought I was in my own cabin but someone had reversed it while I slept, turned everything backward. It's the same cabin, really, isn't it, just on the other side of the mirror. Of the ship. It's as good as being in my own bed, just entirely different. Don't listen to me. I'm asleep."

"Don't worry, I am, too. Here, let me move my arm—there. That's nicer. I like my backward cabin. Everything is polished, everything shines. The bed is not so large, but who knew? Eh? Who knew? You should have heard me, persuading my supervisor that to really film the voyage, I had to have a first-class cabin. Why, if I had not spoken up, Pathe happily would have engaged me a closet beside the boiler room, and then how would I ever have met the famous Miss Dorothy Gibson, the toast of two continents? How would I have seen that special look that she does so well?"

"You're a villain, a cruel and heartless villain to tease me so, and you will pay for it one day, I'm sure you will. But . . . Noel. You might have met me just fine, even in steerage. I'll tell you a secret now."

"You are not Miss Dorothy Gibson at all? Let me guess. You are none other than . . . Sarah Bernhardt!"

"You're awful. No, Mother and I weren't booked for first class at all. We decided we could splurge and afford second class, because we didn't want to settle for one of the lesser ships and miss our only chance to be part of—well, part of *history*, but we knew it was the off-season and so the first-class cabins were unlikely to be *entirely* filled, and so the first place I went when we got on board was the Purser's Office, and I asked so nicely, and the man there, well, he was very understanding . . . most understanding indeed . . . and so he moved us up a notch. Or two."

"What did he want in return?"

"He wanted quite a lot, actually. But what he *got* was money."

"You are just as persuasive as I am."

"Of course. Isn't that obvious? I mean, here we are."

"Here we are."

"Noel. Do you think that I shall be famous one day?"

"I am sure you will be."

She sat up, rolled away from him, ripped the sheet from his body, wadded the cloth, threw it into the dumbwaiter. The bed was too small to get far. He clasped her ankle, and she jerked. "No, goddammit!" she said. "Tell me the truth. Tell me!"

"I don't know."

"It's possible, isn't it? It *might* happen. Something. Anything." She sobbed once, twice, but no tears came. "Shit, I'm choking," she said. "Tell me it's possible, but only if you mean it. Tell me."

"It *is* possible. It is not likely. But it could happen."

"And it might not."

"It might not."

"Oh, God." She snatched the passenger list off the bedside table, opened it. "That's all right," she said. "That's all right. We aren't even listed. Printed ahead of time, I'm sure. Weeks. That's all right." She threw the list aside, leaned over him, touched his face. "Don't. Don't cry, Noel. Please stop. I wouldn't mind. Really I wouldn't."

"I know."

"What about you?"

He smiled. "There are no famous cameramen."

"You fool," she said, squirming across the bed and straddling him. "What do you want? Tell me."

"This."

She rubbed herself against him. "You have that. What else?"

"This again."

"Ah, ha. You have that, too."

"This always."

"No," she said. "No, you can't have that." Leaning on her elbows, her forearms cradling his head, she lay atop him, kissed him, their faces wet. "I'm not one of your camera people," she said, reaching down and guiding him in. "I'm not quite as alive as all that. Not yet. Oh, Noel! Oh, Noel . . . Not *yet*."

Harry keeps squeezing the horn. "Come on, people, come on, let us through, please, let us through."

In the backseat, Dorothy closes her eyes and clutches the ceiling strap and twists it around and around, binds her hand up tight. She cannot look at the crowds anymore, she cannot, but with her eyes shut she has to think about something.

"It was dreadful, Mr. Raver, simply dreadful." Mother clicks her compact open and shut. "All we wanted to do was stand on dry land again, but they wouldn't let us off the ship, just herded us from room to room, asking us questions. Oh! I am quite talked out . . ."

The auto. Dorothy will think about this auto. Harry is very proud of it. A Renault, he said. A 35-horsepower Renault. He plans to use it for advertising. He plans to have a sign painter write on each side, Driven to Entertain: Eclair Moving Picture Company, Fort Lee, New Jersey. He will park it in front of theaters showing Eclair pictures. Even Dorothy Gibson pictures. Yes, that is a good thing to think about. All the upcoming Dorothy Gibson pictures. Harry has big plans. He told Dorothy weeks ago, before she and Mother went to England. The car will glide up to the curb, Harry says, and Dorothy Gibson will step out, and a big crowd of reporters and photographers will be there, and people waiting in line will cheer and applaud. Dorothy had never heard of such a thing. Why should there be a big fuss, she asked, about a theater changing its movie? Trust me, Harry said, you'll see, come over here, kid, come here and sit with old Harry, yeah, just think of it, kid, you can hear the applause now, can't you? Sure you can. Sure you can.

Everyone left on deck applauded as the lifeboat swung over the side. They leaned on the rail with their drinks in their hands and smiled and waved down at Dorothy, and one of them, a woman with too many pearls, called to her, Sorry you're leaving the party so soon, dearie. Beside her at the rail, a man with buck teeth lifted his glass. In the glass was a jagged chunk of ice. It steamed with cold. It's iceberg ice, he said, the very coldest, the very best, the captain just had it delivered. His friends shrieked in merriment as Dorothy craned her neck to keep them in view and watch them grow smaller, and the officer above shouted, first boat away, and then Dorothy was knocked off her seat by the jolt as Lifeboat Number Seven dropped into the sea.

The man who claimed to be a Frenchman had more blankets than anyone else in the lifeboat. No, no, he shouted, do not take my blankets, please, I am a sick man, I am consumptive, I will die if I am chilled, no, stop, as the officers struggled with him, yanked at the blankets, played tug-of-war. Shut up, will you, there are two blankets for everybody, the boat's not half full, shut up, you filthy frog, shut up. The Frenchman clawed and bit and wept.

Dorothy and Mother were at the other end of the boat. They shared one big blanket. Mother huddled beneath it and prayed. Her words were muffled. The blanket was thick and coarse. It was not well made. Dorothy's face was frozen and hurting, but she kept her head clear of the blanket. She could not stop watching the waves. Every few seconds, the stars went away. That meant a wave.

People screamed in the night outside the lifeboat. Sometimes only one voice, sometimes many. One instant very near, as if right over Dorothy's shoulder, the next instant faint and far away. Help me, help me, someone please, I'm in the water, it's cold, it's so very cold. The officers scrambled from side to side, saying, for God's sake, the poor devils, where are they? Do you see them? We must help them. We *must*. Dorothy reached out from beneath the blanket and waved, little clutchings of the air, here I am, don't worry about me, I'm here. When she moved her raw and salted fingers they cracked and bled. My face, she thought, my face. No one looked at her. Dorothy watched the waves. Her feet were frozen. She lifted her feet onto the bench, out of the foul icy sloshing in the bottom of the boat. Eventually the screams stopped. She did not hear the last one. But there were no more screams.

Much later, Dorothy stood at the rail of the *Carpathia* and watched the other lifeboats straggle alongside. The people in each stared up at her in silence. They had the faces of the dead. They made no move to come aboard. The *Carpathia*'s crew had to clamber down and get them, winch them up and carry them aboard like cargo. Noel was on none of the boats. But would she have recognized him anyway? His lined cheeks, his sunken eyes, his gaping mouth?

Dorothy opens her eyes. The crowds press against the auto on both sides. Blank faces stare in. Mouths open, close. Palms press against the windows, leave ghost palms that fade, reappear, fade again, as the auto creeps past the streetlamps.

"Dorothy, you still awake?" Harry asks. "You still with us, kid? Listen, I know it'll take you a while to recover from all this. Three, four days, whatever you need, listen, you take it. And then, the best thing you can do, take my word for this, is get right back to work again. Hah? Hah? Am I right? Because you're an *artist*, kid, a real artist, with real talent, and even terrible, terrible tragedies like this one can be turned into art. Really. If you're not too tired right now, honey, take a look at what's in that envelope back there. The one on the seat next to you. Just take a look."

Dorothy untangles her hand from the strap. It's numb and is criss-crossed with welts. She rubs it. She picks up the envelope and holds it in her lap. It's a long wide envelope with the Eclair insignia and address printed on it. She unties the clasp, slides out the stiff sheet of paper.

"It's an eye-catcher, huh, kid? Look how you can see each little porthole light, all the way back! I mean, that's *art*!"

In the middle of the poster, superimposed over the background illustration, is a photograph of Dorothy herself. The photograph is in a circular frame, like a portrait in a locket. It is one of the costumed publicity photographs for *A Woman and Her Past*. Surrounding the photograph, covering most of the poster, is a striking black-and-white illustration of a seemingly endless ocean liner, steaming toward the viewer, its stern impossibly remote in the distance. The liner is ramming a cliff of ice. The prow is buried in the ice, and great ice boulders rain onto the deck.

"Who better to play a survivor," Harry was telling Mother, "than one of the *real* survivors? I mean, the thing is a guaranteed sensation! But we have to work fast. Right, Dorothy? You see why we have to work fast, right? All these crowds, they won't be as interested three months from now. You see what I mean, kid?"

Dorothy is sliding her fingertips across the smooth surface of the poster. The design is mostly black. The black of the ship, the black of the sky, the black of the sea. Only the ice is white. Dorothy opens her mouth to speak, coughs, clears her throat. Perhaps she has lost her voice. "We didn't hit this way," Dorothy rasps.

"Huh? What?"

"We didn't ram the iceberg. We scraped it as we passed. On the side. Most people didn't even feel it. That's why no one cared at first. They thought they were safe. They thought they were okay."

Harry sounds hurt. "And how were we to know that, I ask you? Besides, it's dramatic license. Don't worry about it. What we need, kid, is a *story*. Now here's what I've been thinking. . . ."

While he talks, while Mother looks at her in silence, Dorothy looks at the poster. All she has left is in this car, and on this poster. That's all. It has to be enough. The poster is taut between her hands. Noel, Noel, if you were here, Noel, then we'd show the bastard a real story. Wouldn't we? The poster tears a little in her grip.

I'll have to tell somebody, she thinks, biting the inside of her cheek. I'll have to tell somebody, or I'll go mad. But not yet.

At one point, she had been the only passenger awake, or conscious, on the lifeboat. Just her and the crew. The sea was deafening, a thousand locomotives. The wind pressed her forehead, her cheeks, her lips, smoothed back her hair. Dorothy could see the waves, but she couldn't feel them, not exactly. Dorothy felt the boat moving, yes, but not up and down. She felt only a mad rush forward, as if she were tumbling down the rapids and over the falls and then another falls and then *another*, out of control, hurtling on, on, on, a chip of wood in the torrent. The feeling had not been unpleasant. She would never admit that to her mother, of course, and certainly not to Harry; but *Noel* knew, she was sure he knew; and one day, when she could weep again, she would weep with shame for that.

Tuesday, May 14
Eight O'Clock Sharp

SAVED from the TITANIC

Eclair's World Sensation
MISS DOROTHY GIBSON,
a survivor of the sea's greatest disaster, tells the story of the shipwreck,
supported by an all-star cast, in the film marvel of the age.

ART POSTERS, PHOTOS, and HERALDS are ready.

Tuesday, May 14 at 8—Tuesday, May 14 at 8
ECLAIR FILM CO.
Fort Lee, New Jersey
Sales Company, Sole Agents

Not too bad, Dorothy decided, stepping backward across the sidewalk and squinting at the poster. Mother wore spectacles at nineteen; Dorothy would hold out until twenty-nine, at least. Yes, still perfectly legible, even at the edge of the curb. She tilted her head as far as she could to the left, then to the right. She wished she could screw her head all the way around, like an owl. But however she contorted herself, the poster still was a striking design. Harry was right; the crumbling ice was better than real.

Three strolling couples, their attention arrested, stopped between her and the poster.

"My God! Do you suppose they have film of it?"

"Surely not. It's possible, I suppose."

"I hope they don't just show that damn christening again. That's all I've seen in the theaters for weeks, and I'm heartily sick of it."

"Couldn't get *me* aboard one of those things."

"She's lovely, isn't she? Poor little thing. How terrible it must have been for her."

"All it does is slide down the ramp into the water, over and over again. I mean, the bloody thing wasn't even *finished*. Why is that worth seeing, I ask you?"

"I wonder who rescued her? Some gallant officer, I'm sure."

"We all should be so lucky."

"We must come back, after dinner."

"Of course, my dear."

"If it's the damn christening again, I shall demand my money back."

"Please do that, Gerald."

"Gerald, why don't *you* take a cruise one day? A nice slow one."

"Couldn't get *me* aboard one of those things."

"No one's making you, dear."

"Perhaps he was the first officer. Perhaps now he will receive a ship of his own, and they will be married on the bridge."

"We are expected at six, my friends, let's not be late."

"We'll come back, then."

"Yes, we'll come back."

Come back, Dorothy thought, come back. She stepped over the curb, lost her balance, almost fell backward; she flailed her arms and caught the lamppost. One of those beastly motorcars blared at her. Steady, girl. Steady. Time to get upstairs, get yourself put together. Time to look like a heroine.

The side door hung crooked on its hinges; the stairwell was narrow and dark and dank. Why was it colder inside than out? We'll make sure not to bring the journalists back here, she decided. She gripped the banister and peered up into the murk as she climbed. Her rustling, clinking bags of clothing and supplies bumped her thigh. The *Dramatic Mirror* was coming, Harry said. That was a good sign, surely. Also *Moving Picture News*. Perhaps even the *World* and the *Sun* and the *Evening Post*. Well, they might come. They might. Anything could happen. This wasn't a theater, it was an icebox! A very *dark* icebox. Dorothy shivered and hurried. She clattered upstairs, chanting: the world and the sun and the eve-ning post and the world and the sun and the eve-ning—

"Harry?"

As her head crested the top landing, had the door to her "dressing room" just swung shut?

"Harry?"

She fumbled for the key Harry had given her. "It's a couple of rooms," Harry had said. "A washbasin, a mirror, a bed, some tables. He does business there sometimes. You own a business, you need a few rooms like that, you know?" She knew. She had told Harry, quite firmly, that she would meet him downstairs at seven-thirty. Maybe he couldn't wait. Or maybe—Dorothy stopped, key poised—maybe it was the theater manager. Maybe that was part of the deal. But no, Harry had said it was the *manager* who owed *Eclair* money, not the other way around. Slightly relieved, she unlocked the door, pushed it inward a few inches. "Harry?" she called. Damn, it *was* like an ice-box in there . . . frigid air just pouring onto the landing. Oh, well, she thought, Biograph it ain't. She cried out when the doorknob twisted in her hand; she jumped back as the door swung inward, revealing a dark, cold room.

"Who's there?" she called.

He peered around the door. "Beware the cameraman," Noel said.

"My God!" Dorothy said. She dropped her bags. They made a satisfying crash and then, sighing, collapsed on themselves. A lipstick tube rolled across the landing and down the stairs in skips and taps. "My God! My *God*!"

"May I presume," Noel asked, "that in my absence, you have become famous?"

Without looking away from him, she knelt, seized her bags, stood up again, regained her balance. She realized it had looked like some sort of stiff curtsy. "*Damn* you!" she said. She flung her bags, one by one, into his face, starting with the softest one, and he hid behind upraised arms, knocking the bags asunder. When she was done, clothes and jewelry littered the floor. A silken sleeve draped his foot; he tried to gently kick it aside, got entangled, then knelt and began feeding it back into the bag, his long delicate fingers rolling the fabric like a spool of film. She fell on him, knocked him backward. It might have begun as a faint but she recovered quickly, clambered atop him, wrestled with him, both of them grunting and laughing. She sat on him. With her knees she pinned his shoulders to the floor.

"Murder! Murder!" he cried, eyes rolling. "Where are the police, I ask you? In Paris, this would never happen."

"In Paris this would happen all the *time*," Dorothy said, yanking his hair for emphasis. She ran her hands over his cold face. "You are a bastard, Noel, a beautiful bastard, a magnificent bastard, but a beastly beastly bastard all the same."

"It is true," he said.

"And you're *freezing*," she said. "You're like ice. Why didn't you turn on the pipes?"

"Without you, I was cold," he said, running his hands up her thighs. "I am much warmer now."

She slapped him, a furious *crack* that numbed her hand. She clamped that hand over her mouth, fingers spread, denting her cheeks, and gasped with laughter. Noel blinked, wiggled his jaw comically, and laughed, too. "Oh, God, Noel, that was harder than I meant. But I *did* mean it, you shit! You missing *shit*! They misspelled your name terribly, you know. Serves you right. You weren't there to set them straight."

"Where? On the poster outside?" His dimple, my God, his dimple. "I saw your name, but somehow mine was left off."

"On the *casualty* list, you shit! Don't you read the papers? Even the *French* papers? The list of the people who—the people who—" She clamped his head in her hands, squeezing, clutching. She bent double and rubbed her face against his, her eyes closed. Her face slid across his cold forehead, his cold cheeks, his warm lips. "Noel," she whispered. "Noel."

She stayed on top. They didn't remove their clothes. They didn't even close the door. His feet stuck out onto the landing, in plain sight, but no one interrupted them. No one could have.

Afterward, lying atop him, motionless and spent, but yet so deliciously full of him, she realized that the room was colder than ever. She began to shiver. She couldn't help it. He held her, stroked her face. Her teeth chattered.

"I couldn't find you," she said.

"Shh," he said. "Shh."

"I was afraid to leave Mother, and afraid the lifeboat would launch without us, and the crew members were dashing around so, they weren't able to look for you, either—"

"I was below, talking to the emigrants. In Third Class."

"Oh, God."

"I wanted to film them. Such large families. So excited. So talkative. Two brothers from Belfast entertained me after everyone else was asleep. Shipbuilding stories. They were very proud. 'Three million rivets!' they said. They pounded the wall with their fists. 'Three million rivets, and all of them by hand, by God!' Then the stewards went down the corridor banging on doors."

"Mother and I had been playing late bridge with two silly men. The stewards closed the saloon around us, threatened to turn out the lights. You should have heard the whining. 'See here, my good man. See here.' Such dreary men. We were still on the deck when the alarm came. Noel, why were we apart Sunday night? Why did we think that was a good idea?"

"I don't know."

"It's never a good idea. My bridge game was awful."

"I was not too interested in rivets, either."

"What time is it?" she asked. "I have to be downstairs. *We* have to be downstairs. Oh, Noel, you'll get to see one of my pictures, isn't that exciting? And I don't even get killed in this one."

"I look forward to it."

"And the fellow who plays Ensign Jack, listen, Noel, I hardly know him, his breath is awful, I hated kissing him, he can't act, his hands are like great big hams. He looks good on screen, that's all. He won't last." She kissed him, fiercely, anxious for any trace of warmth. She pulled back with a smack. "He won't last," she said. "Wait till you see the shipwreck scene."

"Is it the film marvel of the age?"

She laughed. "Well, let's see," she said, ticking off on her fingers. "The iceberg is plywood. And the North Atlantic is a swimming pool. And the ship is about as long as—well, you know." She held her hands a familiar distance apart. "But since you asked: *I* am quite good in it, Noel, *I* am quite good indeed."

"I think you will be surprised," he said. "Because the audience will see it for the first time, *you* will see it for the first time. It may be more realistic than you think." He sat up, gazed down at her, stroked her cheek with a touch of ice. "I hope you are not frightened by what you see," he murmured.

She closed her eyes. "Of course not," she whispered.

"Remember, they are images, only images. They cannot harm you."

"Nothing frightens me," she whispered, "anymore."

"I would never harm you," he said. "I am here only to help you."

She opened her eyes. "Whatever are you talking about, Noel? Whatever is the matter?"

He turned and began raking her things together. "You will be late," he said. "That is the matter. Come, Madame, I will be your dresser for the evening. I undress Madame, I dress her as well. So! Up up up!"

He took her hand and tugged at her. She felt a sudden exultant chill.

"You're leaving," she said.

His face was grim in the darkened room.

"You can't stay," she said.

His hand was positively clammy.

"It's hard for you to stay," she said. "It's hard for you even to be here *now*. In fact, it's impossible. Isn't it, Noel? Isn't it?"

He held her hand and said nothing.

"Oh, Noel," she said. "Oh, my poor dear Noel. I'm so sorry they misspelled your name."

The long, narrow room was packed. Harry wanted her down front beside him, but she refused. She was too nervous. Also, she was waiting on Noel. She wasn't sure that Noel could . . .well, she didn't know how Noel would fare in a crowd. She stood in the back, against the wall, near the exit: in case, she told herself grimly, I have to head for the lifeboats again. The floor was sticky, and the wall plucked at her dress when she brushed against it. She was glad the lights were out. Where *was* he, anyway? The piano player was already banging dramatically away.

The journalists nearly had smothered her when she came in. No unexpected questions, thank God. Yes, in the picture I wear the very clothes I wore in the lifeboat. The black pumps are ruined, I'm afraid. No, Mother declined to appear in the picture. Miss Agnes Stuart observed Mother at some length, however, and she delivers a fine and sensitive performance. In fact, the two women have become fast friends. (Harry nodded enthusiastically at this impromptu absurdity.) Yes, if called upon, I will tell Senator Smith's committee all of what little I know about the disaster. No, I never had the pleasure of meeting the Astors.

Damn you, Noel, she thought as the first titles appeared on the screen. You'll miss the whole damn thing. But then she shivered suddenly and uncontrollably, and she knew that Noel was beside her in the dark. "Thank you," she whispered, reaching for him. His sleeve was damp.

"I am sorry," he said. "It is difficult."

"I know," she said. "It always is."

The picture wasn't much, she knew, but considering everything, it wasn't bad. "Scenes on land are cheaper," Harry had said. And so *Saved from the Titanic* began on land, with the handsome and muscular Ensign Jack, who

CANNOT BEAR BEING SEPARATED FROM HIS BETROTHED,

HIS BELOVED DOROTHY.

Impatient for his fiancée to return from her transatlantic cruise, he visits his friend Bill, a wireless operator.

"I MUST TELL HER I LOVE HER—I MUST!"

Bill dutifully prepares to relay this message, but the two chums are interrupted by an emergency transmission.

"IT'S A C.Q.D., JACK! SOME SHIP IS IN BIG TROUBLE OUT THERE!"

Bill listens to the instruments, eyes wide with horror.

"JACK, IT'S DOROTHY'S SHIP—THE TITANIC!"

Jack reels, gnashes his teeth, and tears his hair. So, back home, do Dorothy's stooped and aged parents, when Jack brings the awful news. A long vigil ensues, until a telegram arrives: Dorothy is safe! Home again, Dorothy agrees to tell her loved ones the story of her ordeal.

Here the flashback, and the real interest of the picture, began. There was footage of the great ship's christening (which prompted a snort of derision from someone in the audience), then footage of the miniature ship bobbing across the swimming pool as chunks of ice floated past, then shots of Dorothy and her fellow actors falling about on the deck as

A TERRIBLE CRASH

ensued. The onscreen Dorothy reeled at the sight of the massive plywood iceberg looming overhead. A retired old stage actor, a cousin of Harry's by marriage, but very good despite it, lifted a megaphone.

"ABANDON SHIP!"

So far, so good, Dorothy thought. She watched herself on the screen as she settled into the lifeboat and gravely saluted the gallant officers on deck. She embraced and comforted the curly-headed moppet beside her as the lifeboat dropped out of sight.

That was about it for the shipwreck scene, Dorothy knew, and she started to let out her breath. But then she seized Noel's hand as the shipwreck scene . . . continued.

The room was utterly quiet. Only the clatter of the projector could be heard. Harry's voice in the front, though only a murmur, was clearly audible: "What the . . . ?"

Noel's lips were cold against Dorothy's ear. "Do not be afraid," he said. "The new scenes will add a great deal, I think."

A crowded lifeboat is swung over the side as dozens of men left on deck claw at it. They fight each other and fight the crew members trying to hold them back. One officer crouches atop the winch, shouting at the mob and waving a revolver. He fires into the air. Several of those on deck jump for it; one manages to grab hold of the edge of the boat and kick his legs for a few seconds before dropping. As the lifeboat is lowered, another man swings his leg over the rail and clutches at it. The officer shoots him, and he falls.

"You filmed this," Dorothy whispered. "You set up your camera, and filmed the sinking."

"I had a couple of hours," Noel said. "I had plenty of film. What else could I do?"

Two portly men in tweed jackets scramble up the deserted, tilting deck of the ship, hand in hand. As they pass, the companionway doors are flung open, and hundreds of people surge onto the deck from below, engulfing the two stragglers. The men wear dark knee-length coats and caps, and many are bearded; the women wear scarves tied beneath their chins; the children are shapeless bundles of warm clothing. The families mill about in circles on the deck, beneath the empty sockets where the lifeboats were stowed.

"I'm tired," Noel said. His voice was faint, as if he were speaking into her ear from the far end of a pipe.

"Thank you for the pictures, Professor Malachard." She didn't know whether she had voiced the statement or merely thought it.

Thank you for ours, came the answering thought. Then her hand was empty, and she realized that if she turned her head, Noel would be gone. So she didn't turn her head.

A man sits alone on the grand staircase, hands dangling between his knees, head bowed. He has the beginnings of a bald spot. Below him, the ocean is flowing up the stairs. It moves slowly put perceptibly, lapping at each stair, then overrunning it. The reflected water shimmers in the glass of the framed maps and charts along the walls. Above, the chandelier hangs at an odd angle. After a few seconds, it twitches sideways, goes even farther out of true, as if pulled by a magnet in the ceiling. The ocean laps at another stair. The man looks up, faces the camera. It is a look no one in the audience will forget.

Dorothy could not breathe. Saying anything would have been beyond her, even good-bye. She wrapped her arms around herself and held on tight, trying to stop the shaking.

Finally, the new footage ended, and the tired old hokum Harry had slapped together resumed. Chairs squeaked and clothes rustled as the audience relaxed.

The queasy giddiness of the past few hours was gone. Dorothy was alone, utterly alone. What would she do? What would become of her? In minutes, the lights would come on, and all these strangers would press around her, wheedling and pleading and plucking at her clothes. Harry would be the most insistent; what would she tell him? How could she explain? She wanted to run from the room, run upstairs, slam the door, lie where he had lain, hug her knees and rock back and forth and wish herself into the place where he was, no matter how dark and cold that place might be.

That's not what I wanted, she heard Noel say. That's not why I came back.

She forced herself to open her eyes, to relax her fists, to stand up straight. No, it was *their* picture now, hers and Noel's, and she would not run away from it. She would do whatever she had to do.

She pursed her lips. She tilted her head just so. She tilted her shoulders in counterpoint. She raised one eyebrow just the tiniest fraction. Then she waited, frozen, at the back of the theater for the lights to come up, and for everyone to turn and applaud. On this picture and the next one and the next, she would keep doing all those things she did so well, and the years would pass, and she would see all of it, all, and one day she would see Noel again, and then life would resume. But until then, moving pictures would have to do.

Dorothy leans against the rail and laughs silently, the ribbon of her hat almost horizontal in the wind. Noel trots to join her. Facing forward, he mouths an instruction, twirls his finger: keep going, keep going. He puts his arm around Dorothy. She sticks out her tongue, laughs again. The wind lifts Noel's hat, and he clamps his free hand over it. Dorothy grabs it with both hands, mashes it down over his ears. He struggles, pulls her hands free, and kisses her. She wraps her arms around him, slowly lifts one foot behind like the lovers in Vogue. *After a pause, he lifts one foot behind, too. They maintain this awkward two-legged embrace as the sky and the deck around them become peppered with flecks and streaks in the film. For this is an old, old picture, one that cannot last. Now the picture is shot through with twitching threads of age. Soon a great swirling boil of white will blossom in one corner and engulf the frame. Even the piano player has begun to falter, slow down, muff a few notes. The audience knows what will happen to this picture, to this ship, to these lovers, to this sky, to this sea—to this piano and the man who plays it. The lovers know it, too, always knew it, and yet, there they are. Just look at them at them. There they* are.

THE ABBESS'S PRAYERS

L. Timmel Duchamp

Here's a vivid and passionate look into the distant past that shows us that rules are made to be broken, even God's Rules, if the reason is compelling enough—and that fires can burn very brightly indeed even when fed on the driest of fuels . . .

New writer L. Timmel Duchamp has become a frequent contributor to *Asimov's Science Fiction* and *The Magazine of Fantasy and Science Fiction*, and has also made sales to *Full Spectrum, Pulphouse, Starshore, Memories and Visions, The Woman Who Walked Through Fire*, and elsewhere. She lives in Seattle, Washington.

THE ABBESS'S PRAYERS

1.

The Oratory is spare and simple, as churches go. The Master's students built it with their own hands, under his direction. The only thing in it to look at was the altar and the massive wooden cross suspended from the rafters above it—until, after the Master's death on April 21, 1142, the Abbess, consumed with grief, ordered that a tomb be built as close to the altar as propriety allowed. For more than a year the tomb lay empty, prominent, gleaming almost spectrally white in that so dimly illuminated space, a constant sign of the Master's death—though who could forget it, given the Abbess's perpetual sadness?—and a strangely eerie reminder that his bones lay elsewhere. The Abbess and sisters face it whenever they perform the Offices, which is to say, several times day and night. And since the Abbess's authority is complete, no one dared question the fact of the magnificent, empty tomb.

On November 15, 1143, Peter the Venerable, the Abbot of Cluny, secretly delivered the Master's remains to the Paraclete. The Abbess placed a candle four feet tall and the thickness of a peasant's thigh at the foot of the tomb and ordered that it always be kept burning, and that it be replaced before its flame guttered. Heretofore a model of moderation in all aspects of the religious life, the Abbess mounted a nearly constant vigil, on her knees, at its head.

The sisters pray for the Master's soul and say nothing to the Abbess about her sudden immersion in devotion. For who would dare to question the Abbess's judgment? And who would take it on herself to articulate concern about another's praying too much? Certainly no one in the Paraclete, certainly no one in the county of Troyes and Champagne, certainly no one in the kingdom of France, much less anyone else in all of Christian Europe.

2.

Beneath her shift, between her breasts, rolled tightly into a thin cylinder, Sister Sebastienne carries her lover's verses. *Your naked hand will*

touch my naked page . . . You can safely lay it in your lap . . . Her lips sing
the *Nunc Dimittis* of Compline in perfect outward obedience, while his
words burn in carnal conflagration within her body and mind, spark-
ing new words—her own words—in her tantalized, torrid thoughts.
Hoc jacet in gremio dilecti schedula nostri, Ecce locata meis subjacet uberibus.
It burns on her breast, yes, the record of their desire. And when she
lies down to sleep, it will be with the naked pages placed under her
left breast, so that the words on them may be close to her heart,
scorching her body and soul, filling her dreams with the fire of his
desiring. *Her* verses—for already she knows she will match him couplet for couplet, all eighty-nine—will tell of it, yes, of how his pages,
lying pressed to her breast, set her womb on fire . . .

The others neither know nor suspect her passion. What could a
correspondence in Latin signify to them? *They* have not read the
Abbess's correspondence with the Master. *They* assume that anything written in Latin must be either studious or holy. Latin, everyone knows, is the language of law, the language of erudition, the
language of the Fathers. *Salve regina*, they sing. *Vita, dulcedo, et spes
nostra, salve.* Banished children of Eve? It had always seemed so—
until now. *O dulcis Virgo Maria*, they sing. And so to bed, though not,
in her case, to sleep.

Matins comes cruelly soon, especially to those whose hours for
sleep are spent caressing the naked words of a lover.

3.

Sister Sebastienne is awake when the bell summons them to
Matins. The sisters' footsteps are quiet, their voices mute as they file
down the stairs and in through the choir. Only the creaking of the
risers, the muted clicking of rosary beads, and the swish of their
heavy wool habits nudge the shivery stillness of deep, dead night.

The sisters find the Abbess in the Oratory before them. As they
chant, their voices crack and strain with middle-of-the-night dryness
and disuse. The utter dark, except for the trembling pools of light cast
by the candles, renders the stillness between moments of vocalization thick, obdurate, pressing. Night in the Oratory is unlike night
anywhere else. Out of doors, night is dangerous, unbounded, endless. In the dormitory, night is a timeless field for unleashed imagination and the luxury of invisibility. And in the cloisters, under the
stars, night is breath and wonder. But the Oratory belongs to God.
The Oratory traps night and imposes a stifling silence, as though
encasing all that enters it within a thick, hard, dark crystal their
voices futilely strain to shatter.

For some unfathomable reason, it happens often during Matins

that Sister Sebastienne recalls how she, now a Bride of Christ, was
bartered by her parents to God in exchange for her brother's recovery from the fever that threatened his life. *We will give you our daughter Sebastienne, God, if you spare our firstborn son*, they solemnly vowed,
before a priest and the entire household. It is a female's lot to be
bartered, she knows, but she has always found it especially disre-
gardful of her that her parents exchanged her for her brother's life
rather than for a parcel of land. (Actually, they endowed her with a
parcel of land to administer to the benefit of the convent.) Everyone
said, when she took the veil, that being given to God was an honor
greater than marriage. (Sebastienne, of course, knew that they did
not really believe it.) Herself, she feels as though she had been des-
ignated a human sacrifice, offered to an exacting, extorting God
determined to have his pound of flesh in one form or another.

   This particular middle-of-the-night, standing in the icy presence
of the God who demands recognition at those times most mortals
give over to sleep, as Sister Sebastienne feels God in the dark corners and thick silences that persist whenever their voices cease, the
secret in her heart gives her the special strength and vitality of the
young wife kept locked up by her ancient, cold-tempered husband,
enjoying as much the thought that she is flouting his dismal constraints as the pleasure of the adultery itself.

4.

In the morning, after Mass, as they go about their daily tasks, a
whisper flies from sister to sister that the Abbess has again spent the
night in the Oratory.

   As she does several times every day but the Sabbath, Sister
Sebastienne goes to her place in the scriptorium. It is fortunate, she
thinks, that the Abbess will again be missing the lesson. Though
Sister Sebastienne's years number a mere twenty-two, she is
exhausted from a night of seductive sensuality, a night spent revel-
ing in certain words and the sensations they conjured up. In the
damp chill of early December, her cheeks, her breasts, her most
moist and private places, burn unslaked. Passion for an absent lover
is an exhaustingly fiery affair.

   Earlier that morning, after Chapter and before Terce, Sister
Sebastienne, not fearing immolation, replaced the satires of Juvenal
she had been studying with the Heroides. Ovid, of course, must be
her mentor in grasping her correspondent's many allusions and wit-
ticisms, strategically placed like kindling to set the entire edifice
burning, as well as her muse in matching him couplet for couplet.
Two particular lines of Ovid popped into her head before she even

laid hands on the book. *Love came to me more deeply for being late—I am burning within; I am burning, and my breast has a hidden wound.* Yes, yes, it must be to Phaedra's elegy to Hippolytus that she turns first. *I burn in silence with a knowing love.* She has no choice but to keep silent about her burning. She has joined those sisters with secrets never to be bared outside the confessional.

For the first time since the Abbot of Cluny's visit, the Abbess enters the scriptorium. She surprises and delights them all by going to her desk exactly as she always used to do. The Prioress—who occupies the Abbess's desk when the latter is absent—rises and bows with the formality that the sheer grace and authority of the Abbess's person inspires in all who come into her presence. Indeed, all the sisters rise from their benches and stools and bow to acknowledge the Abbess's arrival, their mouths and manners appropriately grave, but their eyes joyful to see the Abbess now visibly about her duties, looking more radiant and serene than they have ever seen her, veritably brightening the thin wintry gloom that passes for daylight, as though she had not been going nearly sleepless for the last three weeks.

The Abbess gestures Sister Sebastienne to join her. The sister obeys, aware that all eyes are on her, confirming that she is still the Abbess's favorite. "The Heroides?" the Abbess says, making room on her bench for the sister. "Did you get through the Juvenal so quickly, then?"

Blood rushes to the sister's neck and face. "I thought I would put him aside for a while," she said softly. "He's so harsh. By your leave, I'll return to him when I've done with these."

A flash of gaiety, a hint of playfulness warms the Abbess's face. "Frustrated love being less harsh?"

The sister can't find the words to answer. She's only glad that the Abbess hasn't rebuked her with a query as to whether her choice may not have something to do with Ovid's being so much easier to read than Juvenal.

"His elegiac couplets are moving and beautiful, all the same," the Abbess says. "So, let us begin with Penelope. Read the whole of it aloud first, and then give me a translation."

The recitation makes such demands on her concentration that Sister Sebastienne forgets everything but the lesson, even her lover's couplets. The Abbess corrects her only after she has finished the entire translation, then calls her attention to the text's interesting figures, until the bell rings calling them to Sext.

The Abbess and the sisters rise and walk in a slow, silent file to the Oratory to perform the Office. As they chant, Sister Sebastienne realizes she is ravenously hungry. The office for Sext is short, but seems interminable. Finally they go to the refectory for the midday meal of lentils, leeks, coarse brown bread, and the reading of one of the Master's drier, denser sermons. Afterward, Sister Sebastienne returns to the scriptorium, knowing that the Abbess, who has other duties, will return only after Nones, to work with a group of novices and boarders struggling to learn Latin grammar. The sister is happy, confident that it will be an afternoon of clandestine, personal pleasure. Laudri's eighty-nine verses—and not Ovid—will be her text. Laudri may be no Master Abélard, and she may be no Lady Héloïse, but the pair of them are close enough, she thinks, to play the moon to their betters' sun.

                                5.

An hour before Lauds, Sister Philippa cries out in her sleep, waking everyone in the dormitory, including herself.

In the Abbess's absence, the Prioress lights a candle to investigate.

"Oh!" Sister Philippa gasps, her worn, knobby hand fluttering at her breast. "I had *such* a dream, *such* a dream that I'm sure I'm meant to tell it!"

Many of the younger sisters would rather go back to sleep, but they dutifully sit up to listen.

"In the dream," Sister Philippa says, her thin, reedy voice trembling and quavery, "we were at Vespers, singing the Magnificat. As we finished, and were turning to file out, I caught sight of a cloud of light hanging above the Master's tomb. Startled, and feeling an urgent need to make everyone else see it, too, I said, loud enough for everyone to hear, 'Sisters, sisters, do you see the cloud of light hovering above the Master's tomb?' And lo, even as I spoke, the cloud resolved into perfect clarity, the image of a robe's sleeve rising up, out of the tomb, and of a hand rising up from the sleeve falling away from it, thrusting high a shining silver crucifix. I knew all of you saw what I saw, for up and down the line there were gasps and whispers, and many of us fell to our knees in startled, holy awe. And lo, a form sat up, out of the tomb, then stood in the air above it. And lo, sisters, I recognized, without doubt, our Master himself, wearing that stern aspect that we who came with the Abbess to the Paraclete saw when he first visited us here, more severe in its expectations and austerity than has ever been seen even in the Abbot of Cîteaux himself. And the figure opened his mouth and a terrible howling and wailing proceeded from it, causing a great wind to spring up in the Oratory, sweeping and seizing our habits, even scouring the walls and and ceiling, such that all the candles in the Oratory were extinguished. 'Hear me,' the figure thundered at us. 'Sisters, hear me!' Those who were still standing fell to their knees and bent low their necks. 'It is written,' the figure said. 'It is written that women must keep silent! It is written that the Devil prowls about, ravening like a hungry lion, seeking to devour us. Guard yourselves strictly, you handmaids of Christ, that the uncleanness in your hearts does not invite devils into holy places. Cleanse your hearts and pray without ceasing! I exhort you, I implore you, I command you, sisters! God watches! God knows all! And God will not be mocked!' And so saying, the figure became again a cloud of light, which, as a blinding whirlwind, rose high in the air above the altar, where it was sucked into the cross itself. As there was great confusion in my mind, I remained on my knees, too stunned to take in the wondrous sign that had been granted us. But suddenly I came to myself, and realized that all of you, my sisters, had risen to your feet and were moving past me, out of the Oratory. I knew that we must not do this, that it would be disobedient for us not to stay there and pray. So I cried out to the Abbess, who stood to one side, as she sometimes does, watching us as we file out, 'My lady, this must not be! The sign is clear: we must pray without ceasing!' And the Abbess looked at me, and raised her fingers to her lips, indicating to me that by speaking out I had disobeyed the rule. It was then that I awoke."

Sister Philippa looks dazedly around her. "Sisters," she says, "you all saw! You all saw the sign we were given!"

Sister Agnes, the granddaughter of a duke, laughs. "Sister Philippa," she says, "I can assure you that *I* did not see the sign."

"Nor I," Sister Anne, the daughter of a viscomte, says.

"Nor I," says Sister Eleanor, like Sister Philippa—and Sister Sebastienne, too—the daughter of a mere knight.

"But you *did*, Sister Agnes, and you, too, Sisters Anne and Eleanor," says Sister Philippa, all anxious protest and stubborn insistence. "You did see the sign! In the dream it was—"

"Silence!" the Prioress says sharply. "It is forbidden to talk idly at any time of the day or night. If there is to be discussion of this matter, it will take place in Chapter, as the Abbess directs."

The Prioress snuffs the candle, and dark and silence return to the dormitory. Sister Sebastienne thinks of the tomb and shivers. Night in the dormitory has been disturbed, as though the heavy, stifling, icy dark of the Oratory has crept up the stairs and penetrated the dormitory. In her thoughts there is only the tomb and the awful, dread-filled sense of God's cold demands on his brides. The sister feels strangely like crying, though no tears fill her eyes much less touch her cheeks. Sister Philippa's a silly old hag, she tells herself. But it is not the dream or Sister Philippa's high, quavery voice that she is really thinking about, but the tomb, the tomb now holding the Master's bones.

6.

That morning, as they are performing the office of Prime, Sister Agathe is taken by a fit of hiccoughs that mars the perfection of the psalm. She leaves the Oratory, but the damage has been done.

Later, as Sister Agathe chastises herself for her sin, Sister Philippa is heard to say that the Devil found his way in, even into the holiest of places, the very house of God, through their lack of attention to the sign given them. "Nonsense!" the Infirmarian says briskly. "Sister Agathe simply ate the morning gruel too quickly. She should have known better."

7.

In Chapter, the Abbess neither questions Sister Philippa about her dream nor introduces the subject for discussion. She asks the Prioress, who has a strong, steady voice, to read yet another of the Master's sermons, which everyone knows the Abbess esteems highly.

Afterward, when dismissing the sisters, she gestures slightly to Sister Sebastienne. When the novices and other sisters have gone, the Abbess says, "The Porteress tells me you've received another letter from Brother Laudri."

Sister Sebastienne's heart pounds; she flushes. Has all been lost? She pales—and acknowledges to the Abbess that she has indeed done so.

"I do not ask to see it," the Abbess says. Her fine, high forehead remains smooth, her voice light and even. "I'm sure that if you perceive a reason for my reading it, you will tell me."

Sister Sebastienne bows her head. Her breath expels all at once, and she realizes she's been holding it.

"And yet I would ask you, Sister, to have a care for what you are about," the Abbess says. "I mark the signs of too little sleep on your face. Words scribed in ink have more potency—as do things of the mind generally—than any of us cares to believe. This is the reason we strive to keep speech in our community to a minimum. I am not your spiritual advisor. Truly, I do not wish to know what is in your—or any other sister's—heart. My concern is only for the perfect performance of the Offices, which is our first duty, and for the modesty and decorum of all the inmates in the houses under my care." The Abbess looks down at her hands, so shapely and graceful, so coolly marmoreal against the thick black wool of her habit, folded quietly in her lap. Briefly, her knuckles blanch. "The Heroides is heady wine for a young woman without experience of the world.

May God keep you safe, child." The Abbess rises. "Go to your desk now, Sister. Business affairs claim me, requiring that I miss our lesson today."

Sister Sebastienne fairly flies to the scriptorium. Her heart is bursting with adoration for the Abbess. She has loved her almost since first seeing her. Shortly after Sister Sebastienne's parents brought her to the Paraclete to hand her over to God, the Abbess spoke privately with her. "You are not the only inmate here who comes at the will of others, rather than through vocation. While it would be best for you if you did acquire a vocation, it is not my concern to force you to the appearance of one. Once a woman has taken the veil, she can never be permitted to leave the cloister, because it would be considered an affront to the honor of God. With men, it is otherwise. The estimable Abbot of Cîteaux, for instance, accepts vast numbers of professions from the young men he inspires, most of whom a year or two later tire of the life and choose to leave. God's honor, in such cases, is not impugned, for brothers are not called the Brides of Christ, and are not required to be kept strictly enclosed. But then women are seldom allowed to speak even the frailest word about their own disposal. What I say to you now, Sebastienne, is that you must accept your fate, which is to spend the rest of your life within these walls, and learn to live within our rules, with decorum and discretion. The best outcome would be your acquiring a true profession; the second-best would be your developing a passion for any of the kind of work we do here—a passion for study, for scribing and illuminating, for healing, for music, needlework, or gardening. You will otherwise find your life utterly tedious and your spirit intolerably vexed."

These words subtly alleviated her sense of grievance at having been thrown to God as a hostage for her brother's life. Later, after she had discovered an aptitude and delight in learning, and well after she had mastered Latin grammar, the Abbess allowed her to read the voluminous correspondence between herself and the Master, who had been both lover and husband to her. Though the bulk of the correspondence concerned the rule of the community, the first few letters were personal—exceedingly personal, and more impassioned than any romance Sebastienne had ever read or heard. Of course the Abbess and the Master were famous personages; even before her novitiate, while still out in the world, she had heard something of their story. She knew that the Master, Pierre du Pallet, the firstborn son of a Breton noble—known to all the world as Abélard—was a famous scholar and brilliant teacher who had taken his pupil, the Lady Héloïse, who was almost equally famous for her erudition, as a lover. When she bore the Master a child, her uncle demanded they be married. They acceded to this demand, but kept their marriage secret. When the Master dressed the Lady Héloïse in a novice's habit and sent her to live at Argenteuil, the convent in which she had been raised, where he often visited her and flagrantly took his pleasure of her in even the most sacred places of the convent, Fulbert, the Lady Héloïse's uncle, furious that the marriage was not openly declared, had the Master castrated. Immediately after his castration, the Master forced the veil on the Lady Héloïse (because, Sebastienne has always believed, he did not trust her to remain chaste), and himself took holy orders, and later become an abbot. The Master thought his wife forever immured at Argenteuil, and of no further concern to him. But after a few years, the Abbé Suger evicted Argenteuil's nuns from their convent; for weeks, the Lady Héloïse, who had been Prioress there, led a band of them about, begging food and shelter wherever they went, churning up a torrent of talk at the scandal. Concerned for his own honor, the Master offered the Paraclete as a home for the wandering nuns. The sisters who followed the Abbess to the Paraclete so honor and obey her as their wise, caring superior that they have created an atmosphere of reverence for her, causing each new sister and novice to adopt their attitudes. This is the reason, Sebastienne thinks, that the Abbess has never resorted to the rod for correction. Most sisters correct themselves, for a word of quiet reproof from the Abbess is enough to crush any of them.

Sister Sebastienne knows the Abbess allowed her to read the correspondence so that she would understand that the Abbess herself took the veil under protest, being handed over to God not by her parents, but more treacherously and hurtfully by her lover and husband, who the Abbess always declared was God enough for her. With what new eyes the sister beheld the Abbess after reading the letters! Her theological acumen, evident in the later letters, of course impressed her. But when (as she often does) she ponders the torment and agony the Abbess suffered—might even still be suffering—the sister finds herself repeatedly amazed at the Abbess's appearance of serenity, goodness—even purity. Though she has known a love that was not only carnal but frequently blasphemous, though her body once gave birth to a child, she radiates so powerful a purity and grace it seems at extraordinary odds with her past declarations that she would rather risk damnation with the Master than seek heaven without him.

Sister Sebastienne enters the scriptorium and goes to her desk. A thought strikes her, an observation that somehow previously escaped her notice. After the Master's death, the Abbess's face took on the deep, anguished sadness of grief (which nevertheless remained entirely private). When, just a few weeks ago, the venerable Abbot of Cluny brought them the remains of the Master, the community breathed a collective—though unacknowledged—sigh of relief, tacitly reasoning that the Abbess must have known all along that the costly but plain white marble tomb would one day be filled. The bones were respectfully interred; a special Mass was celebrated. The Abbot departed, and the Abbess began to spend her nights in the Oratory—kneeling always at the head of the tomb. Praying, presumably. Praying for the Master's soul, as they all did at frequent intervals. But, Sister Sebastienne realizes, the Abbess has been marvelously altered since the Abbot's visit. For a year and a half, the Abbess was grave and sad, always in the lowest of spirits. She spent long hours in her cell, often through the night. Her face frequently bore the marks of weeping, her eyes the ravages of insomnia. But now—of a sudden—all is changed. The Abbess moves with a light, youthful step. Her voice has something new in it, something Sister Sebastienne never heard before. She glows with happiness, beyond her own usual unique radiance.

The sister opens Ovid to Phyllis, which she must prepare for her next lesson. She will work hard; she will prove to the Abbess that the games she plays with Brother Laudri inflict no torment on her spirit. She plays with fire, certainly, but easily, happily, *chastely*.

8.

Sister Sebastienne spends as much time studying her lover's *carmen*—seeking to flush out his every allusion, pun, and witticism—as she does studying Ovid. She notes down the phrases that have been floating in her thoughts, tantalizing little snippets of pleasure, scribing one couplet here, another there, without yet knowing the shape her own *carmen* will ultimately take. *Custom and law guard our love, A chaste life justifies our games.* This she writes after the Abbess's talk with her, needing to be clear that for all its wild excitement, for all it makes her body burn, it *is* a game, of words and thoughts, exciting but erudite, flirtatious but without scandalous consequences.

It is really all just playing with the Heroides, she imagines saying to the Abbess. Playing so gleefully. So *hungrily*. One mind to another, speaking one body to another. *Chastely*.

It is not even anything she need mention at confession (which will soon be upon them, since they always communicate at the feast of Christ's nativity).

So many heroines in Ovid, all longing and wanting and desiring—and in every case fruitlessly, if articulately. Laudri could not have found better inspiration for seducing her into the playful poetics of love.

9.

Daily, the sisters perform the Offices, repeating each gesture and movement and vocalization perfectly again and again and again, as God's handmaids must. Matins, Lauds, Prime, Terce, Sext, Nones, Vespers, Compline—always the same, always perfect, an anthem here, an antiphon there, each psalm in this way, the doxology in that, all of God's Brides moving in unison—rising to their feet at this time, falling to their knees at that, bowing their heads, making the sign of the cross, chanting, chanting, chanting modestly, correctly, adoringly, giving praise, giving thanks, giving reverence to their Lord. Brides (though not all of them virgins) cloistered, suspended in time, waiting to be taken by their Bridegroom. Filing into the Oratory, then out, the black robes and the white, silent, orderly, perfect.

Increasingly often now, when the sisters file into the Oratory to perform the Offices, they find the Abbess there before them. The Master, it is true, has always been at the top of their list, and his name has now been entered into the Paraclete's necrology, as one of the souls they will constantly be praying for. And who should know better than the Abbess how much the Master needs their prayers! Their correspondence, Sister Sebastienne recalls each time she sees the Abbess rising from her place at the head of the tomb, their correspondence alluded often to the blasphemous character of their lovemaking and to the special pleasure they took in its blasphemy. From the moment the Master installed the Lady Héloïse and her sisters at the Paraclete, his chief concern had been that they pray for him. And is that not the hope of all the relatives of the sisters, and their reason for endowing them with gifts and rents and tithes and mills and harvest bounties? The sisters pray even for Fulbert, the uncle of the Abbess, the man who ordered the Master's castration. And did not the Abbot of Cluny beg their prayers, and was that not the reason he brought the Master's body? Because of all things, the sisters excel in praying? It is the reason they must take care always to perform the Offices perfectly. The perfect performance of the Offices makes their prayers more pleasing to God. By the time a novice makes her profession, this at least she understands. Of all things, they must know their *raison d'être* in the world.

The Abbess's prayers, Sister Sebastienne thinks, must be superior to those of the other sisters. The Abbot of Cluny addresses her as "Your Sanctity." In fact, before his visit, the Abbot wrote in a letter to the Abbess, *If only our Cluny possessed you, or you were confined in the delightful prison of Marcigny, our daughter house, with the other handmaids of Christ who are there awaiting their freedom in heaven!* But is the Abbess's new radiance and ease in manner solely due to gratification in shortening the Master's time spent in Purgatory? Sister Sebastienne has read the correspondence. She knows the Abbess is much more than greets the eye of the Abbot of Cluny. The Abbess's apparent elation mystifies her.

10.

They go to bed so early in the winter. Halfway to Matins, Sister Sebastienne composes—in her head, certain she will remember it in the morning: *Love that has been wakened knows no night.* Her stomach is burning with gas; she can't stop belching. At the evening meal they ate braised cabbage and onions with their coarse brown bread. Worse, Sister Sebastienne is exhausted in both body and mind from too many nights of scanting sleep, her eyes red and sore, her limbs cramped and aching. She must get her *carmen* written, for her body cannot take much more—of going without sleep, of constantly juggling Latin phrases in her mind, trying to get them to scan as they must.

To be sure, it is not just her stomach that burns! What she would like to make clear in her reply to her lover is that she burns as only women do—not with the dry heat Aristotle says is the normal healthy state of man, but with the passion of a woman. The steaming, liquid molten heat of shifting magma and flowing lava, lava that can be shaped into poetry not with the arid perfection of a monk playing games, but in the purest sculpting of a passion that erupts as a fluid and then cools into gleaming, smooth hard rock.

Sister Sebastienne listens to her sisters' slow, even breaths. Sister Adele snores in her usual rhythm of explosive, toneless puffs. Their digestion of cabbage and onions has created its own winter fragrance, binding them in sharing, wordless intimacy.

Sister Sebastienne reflects on the purpose that fires her brain: it is a matter, she intuits, of exalting the flesh, of putting its passion into words, which are themselves chaste, and making it soar. Solomon, reputed to be one of the wisest men ever to live, though not a woman, surely understood that. The thought makes Sister Sebastienne smile, and sends her drifting warmly, quietly, off to sleep.

11.

The days grow very, very short, and what little light they afford is thin and gray with constant rain. And it is the dark of the moon, and everyone who is neither aged nor ill has the flowers. Every one

of them is unusually cranky and irritable. The cramps in their bel-
lies and the aches in their backs and heads impel them in a nearly
constant stream to the Infirmarian. They are all so cranky, in fact,
that when two lay sisters have to be rebuked for their exchange of
sharp words over the washing of so many rags, no one is shocked
by the raucous openness of their conflict.

The Abbess gives Sister Sebastienne a lesson. The sister reminds
her that they last read Phyllis and says she therefore will read Briseis.
"No, not Briseis," the Abbess says sharply. Sister Sebastienne catches
her breath in amazement. The Abbess is almost never cross. And
Briseis is next. *"Discedens oscula nulla dedi,"* the Abbess quotes in a
tone of voice too grating to be recognizable as hers. Sister
Sebastienne recalls that when as a girl the Abbess studied with the
Master, he required her to recite every text she studied from memory. "It is an inferior dialogue," the Abbess says, "unworthy of Ovid,
in my judgment. We won't waste our time on it."

Unworthy of Ovid! It would be improper for Sister Sebastienne
to question the Abbess. But never has the Abbess said such a thing
about any text in the house's possession. "Phaedra, then?" Sister
Sebastienne asks.

"Quam nisi tu dederis," the Abbess says, gesturing the sister to continue.

Phaedra is the sister's favorite text, the text that will lie burning
beneath the words of her *carmen* to Laudri. Yes, yes: *What modesty
forbade me to say, love has commanded me to write.*

12.

They celebrate the special Mass after Terce on Christmas, all of them
not only seeing God, as they do every morning at Mass, but eating
Him, too. They celebrate the feast of St. Stephen on the day following, then finally, finally, they celebrate Epiphany, feasting on meat
as they rarely do and growing giddy and merry drinking wine. The
novices and boarders perform a mystery play. Most of the house's
inmates dance in a chain around the periphery of the refectory. The
sound of frank laughter, lilting voices, clapping hands fills the room.

But they don't neglect to perform the Offices—perfectly, as they
must.

They go to bed as usual after Compline. Sister Adele puffs more
violently than usual, fueled by meat and wine—making other sisters
wakeful and needing the privy. Sister Sebastienne tries to ignore the
fullness of her bladder, hoping to wait—as she usually does in winter—to void it after Matins. Her head is reeling; her pulse is racing.
Since her thoughts are too jumbled to make poetry, sleep is what she

most desires. But as the others gradually drop off—and more of them begin to snore in addition to Sister Adele, for instance Sister Stephanie, at a pitch and rhythm completely dissonant with Sister Adele's more modest production—her mind remains stubbornly stimulated, and the physical discomfort becomes impossible to ignore. Sister Sebastienne has no choice but to leave her warm bed and face the clammy cold and descend the rickety stairs to the privy.

She rushes through the cloister, which, in the thick, winter fog is impenetrably dark. The only trace of light is the faint glow that strikes the Oratory's few panes of stained glass from whatever candles may be lit within. The seat of the privy feels even colder on the bare skin of her buttocks than the open air of the cloisters on her face; but of course it is not so cold yet to make resort to a chamber pot necessary (chamber pots being a luxury restricted to the ill in all but the bitterest of seasons). Sometimes, when returning from the privy, Sister Sebastienne pauses in the cloisters to look up at the stars. Not so this night, so overcast, so chilly, so moist. And yet something, some sound, perhaps, makes her stop. For several seconds she stands motionless, holding her breath. Then, yes, a noise comes to her, borne on the dense, damp air. Cries, perhaps, or whispers, or maybe even murmuring . . .

Sister Sebastienne thinks of the Abbess, often praying long into the night, on her knees in the Oratory.

What she hears does not sound like praying.

Sister Sebastienne hesitates until a great cry, something between a sigh and a scream, penetrates the fog. The sister must know, she *must* know, she must know if it is the Abbess . . . grieving secretly. *Seeming so radiant and happy, when all along she is mourning in secret . . .*

Sister Sebastienne creeps soundlessly and precisely through the choir. No passage is as familiar to her as this one, though without a sister going before her and another following it feels larger and alien. When she reaches the nave, she stands silently in the darkness that makes her invisible. She stares, but does not understand what she sees. A man, naked, is standing near a brazier of glowing coals, set only a foot or so from the tall, thick candle that is always kept burning at the foot of the Master's tomb.

Sister Sebastienne hears the Abbess say, "As I wrote to you years ago, nothing is less under our control than the heart." Sister Sebastienne looks around for the Abbess, and then realizes that that lady is lying— also naked!—on her back, on the tomb itself, her skin nearly as colorless as the marble, only tinged here and there with a rosy flush. A memory comes to the sister of a passage in the Master's letters to the Abbess, a passage both vivid and icy, telling the Abbess that on her death she must be sewn naked into her shroud, as a superior's special example of humility to her flock.

"The power of our love is plain," the Abbess says. "That you rise from the dead, with your manhood intact, itself always rising to greet me, to claim me, to *take* me, is proof enough! This miracle of the flesh is your gift to me. And yet you never cease trying to deny it! That you should come to me like this, so perfectly—as it is written, *And the dead shall be raised—incorruptible! And the maimed made whole!*"

As she speaks, the Abbess rolls gracefully off the tomb to her feet—her breasts, the sister sees, full and firm as one never imagines a nun's—then moves swiftly to kneel before the man, twining her arms around his waist, pressing her head against his round, hairy belly, stroking him boldly, passionately, possessively.

"This is blasphemy, blasphemy!" the man says angrily. "All the worse that I myself taught you to blaspheme. This madness must end! You keep my soul from Purgatory and would drag me to Hell with you! All your talk of miracles mocks God!"

Sister Sebastienne is astounded. *This* is the Master? But she saw him once, briefly, when she was a novice. He was emaciated, gray, ill—nothing like this full-fleshed, vital man! She wonders, irrelevantly, whether he had been sewn naked into his shroud, having once been an abbot himself.

The Abbess's voice is soft but exultant. "*You* are my God! You made yourself my God. I worshiped you! I still worship you, and will always do so. And so I *do* not mock God—not *my* God. Though maybe *yours*—which is nothing to me."

The Master's voice grows hoarse. "It is said, truly, that there is nothing so monstrous as a woman's lust! What you do, what you are, is monstrous. Renounce this, I command you! And release me from your monstrous will!"

The Abbess rocks back on her heels and looks up into his face. Sister Sebastienne, heart pounding, glimpses the Master's member, engorged, ruby-eyed, trembling. A wave of heat flows over her. She feels as though she is suffocating.

"*Mon coeur, mon coeur,*" the Abbess says. Her voice, sweet and low, is a tender murmuring, relentless and wholly without gentleness. She laughs softly and strokes the Master's member. "When you renounce *this*," she says, "when you renounce *this* miracle of the flesh."

The Master groans and sinks to his knees. He takes the Abbess's face between his hands. "If you love me, obey me," he says, his hoarse voice breaking with emotion.

The Abbess places many and many kisses on his face. The moist, sucking sound of them thrills the sister. The Abbess sighs. "Though I'm no Briseis, I've always obeyed you, even when I knew it was wrong. When I first gave myself to you, all the times I blasphemed with you, when I married you, when I took the veil, when I kept silent about what you from the beginning called my 'old complaint'—always I obeyed you, to keep your love. I told you, and you knew it, that I would do anything to keep your love, give up anything, even the hope of salvation. And now you would have me obey you, to fling that love away?" The Abbess embraces the Master and rains even more kisses on his neck and eyes, his cheeks and lips. "Give up a love that has triumphed over the grave? Never, and never, and never! You are physically as you were the day you walked into my uncle's house. Our bodies are of an age now, my dearest. When I weary of love as you did, ask me *then*, my darling. Now love me again, I command you, before the bell is rung for Matins!"

In the Oratory's nighttime silence that the sister has always thought of as God's, in the shimmering pool of light cast by the great, thick candle, the Abbess's fingers, tongue, and lips draw great gasps and cries from the Master. It is the Master who obeys the Abbess, not the Abbess him, speaking words the sister knows only from the fabliaux she heard as a child in her father's Hall, overpowering the Abbess with embraces fiercer and wilder than any act of love the sister has dared to imagine, until at long last the Abbess, crying out, impales herself on his member.

Sister Sebastienne creeps soundlessly back to the dormitory. Her teeth are chattering, her knees trembling, but her private places are thrilled and moist, burning with an intensity she had not known possible. What she saw cannot be, she is certain. It must be that the meat and wine have given her this lewd, wanton vision, sending her imagination to places it has never before visited. So vivid, yes, so real, but surely impossible . . .

13.

Carefully, lovingly, Sister Sebastienne copies out the first couplet of her *carmen* onto the smooth, clean vellum a lay sister prepared for her. *Perlegi vestram studiosa indagine cartam, Et tetigi nuda carmina vestra manu*— "I read your letter with embracing zeal, And with your hand I have touched your naked songs." It is a joy to write out her verses, a joy to see them written on the vellum—giving her almost as great a pleasure as she took composing them.

Sister Sebastienne glances over at the Abbess, seated at her desk, the sunlight pouring down on her head like the radiance enveloping a saint in a painting. She writes, "At last, weary, I tried to get to sleep, but love that has been wakened knows no night . . ." Hearing her own words in the privacy of her mind makes Sister Sebastienne's palms tingle, as though filled with the sweet shapeliness of her soft, naked breasts. *Love that has been wakened* . . .

How much the Abbess has taught her! She may be a handmaid and hostage of God, but she knows now, in her heart, that not only are the delights of a life of study prodigious, but that the power of love surpasses that of the grave—and that of the Master himself!

THE ASHES OF
NEW ORLEANS
Tony Daniel

You know what they say about that Road to Hell? Well, as the silky smooth and razor-edged story that follows demonstrates, even in today's modern world, it's *still* paved with good intentions . . .

One of the fastest-rising new stars of the nineties, Tony Daniel grew up in Alabama, lived for a while on Vashon Island in Washington State, and in recent years, in the best tradition of the young bohemian artist, has been restlessly on the move, from Vashon Island to Europe, from Europe to New York City, from New York City to Alabama. At last report, he had just moved back to New York City again. He attended the Clarion West Writers Workshop in 1989 and since then has become a frequent contributor to *Asimov's Science Fiction*, as well as to markets such as *The Magazine of Fantasy and Science Fiction*, *Amazing*, *SF Age*, *Universe*, *Full Spectrum*, and elsewhere. His first novel, *Warpath*, was released simultaneously in America and England in 1993; he subsequently won $2,000 and the T. Morris Hackney Award for his inexplicably as-yet-unsold novel *Ascension*. His story "Life on the Moon" was a finalist for the Hugo Award in 1996. He is currently at work on a new science fiction novel.

THE ASHES OF NEW ORLEANS

I rise an hour earlier than most so that I can spend time playing with my long blond hair. A hair stylist told me once that people paid good money for the sunny highlights that have naturally streaked into mine over the years. There are times when I will stand for a good fifteen minutes before the mirror, deciding whether or not to wash my hair, or to go for a more down-and-dirty tangle. I think about who will be looking at me that day, the women I might chance to meet. I spend another thirty minutes picking out my clothes.

Take a particular day of a week ago. I pulled on chocolate brown Dickies—the work pants you can get at Wal-Mart (although I do not shop there)—over narrow-cut cotton boxers, then donned a wide black belt with a curved silver buckle, and a dark blue bowling shirt with off-white piping on the collar and pockets. The name "Larry" was embroidered on the left pocket flap, though my name, of course, is Gerald Dunn. Over the shirt, I wore a vintage brown suede jacket with white stitching, lighter than the pants. I deliberated on the shoes for some time. I had to make a presentation this day, so something besides sneakers was called for. I settled on zipper dingo boots—they were a faded brown—with a metal loop on each ankle. These I'd found in the back of my father's closet after he died. They must have dated from the early seventies. I put them on over dark blue socks with little planets and stars woven subtly into the stretch fabric. Nobody but me would know about those, but detail is everything when you want to *feel* as good as you look.

Obviously, I am something of a modern Southern dandy. While there are times when I'm reluctant to admit that I'm a clotheshorse, for the most part I am not ashamed of this trait, for the simple fact is that I get laid more often on account of it. I am an advertising man—that is, I am *in* advertising, and even in conservative Birmingham, Alabama, it is not unseemly for an advertising man to sport long hair and snappy togs, especially if he is the agency's eccentric creative talent. On the other hand, I do come in for a certain amount of ribbing from my male coworkers, and such ribbing in Alabama is often a shuffle-step away from homophobia.

Of course, most advertising men in Birmingham do not dress as I do, but affect a yuppie, frat-boy standard. If they are particularly daring, you may find them sporting a denim button-down or a loud tie. *They* shop at the Galleria; *I* haunt the thrift stores, with which Birmingham is copiously endowed. As a matter of principle, I refuse to pay more than fifteen dollars for a shirt or a pair of pants. This requires a concomitant heroic diligence in shopping. You may not realize the sacrifice and effort that goes into looking the way that I do, but it is there, underlying the look, nonetheless. When a client is impressed with my creative dress, say, or when a woman in a restaurant gives me a long glance, neither realizes that they are admiring my moral commitment as much as my fashion sense. Or so I like to think.

I like to think well of myself. Why not? I have made a place for myself, spun a cocoon on the south side of the city, where you will find Birmingham's two-block stab at a bohemian neighborhood. I am the top apartment on the left in Marty Lane, a renovated warehouse. I have a loft that overlooks what there is of a city here in the Jones Valley. I like to think well of myself and my life. I get plenty of sex and I'm making money. I support progressive causes; I buy art and go out to music. I've been known to read a book that doesn't have a lawyer as the main character. The good Baptist folk tell me that my existence is hollow, that I must get right with the Lord Jesus Christ, that I must get a haircut. But at work, I am, as they say, a team player with a can-do attitude, and they've just made me a partner. I'm white. I went to a good school. It isn't hard to play along. It's a running game against a passing game, after all. I like to think that if Jesus came back today, he would have a beer with me at Hart's. *He* would appreciate the look I was going for on that particular day.

Hart's is the bar we've all been hanging out at since college. It's basically an old service station into which Charlie Boone put a beer cooler, tables, and a jukebox. There is neon in the windows, but the only sign outside is an unlit piece of metal on a pole that says "Beverages." Nobody has any idea why we call it Hart's.

On the day I wore my brown suede jacket, I met Vincent and Xavier at Hart's after work. I've known them both since my freshman year at Birmingham-Southern. Vincent (everybody but me calls him Vince—but he is skinny and short, with a preternaturally youthful appearance, and he just doesn't *look* like a Vince) is an overdue-loan collector for First Alabama Bank. Vincent lives in a bare apartment in the suburbs. He doesn't like his job and he doesn't have very many friends. In a way, I feel sorry for him. But in another way, being around him fills me with relief at how far I've come from the shy social enigma I was just out of high school. Vincent is constantly on the make. As with many Southern men, women are for him objects of desire and loathing, but always, *always* objects. He is on a testosterone high that hasn't abated in the fifteen years that I've known him. It is a wonder that the vertebrae in his neck haven't ground themselves away from such constant head jerking to look at legs, breasts, shoulders. Vincent is not exactly the master of the sidelong glance.

He was the first to show up, and he joined me at our usual booth with his usual nervous handshake. I have no idea why he felt it was necessary to shake hands every time we met. I knew that he wasn't really comfortable *touching* anyone. Over the years and after one bender or another, I'd wound up at his place of an evening, and the elaborate precautions he took in the morning *not to be seen*, to cover up, were amusing. He closed—and *locked*—the bathroom door. His big robe nearly swallowed him. For a time I toyed with the idea that he was gay and in denial, but what was up with Vincent went deeper than that. The man was fundamentally uncomfortable *being* in the world. There was always a moment when it appeared that Vincent was deciding—wholly unconsciously—whether it would be more appropriate to hit you or to shake your hand. What am I supposed to *do*? you imagined his brain shouting. We've got a situation here!

"Did you see that one over in the corner?" Vincent said as he sat down across from me. "Those are some nice tits!"

"No. She came in after me." Of course I *had* noticed the woman he was talking about—we'd exchanged glances when I'd come in—but to begin a discussion about her breasts . . . with Vincent, that way lay madness.

"She can't be twenty-five. Probably in college. She's got one of those nose piercings."

"I'll take your word for it."

"All in black. You like those gothic girls, right? You sure you don't want you some of it tonight? How long's it been since Shelly moved to Nashville?"

"Two months. We weren't really together, you know."

He looked over my shoulder at the woman. "This one's fine. Jet black hair. White skin. Probably soft as a lily."

"Jailbait," I said.

"I thought you hadn't seen her?" Vincent sat back and grinned.

"I'm just going by your description."

Fortunately, Charlie arrived with a beer for Vincent and a vodka tonic for me. I squeezed the lime and dropped it in, where it floated greenly in the concoction.

"X coming?"

"She said she was."

"Good, because I could really use a little Deb tonight."

"Me, too."

Vincent took a pull on his beer. "What about them Blazers?" he said. "Think Auburn's gonna whoop up on 'em?"

This must have been a carryover from work, because Vincent knew how little I cared about college football. I gazed off into the smoke of the bar. "It's a running game against a passing game," I replied.

Xavier came in in her hospital greens. Yet, even wearing such a sexless get-up, X managed to give off an air of dominating passion, of out-and-out lust. I imagined her tall, black form passing through the sterile corridors of the hospital where she worked. Terminally ill patients turning their heads for a last, longing look at the desire they could no longer feel because of the pain and dope.

X was a nurse practitioner at UAB — the University that Ate Birmingham—at the medical center. Her specialty was neurological medicine. She managed the head and spinal-trauma cases.

X sat down beside me. She always sat beside me in the booth. I suspected this was because Vincent had groped her once or twice, for all the good it would ever do him with X. She was bi, even poly-sexual, but none of her twists and turns included a kink for *Vincent*.

"Techmed pumps are in," was the first thing X said.

"You are so out of it, girl," I said. "Those were the rage in Paris four *months* ago. We've moved on since then."

X cracked a smile. That's what X always did. Tight-lipped. You had to look carefully at her when she talked if you wished to find out whether or not X had teeth. "Implantable drug pumps for continuous dosing. They go in just under the shoulder blade. The new ones came in today. We're going to put one in a Parkinson's patient tomorrow."

"What's in it?" Charlie asked, setting X's beer—a porter—on the table.

"Muscle relaxant in that one. You can put anything in them. Morphine for pain control is what's in a lot of them these days. You inject a couple of month's worth through the skin and into the pump's reservoir."

Vincent cough-laughed, cleared his throat. "Did you see that one when you came in?" he asked her.

X frowned at the interruption. She frowned as slightly as she smiled. "The curvy one?"

"That's what I mean. Gerald says jailbait."

X languidly turned and looked at the woman. What in Vincent would be nigh on *stalking* behavior was sexy as hell when Xavier did it. "Oh, I don't know," X said. "She's fine."

Well, scratch that one for me tonight, I thought. She's liable to think we're all looking to cook and eat her by this point. But, in any case, I had other plans for the evening.

"Sort of like Deborah," X said, turning back around. "The eyes, I mean."

"Not really," I said. "I didn't think so."

Vincent pointed his beer bottle at me. "You *are* looking!"

"Speaking of which, I'd just as soon go ahead now. Unless either of y'all have another plan."

"Let's," Vincent said.

"All right." I downed the remainder of my drink and stood up. "Let's tell Charlie and go in the back."

Charlie saw where we were headed and nodded to me. We crowded into the small backroom at Hart's, and X flinted on the little propane torch that Charlie kept back there for odd jobs—and for us.

We all stood around the tiny flame as if it were a campfire. For an early autumn evening, it had gotten chilly in the bare concrete room.

Then Charlie came in with the black film canister where we kept a year's supply of Deborah.

Of course Charlie had no idea what was in the canister. Or what was in the Red Diamond coffee can we asked him to place in his safe those many years ago. That was why he was the perfect keeper, the perfect dealer. None of us—me, Vincent, X—would have trusted the others with Deborah. And we were *right* not to. I have no idea what Charlie thought was in there. He never asked about it, even when he was at his most garrulous. After X took the canister from him, he left us to our devices.

X took a bent spoon from her handbag and set it up on the room's plain wood table. She shook a few crystals—about a salt packet's worth—from the powder in the container into the bowl of the spoon. She moistened the crystal with saline from a syringe, then carefully held the propane torch close to the metal. With the finest flicking motion, X heated the metal until the brown-black crystals began to dissolve in the saline. As always, she heated it until the saline just started to boil, then backed off. She was very good at this. It was X who first came up with the idea of the *injections*.

Time. Quickly, she filled three syringes with the liquid from the spoon, handing one to Vincent, one to me, and taking one for herself.

Vincent and I had already popped veins up in the bend of our elbows. I turned from the others, faced a gray wall. I looked at what was in my hand.

Deborah was in my hand. My first and only true love. I took a breath. Prepared.

"Damn it," said Vincent. "I can't hit the damn vein." I did not look back at him. "Ouch—shit. X, can you—"

"All right," X said. I waited. "There now," she finally said. "How's that?"

"Fucking marvelous," Vincent replied. "Fucking . . ." And then he was lost in it, in her. She was *there* for him. She would soon be there for me.

I looked down at the bare white of my arm. My suede jacket was lying in the corner. My shirt was short-sleeved. My vein was very, very blue. With a quick thrust, I slid the needle through the skin, into the wall of the blood vessel. My thumb came down on the plunger with the same motion. Smooth and easy. I'd learned to do this well.

Deborah flowed into my blood and bones.

I breathed out, long; breathed in deeply. I looked up at the lightbulb hanging on black cord from the ceiling. Light, pure white. Pure white, but softening. As soft as the sun through Alabama rain. The sun through rain, scintillating now to the prismatic, to prism hues.

And *she* was there. Like the colors of light inside me.

I couldn't *see* her. I would never see her again. It was her *presence* I felt, more than anything. The way it felt to be around her, to breath her in. To touch and be touched by her, by my old lover, Deborah Vines. Her fingernails on my skin, as she ran the back of her hand across my cheek—

"Gerald."

"Hmm?"

"Gerald, it's X."

"Yes. What?"

"Vince is totally gone."

"He always does. He always does."

"I want to go with her."

"Then go. Go with her, X."

"Let's call Charlie."

"Okay." I rapped on the door three times. After a moment, Charlie came in and took the film canister away. Just us now. The three of us. And the night to spend with Deborah.

I gazed around the room. Vincent was in a corner, slumped on my jacket. His eyes were closed and his eyeballs twitched underneath his lids.

"I think Vincent will stay here tonight," I said. "Charlie'll look after him."

X nodded. "I . . . do you mind if I come to your place tonight?" she asked me. "Allison is staying with me at the house this week."

"Come home with me, then," I said. "But let's take two cars."

"All right."

I looked at X. Tears were forming in her eyes. Tears ran down her face. "Deb," she said. "Oh, Deb." But she wasn't talking to me.

"Are you okay to drive?"

X wiped her nose, sniffed. "I'll be all right. Let's go."

I pulled my jacket out from under Vincent. He toppled over, lay on his side, but didn't seem to notice. On the way out, I passed the woman he and X had been looking at. She wasn't really very special. Nothing special at all when compared to Deborah.

Driving the streets of Birmingham with Deborah inside me. Her fingers on my skin *from the inside*, caressing, touching me in places no other woman has, where no other woman can. Every wait at a traffic light is an eternity of longing. But an eternity I can endure, use to gather strength within. Streetlights of the Southside, the colors of a dark rainbow. We'd driven this way so many times together. Up Twentieth, up Red Mountain, toward the television antennas. Up to the giant iron man on the summit, the Vulcan, symbol of Birmingham's lost steel-mill past.

Under the god's feet, under his white marble tower, where Deborah and I went to be alone, back when we both lived in the dorms. Back when we'd first fallen in love and couldn't get enough of one another. I could never get enough of her back then.

I parked and walked to my apartment. X was already there, waiting for me at the outside door, although she'd had a key for many years. We climbed up the three flights of stairs in silence, each lost in our separate thoughts. But together, too.

I put X on the futon, and I sank into my big chair. I turned it to face the window, to face out over the lights of the city. Finally, I gave myself completely to Deborah. I gave myself to the memories coursing through my blood.

Gerald, where are you?
    Here.
    Where?
    Birmingham.
    I thought. I thought you were going to leave. Go to New Orleans. Go to New York. What about your play?
    My what? Oh. You can't have old manuscripts in your bottom drawer if you want to make partner. I don't want to talk about that, Deb.
    Okay. I love you.
    I love you, too.
    You were so intense. *We* were so intense. Everything *mattered* so much to you! God, I would come just thinking of you, all bunched up inside like that, ready to explode. You were going to take off like the fireworks, baby. Remember the fireworks on the Fourth? Sitting under Vulcan watching them and they were *right on top of us,* like we were making love *in* them, like we were one of them.
    Yes. Yes.
    All of us. Me, you, X, and Vince. Did y'all ever get a place together in New Orleans like we talked about?
    We got a place here.
    Oh. Was it nice?
    For a while.
    Oh.
    You weren't there. It wasn't. It didn't. Work out.
    I wasn't there.
    No.
    Gerald?
    Yes?
    How did I die? I can remember everything but that.

*   *   *

The blue sadness was as delicious as the rapture. I'd found that out over the years. That was why I always let her ramble on. Why I always let her ask that question. And I could answer. I could answer if I wanted to, because she'd never remember the answers the next time.

She was always and forever twenty-two years old. Ghost in my blood. How could we have done this to her? How could *I* have done this to her?

It was easy, really.

I was the theater major, and it was I who had done the research on ritual magic, ritual murder. For my play, of course. It was to be a mock renaissance drama. I was going to out-Marlowe Marlowe, by heaven and hell. A postmodern Faust, where the good doctor wins.

The weird kids, the freaks kids, get very close in Southern colleges. We come from small towns, from hick neighborhoods in the city, and no one has ever been like us before. All we knew were Bible thumpers, good old boys, or nouveau riche playing at being old gentry. Nobody like *us*. Until we go off to school. And there they are: *our kind. My* kind. It was such a relief. I cannot tell you. *There were other people like me!*

The artist. Oh, Vincent was a male chauvinist pig, but he was a pig with a genius for paint. A demon who has stared down into himself and found his own hell, and come back with a picture of it to show around to his friends. Vincent used to paint like a fallen angel. I still had some of his work in my apartment.

X, whose *life* was a work of art in progress, whose brush was her sex, the living organ of her skin. What a rare and amazing thing to body forth out of the South! She wanted to be a nurse so she could be *around* bodies. Beautiful bodies in all their lovely and hideous forms.

X, who had drawn us all together in a tight knot of intimacy and desire. A tight knot whose name was Deborah.

X, who worked part-time at the crematorium.

And Deborah. Deb, who sang. Who sang us dark lullabies after we made love. X and me. Vince and Deb. X and Deb. Then Deb and me. She was *my* girlfriend, after all.

Deb, whose voice was as chilly as a night wind, and as lovely.

Maybe we'd all gotten a little *too* close. We were all terrified that we would end up back where we came from, back in the 'burbs and small towns where they'd looked at us funny for *wanting*. Not wanting something *more*. Not really. Just something *else*.

There is no good and bad. There is only the ugly and the beautiful.

We wanted beautiful lives. And that was all it took to earn people's distrust. Their hatred.

We had thought we were working a magic against the possibility of return. One of us would give himself for the others, so that *that* horror would never come about. So that the others would get what it was they most wanted. Never to go *back*. One of us would give herself.

We loved each other so much.

We took up kitchen knives in our right hands and drew straws with our left. Well, except for Vincent, who is left-handed.

And the magic worked.

Look at us now, fifteen years later. The magic worked, and we never had to go home again.

The next morning, I woke and found X making me breakfast. She was poaching the eggs, just as she knew I liked them. I sat down at my kitchen table, rubbed my eyes. The hangovers could be bad, but so far this one was only mild. A mild and sweet blue in my heart. It might have matched my shirt.

"My shift doesn't start until eleven today," she said. "So I thought I'd get you going."

She poured me coffee in a tea cup and set it down black on the blond wood of the tabletop.

"Thanks."

"You all right?"

"I guess. Yes, I'm fine."

"Me, too."

The eggs were soon ready, and X sat down across from me with her own cup of coffee. She put the slightest touch of milk in hers. Macchiato. Like her skin. Touched with cream.

"How's Allison?" I asked.

"Fine, I guess." She sipped, swallowed. "I think we're breaking up."

"What? Oh, that's too bad. Why?"

"I come home and there's just . . . nothing. It's like we're both waiting for the other to say something. Only I don't know what it could be."

"Do you fuck?"

X smiled, tight as usual. "Not much," she said.

"That's too bad."

"Yeah. Listen, there's something I wanted to talk to you about. Away from Vincent. I *know* he would go for it."

"Go for what?"

"Remember those pumps I was telling you about?"

"The drug pumps?"

"The implantable pumps, yes. They're very safe these days. Almost routine. As a matter of fact, I have one."

"You *have* one?"

"Yeah. I got one of the docs to put it in when I had my eye surgery. For pain control. It's very efficient and effective. Better than any nurse."

"I'll bet."

"Listen. We could. You could get one."

"Get one?" I swallowed hot coffee, choked back a cough. I set my cup down. "For *Deborah*, you mean?"

"We could divide her up fairly then. For continuous dosage. No more sleazy back room at Hart's. We could charge it up for six months at a time. The technology is not at all experimental any more. It's practically routine."

I couldn't reply to this. I sat there and absentmindedly finished my coffee. Deborah. All the time, a bit of Deborah trickling into me.

X's touch on my hand brought me out of my reverie.

"There's another thing I wanted to ask," she said. She sighed, touched my cheek. What was she doing? "I'm lonely, Gerald. Allison is so far away, and I'm lonely. Sometimes I think we missed something along the way, you and I. That there was something there and we just weren't paying attention to it. Do you think . . . before you go to work . . . do you think we could . . . *be* together? For old time's sake?"

What was she doing?

"Oh Christ, X," I said. "It's pretty late. I have to get dressed." I stood up, rattling the bleached table. "I have to get dressed. I have a presentation."

Today I am up at six so that I can wash my hair. Deborah always liked it better freshly washed. The grungy look came in long after she had passed on. I examine my pretty blond locks in the mirror, and I see Deborah smiling through my eyes.

X was right. The implanting procedure took all of half an hour. She performed the operation herself, in an unused examining room at the UAB medical complex. Vincent first, then me. Snipped us open and taped us shut, and that was it. I was already healing. Maybe the incision wouldn't even scar up. But it was on my back, so I would never see it in a mirror. Nothing to worry about. X is blindingly efficient.

Now we only have to meet every six months. No more sleazy back room at Hart's. No more Hart's, really, because I have to admit there was only one reason I ever went there anymore. I think the others felt the same way, too. Underneath it all.

Big fat corduroy is in, and today I'm wearing a beige shirt over slouchy black pants, suitable for bowling. What a hoot; I haven't been bowling since college. I like to think well of myself. Why not? I'm going to dare the fashion gods, I decide, and I pull a corduroy jacket *over* my corduroy shirt. It's a running game against a passing game.

The effect works. Surprisingly well. I am a wizard, a goddamn wizard of texture.

"You are a wizard of texture," I say to my reflection.

Do you remember how long we used to take getting ready to go out? Hours, sometimes.

It was like getting ready was more important than whatever it was we were going to *do*. We'd pass windows and look at ourselves walking by. Silly.

Sweet.

We were just kids.

I'm not a kid. I'm twenty-two. I'm not a kid anymore.

No. You're a woman, my love.

A woman. That's better.

I sit down on the futon and lace up my shoes—black Converse All Stars. Oxford cut, not ankle-highs.

Gerald?

Hmm?

I know I must have asked you this before, but I keep forgetting.

That's okay. That's okay, my love.

How did I die?

Gerald?

I like the color of the Gulf of Mexico. It is a pleasant blue-green. And warm. It is like swimming in your own body, your own blood. We all went to New Orleans for spring break of our senior year, and Deborah and I drove over to Biloxi and we lay out on those bone-white beaches, and we swam under those heavy, humid Southern skies. And we made love in the sandy night.

And after two days, we went back to New Orleans and found Vincent and X, and we all were so excited we couldn't get enough of it all, of the city, of everything all at once, everything happening all at once. So we walked the streets of the French Quarter, and we looked at the tangle of iron and masonry, and we all said how wonderful it was, how exquisite and beautiful, and we are all going to move here together, live here together, and it will be a life like nobody has ever had before. Everything will be amazing, exquisite, and beautiful. And we are all going to live in beautiful, beautiful New Orleans and go swimming in the sea.

So we remained in Birmingham? So we live as we do live? The world is *still* beautiful, only it's more beautiful on the inside than the out—at least mine is. I don't feel that I betrayed anything, not really. Deborah's sacrifice wasn't meaningless. And she is alive, still alive, in my living body. It's a peculiar kind of life—but then, so is mine.

It's not so bad for either of us. We are always young, always together, and always committed to intensity and passion. What better way is there to live? This is how I will honor my past. This is what I will do with the time that remains. It *is* a peculiar kind of life—but then, so is *yours*. So is everyone's on the inside of the skin, in the coursing of the blood.

How did I die?

Gerald?

Gerald?

MULTIPLES
Robert Silverberg

Robert Silverberg is one of the most famous SF writers of modern times, with dozens of novels, anthologies, and collections to his credit. Silverberg has won five Nebula Awards and four Hugo Awards. His novels include *Dying Inside*, *Lord Valentine's Castle*, *The Book of Skulls*, *Downward to the Earth*, *Tower of Glass*, *The World Inside*, *Born with the Dead*, *Shadrack in the Furnace*, *Tom O'Bedlam*, *Star of Gypsies*, *At Winter's End*, and two novel-length expansions of famous Isaac Asimov stories, *Nightfall* and *The Ugly Little Boy*. His collections include *Unfamiliar Territory*, *Capricorn Games*, *Majipoor Chronicles*, *The Best of Robert Silverberg*, *At the Conglomeroid Cocktail Party*, *Beyond the Safe Zone*, and a massive retrospective collection *The Collected Stories of Robert Silverberg, Volume One: Secret Sharers*. His most recent books are the novels *The Face of the Waters*, *Kingdoms of the Wall*, *Hot Sky at Morning*, and *Mountains of Majipoor*. He lives with his wife, writer Karen Haber, in Oakland, California.

In the fascinating examination of Unearthly Love that follows, Silverberg turns his coolly sardonic eye toward a strange kind of future singles bar, where things are not *supposed* to be as they seem, and the customers have a great deal more to offer each other than it would at first appear . . .

MULTIPLES

There were mirrors everywhere, making the place a crazyhouse of dizzying refraction: mirrors on the ceiling, mirrors on the walls, mirrors in the angles where the walls met the ceiling and the floor, even little eddies of mirror dust periodically blown on gusts of air through the room, so that all the bizarre distortions, fracturings, and dislocations of image that were bouncing around the place would from time to time coalesce in a shimmering haze of chaos right before your eyes. Colored globes spun round and round overhead, creating patterns of ricocheting light. It was exactly the way Cleo had expected a multiples club to look.

She had walked up and down the whole Fillmore Street strip from Union to Chestnut and back again for half an hour, peering at this club and that, before finding the courage to go inside one that called itself Skits. Though she had been planning this night for months, she found herself paralyzed by fear at the last minute: afraid they would spot her as a fraud the moment she walked in, afraid they would drive her out with jeers and curses and cold mocking laughter. But now that she was within, she felt fine—calm, confident, ready for the time of her life.

There were more women than men in the club, something like a seven-to-three ratio. Hardly anyone seemed to be talking to anyone else: most stood alone in the middle of the floor, staring into the mirrors as though in trance. Their eyes were slits, their jaws were slack, their shoulders slumped forward, their arms dangled. Now and then as some combination of reflections sluiced across their consciousnesses with particular impact they would go taut and jerk and wince as if they had been struck. Their faces would flush, their lips would pull back, their eyes would roll, they would mutter and whisper to themselves; and then after a moment they would slip back into stillness.

Cleo knew what they were doing. They were switching and doubling. Maybe some of the adepts were tripling. Her heart rate picked up. Her throat was very dry. What was the routine here, she wondered? Did you just walk right out onto the floor and plug into the light patterns, or were you supposed to go to the bar first for a shot or a snort?

She looked toward the bar. A dozen or so customers sitting there, mostly men, a couple of them openly studying her, giving her that new-girl-in-town stare. Cleo returned their gaze evenly, coolly, blankly. Standard-looking men, reasonably attractive, thirtyish or early fortyish, business suits, conventional hairstyles: young lawyers, executives, maybe stockbrokers, successful sorts out for a night's fun, the kind you might run into anywhere. Look at that one, tall, athletic, curly hair, glasses. Faint ironic smile, easy inquiring eyes. Almost professorial. And yet, and yet—behind that smooth intelligent forehead, what strangenesses must teem and boil! How many hidden souls must lurk and jostle! Scary. Tempting.

Irresistible.

Cleo resisted. Take it slow, take it slow. Instead of going to the bar she moved out serenely among the switchers on the floor, found an open space, centered herself, looked toward the mirrors on the far side of the room. Legs apart, feet planted flat, shoulders forward. A turning globe splashed waves of red and violet light, splintered a thousand times over, into her face. *Go. Go. Go. Go.* You are Cleo. You are Judy. You are Vixen. You are Lisa. *Go. Go. Go. Go.* Cascades of iridescence sweeping over the rim of her soul, battering at the walls of her identity. Come, enter, drown me, split me, switch me. You are Cleo and Judy. You are Vixen and Lisa. You are Cleo and Judy and Vixen and Lisa. *Go. Go. Go.*

Her head was spinning. Her eyes were blurring. The room gyrated around her.

Was this it? Was she splitting? Was she switching? Maybe so. Maybe the capacity was there in everyone, even her, and all it took was the lights, the mirror, the ambience, the will. I am many. I am multiple. I am Cleo switching to Vixen. I am Judy and Lisa. I am—

No.

I am Cleo.

I am Cleo.

I am very dizzy and I am getting sick, and I am Cleo and only Cleo, as I have always been.

I am Cleo and only Cleo and I am going to fall down.

"Easy," he said. "You okay?"

"Steadying up, I think. Whew!"

"Out-of-towner, eh?"

"Sacramento. How'd you know?"

"Too quick on the floor. Locals all know better. This place has the fastest mirrors in the west. They'll blow you away if you're not careful. You can't just go out there and grab for the big one—you've got to phase yourself in slowly. You sure you're going to be okay?"

"I think so."

He was the tall man from the bar, the athletic professorial one. She supposed he had caught her before she had actually fallen, since she felt no bruises. His hand rested now against her elbow as he lightly steered her toward a table along the wall.

"What's your now-name?" he asked.

"Judy."

"I'm Van."

"Hello, Van."

"What about a brandy? Steady you up a little more."

"I don't drink."

"Never?"

"Vixen does the drinking," she said. "Not me."

"Ah. The old story. She gets the bubbles, you get her hangovers. I have one like that, too, only with him it's Hunan food. He absolutely doesn't give a damn what lobster in hot-and-sour sauce does to my digestive system. I hope you pay her back the way she deserves."

Cleo smiled and said nothing.

He was watching her closely. Was he interested, or just being polite to someone who was obviously out of her depth in a strange milieu? Interested, she decided. He seemed to have accepted that Vixen stuff at face value.

Be careful now, Cleo warned herself. Trying to pile on convincing-sounding details when you don't really know what you're talking about is a sure way to give yourself away, sooner or later. The thing to do, she knew, was to establish her credentials without working too hard at it, sit back, listen, learn how things really operate among these people.

"What do you do, up there in Sacramento?"

"Nothing fascinating."

"Poor Judy. Real estate broker?"

"How'd you guess?"

"Every other woman I meet is a real estate broker these days. What's Vixen?"

"A lush."

"Not much of a livelihood in that."

Cleo shrugged. "She doesn't need one. The rest of us support her."

"Real estate and what else?"

She hadn't been sure that multiples etiquette included talking about one's alternate selves. But she had come prepared. "Lisa's a landscape architect. Cleo's into software. We all keep busy."

"Lisa ought to meet Chuck. He's a demon horticulturalist. Partner in a plant-rental outfit—you know, huge dracaenas and philodendrons for offices, so much per month, take them away when they start looking sickly. Lisa and Chuck could talk palms and bromeliads and cacti all night."

"We should introduce them, then."

"We should, yes."

"But first we have to introduce Van and Judy."

"And then maybe Van and Cleo," he said.

She felt a tremor of fear. Had he found her out so soon? "Why Van and Cleo? Cleo's not here right now. This is Judy you're talking to."

"Easy. Easy!"

But she was unable to halt. "I can't deliver Cleo to you just like that, you know. She does as she pleases."

"Easy," he said. "All I meant was, Van and Cleo have something in common. Van's into software, too."

Cleo relaxed. With a little laugh she said, "Oh, not you, too! Isn't everybody nowadays? But I thought you were something in the academic world. A professor, perhaps."

"I am. At Cal."

"Software?"

"In a manner of speaking. Linguistics. Metalinguistics, actually. My field's the language of language—the basic subsets, the neural coordinates of communication, the underlying programs our brains use, the operating systems. Mind as computer, computer as mind. I can get very boring about it."

"I don't find the mind a boring subject."

"I don't find real estate a boring subject. Talk to me about second mortgages and triple-net leases."

"Talk to me about Chomsky and Benjamin Whorf," she said.

His eyes widened. "You've heard of Whorf?"

"I majored in comparative linguistics. That was before real estate."

"Just my lousy luck," he said. "I get a chance to find out what's hot in the shopping-center market and she wants to talk about Whorf and Chomsky."

"I thought every other woman you met these days was a real estate broker. Talk to them about shopping centers."

"They all want to talk about Whorf and Chomsky."

"Poor Van."

"Yes. Poor Van." Then he leaned forward and said, his tone softening, "You know, I shouldn't have made that crack about Van meeting Cleo. That was very tacky of me."

"It's okay, Van. I didn't take it seriously."

"You seemed to. You were very upset."

"Well, maybe at first. But then I saw you were just horsing around."

"I still shouldn't have said it. You were absolutely right: this is Judy's time now. Cleo's not here, and that's just fine. It's Judy I want to get to know."

"You will," she said. "But you can meet Cleo, too, and Lisa, and Vixen. I'll introduce you to the whole crew. I don't mind."

"You're sure of that?"

"Sure."

"Some of us are very secretive about our alters."

"Are you?" Cleo asked.

"Sometimes. Sometimes not."

"I don't mind. Maybe you'll meet some of mine tonight." She glanced toward the center of the floor. "I think I've steadied up, now. I'd like to try the mirrors again."

"Switching?"

"Doubling," she said. "I'd like to bring Vixen up. She can do the drinking, and I can do the talking. Will it bother you if she's here, too?"

"Not unless she's a sloppy drunk. Or a mean one."

"I can keep control of her, when we're doubling. Come on: take me through the mirrors."

"You be careful, now. San Francisco mirrors aren't like Sacramento ones. You've already discovered that."

"I'll watch my step this time. Shall we go out there?"

"Sure," he said.

As they began to move out onto the floor a slender T-shirted man of about thirty came toward them. Shaven scalp, bushy mustache, medallions, boots. Very San Francisco, very gay. He frowned at Cleo and stared straightforwardly at Van.

"Ned?" he said.

Van scowled and shook his head. "No. Not now."

"Sorry. Very sorry. I should have realized." The shaven-headed man flushed and hurried away.

"Let's go," Van said to Cleo.

This time she found it easier to keep her balance. Knowing that he was nearby helped. But still the waves of refracted light came pounding in, pounding in, pounding in. The assault was total: remorseless, implacable, overwhelming. She had to struggle against the throbbing in her chest, the hammering in her temples, the wobbliness of her knees. And this was pleasure, for them? This was a supreme delight?

But they were multiples and she was only Cleo, and that, she knew, made all the difference. She seemed to be able to fake it well enough. She could make up a Judy, a Lisa, a Vixen, assign little corners of her personality to each, give them voices of their own, facial expressions, individual identities. Standing before her mirror at home, she had managed to convince herself. She might even be able to convince him. But as the swirling lights careened off the infinities of interlocking mirrors and came slaloming into the gateways of her reeling soul, the dismal fear began to rise in her that she could never truly be one of these people after all, however skillfully she imitated them in their intricacies.

Was it so? Was she doomed always to stand outside their irresistible world, hopelessly peering in? Too soon to tell—much too soon, she thought, to admit defeat—

At least she didn't fall down. She took the punishment of the mirrors as long as she could stand it, and then, not waiting for him to leave the floor, she made her way—carefully, carefully, walking a tightrope over an abyss—to the bar. When her head had begun to stop spinning she ordered a drink, and she sipped it cautiously. She could feel the alcohol extending itself inch by inch into her bloodstream. It calmed her. On the floor, Van stood in trance, occasionally quivering in a sudden convulsive way for a fraction of a second. He was doubling, she knew: bringing up one of his other identities. That was the main thing that multiples came to these clubs to do. No longer were all their various identities forced to dwell in rigorously separated compartments of their minds. With the aid of the mirrors, of the lights, the skilled ones were able briefly to fuse two or even three of their selves into something even more complex. When he comes back here, she thought, he will be Van plus X. And I must pretend to be Judy plus Vixen.

She readied herself for that. Judy was easy: Judy was mostly the real Cleo, the real estate woman from Sacramento, with Cleo's notion of what it was like to be a multiple added in. And Vixen? Cleo imagined her to be about twenty-three, a Los Angeles girl, a onetime child tennis star who had broken her ankle in a dumb prank and had never recovered her game afterward, and who had taken up drinking to ease the pain and loss. Uninhibited, unpredictable, untidy, fiery, fierce: all the things that Cleo was not. Could she be Vixen? She took a deep gulp of her drink and put on the Vixen-face: eyes hard and glittering, cheek muscles clenched.

Van was leaving the floor now. His way of moving seemed to have changed: he was stiff, almost awkward, his shoulders held high, his elbows jutting oddly. He looked so different that she wondered whether he was still Van at all.

"You didn't switch, did you?"

"Doubled. Paul's with me now."

"Paul?"

"Paul's from Texas. Geologist, terrific poker game, plays the guitar." Van smiled, and it was like a shifting of gears. In a deeper, broader voice he said, "And I sing real good, too, ma'am. Van's jeal-ous of that, because he can't sing worth beans. Are you ready for a refill?"

"You bet," Cleo said, sounding sloppy, sounding Vixenish.

His apartment was nearby, a cheerful airy sprawling place in the Marina district. The segmented nature of his life was immediately obvious: the prints and paintings on the walls looked as though they had been chosen by four or five different people, one of whom ran heavily toward vivid scenes of sunrise over the Grand Canyon, another to Picasso and Miro, someone else to delicate impressionist views of Parisian flower markets. A sun room contained the biggest and healthiest houseplants Cleo had ever seen. Another room was stacked high with technical books and scholarly journals, a third was set up as a home gymnasium equipped with three or four gleaming exercise machines. Some of the rooms were fastidiously tidy, some impossibly chaotic. Some of the furniture was stark and austere, and some was floppy and overstuffed. She kept expecting to find room-mates wandering around. But there was no one here but Van. And Paul.

Paul fixed the drinks. Paul played soft guitar music and told her gaudy tales of prospecting for rare earths on the West Texas mesas. Paul sang something bawdy-sounding in Spanish, and Cleo, putting on her Vixen-voice, chimed in on the choruses, deliberately off-key. But then Paul went away and it was Van who sat close beside her on the couch, talking quietly. He wanted to know things about Judy, and he told her a little about Van, and no other selves came into the conversation. She was sure that that was intentional. They stayed up very late. Paul came back, toward the end of the evening, to tell a few jokes and sing a soft late-night song, but when they went into the bedroom she was with Van. Of that she was com-pletely certain.

And when she woke in the morning she was alone.

She felt a surge of confusion and dislocation, remembered after a moment where she was and how she had happened to be here, sat up, blinked. Went into the bathroom and scooped a handful of water over her face. Without bothering to dress, went padding around the apartment looking for Van.

She found him in the exercise room, using the rowing machine, but he wasn't Van. He was dressed in tight jeans and a white T-shirt, and somehow he looked younger, leaner, jauntier. There were fine beads of sweat along his forehead, but he did not seem to be breath-ing hard. He gave her a cool, distantly appraising, wholly asexual look, as though she were a total stranger but that it was not in the least unusual for an unknown naked woman to materialize in the house and he was altogether undisturbed by it. He said, "Good morning. I'm Ned. Pleased to know you." His voice was higher than Van's, much higher than Paul's, and he had an odd overprecise way of shaping each syllable.

Flustered, suddenly self-conscious and wishing she had put her clothes on before leaving the bedroom, she folded one arm over her breasts, though her nakedness did not seem to matter to him at all. "I'm—Judy. I came with Van."

"Yes, I know. I saw the entry in our book." Smoothly, effortlessly, he pulled on the oars of the rowing machine, leaned back, pushed forward. "Help yourself to anything in the fridge," he said. "Make yourself entirely at home. Van left a note for you in the kitchen."

She stared at him: his hands, his mouth, his long muscular arms. She remembered his touch, his kisses, the feel of his skin against hers. And now this complete indifference. No. Not *his* kisses, not *his* touch. Van's. And Van was not here now. There was a different tenant in Van's body, someone she did not know in any way and who had no memories of last night's embraces. *I saw the entry in our book.* They left memos for each other. Cleo shivered. She had known what to expect, more or less, but experiencing it was very different from reading about it. She felt almost as though she had fallen in among beings from another planet.

But this is what you wanted, she thought. Isn't it? The intricacy, the mystery, the unpredictability, the sheer weirdness? A little cruise through an alien world, because her own had become so stale, so narrow, so cramped. And here she was. *Good morning, I'm Ned. Pleased to know you.*

Van's note was clipped to the refrigerator by a little yellow magnet shaped like a ladybug. *Dinner tonight at Chez Michel? You and me and who knows who else. Call me.*

That was the beginning. She saw him every night for the next ten days. Generally they met at some three-star restaurant, had a lingering intimate dinner, went back to his apartment. One mild clear evening they drove out to the beach and watched the waves breaking on Seal Rock until well past midnight. Another time they wandered through Fisherman's Wharf and somehow acquired three bags of tacky souvenirs.

Van was his primary name—she saw it on his credit card at dinner one night—and that seemed to be his main identity, too, though she knew there were plenty of others. At first he was reticent about that, but on the fourth or fifth night he told her that he had nine major selves and sixteen minor ones, some of which remained submerged years at a stretch. Besides Paul the geologist, and Chuck who was into horticulture, and Ned the gay one, Cleo heard about Nat the stock-market plunger—he was fifty and fat, and made a fortune every week, and liked to divide his time between Las Vegas and Miami Beach—and Henry the poet, who was very shy and never liked anyone to read his work, and Dick who was studying to be an actor, and Hal who once taught law at Harvard, and Dave the yachtsman, and Nicholas the cardsharp—and then there were all the fragmentary ones, some of whom didn't have names, only a funny way of speaking or a little routine they liked to act out—

She got to see very little of his other selves, though. Like all multiples, he was troubled occasionally by involuntary switching, and one night he became Hal while they were making love, and another time he turned into Dave for an hour, and there were momentary flashes of Henry and Nicholas. Cleo perceived it right away whenever one of those switches came: his voice, his movements, his entire manner and personality changed immediately. Those were startling, exciting moments for her, offering a strange exhilaration. But generally his control was very good, and he stayed Van, as if he felt some strong need to experience her as Van and Van alone. Once in a while he doubled, bringing up Paul to play the guitar for him and sing, or Dick to recite sonnets, but when he did that the Van identity always remained present and dominant. It appeared that he was able to double at will, without the aid of mirrors and lights, at least some of the time. He had been an active and functioning multiple as long as he could remember—since childhood, perhaps even since birth—and he had devoted himself through the years to the task of gaining mastery over his divided mind.

All the aspects of him that she came to meet had basically attractive personalities: they were energetic, stable, purposeful men, who enjoyed life and seemed to know how to go about getting what they wanted. Though they were very different people, she could trace them all back readily enough to the underlying Van from whom, so she thought, they had all split off. The one puzzle was Nat the market operator. It was hard for Cleo to imagine what he was like when he was Nat—sleazy and coarse, yes, but how did he manage to make himself look fifteen years older and forty pounds heavier? Maybe it was all done with facial expressions and posture. But she never got to see Nat. And gradually she realized it was an oversimplification to think of Paul and Dick and Ned and the others as mere extensions of Van into different modes. Van by himself was just as incomplete as the others. He was just one of many that had evolved in parallel, each one autonomous, each one only a fragment of the whole. Though Van might have control of the shared body a greater portion of the time, he still had no idea what any of his alternate

selves were up to while they were in command, and like them he
had to depend on guesses and fancy footwork and such notes and
messages as they bothered to leave behind in order to keep track of
events that occurred outside his conscious awareness. "The only
one who knows everything is Michael. He's seven years old, smart
as a whip, keeps in touch with all of us all the time."

"Your memory trace," Cleo said.

Van nodded. All multiples, she knew, had one alter with full awareness of the doings of all the other personalities—usually a child, an
observer who sat back deep in the mind and played its own games and
emerged only when necessary to fend off some crisis that threatened
the stability of the entire group. "He's just informed us that he's
Ethiopian," Van said. "So every two or three weeks we go across to
Oakland to an Ethiopian restaurant that he likes, and he flirts with the
waitresses in Amharic."

"That can't be too terrible a chore. I'm told Ethiopians are very
beautiful people."

"Absolutely. But they think it's all a big joke, and Michael doesn't
know how to pick up women, anyway. He's only seven, you know.
So Van doesn't get anything out of it except some exercise in comparative linguistics and a case of indigestion the next day. Ethiopian
food is the spiciest in the world. I can't *stand* spicy food."

"Neither can I," she said. "But Lisa loves it. Especially hot
Mexican things. But nobody ever said sharing a body is easy, did
they?"

She knew she had to be careful in questioning Van about the way his
life as a multiple worked. She was supposed to be a multiple herself,
after all. But she made use of her Sacramento background as justifi-
cation for her areas of apparent ignorance of multiple customs and
the everyday mechanics of multiple life. Though she, too, had known
she was a multiple since childhood, she said, she had grown up outside the climate of acceptance of the divided personality that pre-
vailed in San Francisco, where an active subculture of multiples had
existed openly for years. In her isolated existence, unaware that there
were a great many others of her kind, she had at first regarded herself as the victim of a serious mental disorder. It was only recently, she
told him, that she had come to understand the overwhelming advan-
tages of life as a multiple: the richness, the complexity, the fullness of
talents and experiences that a divided mind was free to enjoy. That
was why she had come to San Francisco. That was why she listened
so eagerly to all that he was telling her about himself.

She was cautious, too, in manifesting her own multiple identities. She wished she did not have to be pretending to have other

selves. But they had to be brought forth now and again, Cleo felt, if only by way of maintaining his interest in her. Multiples were notoriously indifferent to singletons, she knew. They found them bland, overly simple, two-dimensional. They wanted the excitement that came with embracing one person and discovering another, or two or three. So she gave him Lisa, she gave him Vixen, she gave him the Judy-who-was-Cleo and the Cleo-who-was-someone-else, and she slipped from one to another in a seemingly involuntary and unexpected way, often when they were in bed.

Lisa was calm, controlled, straitlaced. She was totally shocked when she found herself, between one eye blink and the next, in the arms of a strange man. "Who are you—? Where am I—?" she blurted, rolling away, pulling herself into a fetal ball.

"I'm Judy's friend," Van said.

She stared bleakly at him. "So she's up to her tricks again. I should have figured it out faster."

He looked pained, embarrassed, terribly solicitous. She let him wonder for a moment or two whether he would have to take her back to her hotel right here in the middle of the night. And then she allowed a mischievous smile to cross Lisa's face, allowed Lisa's outraged modesty to subside, allowed Lisa to relent and relax, allowed Lisa to purr—

"Well, as long as we're here already—what did you say your name was?"

He liked that. He liked Vixen, too—wild, sweaty, noisy, a moaner, a gasper, a kicker, and thrasher who dragged him down onto the floor and went rolling over and over with him. She thought he liked Cleo, too, though that was harder to tell, because Cleo's style was aloof, serious, baroque, inscrutable. She would switch quickly from one to another, sometimes running through all four in the course of an hour. Wine, she said, induced quick switching in her. She let him know that she had a few other identities, too, fragmentary and submerged, and hinted that they were troubled, deeply neurotic, almost self-destructive: they were under control, she said, and would not erupt to cause woe for him, but she left the possibility hovering over them, to add spice to the relationship and plausibility to her role.

It seemed to be working. His pleasure in her company was evident, and the more they were together the stronger the bond between them became. She was beginning to indulge in pleasant little fantasies of moving down here permanently from Sacramento, renting an apartment somewhere near his, perhaps even moving in with him— a strange and challenging life that would be, for she would be living with Paul and Ned and Chuck and all the rest of the crew, too, but how wondrous, how electrifying—

Then on the tenth day he seemed uncharacteristically tense and somber, and she asked him what was bothering him, and he evaded her, and she pressed, and finally he said, "Do you really want to know?"

"Of course."

"It bothers me that you aren't real, Judy."

She caught her breath. "What the hell do you mean by that?"

"You know what I mean," he said, quietly, sadly. "Don't try to pretend any longer. There's no point in it."

It was like a jolt in the ribs. She turned away and stared at the wall and was silent a long while, wondering what to say. Just when everything was going so well, just when she was beginning to believe she had carried off the masquerade successfully—

"So you know?" she asked in a small voice.

"Of course I know. I knew right away."

She was trembling. "How could you tell?"

"A thousand ways. When we switch, we *change*. The voice. The eyes. The muscular tensions. The grammatical habits. The brain waves, even. An evoked-potential test shows it. Flash a light in my eyes and I'll give off a certain brain-wave pattern, and Ned will give off another, and Chuck still another. You and Lisa and Cleo and Vixen would all be the same. Multiples aren't actors, Judy. Multiples are separate minds within the same brain. That's a matter of scientific fact. You were just acting. You were doing it very well, but you couldn't possibly have fooled me."

"You let me make an idiot of myself, then."

"No."

"Why did you—how could you—"

"I saw you walk in, that first night at the club, and you caught me right away. And then I watched you go out on the floor and fall apart, and I knew you couldn't be multiple, and I wondered, what the hell's she doing here, and then I went over to you, and I was hooked. I felt something I haven't ever felt before. Does that sound like the standard old malarkey? But it's true, Judy. You're the first singleton woman that's ever interested me."

"Why?"

He shook his head. "Something about you—your intensity, your alertness, maybe even your eagerness to pretend you were a multiple—I don't know. I was caught. I was caught hard. And it's been a wonderful week and a half. I mean that. Wonderful."

"Until you got bored."

"I'm not bored with you, Judy."

"Cleo. That's my real name, my singleton name. There is no Judy."

"Cleo," he said, as if measuring the word with his lips.

"So you aren't bored with me even though there's only one of me. That's marvelous. That's tremendously flattering. That's the best thing I've heard all day. I guess I should go now, Van. It *is* Van, isn't it?"

"Don't talk that way."

"How do you want me to talk? I fascinated you, you fascinated me, we played our little games with each other, and now it's over. I wasn't real, but you did your best. We both did our bests. But I'm only a singleton woman, and you can't be satisfied with that. Not for long. For a night, a week, two weeks, maybe. Sooner or later you'll want the real thing, and I can't be the real thing for you. So long, Van."

"No."

"No?"

"Don't go."

"What's the sense of staying?"

"I want you to stay."

"I'm a singleton, Van."

"You don't have to be," he said.

The therapist's name was Burkhalter and his office was in one of the Embarcadero towers, and to the San Francisco multiples community he was very close to being a deity. His speciality was electrophysiological integration, with specific application to multiple-personality disorders. Those who carried within themselves dark and diabolical selves that threatened the stability of the group went to him to have those selves purged, or at least contained. Those who sought to have latent selves that were submerged beneath more outgoing personalities brought forward into healthy functional state went to him also. Those whose life as a multiple was a torment of schizoid confusions instead of a richly rewarding contrapuntal symphony gave themselves to Dr. Burkhalter to be healed, and in time they were. And in recent years he had begun to develop techniques for what he called personality augmentation. Van called it "driving the wedge."

"He can turn a singleton into a multiple?" Cleo asked in amazement.

"If the potential is there. You know that it's partly genetic: the structure of a multiple's brain is fundamentally different from a singleton's. The hardware just isn't the same, the cerebral wiring. And then, if the right stimulus comes along, usually in childhood, usually but not necessarily traumatic, the splitting takes place, the separate identities begin to establish their territories. But much of the time multiplicity is never generated, and you walk around with the capacity to be a whole horde of selves and never know it."

"Is there reason to think I'm like that?"

He shrugged. "It's worth finding out. If he detects the predisposition, he has effective ways of inducing separation. Driving the wedge, you see? You do *want* to be a multiple, don't you, Cleo?"

"Oh, yes, Van. Yes!"

Burkhalter wasn't sure about her. He taped electrodes to her head, flashed bright lights in her eyes, gave her verbal association tests, ran four or five different kinds of electroencephalograph studies, and still he was uncertain. "It is not a black-and-white matter," he said several times, frowning, scowling. He was a multiple himself, but three of his selves were psychiatrists, so there was never any real problem about his office hours. Cleo wondered if he ever went to himself for a second opinion. After a week of testing she was sure that she must be a hopeless case, an intractable singleton, but Burkhalter surprised her by concluding that it was worth the attempt. "At the very worst," he said, "we will experience spontaneous fusing within a few days, and you will be no worse off than you are now. But if we succeed—ah, if we succeed—!"

His clinic was across the bay in a town called Moraga. She checked in on a Friday afternoon, spent two days undergoing further neurological and psychological tests, then three days taking medication. "Simply an anticonvulsant," the nurse explained cheerily. "To build up your tolerance."

"Tolerance for what?" Cleo asked.

"The birth trauma," she said. "New selves will be coming forth, and it can be uncomfortable for a little while."

The treatment began on Thursday. Electroshock, drugs, electroshock again. She was heavily sedated. It felt like a long dream, but there was no pain. Van visited her every day. Chuck came, too, bringing her two potted orchids in bloom, and Paul sang to her, and even Ned paid her a call. But it was hard for her to maintain a conversation with any of them. She heard voices much of the time. She felt feverish and dislocated, and at times she was sure she was floating eight or ten inches above the bed. Gradually that sensation subsided, but there were others nearly as odd. The voices remained. She learned how to hold conversations with them.

In the second week she was not allowed to have visitors. That didn't matter. She had plenty of company even when she was alone.

Then Van came for her. "They're going to let you go home today," he said. "How are you doing, Cleo?"

"I'm Noreen," she said.

There were five of her, apparently. That was what Van said. She had no way of knowing, because when they were dominant she was gone—not merely asleep, but *gone*, perceiving nothing. But he showed her notes that they wrote, in handwritings that she did not recognize and indeed could barely read, and he played tapes of her other voices: Noreen a deep contralto, Nanette high and breathy, Katya hard and rough New York, and the last one, who had not yet announced her name, a stagy voluptuous campy siren-voice.

She did not leave his apartment the first few days, and then began going out for short trips, always with Van or one of his alters close beside. She felt convalescent. A kind of hangover from the various drugs had dulled her reflexes and made it difficult for her to cope with the traffic, and also there was the fear that she would undergo a switching while she was out. Whenever that happened it came without warning, and when she returned to awareness afterward she felt a sharp bewildering discontinuity of memory, not knowing how it was that she suddenly found herself in Ghirardelli Square or Golden Gate Park or wherever it was that the other self had taken their body.

But she was happy. And Van was happy with her. As they strolled hand in hand through the cool evenings she turned to him now and again and saw the warmth of his smile, the glow of his eyes. One night in the second week when they were out together he switched to Chuck—Cleo saw him change, and knew it was Chuck coming on, for now she always knew right away which identity had taken over—and he said, "You've had a marvelous effect on him, Cleo. None of us has ever seen him like this before—so contented, so fulfilled—"

"I hope it lasts, Chuck."

"Of course it'll last! Why on earth shouldn't it last?"

It didn't. Toward the end of the third week Cleo noticed that there hadn't been any entries in her memo book from Noreen for several days. That in itself was nothing alarming: an alter might choose to submerge for days, weeks, even months at a time. But was it likely that Noreen, so new to the world, would remain out of sight so long? Lin-lin, the little Chinese girl who had evolved in the second week and was Cleo's memory trace, reported that Noreen had gone away. A few days later an identity named Mattie came and went within three hours, like something bubbling up out of a troubled sea. Then Nanette disappeared, leaving Cleo with no one but her nameless breathy-voiced alter and Lin-lin. She knew she was fusing again. The wedges that Dr. Burkhalter had driven into her soul were not holding; her mind insisted on oneness, and was integrating itself; she was reverting to the singleton state.

"They're all gone," she told Van disconsolately.

"I know. I've been watching it happen."

"Is there anything we can do? Should I go back to Burkhalter?"

She saw the pain in his eyes. "It won't do any good," he said. "He told me the chances were about three to one this would happen. A month, he figured—that was about the best we could hope for. And we've had our month."

"I'd better go, Van."

"Don't say that."

"No?"

"I love you, Cleo."

"You won't," she said. "Not for much longer."

He tried to argue with her, to tell her that it didn't matter to him that she was a singleton, that one Cleo was worth a whole raft of alters, that he would learn to adapt to life with a singleton woman. He could not bear the thought of her leaving now. So she stayed: a week, two weeks, three. They ate at their favorite restaurants. They strolled hand in hand through the cool evenings. They talked of Chomsky and Whorf and even of shopping centers. When he was gone and Paul or Chuck or Hal or Dave was there she went places with them, if they wanted her to. Once she went to a movie with Ned, and when toward the end he felt himself starting to switch she put her arm around him and held him until he regained control, so that he could see how the movie finished.

But it was no good, really. She sensed the strain in him. He wanted something richer than she could offer him: the switching, the doubling, the complex undertones and overtones of other personalities resonating beyond the shores of consciousness. She could not give him that. And though he insisted he didn't miss it, he was like one who has voluntarily blindfolded himself in order to keep a blind woman company. She knew she could not ask him to live like that forever.

And so one afternoon when Van was somewhere else she packed her things and said good-bye to Paul, who gave her a hug and wept a little with her, and she went back to Sacramento. "Tell him not to call," she said. "A clean break's the best." She had been in San Francisco two months, and it was as though those two months were the only months of her life that had had any color in them, and all the rest had been lived in tones of gray.

There had been a man in the real estate office who had been telling her for a couple of years that they were meant for each other. Cleo had always been friendly enough to him—they had done a few skiing weekends in Tahoe the winter before, they had gone to Hawaii once, they had driven down to San Diego—but she had never felt anything particular when she was with him. A week after her return, she phoned him and suggested that they drive up north to the redwood country for a few days together. When they came back, she moved into the handsome condominium he had just outside town.

It was hard to find anything wrong with him. He was good-natured and attractive, he was successful, he read books and liked good movies, he enjoyed hiking and rafting and backpacking, he even talked of driving down into the city during the opera season to take in a performance or two. He was getting toward the age where he was thinking about marriage and a family. He seemed very fond of her.

But he was flat, she thought. Flat as a cardboard cutout: a singleton, a one-brain, a no-switch. There was only one of him, and there always would be. It was hardly his fault, she knew. But she couldn't settle for someone who had only two dimensions. A terrible restlessness went roaring through her every evening, and she could not possibly tell him what was troubling her.

On a drizzly afternoon in early November she packed a suitcase and drove down to San Francisco. She arrived about six-thirty, and checked into one of the Lombard Street motels, and showered and changed and walked over to Fillmore Street. Cautiously she explored the strip from Chestnut down to Union, from Union back to Chestnut. The thought of running into Van terrified her. Probably she would, sooner or later, she knew: but not tonight, she prayed. Not tonight. She went past Skits, did not go in, stopped outside a club called Big Mama, shook her head, finally entered one called The Side Effect. Mostly women inside, as usual, but a few men at the bar, not too bad-looking. No sign of Van. She bought herself a drink and casually struck up a conversation with the man to her left, a short curly-haired artistic-looking type, about forty.

"You come here often?" he asked.

"First time. I've usually gone to Skits."

"I think I remember seeing you there. Or maybe not."

She smiled. "What's your now-name?"

"Sandy. Yours?"

Cleo drew her breath down deep into her lungs. She felt a kind of light-headedness beginning to swirl behind her eyes. *Is this what you want?* she asked herself. *Yes. Yes. This is what you want.*

"Melinda," she said.

ANOTHER STORY
Pat Cadigan

Pat Cadigan was born in Schenectady, New York, and now lives with her family in London, England. She made her first professional sale in 1980 and has subsequently come to be regarded as one of the best new writers in SF. Many of her stories have appeared on major award ballots, and one of them, "Pretty Boy Crossover," has recently appeared on several critics' lists as being among the best science fiction stories of the 1980s. She was the coeditor of *Shayol*, perhaps the best of the semipro zines of the late seventies; it was honored with a World Fantasy Award in the "Special Achievement, Non-Professional" category in 1981. She has also served as Chairman of the Nebula Award Jury and as a World Fantasy Award judge. Her short work has been assembled in the landmark collection *Patterns*. Her first novel, *Mindplayers*, was released in 1987 to excellent critical response. Her second novel, *Synners*, won the prestigious Arthur C. Clarke Award, and her third novel, *Fools*, won the Clarke Award as well, the only time this award has ever been won twice by the same author. Her most recent book is a new collection called *Dirty Work*. Coming up is a new novel, tentatively entitled *Parasites*.

Here she serves up a scary and deliciously erotic look at how misery not only loves company, sometimes it *demands* it . . .

ANOTHER STORY

The post office box was full again today. Dan unlocked it and gathered up the pile of manila envelopes, checking the addresses as he slipped them into the soft-sided shoulder bag with the *Ministry of Sound* logo on it. Every single one was addressed to The Manuscript Doctor, which meant that every single one would have a money order or cashier's check that was as good as gold, attached to a manuscript as good as dogshit.

Dan smiled flatly to himself as he hefted the bag and went over to check the second, smaller post office box he had rented. *Frustrated by rejection? Eager for editorial guidance instead of a form letter? You don't need a shrink, you need a specialist! The Manuscript Doctor will diagnose your troubles and prescribe what you need to get going as a writer. Send a SASE for current rates. Fiction, non-fiction, plays, TV and movie scripts. Sorry, no poetry.*

There were half a dozen white business-size envelopes in this box. Dan pulled them out and jammed them into the bag without bothering to look at them. How much per thousand words of futility? How much per thousand words of hopelessness? How much per thousand words of completely unremarkable mediocrity?

"How much per thousand words of overwrought melodrama?" Dan muttered, unlocking the passenger-side door of his Geo Metro and tossing the shoulder bag on the front seat. The woman in the car next to him glanced up suspiciously from a handful of mail. He smiled at her and shrugged. "Looks like a lot of bills." Offended, she rolled up her window.

He couldn't help laughing as he slipped behind the wheel and pulled out. Anyone not suspicious of him was merely offended. He supposed the sight of a man with gray hair well past his shoulders, dressed in relentless old denim—not just aged, but legitimately old—driving a subcompact gas miser with an Amnesty International decal on the window and a Nine Inch Nails bumper sticker was both suspicious and offensive even in these postmodern and parlous times.

Well, he had conceded a great deal over the years, little by little, as so many of his contemporaries had. But some things he simply would not give up. The majority of those things seemed to be of the type that he couldn't articulate, and what he could articulate only sounded unbearably trite if he did. So he left it unspoken that he would *not* carry a briefcase, would *not* buy a suit (or a tie), would *not* get a regular job, and would *not* keep holy the Sabbath day.

It was all for the sake of his (sort of, kind of, not really but in a way) dormant writing career. The thing about writing was, you could be a blazing success at any time, with absolutely no warning, even after years of obscurity, or outright failure (like from being badly blocked—no, don't say the b-word, that only made it more real). He wasn't going to let some unrelated job drive a wedge between himself and his real work. If there was anything he didn't need, it was another stumbling b-word.

Besides, the only thing he knew how to do other than write was edit. There was currently a severe shortage of editing jobs around, and the ones that did exist all seemed to demand expert knowledge of things called *Quark* and *PageMaker* and *Adobe*, which, as far as the thoroughly unplugged Dan Dietrich could tell, had a lot more to do with page layouts than real editorial work. Desktop publishing only seemed to have made it easier for overpaid bean counters to demand more and pay less for it. But then, what hadn't?

Amen, and amen again to that, Jordan would have said. Jordan had been one of the few commercial (well, all but) successes to come out of the MFA program all those years ago, back in grad school, when it seemed extremely likely that a bright young writer could, by dint of sheer brilliance, burn up twentieth century litera-ture. From the beginning, Jordan had aspired to being the Maxwell Perkins of their generation, and while he had fallen somewhat short of that goal, he had managed to publish a number of high-quality books by genuinely talented writers under an imprint that he had kept alive, sometimes seemingly by sheer willpower, at a publishing house that had been sold half a dozen times in fifteen years. It was the seventh time—unlucky seven—that had been the end, not of the imprint, but of Jordan's tenure.

"The new owners don't actually have anything to do with publish-ing," Jordan told him over the phone. "They dumped me because—and I quote a source who insists on not being quoted in any official capacity—they can get any bright-eyed kid off the street to do the same thing at half my salary."

"But it *wouldn't* be the same thing," Dan had said. "Not your experience or your perception—Jesus, I mean, your authors have won literary awards—"

"I don't think they care about that," Jordan had said stiffly, and Dan had had a sudden, blinding satori: even success could end in fail-ure without you having anything to do with it one way or another. You could be your own best friend or your own worst enemy—the machine would grind you under or pass you by on a schedule all its own.

The lesson was clear—no meteorologist needed to discern from which point of the compass the air mass would be approaching, as one of the Manuscript Doctor's patients would have said: stay the fuck out of the way of machines.

Or, to put it another way: when life gives you lemmings, make tetrazzini. It'll just taste like chicken. Everything does.

"Everything does," said the Manuscript Doctor, cruising through a yellow light on the traffic way.

He settled down in the hammock with the manuscript envelopes resting on his stomach, and a large whisky and soda on the rocks on the small table next to him. The hammock was another of his little defiances, what he had instead of a couch. It was the sort of hammock that swung within a framework, for those yards without two conveniently placed trees. Yards, or living rooms—at one time, he had contemplated potted trees, a sort of bonsai, but on a much larger scale than regular bonsai, except he knew that even if such a thing were actually possible, neither of his thumbs was anywhere near green enough. The hammock was fine as it was, with the added advantage that it didn't need watering, and wouldn't be attacked by bag worms or Dutch elm disease.

He opened the first manuscript. Money order and self-addressed, stamped envelope enclosed—good work, the Manuscript Doctor will see you now. He turned his attention to the cover letter.

Dear Doc: Well, here it is, the great work of art I promised you when I sent for your rate card—well, actually, it's the first fifty pages of the great work of art that I promised you, just like you said on your rate card. None of my friends think I have the nerve to send this to a real writer who knows all the ins and outs of the business as well as the actual art—creating, which is to say, the writing, I'm sure you will agree with me when I say that all writers are artists, just as much as those who work with paint, because we paint pictures with our words. I really hope you can help me out with this particular painting, as I am not at all sure of the technique I should use. I mean, it's easy for painters, they can just decide to be cubist or whatever, but us writers have to follow the demands of the story where it takes us. And it hardly ever says, be cubist (ha, ha).

"Oh, I don't know about that," said the Manuscript Doctor, genially, taking a big sip of his drink. There were times when he thought he should be smoking grass while reading some of these rather than drinking, but he had no idea where to get any. Even if he had, he'd have been too afraid to buy so much as a joint, not because it was illegal, but because it might cause him to take up smoking cigarettes again, and quitting those was the worst ordeal he'd ever been through. He had to be cubist on that one. Definitely cubist. Story of his life; perhaps that was story enough.

The story paperclipped to the letter was not the story of his life, or anyone else's. It was impossible to see what story there was, or might have been intended. The Manuscript Doctor leafed through it, skimming pages here and there just to make sure that it didn't make sense, and then dropped it on the floor on his left. The Incoherent Pile was starting early today. On to the next.

Check? SASE? Good, the Doctor will see you now. Ah, the story of *your* life, yes, how fascinating. Of course, when you're eighty, you've got a lot of life to write about, and the first fifty pages hardly conveys the richness and variety of such a long life. In fact, it doesn't even get you out of the nursery. As a work of literature, it's iffy, but as a soporific, it's almost completely—the Manuscript Doctor yawned—completely successful. At least it was the start of a new pile. Next case.

Dear Doctor, I know you said no poetry but I just had to send you this because it is not your ordinary run-of-the-mill poem. If you are schooled in the classics—and you must be if you are really a doctor—you will see that this is an epic poem in the style of The Iliad, *and tells the story of a great hero based in part on Achilles, but also with elements of Confucius, Jesus Christ, and Sherlock Holmes. I have of course enclosed a check in the amount for the full fifty-page prose evaluation, as I know that epic poetry is much more demanding a read than . . .*

Reluctantly, the Manuscript Doctor started a Return Check and Manuscript pile and opened the next envelope.

Hi, Doctor, remember me? I sent you the young adult novel about the dolphins and the boy who wanted to be a mermaid. I've decided now that I really ought to write for adults, so here's my newest project, which is a fictionalized account of my struggle to come to terms with my sexuality. It also contains many elements that I think of as being "cyberpunk," if you get my drift . . .

Cyberpunk sexuality, thought the Manuscript Doctor, might actually be commercial. It was hard to tell when you had Luddite tendencies. *Send me a story I can understand—the struggle to come to terms with your technophobia, containing many elements that you think of as being "sexual." If you get* my *drift.* The Manuscript Doctor shook his head. *If* I *get my drift.*

The next submission contained no self-addressed, stamped envelope, no cover letter, and, worst of all, no check. "Tsk, tsk," said the Manuscript Doctor, having another healthy pull on the whisky and soda. "No diagnosis for *you.* What do you think this is, England?" He was about to toss the manuscript down as a Return Unread when the name on the first page leaped out at him.

Paula Woodbine.

Dan froze, holding the manuscript up in front of his face for several seconds before slowly lowering it to his drawn-up knees. Paula Woodbine. God, how many Paula Woodbines could there be in the world? At least a few, that was a statistical certainty. He looked at the envelope again, but there was no postmark to tell him where it had come from. Well, Paula Woodbine was a distinctive name, not common but hardly unusual—not *really* unusual—

You Know What I Need

by

Paula Woodbine

"Hello, Paula," he said quietly. "What's new?"

Whatever might be new, it wasn't the story. He had seen the first draft twenty-five years ago, in those happy horseshit days of grad school. And the woman who had written it, Paula Woodbine—well. It would have been so easy if she'd been immensely talented and enormously fat, or incredibly, delicately, exquisitely beautiful and into lyrical free verse, or just gay and anything. But that wasn't Paula.

Of course, that had been the times, too. Men and women, the whole male-female-sex thing, as one of his women acquaintances had put it. It was supposed to be a time of liberation for both sexes, the old constraints and constrictions discarded in favor of frankness, honesty, and nonsexist relationships between men and women. Except maybe his generation had already been too old or something, because it seemed like the first thing they all did in workshop was size up the members of the opposite sex as sex partners. Then writers. Then competitors. The amount of importance for each of these things changed as time went by, but that was the way it was in the very beginning, before anything happened at all.

And now, Dan thought, it didn't seem really to have anything to do with what generation any of them had been in, as he saw the same thing happening between much younger people. When he attended writers' conferences, often (too often) as a fill-in teacher for a last-minute cancellation, he could see the attendees and many of the instructors (too many), sizing each other up as sex partners. The eternal barnyard gavotte—Women's Liberation hadn't cured it; the Sexual Revolution hadn't stopped it; AIDS had had no effect on it. Yeah, so, what the hell, folks, why not just go with it? Paula Woodbine had.

Paula Woodbine had not been incredibly, delicately, exquisitely beautiful, or enormously talented, or gay. She had been difficult. There were days when she looked pretty good, other days when she looked pretty awful, and on a few rare occasions, she was striking.

It was as if she were moving through a cycle, but a cycle completely devoid of any regularity. Her writing was the same—there were flashes of brilliance amid workmanlike declarative text and ghastly purplish prose, and unremarkable, unmemorable, forgotten-as-soon-as-you-read-it prose. Then she had taken up erotica.

You Know What I Need. Everyone in the workshop—every *man* in the workshop—had been sure it had been Paula's secret message to come and get her. And every man had gone ahead and tried, including Dan.

He put both hands over the typescript, as though he wanted to see if he could remember it before reading it. He hadn't thought of Paula or her weird story in years—he'd thrown out his copy right after he'd gotten the MFA, while he was packing up to move out of his apartment—but now that he was thinking of it, the damned thing seemed to be coming back to him.

You know what I need. You've always known. I can tell the way you look at me. The way you pretend not to look at me. Actually, you don't have to look at me at all to know that I'm in need of what you can give me. You know my secrets. You know my dreams. You are intimate with me before you touch me. You are so intimate with me that I can feel your hand slide down my breast so that your thumb comes to rest on my nipple, even as you are only thinking about doing it. Before you touch me, you know where my nipple is through my clothes, because you know me, and you know what I need.

(Okay, so tell the truth, Dan old man—you weren't used to that kind of frankness in a woman's writing, right? But even as he was smiling ruefully at himself and his sexist atavisms, he remembered that *she* had said that to him after the workshop, after the time he had discovered that he did, indeed, know what she needed. Then.)

You know that I need the warmth of your hand cupping me between my legs. You know that I need—

(Does practically *every* sentence have to start with *You know that I need*? someone had asked, one of the women. And the answer had been *Yes*, but it had been one of the men who had said it. Not Paula—she didn't have to.)

You know that I need the pressure of your fingertip between my lips, a little, and a little more, and a little more. You know that I need your finger, wet, to trail up to the sweet place—

(What did you do, bug your own mattress and then transcribe it? someone had asked, and someone else had said, Well, we sure know she didn't bug *yours*, and for a while, there was the potential of nuclear war between the sexes.)

—spread open—

(Did anyone else read that article in the *National Lampoon* about putting all your boring exposition in a hot sex scene? someone had said. Dan had thought it might even have been him at that point, but it was hard to remember now.)

—*squeeze so tight*—

(You know, it's only *leg*-hold traps that are illegal, someone had whispered, giggling, and one of the guys had said that was because you wouldn't chew through anything to get out of *that*.)

—*push it there and*—

(Dan had wanted to make a joke, he'd kept thinking that in the next moment he would open his mouth and make the goddam joke, he'd just say it and release the tension. But then he realized that tension had already been released, and there hadn't been any laughing involved.)

(Some indefinite interval later, they all seemed to come to, and there was a moment when all hell could have broken loose, perhaps even should have, but no one had known what to do, except leave. Paula Woodbine had sat and watched them all go. Some of the guys had avoided looking directly at her, and some of them stared at no one and nothing else. A couple of the women had fled in silent embarrassment, a couple of others had stomped out obviously angry. One guy had given Paula a pitying look and never returned, and one woman had given her a slip of paper with her phone number on it. Dan had tried to act completely neutral, but he had been slow gathering up his things, trying to be last out of the room with Paula. One of the other guys had waited him out, though, and, from the way she was looking at him, Paula wanted the other guy to be last, not him, so he had conceded and left. The other guy's name had been Terry or Tim or Tom, something like that.)

He came back to himself staring at the title page. Damn—he must have read the last pages, he was sure he had, but somehow he'd dropped a stitch or something. It had been like that back then, too, he recalled. You knew you had read the last pages, you were quite aware of *having read* them, but somehow, you could not be aware *of* reading them. Unmemorable prose, maybe just careless—when it was done with you, it just rolled over and went to sleep.

Lying back in the hammock, he stared unseeingly up at the ceiling, picturing Paula's face as it had been. What would she look like now, so many years later? And while we're wondering about this and that, why was she sending this old story out to someone called The Manuscript Doctor, what was *that* about? Dan could imagine any number of terribly mundane scenarios—kids are grown, time to get back in touch with those old dreams; postdivorce determination to make a new start; unexpected discovery of old stories and fragments while cleaning out the attic or the basement and deciding, What the hell, I bet I really *could* sell this; midlife crisis of the omigod-I-forgot-to-become-world-famous variety. Dan had seen all of these and most of their variations in the cover letters attached to the good checks and the bad manuscripts. Sometimes it was stated openly, sometimes it was only present between the lines, and, like the manuscripts themselves, they all believed that no one else had ever thought of it, that it was unique to them, their lives, their circumstances. Like believing that no one saw the same arrangement of stars that you saw in the night sky, or the same colors in the visible spectrum.

Which, now that he thought of it, were the bases and/or tenets of a number of New Age-y type theologies or philosophies, or whatever they cared to call them. We all have our own truth, we've all been Cleopatra in another life. He supposed swallowing that sort of thing could make your disappointments more palatable. I was the Mahatma in my previous incarnation, so I'm taking it easy this time around, gotta get my strength back so I can cure AIDS in my next life.

Which had nothing to do with Paula Woodbine's decades-old sex fest. College eroticism, there was nothing like it. Like your lost innocence, he thought. Or maybe not *like* it, maybe that *was* it. Most people didn't think of themselves as innocent in college, especially on the grad school level, but from the perspective of a quarter of a century or so later, dew had definitely still been on the daisy. Not the power of discovering sex itself, but discovering sexuality, what flavor you were.

Flavor. Dan sighed. The flavor of sex with Paula Woodbine, the flavor of Paula herself. Back in the pre-AIDS era, of course, which might as well have been the Garden of Eden. And come to that, perhaps it was.

It seemed as if he had blinked and the room had suddenly darkened, but he knew he must have dozed off. Dan glanced ruefully at the glass, which was mostly empty. Gotta watch the dosage on that, Doc.

He put Paula's manuscript aside and looked quickly through the rest of the day's haul. When he was satisfied that no Hemingways, Faulkners, or Gardners had reemerged from the reincarnation pool— or at least, not in this pile of manuscripts—he struggled out of the hammock and went into the kitchen to make a sandwich.

He ate standing up at the counter, trying to decide if he wanted to call someone, go out, or just resign from the day in front of the television. Nothing like a blast from the past to put a hitch in your gitalong. Especially when it was a blast like this. That old story turning up among manuscripts sent to a scheme designed to separate modest amounts of money from a large enough number of wannabes so as to provide a living for the schemer who thought it up—that couldn't have meant anything good. Even if the scheme had been launched with the sincerest of intentions, even if it was operated every single day with just as much sincerity (almost), not to mention integrity, even if no one had ever, ever been strung along with praise as false as it was effusive for the sake of steady repeat business. This was for people who could afford to subsidize a little dream so they could feel as if they were making some kind of progress. And what the hell, the occasional talent *did* surface, now and again. He liked to believe that what he told the talented ones provided the kind of encouragement they needed to keep going. Who knew, but that giving someone the right words at just the right moment could provide a turning point in life and give the world a new artist instead of another overpaid bean counter.

He caught his reflection looking smug in the glass front of the microwave oven and suddenly felt very foolish. *Yes, my work is very significant and profound—why, at any moment, I might change the world, and thank God for that. Otherwise, I might have to have been Cleopatra in my previous life and that sounds far less plausible at cocktail parties.*

"It's probably one of the things you mentioned," said Cora, "but I'd bet money on it being a midlife crisis thing that made her send you the story. I don't think it's a come-on or anything." She finished her beer and signaled the bartender for another.

"Well, no, of course not. It being a come-on never crossed my mind," Dan said, a bit startled.

"Are you sure about that?" she asked him, with a teasing smile. "I mean, you just finished telling me how you reacted the last time she showed you this story. Pretty fresh for being twenty-five years in the past, don't you think? I mean, maybe the higher nature of your intelligence knows it isn't a come-on, but the animal nature of your body might be interpreting it as a call-home-all-is-forgiven."

"My animal nature is acquainted with *turn-on*," Dan corrected her. "'Come-on' is a bit sophisticated. If you see the difference."

The bartender, who was putting another beer in front of Cora, paused for a moment looking thoughtful, and then nodded before moving off again. Cora chuckled and passed Dan a long narrow laminated menu. "Bar snacks?"

He was about to push it back at her and then picked it up. The St. Pauli girl was on the cover, looking cheerfully art deco. "Hunger," he said. "That's what it was like. I got the feeling reading that story, at the time and then again yesterday, that Paula Woodbine was *hungry*. And the story was like a menu for *us*, but when *we*—" he paused, trying to think. "'Ate from it' isn't the right way to put it, but after two beers, I'm not especially elegant in the phrase department.

Anyway, what we took from it satisfied *her*." He laughed a little. "Is that daffy or what?"

"I don't know. Ask a woman who *hasn't* had to explain the idea of *enough* foreplay to a bonehead," Cora said archly. "Of course, that's a whole different story, and my horoscope advised against talking about my first husband today."

"I know what you mean, Cora, but that's not it, either, really. That's not what Paula was offering."

"What offering?" Cora laughed. "You said the name of the story is 'You Know What *I* Need,' not '*I* Know What *You* Need.' She's offering you an opportunity to do it for her, not vice versa. Or was she? Did she return the favor?"

Dan made a face. "It was more like, if you're happy, I'm happy, if you see what I mean." Cora didn't. "You know, if you like it, I like it, anything you want."

"That sounds awfully passive, and I don't get the idea this was a terribly passive lady, on paper or in bed," Cora told him. "The way you describe the story, she's telling the reader—or whoever—everything to do. It's hard to reconcile that with 'here it is, please yourself.'"

"But it was," Dan said, staring past her, barely aware that he was speaking aloud. "It was all a turn-on. Everything she wanted you to do, it was a turn-on. Whatever *she* needed was *your* turn-on."

"Do you think that's why everyone was so upset with her?"

Dan finished his beer and pushed the glass away absently. "I think we were so upset with her because we were a bunch of prigs, really. We weren't used to having a woman be so frank about her sexuality. And to be honest, I don't think we'd have liked it any better if it had been a story about a man. It was too . . . graphic. We all knew that Paula had just written down what she said in bed and tarted it up with a few little touches to make it more storylike."

"The problem for me has always been that what you say *in* bed sounds really stupid *out* of bed." Cora ran a hand through her short, dark hair and then massaged the back of her neck. "So when you write it down and then read it, it must sound about three times as stupid, being three removes from bed, where it belongs. If you see what I mean."

"Writers write hot sex scenes all the time and they don't sound stupid," Dan said.

"No, they don't," insisted Cora stubbornly. "They circumlocute. They circle round and round the subject and make you say everything to yourself in your head."

"Not always, though."

"Then not often enough. Go ahead, pick up one of those hot sex scenes that turn you on so much and read it aloud. You'll crack up."

"You're not supposed to read it aloud, it's not meant for that."

Cora shrugged. "Okay, then, read it to yourself. You'll still crack up."

"No, you're missing the point," Dan said, starting to feel irritable. "That would be like reading a musical score and naming the notes. Or watching a movie with the special effects left out and seeing the actors in front of a blue screen."

"Well, that's what happens when you use the wrong medium," Cora said, unperturbed. "You don't sculpt the Pieta in peanut butter and you don't play 'The Ride of the Valkyries' on a kazoo. Therefore, you should never write down what you say in bed."

"Or if you do," said the bartender, reappearing almost magically to put a third beer in front of Cora, "don't ever sign your name to it."

Cora raised her glass to him. "Thanks for the tip."

He was still trying to decide what to do about the manuscript when the next one arrived. There was no name or return address on the outside of the envelope, and again, no postmark. But he knew it was from Paula. He recognized the anonymous printing from the first one. He had to force himself not to open it in the post office or in the car. Obstinately, as if he were refusing a demand outside of his own curiosity, he made himself drive all the way home, going a little more slowly than usual, not cruising through the yellow light on the traffic way, making a business out of getting the car perfectly straight in the parking lot behind the building where he lived, stopping to get his personal mail out of the narrow box in the vestibule and looking at each envelope carefully as he went slowly up the stairs. The manuscript in the shoulder bag nagged at him like a toothache, or he imagined it did.

Won't you feel stupid when you open it up and it's from some other harmless, feckless, sexless wannabe? The thought was mocking, but at the same time, he knew it wouldn't be. It would be from Paula Woodbine, perhaps with a letter this time. Hey, Dan, long time, no see. Guess you're surprised to hear from an old college friend after so many years, blah, blah, and yet more blah.

He deliberately made himself a drink first before easing himself into the hammock. After a hefty sip of whisky and soda, he started to open one of the other manuscripts first. Or rather, he had meant to, but it turned out that he had Paula's envelope in his hands after all, so he went ahead and gave in to his curiosity.

I'm Waiting
by
Paula Woodbine

Dan closed his eyes for a moment, sure he was imagining this one. But when he opened his eyes again, Paula was still waiting.

Carefully, he leafed through each page and examined the envelope, but there was no letter, no address,

Waiting for you is aching in an empty place . . .

He came to rumpled and disarranged, his mouth tasting thick and cottony, his eyes painfully heavy. The room was dark. He felt around himself for some clue as to why he had been dozing in the hammock and finally struggled upright, his legs dangling over the side. Maybe he ought to give up and buy a regular sofa so he could read sitting up, and visitors could have another place to sit, besides the floor and the two old easy chairs.

Or you could knock off the booze while you're reading manuscripts, he thought at himself, annoyed. *The customers aren't paying you to go into a stupor. And whatever they are, or aren't, as writers, they're paying* you, *you're not paying them—*

It seemed to be an even harder struggle to get out of the hammock and stand up. In the darkness, he could see the white sheets of paper, Paula's manuscript, scattered all over the hardwood floor. "Jeez, Paula, what did you do to me?" he muttered. He went to scratch his stomach and discovered that his pants were undone.

Dan had the distinct sensation of his nerves attempting to tie themselves in square knots. There was a drug of a certain kind, he couldn't remember the official name for it, but the police were calling it "the rape drug," because there had been cases of women waking up in strange places with no memory of how they'd gotten there or what had happened, only evidence that someone, perhaps more than one someone, had made use of their bodies.

That's a good one, Einstein. All you have to do is figure out who got into the house and spiked your liquor supply, and then had their way with you. That would be a mere plotting exercise for the fabled Manuscript Doctor. And remember, if you're aiming this at a network movie-of-the-week, it doesn't have to be plausible, just exciting. No talking heads, lots of action—

Dan groped his way across the living room and put on the floor lamp in the corner. The windows were all closed, locked from the inside, and the chain was still on the door. He wiped a hand over his face groggily. On the table next to the hammock, his whisky and soda stood untouched, the ice making faint, slightly musical noises against the glass as it melted.

He put on a pot of coffee and phoned Cora.

An hour later, she called him back. "There were an even dozen Paula Woodbines—or should that be Paulas Woodbine?—with Web pages, none matching the description you gave me, and most of them the wrong age to begin with," she told him, sounding crisp and efficient. "There are lots of Paula Woodbines in various white pages listings. And, probably most interesting, there's a Paula Woodbine conveniently located at that address you gave me."

"In Amherst?" he said incredulously. "But that was over twenty years ago!"

"Don't you know about College Town Syndrome, dude?" Cora teased. "You must have seen it even while you were there, people who go to college and never want to leave. So they don't. They settle down, get jobs or run small businesses, sometimes go through the charade of an advanced degree program or just take this or that continuing ed course. Some of them have been known to prey on naive undergrads. When I was in school, we had one of those actually living in the dorm—Fred the Head. Every semester he'd pick up a new freshman girl and relieve her of unwanted virginity in return for room and board. In those days, floating around with no visible means of support and no fixed address was considered cool."

"Well, that description wouldn't fit Paula," Dan said. "I mean, the part about preying on impressionable students. Pardon my sexism, but women don't really seem to engage in that the way men do."

"Come *on*, you've never seen *The Graduate*?"

"Cora, that's a *movie*—"

"Okay, then, how about toy boys, o ye of little faith?" Cora's laughter had an edge. "Hey, if you *really* think women don't or won't prey on impressionable men—*or* women, for that matter—you've missed about half the movie you're *in*. Personally, I think you've had one touch the hem of your garment at least, and her initials, to give you a hint, are P.W. Got it?"

Dan sighed. "What's the phone number at the Amherst address?"

"Isn't one. I mean, there's no phone. I checked."

"No phone? Then how the *hell* did you find that address on the Internet?"

Cora laughed again, a bit more merrily this time. "She may not have a phone, but she's on a few mailing lists. You really ought to give in and get yourself connected. You can do amazing things with the Internet, all kinds of research things—"

"Yeah, I'm sure. I'm just afraid that if I do that, I'll spend the rest of my life doing research on the Internet. If you see what I mean."

"Nah. Only for the first three weeks. Then you get burned out."

"Lovely. I've been looking for a new way to get burned out. Thanks, Cora."

"You're welcome," she sang, and hung up.

*   *   *

In the end, he decided to drive the two hours to Amherst rather than attempt to communicate by registered letter or telegram. Did they even *have* telegrams any more, he wondered. He remembered something Cora had told him, on one of the many occasions she had tried to convince him to buy a computer and a modem, about Western Union's early attempts to forestall the telephone in favor of the telegraph by terrorizing telephone subscribers. *If a hotel had the nerve to put a telephone at the check-in desk for the convenience of the guests, Western Union would send out a bunch of goons to beat the owner up and sometimes burn the place down as well. They tried hard. Notice how popular Morse code is now? Why, every day millions of people surf the 'graph with Graphscape.*

He had laughed, but buried in there had been a nugget of real question, a what-if that intrigued him, despite the fact that he knew only what little he had picked up by osmosis. What if it had all been arranged differently, so that it had always been pure data transmission and not sound or voice? It sounded like a hard tech question on the surface, something that Dan couldn't have been less interested in. What intrigued him was the question of how communicating might have turned out, if you had to send the data itself any time you contacted someone? Which meant that there was no such thing as calling someone up just to say hi and talk about nothing. You just got right to the point, transmitted whatever you had to transmit, as quickly as you could. What kind of a world would that be, he wondered.

Unbidden, something else Cora had said came to him: *ask a woman who hasn't had to explain the idea of* enough *foreplay to a bonehead.*

So, small talk as foreplay? He wondered what his generative grammar instructor would have made of that. Probably a thesis.

He glanced at the manuscripts sitting on the passenger seat beside him. He had stopped at the post office before he left, to pick up the manuscript he had known would be there. Leaving the other submissions in the box, he opened the unmarked envelope just to look at the title page, to make sure.

It had been from Paula, all right, and the title of this story was, simply, *Come*. No small talk, just the main feature.

He told himself the main thing he wanted to do was ask her why she hadn't at least put a return address on the manuscripts.

Amherst had changed very little, except for the names of some of the stores and their inventory, and perhaps in some cases that was only cosmetic. Head shops had transmogrified into New Age emporia; the hip clothing shops sold designer labels rather than tie-dye or batik; there were hippies mixed in among the very straight and clean-cut, but the former showed a fair amount of gray in their hair while the latter looked like sixth graders. Dan sighed. In the last twenty-five years, he had visited Amherst only twice. Somehow, the reminders of time's passing were too depressing here. Perhaps he might have felt differently, he thought, if he had had his finest hours here, the way some of his contemporaries had. But it hadn't been that way for him. The MFA program had been great, but hardly a pinnacle. To his knowledge, he hadn't had a pinnacle yet.

That's right, Danny-boy—no peaks, no comedowns, no problems as long as you just keep it all flatline. You wouldn't want to risk being thrown out on your ass like Jordan or married and divorced several times like Cora. You wouldn't want something bad *to happen—*

Dan shook his head, bewildered. Where the hell had all *that* come from? He drove into the parking area near the town green and stopped to catch his breath. Two young women dressed in denim cutoffs and tube tops walked across the grass in front of him. They looked so familiar to him, he had a strong feeling that at any moment he would place them, remember their names, but he knew that was just a trick the location played on him. It had happened when he had visited before, the sensation, something like a premonition, that he was about to see someone he knew. Cora had called it an emotion mirage. He started the engine and pulled out again.

The house where Paula had lived was not actually in Amherst, but out in the wilds of South Hadley, which were still pretty much the wilds. Dan couldn't decide if that was surprising or not. He cruised past the dairy farms, still filled with unremarkable black-and-white cows that seemed not to have changed any more than the area itself. How long did cows live? Certainly not twenty-five years? A couple of the barns looked new or newly painted, any-way, but other than that, it might have been a quarter of a century ago.

A quarter of a century; he liked to put it that way, and, at the moment, he liked it a hell of a lot, more than he ever had, because it seemed very, very important to stay aware of the fact that time had passed, a *lot* of time had passed, and *this* was *now* and *that* was *then*, amen. Nothing was *really* the same here; maybe the roads hadn't been widened or made into turnpikes, but he could tell by the ride that the roads had been repaved.

There were more houses than he remembered on the long, twist-ing road to Paula's old place, all of them much more modern and new-looking than the old farmhouses still standing and probably still occupied by groups of students or maybe former students heavily under the sway of College Town Syndrome. For a while, a bonafide commune had flourished in one of the oversized, drafty Victorian monstrosities. He passed an A-frame and got a quick glimpse of what looked like a dinner party through a two-story window. Some of the old hippies, he remembered wryly, had come from some pretty old money.

He rounded a hard bend where a gas station had opened, closed, and then become a convenience store, and saw Paula's house, sitting at the side of the road, looking repainted and refurbished, but very much the same house. He slowed and pulled into the still-unpaved lot that had served the three apartments the house had been divided into, however many years before. Except he saw that there was only one mailbox at the side of the road now. The house must have been converted back into a one-family dwelling.

Slowly, he got out of the car, clutching the manuscripts tightly, and then stood, looking up at the house. So now that he was here, what was he going to do? What was he going to say to her?

You could try asking her why she sent you anything or what she expected you do to about them when she didn't even provide a way to get in touch with her.

He moved toward the front door with a heavy feeling in the pit of his stomach. Now this seemed like a very bad idea indeed. At best, it would probably be depressing as hell, at worst—well, who knew? You could struggle for years to get bad shit from the past out of your system and then, *blam*—something could bring it back.

He looked down at the manuscripts. Bad shit from the past? Or just old shit? Whatever it was, it was no good for him, probably no good for Paula, however she was, whatever she was now. Maybe he should have just tossed them all out instead of going to all this trouble just to say he didn't want to see any more of her erotica. Well, never mind. He was here, he might as well go through with it. Bracing himself, he went up the three steps to the porch and rang the doorbell.

In the few moments that he heard the inner door being unlocked, he had the awful feeling that the door would swing open and he would see Paula as she had been twenty-five years before, unchanged and unsurprised to see him.

Then the door swung open, and, behind the screen door, Paula appeared as she had been twenty-five years before, unchanged and unsurprised to see him. His mouth dropped open and he heard himself make a faint startled noise.

"Come in, Dan," she said, pushing the screen door open. He stepped back, shaking his head slightly. Her smile brought out two dimples he didn't remember her having. "I recognize you from my mother's scrapbook."

And now he could see that, of course, she wasn't Paula. The differences were very slight—the dimples when she smiled, the color of her eyes, the shape of her mouth, and her height—but now he could see them quite well. He tried to hide his relief as he stepped into the living room. His heart was still pounding hard.

"Everybody who knew my mother from her college days has that reaction when they see me," she said.

"Everybody?" he asked, puzzled. "Do you get a lot of visitors?"

"Oh, yes," she said. "Well, especially now."

Dan frowned. "Did something happen?"

Paula's daughter looked up at him in mild amazement. "I thought you knew. I thought that was why you had come."

He closed his eyes. *This is where she tells me Paula's dead, and we go out to the graveyard and we find one last manila envelope on the grave and then I wake up. Or go mad.*

"My mother had a stroke. She's been comatose for weeks."

Dan opened his eyes. "She—what?"

"Completely unexpected. My mother's never been sickly. Anyway, I really appreciate you coming. As you know, comatose patients may be able to hear even if they can't respond or even show they're aware, and the doctors say that familiar voices—"

"Did you send me these manuscripts?" Dan demanded, more harshly than he had intended.

She blinked at him. "Manuscripts?"

He held them out to her. "These. Her stories that she wrote in college."

Paula's daughter looked dazed as she took them from him and flipped the pages briefly. "I knew my mother wrote." She shrugged and turned them over to look at the envelopes. "Wow. It sure *looks* like my mother's writing. But I know it's not mine."

"Yeah. Right." Dan folded his arms.

"I'm sorry, I don't know who sent those to you, and I don't know why you came here originally. But I'd appreciate it if you'd just spend maybe three minutes with my mother. I mean, since you *did* come all the way from wherever you came from, I know you don't live around here. Please? It could help her."

"Yeah, all right," Dan said, resigned. "What hospital is she in?"

"She's right upstairs. In the master bedroom. I'm taking care of her here at home." She gestured at the staircase. "Please."

Okay, Paula, he thought, climbing the stairs. *Here I come, after all these years. God knows why.*

The room had been transformed into a perfect hospital room. He didn't like to think how much the life-support equipment must have been costing. Paula was lost among it, a little form in a snow-white bed, her chin lifted and turned slightly away from the breathing tube in her throat, as if she were repelled by it even in her coma.

Her face was shockingly old; her skin had acquired the pale translucence of someone in her eighties. The sight was terrifying. He pulled a chair over and sat down, feeling breathless. If he had believed in any sort of God, he'd have been tempted to believe this was to remind him that life was short and you had to get out here and gather ye rosebuds while ye may, that after your *on* button got pushed, there were only two others—*play* and *stop.*

"Jesus, Paula," he said. "Who would have thought. I don't know if I ever really meant anything important to you." He took her warm, limp hand. "But—"

Her hand suddenly snapped tight around his like a trap, and he yelled in surprise and pain. He thought for a moment that she was simply having a weird muscular contraction; then the pressure on his hand increased and he could feel the bones grind together.

"Paula!" he yelled. "Hey, someone—you, downstairs, Paula's daughter—"

The pain in his hand turned to liquid fire and began to pour up his arm, into his shoulder, where it radiated out to the rest of his body. He fell to his knees, shaking; the woman's grip continued, impossibly, to tighten. "Paula," he moaned weakly.

A bright light filled his mind, and suddenly he was standing at the front door again, and there was Paula as she had been twenty-five years ago, inviting him in. Not her daughter this time, but Paula herself, unchanged, untouched, and unsurprised to see him.

Come in, she said. *It gets lonely, having to stay in here all by myself, so come in, come in, please come in. I think you'll recognize just about every-one else who's come.*

No, he tried to say, but his voice had gone missing.

I need you, said Paula fondly. *There are so many more stories now.*

Her lust was more like a punch than a caress.

Come in, come in, Dan. Come in and stay this time. Come in and stay.

He was already in, all the way in, and there wasn't the slightest doubt that he would stay, just like all the others.

Paula's daughter removed the emptied clothing, searching it carefully for all official ID. She would have the car towed out to the Smith College campus, after she removed the license plates, where it would be impounded and then forgotten about. And then her mother would call the next one.

It was really amazing how they came. She couldn't imagine why it was so easy to get them here. Must be that lemminglike tendency in human beings, she thought. They were lemmings, and her mother was a lemming predator. She laughed humorlessly.

"How do they taste, Mother?" she asked. There was no answer, only the shushing sound of the respirator. She shook her head. What a question. How did they taste.

Probably like chicken. Everything did.

Goo Fish
Robert Reed

They say that the Devil finds work for idle hands. Well, goddammit, they're *right*, as the creepy and unsettling story that follows amply demonstrates.

Robert Reed is a frequent contributor to *The Magazine of Fantasy and Science Fiction* and *Asimov's Science Fiction* and has also sold stories to *Universe, New Destinies, Tomorrow, Synergy, Starlight*, and elsewhere. His books include the novels *The Lee Shore, The Hormone Jungle, Black Milk, The Remarkables, Down the Bright Way*, and *Beyond the Veil of Stars*. His most recent book is the novel *An Exaltation of Larks*. He lives in Lincoln, Nebraska.

GOO FISH

🌹

Let's just talk . . . about yourself, your brother . . . about how this thing got started . . .

You already know, I'm sure . . . I'm a pretty important business-man in this town . . .

When I was eight, I was mowing lawns. I dropped out of school when I was seventeen, opened my own lawn-care business, then saved practically every penny I ever made. When I had working capital, I bought an equipment-rental place. Which has done pretty well for me, I'd like to think. Later on, I got into dry cleaning and videos and apartments. I bet you guys have used my services, prob-ably a thousand times. Hell, I'm even a partial owner of the third-largest mortuary in the state. Which is just to compare myself to my brother. Just so you know who to trust here.

Donnie's ten years younger than me. And we look like brothers, except he doesn't have my belly yet and he wears what's left of his hair in a ponytail. Girls like long hair, he claims. It must work, because he's usually got one or two hanging around.

Frankly, we've never been close, never been much alike. Donnie looks at work as being a disease, something to avoid at all costs. Mom used to tell me, "I wish he was more like you, Kal. I wish you could teach him how to be a success." She'd usually say that right before trying to coax me into giving my brother another job. "Any kind of work at all," she would beg. "Just to help him through this bad spell." Which is what I did for years. Good-hearted me. I'd put my brother behind counters or in the back somewhere, or I'd invent some half-ass job just for him. But something always went wrong. Always. And I'd end up firing him or forcing him to quit, which would make Mom mad. Which wasn't that awful, frankly. But then she'd get over being mad and come back to me again, saying, "I wish he was. I wish you could." And I was back in the same mess again. You know? You know how it goes?

The thing is, I finally ran out of places to dump Donnie. Honest. My good workers refused to work with him, and I had to tell that to Mom. Point-blank. Which kept her off my back for maybe six months. Half a year without having to deal with Baby Brother. Come to think of it, that's the only vacation that I've ever taken, and I can't imagine a sweeter one.

It ended when Mom arrived out of the blue. She was all smiles,
saying that she had a great idea . . . which meant that Donnie'd had
the idea and put her up to it . . .

She began by saying, "You know how your brother's always
loved keeping fish."

No, I didn't. I half remembered some little tanks bubbling in his
bedroom, but honestly, I wasn't around most of the time.

"Well, he does love fish," she persisted. "Which is why I was
wondering . . . why don't you help him start his own business? A
fish store, maybe. Then he can have something of his own to take
care of, and he'll be independent, and you won't have to worry
about him again."

As if I was worrying about him much in the first place.

"Please, Kal? Will you, son?" She started working me over with
guilt. "If your brother doesn't find himself soon . . . I just don't
know what's going to happen to him!"

I broke down. I agreed to at least check things out, if only to make
sure I had reasons to tell both of them no.

Donnie came over to my house and gave me his pitch. Then I
asked questions until he ran out of answers. But instead of vanish-
ing like I expected, he did his research and came back with fresh
answers, including a proposed location and what he'd need for
working capital. I checked out the location myself, made my own
estimates of costs and sales, and I decided that I'd be losing money
every year. But not much money. Certainly not as much as it would
have cost having Donnie on my payroll, screwing things up daily. So
we made a deal. A pure business arrangement. And not only did I
countersign his loan, I gave him an allowance—just enough to keep
his store going, and give me a say in how my money was spent.

The Fish Stop, he called it.

It fills an old frame building not far from downtown. A sweet
lease, a fair location. But then he made his big mistake. He's got this
lifelong friend, a crazy shit named Pull, who became his entire staff.

A genuine maniac, if you want the truth.

Pull's a nickname, and I don't know where he got it. Pulling-your-
own-pud comes to mind. He was a tall guy, big and strong in an accidental sort of way. Not bad looking, but *wrong* looking. Black hair cut
military-short and big dark eyes, plus this strange little smile that
appeared whenever some poor gal wandered into the store. Pull didn't
have his own girlfriends, but he loved gawking at the customers and
Donnie's girls, and he stood there with his hands shoved in his pockets,
probably playing with his pud the whole time.

Donnie never noticed that his buddy was a jerk.

Or maybe he knew it and just didn't give a shit.

When they opened up finally, Mom promised that running his

own store would change Donnie. Making him more responsible, more like me.

Except I never saw it happening.

I don't know the fish business. I'll admit it. But every business has the same basic rules. "Keep your store clean," I used to tell those two. I'd drop by unannounced, and after my walk-through I'd tell them, "These aquariums look like shit. And what's with all those dead fish? God, no wonder you call this place The Fish Stop. Nothing with fins ever gets out of here alive!"

Pull hated my walk-throughs. He said it with his eyes, shooting fire at me. He said it with the way he stood behind the cash register, grinding his teeth and rarely gutting out a word in my direction.

I really blame Pull for everything. Twenty times more than Donnie, quite frankly.

Things didn't go well with the store . . . did they . . . ?

Even compared to what I thought was likely, The Fish Stop was a disaster.

Its customers were mostly kids and Donnie's other friends. Not a lot of cash to spend, in general. They were exactly the kind of customers that you'd expect in a store where the tanks were filthy, where fish were dying, and the smell of things just about made a grown man want to gag.

"Dead fish are unavoidable," Donnie told me, using a dip net to snag a floating swordtail. "Our stock comes to us under stress. Weak, susceptible to disease. We can't help but lose a few. Everyone in the business does."

"Okay," I said. "But what about this tank?"

I was pointing at a big tank set off from the others, more fish than water in it.

"That's our feeder tank," Pull shouted from behind the register. "It's supposed to look that way."

"That way" meant having ten million tiny goldfish squeezed into a cloudy stinking mess. A lot of the fish had died, and the rest looked half dead. If goldfish ever write histories, that fifty-gallon tank will be remembered as their Dachau.

"People buy these fish to feed to *other* fish," Donnie explained. He had a habit of standing between Pull and me, as if trying to keep us from looking at each other. "That's why we stock so many, and why they're so cheap."

"Yeah," I said, "and I'd like nothing better than to feed sick fish to my expensive ones." A dozen fish were stuck to the tank's heater, their flesh slowly cooking, dead eyes looking out at me. "Do you sell the dead ones, too?"

Donnie acted astonished. "Of course we don't!"

"Then they're a business expense that gets you nothing back. You might as well throw money out the windows."

He didn't say anything, but his face got redder by the minute.

"All I'm saying is this: clean up your store." I looked over at Pull, adding, "You can help, too. Come out from behind that register. Nobody's going to steal it, at least not until you get some money in there."

It was Pull who grumbled loudest. "This isn't your store. Who the fuck are you—"

"Hey," I said. "Don't start with *me*."

He shut up, but only barely.

Then I looked at my brother, saying, "Clean things up in here, and I'll give you something extra. Enough so you can advertise on radio. Okay?"

Donnie's eyes got bigger. Happier. "Really?"

"Why not?" I said. "If you've got a good store, it pays to run ads."

Except I didn't really believe that I'd have to make good on my promise, and Donnie, bless him, saw to it that it never came up again.

When did you see your brother again . . . ?

Well, my own businesses needed a lot of help after that; I was backed up pretty badly for the next few weeks.

When I finally paid the boys another visit, unannounced, I could see exactly how far the two of them had gotten with their house-keeping. I walked down one aisle, marveling at the clean tanks and shiny floor, then turned the corner and just stopped. If anything, the other half of the store was dirtier than ever. The smell alone was enough to make me queasy. But I was trying to sound positive, say-ing, "Well, you've gotten a fair start with things."

Pull gave a snort and looked over at Donnie.

"We meant to finish," my brother told me. "But something hap-pened—"

"They're called sore backs," I groused. "You'll get over them."

Neither spoke for a long minute.

Then it was Pull who said, "Maybe he doesn't want to see what we found. What's eventually going to make us *rich*."

The idiot.

I halfway laughed, asking, "Rich how?"

"Let me show him." Pull came out from behind the counter and pointed at the ugliest tank in the place. No pump was running. According to the thermometer, its filthy water was a feverish hun-dred degrees. A raft of dead fish—all kinds—floated on the surface.

Which explained the smell. But swimming around in that sewage were seven or eight living fish. Goldfish mostly. And despite their circumstances, they didn't look too awfully unhappy.

"Rich how?" I said again.

"I found the first one," said Donnie. "That one there."

He was kneeling, pointing hard at the tiniest goldfish.

"The pump on our feeder tank died on a Saturday night," he explained to me. "By the time we came in Monday, every other fish was dead. And the whole place was starting to stink."

What do you know? My brother had a sense of smell.

"That's one tough fish," said Pull. His face was strange, lit up behind those dark eyes, and with a weird smile making me uneasy. "At least that's what we were thinking, at first. That it was just tough."

I didn't see where they were going, and believe me, I told them so.

Donnie took the reins, trying to explain. "That fish shouldn't have lived. I mean, goldfish are durable, but the water was covered with rotting bodies. Oxygen couldn't get past them, and any oxygen left in the water would have been used up by the decay. Yet there was that one little fish, and he looked perfectly fine."

"We watched him," said Pull, smiling at the memory. "We watched him swimming, then after a while, the little guy started chewing on one of his dead buddies."

They were a pair, those two. Stranger than any fish. "So when do you tell me what it all means?" I asked.

They looked at each other, laughing.

"We thought we had some kind of mutant," said Donnie. "A goldfish that could live with next to no oxygen."

"Billions of feeders are bred every year," said Pull. "In lousy conditions, most of the time. Why shouldn't tougher kinds evolve in those tanks?"

"But you've got eight fish in there," I said. "Did you find even more mutants? Or do the little bastards breed extra fast, too?"

"No," said my brother. "And no."

I looked at both of them, waiting.

Pull said, "That first fish was chewing on a dead one."

"You told me that already," I said, thinking about places I'd rather be.

"While we watched," he told me, "it chewed until one spot was raw."

I had a picture in my head: my brother and this maniac sitting on chairs, watching a cannibal goldfish.

"That's the fish there," Donnie told me. "The one with the black back."

"But that one's alive," I said.

And Pull said, "It was dead, then it *wasn't*."

I said, "What . . . ?"

Then Donnie said, "The chewing took a long time. Because gold-fish don't have real teeth, and the stuff has to work its way into an open wound—"

I interrupted, asking, "*What* stuff?"

They looked at each other, beaming. Then Pull said, "Let me show him."

With a dip net, he snagged one of their prized specimens. "We fig-ured it out a few days ago," he was telling me, setting the fish on the nearest table. "After watching them long enough, we saw what was happening . . ." He yanked a penknife from his pocket, then made a quick deep cut up the side of the body. The poor thing was flipping its tail, but it didn't die. It couldn't die, because it already was. But I didn't know that then. "See what's coming out?" said Pull. "That's what's going to make us a fortune. That stuff there, that *goo* . . . !"

Sure enough, a thick grayish *something* was dripping out of the poor fish.

"We haven't figured out how it's going to make us rich," Donnie confessed. "But sooner or later, we will be—"

"And famous," said Pull.

"Yeah," said my brother. "And that, too."

You didn't believe them, did you . . . ?

Not one word, or smile, or any of it. No.

What was happening, I figured, was that the boys had cooked up a scheme to milk me out of my money. I couldn't tell how they did that trick with the fish, and I had a tough time believing that Donnie would actually turn on me, but as soon as he talked about getting rich and famous, I knew exactly what was what.

Every week or so I came by, always bracing myself for new tales about the important research being done by those junior scientists. Sometimes they talked about the goo being a kind of parasite that took over dead bodies. Probably something from the deepest Amazon. Other times it was a chemical, complicated and able to grow, but not quite alive. They'd set up a lab in their shop's little basement, and they showed me samples under a cheap microscope. The goo looked like tiny squishy Ping-Pong balls dancing around on the slide. Whatever it was, I thought, the goo kept itself awfully busy.

"Now watch this," said Donnie. "Are you watching?"

They had a tiny fish heart ready to go. It was blackish red and very dead, but when it touched the goo it started to turn color, becoming pink, and all at once it was beating, pumping hard, pulling the goo in and out of its tiny arteries and veins.

I didn't buy what I saw, or what I heard.

"The stuff takes over dead organs," Pull told me. "In a dead body, it takes charge of everything. The heart. The guts. Even the dead brain."

I wondered what he thought was in *my* brain.

"This is going to be *huge*," Donnie kept saying.

"I bet so," I said, not meaning it.

"But first," said his con-artist partner, "we need to learn more. We've got to know what we're dealing with here."

Know why I kept coming? Because I wanted to see what was next. It was almost fun, watching their sleight-of-hand tricks, wondering how they could make dead hearts beat on command, and so on. They were working hard to con me, the hardest I'd ever seen my brother work. And besides, I was curious: when would they finally ask me to open up my bank accounts? And would Pull ask for the money, or would Donnie . . . ?

The goo had ways of crossing from one corpse to another, they told me. But it took perfect conditions—hot water and dead flesh, but not too rotten—and even then it didn't happen often. Which, they claimed, was why nobody had ever noticed it before.

Injecting goo straight into a dead fish worked easily. Would I like to try it?

I told them, "Thanks, no."

Species didn't matter. The old feeder tank was reserved for goo fish, a big sign hanging on it. Not For Sale, it read. And packed into the water was every kind of fish, big and tiny, tropical and not, swimming together and eating just a little food now and then. But never much. "Goo fish," Donnie explained, "have very slow metabolisms."

And the magical goo worked on things other than fish, too.

In the basement, in a stained old tank, they had a pack of dead mice. The mice swam underwater, never breathing. While I watched, two mice grabbed hold of the same wheel, stupidly trying to move it in opposite directions. "They aren't as sharp as living mice," Donnie told me. "And they've got to stay underwater. Out of it, they'll just dry up and die all over again."

The way I figured it, I was looking into a bottle set inside the aquarium. Those mice were living in something other than water, and if I reached in there, I'd touch glass.

But I didn't reach. Because that would have proved what I knew, which would have spoiled everyone's fun.

"Huh," I kept saying. Over and over. "Huh, huh, huh."

"Whatever this stuff is," said Donnie, "it's amazing."

Pull took a big breath, then said, "You know, we're going to have to protect what we've found here."

"Protect it how?" I asked.

"A patent," Pull said. "That's our next step, we're thinking."

Here it comes, I told myself.

"Which means lawyers," he said. "And some pretty hefty fees, to begin with."

"A three-way partnership," Donnie said to me. "You can draw up the terms yourself. I'll trust you."

Pull didn't trust me. But he managed to keep quiet.

Even though I expected that moment, I took the words hard. My only sibling was trying to swindle me—that's how I looked at it—and I wasn't ready to blow any whistles. I stared at him, stared at Pull, then decided to delay things. To give Donnie another chance to back out of this ugly game.

"I need something more," I told them. "Something better than bringing people's pets back from the dead."

The two boys wore stupid faces, watching me.

"If I'm going to invest," I said, "I need to see a chance for real profits. Which means doing something *big*. Something that'll make people look at your goo and say, 'Wow! I've got to have some of *that*!'

"That's how you make yourself a fortune," I told them.

And that's all I told them. Nothing more. I don't know what other stories you're hearing, but this one's the truth.

When did you see your brother again . . . ?

Let me think a minute.

(Inaudible.)

It was a couple weeks. I hadn't heard from him, so I stopped by during business hours. Except it was closed and locked up tight. Donnie's old pickup was parked out back, and so was Pull's VW. But nobody answered the door, and when I tried my key—I'd demanded my own when I set things up—I discovered that the pricks had changed locks on me.

It was a couple, three days later when I heard about the catfish.

I caught it on the late news. It was a blue catfish, and it had lived in the same enormous tank for twenty years, eating its fill of crayfish and chicken livers. People called her Old Blue, and the same people were up in arms when they learned that someone had broken into the state aquarium and stolen her. And judging by the blood on the floor, that someone had used a meat hook to do it, dragging her fat body down a hallway and out a window, then into the getaway vehicle.

A witness had seen a pickup truck in the parking lot. An old pickup truck. Because it was a fish and I had fish on the brain, I remember it now. But I couldn't see why my brother would care about Old Blue, and I certainly didn't see why *I* should, and I just sort of filed the story away, then went to bed for my usual five hours.

When I went past the store again, it was open. Donnie was standing behind the counter, not Pull, and I didn't bother asking where his buddy was.

"You don't make money when you're closed," I warned him.

He said he knew that, and he was sorry. But there were a lot of two-man jobs to do. "And still more to be done," he added.

It was strange, hearing my brother talk about work as if it wasn't a fungus between your toes.

"Kal," he said to me, "we've got a helluva plan."

I nodded, sort of. Then I warned him, "I'm going to be a tough sale. Particularly if I even think that you're trying to cheat me—"

"I wouldn't," he interrupted. "Never!"

The thing is, I had this sudden sense that the twerp actually *believed* his crazy words. All of them. And for the first time, just for that little moment, I was wondering what exactly was really real.

I left The Fish Stop. I remember seeing Pull's car in the lot, which means he was in the basement, working away at their big plans. I made a mental note to check back in a day or two, just to keep the boys jumpy. But I got sidetracked. There was a big wreck that night on the Interstate, and one of the dead—that Lindstrom girl—was taken to the third-largest mortuary in the state. The mortuary that I own a share of. An investment I made because people are always dying, so it seemed like steady money. You know . . . ?

Anyway, twelve hours later, her body turns up missing.

I still didn't make the connection. Maybe that sounds stupid, but then again, I still didn't believe in magical goo that could bring the dead back to life.

No, the missing body was just a missing body.

A fucking big headache. But that's all it was for me.

Of course, Donnie used to work at that mortuary, washing hearses for me, and it would have been easy for him to have kept a set of keys.

But that didn't occur to me then.

I was too busy dealing with lawyers and the girl's family and the assholes in the press, not to mention you guys. Seven days of trying to make the trouble go away . . . and then some guy walking in the woods finds something half buried in the brush. Two somethings, actually. White and naked, and very dead.

When I heard the news . . . when I learned that they'd found the girl's legs and *only* her legs . . . that's when everything fell together in my head . . .

Finally.

All at once, I knew what those boys were doing in that basement.

They were building something, with a fish and a woman, and goo.

Why didn't you contact us . . . ?

I know I should have handled things differently. I *know* that. But this was family, this was my brother, and besides, it was *Pull* who was to blame. *He* was the sick son of a bitch between them, and if I wanted to save Donnie, I needed to do it without bringing in the world. That's all I was thinking. God's truth.

I called the store straight off, but nobody was answering.

So I called Donnie's apartment, leaving a string of messages. I told him that we had to meet, just him and me. I told him that I wanted to help, that he didn't have anywhere else to turn. But he never bothered calling me back, which is why I changed my tactics.

I started driving past The Fish Stop, maybe a hundred times in the next couple days.

And nights.

They were closed for business, but I knew they were there. Their cars were always parked out back, even in the middle of the night, and through the milky glass in the basement windows, I could tell that someone was walking slowly, moving back and forth between me and the lights.

It was a week before they finally took a break.

I saw them leaving. I was parked up the street, waiting inside one of my rental trucks. Donnie came out first, then Pull, and I watched Pull lock the back door and test it twice. They were moving like guys who hadn't slept forever. Without saying a word, they got into their cars and took off. And after waiting a couple minutes, I drove up and parked as close to the back door as possible, and, with a little crowbar, I managed to coax the door open.

That store is as much mine as anyone's; I had a perfect right to be there.

The basement stairs were steep, but at least they'd left lights burning. I started down, then stopped and listened. I could hear the air pumps running upstairs, and it seemed like water was sloshing somewhere below. But I wasn't sure. I took a couple more steps, then stopped to listen again. I didn't hear any sloshing that time. I waited, and waited, and I got to thinking about what I was doing, what I thought was happening in that basement, and suddenly it just seemed so stupid. Just crazy. I looked at myself, thinking, that poor asshole, he's going insane.

Which made it easier, not believing it anymore.

I came down the last few stairs, then froze.

The boys had built a homemade tank that stretched along the far wall, lights strung above it and a metal chair set right in the water. I didn't understand the chair, at first. The girl was there, swimming. I was watching her, too stunned to move. She had just enough room to take a stroke and kick once, side to side like a fish, then turn and take another stroke. And that's when she saw me. A big, beaming smile came to that little face of hers, and with her right hand, she waved at me, waving through the glass. She mouthed the word, "Hello." Twice she said, "Hello." And she pressed herself against the glass, her belly and her breasts and her long blue-white tail, too, and I could see her mouth moving, asking me, "Who are you . . . ?"

You planned all along to take her. Didn't you . . . ?

That's why I brought the truck, yeah. But what I was thinking . . . I was thinking that I'd find the rest of her corpse in the basement, mutilated . . . and if the magical goo somehow worked, she'd be the same as the fish upstairs . . . a mindless zombie that could do nothing but swim and chew on the dead . . .

I never expected her to *smile*.

Or try to talk.

I'd planned to take her out into the country and bury her, hopefully putting her deep enough so nobody would discover what those bastards had done to the poor girl . . .

The poor girl . . .

Yeah, I took her. But I first soaked down the packing blankets from the truck, thinking I should keep her wet. And I grabbed a bottle of dechlorinating chemicals from upstairs. Then I came back down and looked through the glass, watching her, trying to get up my courage. What I wanted to do . . . well, it's not the sort of thing that a normal person ever thinks of doing . . . you know . . . ?

"I want to help you," I told her.

I told her, "I'm going to take you somewhere safe."

She was smiling all the time. I asked, "Do you understand?" and she seemed to nod at me. So I did it. I reached into that warm water, smelling that smell that comes with living fish, and she slipped out of my hands once, then again, laughing at me. It was a game to her. So I climbed up into the tank, using that sunken chair as a step, and I cornered her, grabbing one arm and then the other, wrestling her out of the water. And in about two seconds, she was suffocating. Water was pouring from her mouth, and she was dying again.

I carried her upstairs, fast. She wasn't big. Not when she was human, and not as a mermaid, either. I wrapped her in the wet blankets, then ran back inside and filled a bucket with aquarium water, and I shoved her head under the surface, holding her down until I could feel her breathing it in and out, nice and slow.

It took me maybe ten minutes to drive home.

By then, half the water had bounced out of the bucket, and she was suffocating again. So I carried her straight to the best place I could think of. I've got a Jacuzzi in my backyard, big enough for eight people. I put her in, then used the whole bottle of the dechlorinator. Then I watched her swim in that little pool, kicking in circles, praying the whole time that the shock and chemicals wouldn't kill her.

Because she was *alive*.

From that point on, I couldn't think of her as being any other way.

As a human girl, she must have been beautiful. As a mermaid, or whatever she was, she was strangely pretty. That fish tail was shiny and naked—catfish don't have scales—and it and its long fins had a soft blue-white color that seemed to glow when I turned on the Jacuzzi's lights. She narrowed at the waist, becoming human. I could see the sutures, but only when I looked for them. Her human skin looked pale but healthy. When her face was turned down, I could see her spine leading to her fish spine, and how her long straw-colored hair floated where the currents took it. Then she would roll over, and I'd see her face, pretty as pretty can be. Blue eyes, a little nose. That smiling mouth. Her photo on TV didn't do her justice, I kept thinking. And sure, I watched her tits now and again. Any man would have. They floated like the hair floated, obeying the currents, and the nipples were fat and candy-colored, and sometimes she would break the surface with her nipples, or more, looking just as natural as anything.

I watched her for an hour, making sure that she was all right.

Then, just when I thought everything was fine, she sank to the bottom and stopped moving. I could see her drifting hair, and her back, and nothing else. So I climbed into the pool, thinking something was wrong . . . and she grabbed me, holding on tight and pulling at me . . . smiling, like always . . .

It was another game, playing dead was.

She and the boys must have invented it. One boy at a time. That's what the three of them were doing for days and days. And I learned what the chair was for.

The boys sat on it, one at a time.

I'm not a sick son of a bitch. I'm *not*. The girl just seemed . . . I don't know . . . so damned determined . . . sure of herself . . .

Dead or not, she was so pretty in so many ways . . .

So I was sitting in that warm water when the sun finally came up . . . holding the back of her head in my hands . . . and I couldn't stop thinking about how that soft golden hair felt against my legs, once I was naked . . . and how very *good* she was when she was doing that wonderful, wonderful thing . . .

What happened next . . . ?

The doorbell rang at about eight.

I threw on a robe and looked outside before opening the door. It was Donnie. Just Donnie. He had a wild expression and a matching voice. "You didn't do it, did you? I mean, I hope you did . . . because I don't know who *else* . . . but I told Pull that it couldn't be you—?"

"Couldn't be me what?" I asked.

He gave me a helpless look, then said, "You took her. God, you *did!*"

"Get out of here," I said.

"You had no right—"

"What do you know about rights?" I asked him.

He started looking around, eyes full of panic. "You've got to keep her in water. Always. And it's got to be warm water, too."

"She's not here," I told him.

"Then where is she . . . ?" He stopped himself, staring at my robe and wet feet. "She's here, all right. Where? Out back?"

"In the bathtub upstairs," I said.

"I want to see her."

But I put a hand on his shoulder, pushing. I said, "What I want to do is save your ass, Donnie."

He tried to slip past me, but I got him down and grabbed his ponytail, shaking him and telling him, "Stealing a corpse is a felony, you stupid son of a bitch!"

"Let go of me."

"Do you really want to go to prison? *Do* you?"

"But the goo works," he argued. "We brought her back to *life*. Sort of. When her parents see her, they'll thank us—"

"Bullshit."

"And we'll make a fortune, too."

"More bullshit," I told him. Then I let him go and said, "But I'll tell you what I'll do. I'll keep her here with me, and I'll talk to people. My attorneys, whoever. I'll find out what's the very best way to go from here, and I'll get back to you. As soon as I can."

"Promise?" he squeaked.

I lied, saying, "Sure I will."

Then I showed him to the front door, saying, "And another thing. Don't tell Pull what I told you. Or that I've got her with me. Okay?"

He said, "Sure."

I watched Donnie leave, making certain that he really drove off, then I got some breakfast and took it out back, eating and thinking things through, trying to resist the temptation to climb back into that tub with my brand-new mermaid.

Temptation won . . . didn't it, Kal . . . ?

Are you guessing, or do you know?

Okay, I climbed back in with her. But you've got to see it through my eyes here. She was pretty, and alive, and very willing, and I don't know about *you*, but it's damned hard for me to turn down good head.

I told myself that I was trying to see what was left of the Lindstrom girl. Did she still know how to read, for instance? So I got a marking pen and wrote "Hello" on an old plate, then stripped and got in and showed her the plate. She looked at the word, I'm pretty sure, but it didn't seem to mean anything. What mattered was me. What mattered was *doing* me again. The warmest, wettest mouth imaginable, and it was mine, and of course I just sat back, closing my eyes, thinking . . . thinking that a man could get used to that kind of fun . . .

I didn't hear anyone until Pull was standing behind me. Until he cleared his throat, then said, "That's sick, you know. Doing it with a corpse. No, with *half* a corpse . . . "

I tried to stand up, but the mermaid grabbed hold of me. With her arms as well as her mouth.

"She's stronger than she looks," said Pull, laughing. He walked around the patio, getting in front of me, showing me his wild eyes and his sick smile. And the crowbar that I'd left behind at the store. "That's something we learned pretty early. That, and she's got a real healthy appetite, too."

I just sat there, shriveling.

"Know why she likes to suck?" he asked.

I said, "No."

"To see if you're *dead*." Pull couldn't stop smiling. "If you die right now, she'll start chewing instead. Then she'll spit goo up into that stump of yours. And she'll have herself a husband, of sorts."

"Get out of here," I told him.

Pointing with the crowbar, he asked, "What's that there . . . ?"

He meant the dinner plate where I'd written "Hello."

"Yeah," he said, "we tried that trick. And plenty of others, too. But the poor girl doesn't have much left of her old self. Just a few parrot words, and the smiles. Which is best, really. I mean, think about it. You're the capitalist. How much would men pay to have their fun with a perfectly done mermaid . . . ?"

I sat motionless, barely feeling her working and working on my soft prick.

Pull knelt on the far side of the Jacuzzi, twirling the crowbar above the water. "In a lot of ways, she's the perfect woman."

"What are you going to do?" I asked.

"I'm going to take my property back, of course."

"And if I try to stop you—?"

"*Do* that," he told me. Both of his hands took a firm hold on the bar, and he said, "I've hated you forever, you cheap son of a bitch. Go on. Try to stop me."

"No," I said. "You can have her back." I was talking quietly, with a dry mouth. Putting my hands under the water, I pulled her off me as smoothly as I could, then gave her a half turn. "Here. Let me—"

The mermaid was small, and I was hopped up with adrenaline. It was practically easy to throw her out of the water, letting her hands grab at the next living thing. Which was Pull. She took him by his arms and held tight, and he tried to stand but not fast enough, and I got a good grip on the crowbar, jerking it out of his hands.

Then he came at me. I swear it.

He pushed the mermaid into the water and reached for my neck, and I didn't have any choice but to take a swing, or two. Maybe three, at the most. Then Pull dropped into the water beside me, his skull caved in. And sure enough, that mermaid started to chew on one of his thick fingers, working her way down to the knuckle before I had enough energy back in me to drag him up on the patio, up to where he would stay dead.

The bastard.

It was self-defense. Justifiable homicide. Whatever you call it . . .

You've got to believe me. It was him, or it was me . . . !

We believe you, Kal . . .

No, you don't. Do you?

Just tell us what happened next. What did you do . . . ?

I pretty much panicked after that. I admit it. I should have called you people and let things run their course . . . but frankly, I was scared that you wouldn't believe my crazy story, and what it would do to my reputation. My good business name. So what I did was, I dragged Pull into the back end of the truck, then emptied my biggest trash can and put it beside his body, and I filled the can with water and put the mermaid in and fastened down the lid . . .

I drove to the river. Nice and gentle, so she didn't spill.

I dumped Pull at my first stop. Just upstream from where those fishermen found him. What was it? Two days ago now . . .

I drove my mermaid to a different place.

The perfect place.

Don't ask me where. I won't tell. It wouldn't be right for the Lindstroms to get hold of her. Whatever she is, she's not their daughter, not anymore, and I'm saving them a whole lot of grief, believe me.

In the end, I carried the mermaid down to the water and climbed in with her, and for the first and only time, kissed her. Which means that she sort of chewed on my lips, one after another. But smiling, like always. And I was crying like an idiot, telling her to be careful out there and finally letting her go, watching as she took a stroke and kicked twice, her tail disappearing into that muddy water but her bare white body lingering, rolling over, those beautiful breasts breaking the surface just long enough for me to wish that I could have somehow kept her forever . . .

I suppose my brother tells you a different story. Trying to get out from under the blame . . . like he always does . . .

What kind of story would he tell us?

I guess he might try to paint me into a bigger role. That I believed in the goo long ago. Maybe even that I was in charge of things. He might even tell you . . . I'm just speculating here . . . that it was my idea in the first place to steal away the dead Lindstrom girl, and I did it myself, and poor Donnie didn't know what was happening until it was too late.

Which would be a total lie.

And if he says that I took the mermaid out of The Fish Stop so that I didn't have to share her with Pull, that's a lie. And that I killed Pull just because I wanted her for myself, or some such shit . . .

But that's a lie, too. And if you've got two brothers telling two different versions, who's the jury going to believe . . . ?

Except, Kal . . . there's another viable witness, too.

Who?

I mean it, who?

Think, Kal. Who else is in a position to know the truth?

(Inaudible.)

Let's suppose a maintenance crew was working on the cooling system of a nuclear reactor at the other end of the state. Just suppose. They found a mermaid swimming in that warm water, and they managed to net her and take her to the state aquarium, and right now she's swimming in the same tank where that big blue catfish once lived. And a team of experts have been secretly studying her . . . since this happened . . . last week, say . . .

I don't believe you.

And besides, she can't tell you anything.

The poor creature doesn't have enough of a mind left. I never saw any sign of memory, or language—

*Experts can accomplish wonders with people who have suffered traumas.
All kinds of trauma, including being cut in half and sewn onto the back end
of a dead fish, then kept stuffed inside a tiny tank while strange men forced
themselves on her . . .*

(Inaudible.)

What was that, Kal?

I don't believe you. No, I'm not falling for your games.

The ungrateful (inaudible), I should have (inaudible) . . .

What was that?

Nothing.

*But hey, Kal . . . we were wondering, all of us were . . . if anyone is guilty
of anything, and if the girl was a witness, even if she wasn't a very credible
witness . . . why would anyone take the trouble to put that witness in the
warm water downstream from a nuclear power plant? The only environ-
ment where she would have a chance of surviving . . . ?*

I don't know.

It was love, wasn't it?

*Of a sick sort, sure. That's a given. But isn't that why you couldn't just
pull her out into the sun and let her die a second time.*

You loved her, didn't you—?

(Inaudible.)

I want my lawyer.

(Inaudible.)

. . . and after all I *did* for that girl . . . !

YESTERDAY'S HOSTAGE
Michael Bishop

Michael Bishop is one of the most acclaimed and respected members of that highly talented generation of writers who entered SF in the 1970s. His renowned short fiction has appeared in almost all the major magazines and anthologies and has been gathered in four collections: *Blooded On Arachne, One Winter in Eden, Close Encounters With the Deity*, and *Emphatically Not SF, Almost*. In 1981 he won the Nebula Award for his novelette "The Quickening," and in 1983 he won another Nebula Award for his novel *No Enemy but Time*. His other novels include *Transfigurations, Stolen Faces, Ancient of Days, Catacomb Years, Eyes of Fire, The Secret Ascension, Unicorn Mountain*, and *Count Geiger's Blues*. His most recent novel is the baseball fantasy *Brittle Innings*, which has been optioned for a Major Motion Picture. Bishop and his family live in Pine Mountain, Georgia.

Here he sweeps us along with a man taking a trip through Europe who is about to have a Close Encounter with Unearthly Love, and to discover that some relationships you can *never* forget—no matter how hard you try . . .

Yesterday's Hostage

They did not "meet cute"—if anything, the opposite. In fact, they met so ugly that for an instant Rodgers feared that he'd either killed her or inoculated her with the pox of irreversible blood poisoning. Outside storybooks and plays, death and septicemia seldom amuse people, even people amusing themselves in a museum whose founders have devoted it to the display of Finger Bolts, Shame Masks, Neck Violins, Stretching Benches, Slander Stones, Execution Chairs, and other medieval tools of humiliation and torture. On a fine summer's day nearly three months before Germans on both sides of the Berlin Wall fell to a gleeful demolition of that barricade, these items had amused Rodgers, and dozens of other eager tourists in the Mittlealterliches Kriminalmuseum in the historic old city of Rothenburg-ob-der-Tauber.

In his amusement, and incredulity, Rodgers Hart scribbled notes in a palm-sized memobook, copying out the English-language squibs for the Iron Maiden ("mantle of infamy for women and girls, 16th century"), the Rosary Stocks ("church punishment for people who did not go to church or fell asleep during the service"), the Ducking Cage ("for bakers who sold too small loaves"), and so on.

Eventually, he dashed off a tiny illo of a ten-foot—no, a three-*meter*—pole that the diorama's caption labeled a "Witch Catcher," for one could drag or push along an accused witch by the fanged collar at the pole's business end without fear of stumbling into her clutches.

Such ingenuity. How those medieval burghers loved the Law, how grotesquely they upheld in practice as well as fancy its fussiest statutes.

An American college kid in a backward Yankee cap nudged Rodgers, hard. "How'd you like to nail *that* babe, hey?"

A quick pivot from the Witch Catcher display to find the kid's lust object. (Rodgers liked nailable females as much as had Old Rothenburg's literal-minded Polizei, if in a different way.) The ultra-fine point of his pen jabbed the young woman's bare midriff. She cried out: not so much a scream as a blurt of alarm.

Rodgers glimpsed a cutoff tee, hiking shorts, a band of tan belly, legs that moved like flowing honey into jaunty Italian sandals. He also saw blood—oh no, not *here*! no Blut in the holy precincts of the Mittelalterliches Kriminalmuseum!—for his pen dangled from her wound like a misplaced prosthetic dug: ugly, so ugly.

In a panic, Rodgers seized the pen and pulled. She put out a hand, a bridge to his shoulder, and he reacted—abreacted—by jabbing the pen upward into her throat, an involuntary (surely) reflex summoning a fresh puncture, a fresh red gout, a look of such shock that *he* would die if she didn't. Of mortification, formal guilt, the need to bury himself ahead of the burial owing his clumsy animal self.

"Jesus!" cried the college kid. "You vicious spaz!"

Despite his chagrin, Rodgers had either the savoir faire or the insensitivity to say, "One or the other, not both."

"What? *What?*"

"Either I'm vicious or I'm a spaz, one or the other."

The kid nodded at the young woman. "The longer you let her bleed, the shakier your argument, man."

Exactly. Rodgers saw her eyeballs clocking, her lissom body trembling toward a faint. Two barrellike Teutonic males and their wives looked ready to intervene, to seize the girl and maybe even to report him to the museum's guardians, who would . . . what? slam him in the stocks? make him wear a bell-shaped brass overcoat? lay him on a table with a roll of spikes at his lower back? Even the callow Yankee fan wanted to help, probably as a prelude to trying to get into her pants.

Rodgers steadied the woman—girl? ingénue? jailbait?—with one arm, and pressed his soiled handkerchief against her throat puncture. (He *could* have pierced the jugular, or her windpipe or esophagus.) She pushed him away but kept a grip on his handkerchief, pressing it to the second of the two wounds he'd inflicted on her. (The first, at her midriff, had already ceased to bleed. Her clotting agents worked *fast*.)

Glancing down, Rodgers saw his pen lying on the floor. He picked it up and, with a look of penitential self-reproach, faced the young woman. "God, I've never done anything so stupid in my life."

"Oh, I'm fine," pressing the darkening linen to the wound, regarding him warily. "Thanks for asking."

"You can't imagine how much this has embarrassed me."

"You stuck me *twice*." A hit at his boorish self-concern.

"Swab both punctures with alcohol or hydrogen peroxide."

The fretful German couples, seeing Rodgers and her talking, ambled off to the next exhibit. The Yankee fan kept eyeing them, but moved along when Rodgers, older and taller, gave him an emphatic thumb-jerk.

Rodgers touched her shoulder. "*Are* you okay? I'm *really* sorry."

"Twice," more bewildered now than accusing.

The design on her tee—a horizon line with a half circle atop it and a robed man dividing the half circle's upper curve—featured the legend SON*RISE over the man's head. This T-shirt design spoke libraries.

"Can't you forgive me?" he said.

She eyed him shrewdly, still pressing his handkerchief to her throat. The stain in the linen did not seem to have spread much. "I think I could stand to sit for a minute."

Rodgers smiled. "Whoa. A contradiction in terms."

Her empty stare hinted that he had lost her.

"Standing to sit," he said. "Most people *sit* to sit." He worked like a Bible salesman to fold a consoling sincerity into his patronage.

She teetered between dislike and sympathy. He stopped his breath, the lungs behind his ribs like lacquered paper sacks.

"Oh," lip corners quirking up. "Well, I could *still* stand to sit." She returned his handkerchief. "Thanks."

"Least I could do." She had great coagulants, but the cloth remained sticky, warm, laminated like a piece of floppy umber mica. What to do with it?

As, glancing back, she led him toward the stairwell and a window seat above the so-called Tauber Riviera—a limited view of the green valley and a coil of the river—Rodgers tossed the handkerchief on a display case. No one, not even the girl, saw him, and he escorted her to the window seat, amid the tourists, with a heady sense of vindication and relief.

"Gisela Gestern," she said.

"Say again?"

She repeated her name. He asked her to say it again, and yet again. She said her given name *GUI-se-la*: a hard G in an accented first syllable. Just remember, she said, that Gisela rhymes with *feasible*. Sort of. *Gestern*, also with a hard G, rhymes with *western*; Rodgers could not help imagining gazelles wheeling across an Arizona steppe.

"No," Gisela said. "My name doesn't mean 'gazelle,' but 'pledge' or 'hostage.' It has Old German origins, and if you saw me run, you'd see that I do it much more like an old lady in chains than a Serengeti gazelle."

"I doubt that," ingratiatingly chivalrous, "given your, ah, athletic build."

"You're politely calling me skinny."

"I'm discreetly calling you built."

She flushed, even through her tan, and he began to regret that after stabbing her twice with his Pilot Precise V-5 pen, he'd thought first of how he had looked to others and second of how he could recover his pen and escape.

Gisela Joyce Gestern hailed from LaGrange, Georgia, a scion of German immigrants whose latter-day generations no longer spoke the language. She had attended LaGrange College, a small Methodist-affiliated institution, before going on to graduate school in German at Emory in Atlanta. En route to her masters, she had interrupted her studies to teach English as a foreign language in the *Sprachlabor* at the University of Kiel, a city she found bracing but cold, meteorologically and relationally. Its leaden skies and everlasting winter heightened her sense of the emotional barrenness of many student liaisons there. She had made some friends in the language department, but none who shared her spiritual outlook. So it often struck her that the magnificent churches and cathedrals in European cities had dwindled from living transmitters of the faith to architectural relics—tourist attractions—formidable shells from which the scientific and mercantile dynamics of the twentieth century had sucked the irrigating marrows of fealty and conviction. She actually said "irrigating marrows," without self-consciousness, thus declaring herself something other than a valley girl on holiday. Probably, he should run. He couldn't, though. Her combination of beauty and intellect—even if she smutched them both with a cryptic religiosity—excited him. Even saints had genitals, and many did not achieve canonization until they had passed through the flame . . .

"Listen, *I* see Germans as a jolly people."

Gisela laughed. "The beergardens. The oom-pah festivals. Yes. Maybe *too* jolly."

"You'd refuse if I offered to buy you a beer?"

"Oh, no. I like beer, and the Germans make it better than most. The jolliness *I* deplore has no root system, only a crown of showy but blighted leaves."

"They enjoy the Law," nodding toward the ghoulish machines in the crime museum. "They won't cross a street against a Don't Walk sign even if it's one A.M. and not a car in sight. They like to humiliate scofflaws. They get off on torture."

"We all do," Gisela said. "Even on torturing ourselves."

Rodgers watched as a trio of youth-hostel refugees, female hikers even younger than Gisela, came giggling down the narrow stairs, one in ragged cutoffs, another in Spandex biking pants, the third in a tight striped mini.

"Hello," Gisela said pointedly to Rodgers.

He turned back to her. "By and large, we torture ourselves with guilt. I try not to. So, after taking a gander at your shirt—" gazing hard at its logo "—I'm *pleeeeased*, Miss Gestern, to learn that you eschew total teetotalism."

"I witness in this shirt, but the first miracle involved wine, you know. How could I teetotal, totally?"

"Doesn't your shirt get a little gamy after a week or so of bosoming your faith around? I mean, if the Son only rises when you're modeling him?"

Gisela, offended, "I change or rinse out my stuff daily."

"Cleanliness, godliness—I remember. What about presenting a consistent witness?"

"The Son also rises in our actions. Even now I risk your interest, your *indulgence*, with too much talk."

The Son also rises . . . Wow. Pretty slick kid.

Cagily, Gisela directed their talk to Rodgers, who could not help noting that the inoculation wounds on her belly and throat now resembled, well, mere freckles. Great coagulants; great tan.

"Your parents—?" she prompted.

"The Harts of San Diego, California."

"—named you *Rodgers? Rodgers Hart?* Isn't that a little like naming you, ah, Gilbert Sullivan?"

"Just about exactly. Or try Laurel Hardy, Martin Lewis, Dion Belmonts."

Gisela smiled. "Abbott Costello," she said. "Anthony Imperials. Herman Hermits. Bob Ray." She paused, thought, continued: "Ferrante Teicher. Lerner Loewe. Smith Wesson. Procter Gamble. Simon Garfunkel . . ."

"Hey, my folks loved Richard Rodgers. And I came along late in their marriage, before Mom hit forty-two. I'm amazed Rodgers and Hart means diddly to *you*, though."

"In college, I was in the chorus of a student production of *Pal Joey*." She asked what, if anything other than tourism, had brought him to Germany.

Business, he explained. He sold pharmaceuticals stateside and occasionally had to visit overseas drug firms specializing in research and development. He spoke no French, no Italian, no Swedish, and only a very little Spanish and German, but could generally rely on European business executives to bail him out with the rudimentary English they'd learned in their countries' secondary schools. And some spoke English very well. Still, it was often a hassle to get around by pointing, smiling, or tapping the guidebook phrases necessary to secure comfort, even survival, on a sight-seeing trip. He'd come to Rothenburg, his business concluded, to improve his German (so far, a failure) and to absorb the medieval ambience (so far, given the museum's period grotesquery, a success).

"I love hiking through the works of this neurotic Bavarian cuckoo clock of a village. And you?"

"I came south to get warm," clutching her shoulders.

"Surely you don't feel cold today?"

"Always. Everywhere."

Rodgers believed her, felt for her.

"But Kiel, on Kieler Bucht, on the ice-clotted Baltic, the Germans call it the East Sea: that town kept me frozen for nine hellish months. I rocketed out of there as soon as the spring session ended, to thaw my wits and give birth to my old peachy self. Even here in Bavaria, though, I'll catch a whiff of the arctic and shiver . . ."

"Let me get you that beer."

Gisela shrugged, smiled, put her arm through his and asked him to escort her to the floor where they could see a display of metal Shame Masks. They could walk to a pub as soon as they'd visited this exhibit. Rodgers, who'd had almost enough of the crime museum, acquiesced, and they soon stood, Gisela tapping a finger on her breastbone, in front of the sadistic, and funny, helmets in which Rothenburg's burghers had confined the heads of gossips, snitches, buffoons, kibitzers, and other nonviolent reprobates.

"Do you see, Gilbert Sullivan, how the wily Teutons strove to make the punishment fit the crime?"

"Ma'am?"

"The masks for busybodies have big ears; those for gossips, long curly tongues."

"Clever."

"Gluttons got to wear the heads of pigs."

"I don't see a mask for the hypocritically pious."

Gisela regarded him sidelong. "What would you suggest?"

"A halo with inward-pointing spikes. An upside-down miter of the heaviest marble available."

"You're talking headgear, not masks—that's another display case." Locking on his eyes: "What made you think of those?"

"Just trying to fit a crime—annoying piety—to a dead-on punishment. With your brains, you could come up with something a lot more clever."

"What would *you* design for a really sneaky flatterer?"

Rodgers cogitated. "A sculpted tin bum, with a long pointy nose going tip-first into the crack."

An inscrutable stoneface. "Oh, *that* would become you."

"Depending on who posed for the cheeks, for once in my life I might enjoy shaving."

The stoneface shivered, split. Despite herself, Gisela laughed—a guffaw that turned a dozen or more people around. Rodgers touched a hand to his forelock, to salute each onlooker in turn, and, gratifyingly, Gisela guffawed again.

In a touristy café inside the old city, they had a beer; two. The hops lubricated Gisela-sort-of-rhymes-with-*feasible*; Rodgers began to think that he might feasibly maneuver her SON*RISE tee over her head and her hiking shorts down at least to her ankles—*not* here among the guzzlers, camera-bandoliered Japs, and Scandinavian bluehairs, but, if he could get her to travel with him, somewhere on the road, among the trees, in the timbered shade of a pension hideaway, or upright beneath the stars with the whole continent revolving under them like a vast lazy- Susan of duchies and principalities, the night smelling of sunflower stalks and dairy-cow manure.

Suddenly she said, "I can see it in your eyes, even with a muzzy two-beer glaze on them."

Taken aback: "See what?" He already knew.

"Lust, Rodgers Hart. Ravenous manipulative lust. It shows even in your blue-veined eyelids."

"Sorry." He leaned back, truly sorry, but whether for his leer or for her catching him out in it he couldn't say, except that he could. "Don't you ever lust, Gisela?"

A hand to her breast, four fingers caging Jesus's head: *"Moi?* Empedestaled womanhood? Me, lust?"

"Well?"

"Not if I think on other things. If I don't, then, yes, I guess you could say I get an itch."

"An itch?"

"Worse than that, sometimes. Or better. A moist fever."

Rodgers liked that. "What do you do for it?"

"Wait. Divert my focus. Pray."

"Cold showers? Saunas? Self-flagellation with evergreen fronds?"

"Every shower in Kiel'll freeze you. I loathe saunas. And whipping strikes me—pun intended, I guess—as the sickest sort of, of solipsistic masochism."

Solipsistic masochism: two polysyllables in a row. Rodgers chewed on them. Then: "Maybe you'd like it better if somebody else did it for you?"

"You know, Mr. *Hart*, I don't think you have one," slugging back all that remained in her pilsner glass, wiping her plummy mouth. "I'm not sure I like you much."

"No sympathy for guys who poke you twice before you've had a proper introduction?"

"For scoffers."

"For truth-speakers who admit that lust exists and that it ain't necessarily the Devil's work?" He made himself shut up. He would lose her if he said too much. Did he care? My God, he did. Gisela could stand toe-to-toe with him, yet he had the sense that if he stayed tactfully after her, feinting, jabbing, he could win the bout—on a decision, if not a knockout.

"Rodgers," Gisela squinting, "you have no heart."

"Hey, we've known each other less than an hour, am I right, and already I *care* about you."

"How lucky I am to've won the regard of a horny nihilist! The part of me you care about you want around a lowdown part of yourself, after which you'd cut and run. The heart is *not* the part you lead with, Mr. Rodgers."

Rodgers had a pair of cuticle scissors in his fanny pack. He produced them and used them to cut a heart out of the café's laminated menu. Finished, he gave it to Gisela. Then stood, put a hand over his, yes, his *heart*, and crooned:

> *My prudish valen-tine,*
> *Scared, screwed-up valen-tine,*
> *You make me squirm, with your qualms.*
> *Your bones are jump-able,*
> *So ve-ry hump-able:*
> *Please let me kne-e-e-ad them, with my palms.*
> *Is your life unhiply chaste?*
> *Do you fear to grab a taste?*
> *When you con-tem-plate the waste,*
> *Are you ca-a-alm?*
> *Don't wear the veil for me,*
> *No sack-cloth sail for me—*
> *Bite, hungry valen-tine, bite!*
> *Each night is, Valen-tine's Ni-i-i-ight!*

Everyone in the joint gaped at Rodgers as if a clockwork nightingale had just erupted from his larynx.

"You," Gisela vehemently accusing, "made that up."

"Of course I made it up." Rodgers bowed, sat back down before somebody gave him the heave-ho. (No one had applauded, as they would've in the movies, but nobody'd tossed him out on his can, either.) "Didn't you like it?"

"I meant, you didn't make it up *just now.*"

"Never claimed to've."

"Then you didn't sing it to me off the top of your head, and you can't claim the virtue of utter spontaneity."

"The spontaneity came in standing up and singing it to you in front of all these—" gesturing "—clueless foreigners. Don't I get any points for that?"

"For a vulgar Rodgers and Hart knockoff?"

"I call it clever, not vulgar. Don't I get points for inventiveness? For balls?"

Gisela leaned back, chin on the puncture-freckle that the tip of Rodgers's pen had left on her throat. "Well, sure," she said. "A few."

That night they stayed in a pension in the nearby hamlet of Insingen, a postcard enclave of salmon-colored houses with red-tiled roofs. They slept in the same room, but not in the same bed, under puffy lavender-and-ivory-striped bolsters that felt at once billowy and crinkly. (It was too hot to fret the lack of other cover.) Frau Glocke, mistress of the pension, showed them how to tilt the room's windows out, how to use a canvas strap feeding through a wall bore to raise or lower the latticelike shades, and where to find the water-closet. Rodgers liked that she had taken Gisela and him for married; also, her disinclination to blather or pry.

Of course, Gisela had left Rothenburg with him only because he'd sung to her *in public*; or only because she'd knocked back three beers; or only because, after how many weeks on the road, she'd wearied of waking up, eating, and traveling alone. How many "only becauses" could he posit for her abandonment of her self-denying standards of propriety, of virtue? Maybe Gisela saw in him something . . . promising? attractive? worthy of redemption? (He'd had too much to do with gameplayers, innocents, even otherwise upright women who wanted to put him in jesses, to credit the concept.) Who knew what Gisela, drunk, saw in him other than company on the road, a half-open wallet, a potential conquest for God?

As she slept, she snored—no, not a snore: a whispery psalm of fatigue, maybe even trust, so that Rodgers saw her with more tenderness and less animal hunger than he could recall looking upon any other woman. He was probably deluding himself, filtering Gisela and his take on her through a flimsy metabolic seine of German sunlight and malt . . .

O Gisela. My feasible, squeezable Gisela.

On the end of his bed, looking at and listening to Gisela, Rodgers felt a presence—neither malignant nor benign, neither dreadful nor wholly reassuring—larger than the two of them; larger than both this pension and Insingen itself; larger than Bavaria, Deutschland, Europe, the hemisphere, the planet, the solar system. Et cetera.

Stupid, then, that as he studied Gisela and sensed this vague overwraith, his penis should nose its way out and stand in the twilight as if summoned. Stupid because Rodgers did not feel lust, but a sweet, unsettling awe. Gisela lay under her bolster, oblivious, as he appraised his rigidness. He would not make it slump by abusing it, though; at length, or at scant length, it fell back through his boxers' lips to nestle dispiritedly in his groin. His awareness of a transcendent presence, as real as a toothache, did *not* collapse—not even when he lay back and slept, both feet on the floor.

In the morning, Gisela woke him. She had already showered and tied a ribbon through her hair; heedless of his dishabille, she dragged him to the window to see a flock of black-and-white scissor-tailed birds (more like martins than any other species he could name, although here he hesitated to play Linnaeus) skylarking between the pension and the nearest house, diving like mosquito-hawks. Gisela oooohed and aaaahed as if watching fireworks. All Rodgers registered was a penetrating belly hunger and a similar emptiness in his anticipation of the day. This last surprised him.

"Didn't you sleep well?" picking up on his malaise. "You looked happily zonked a minute ago."

"We spent the night together, and *didn't* spend it together, if you know what I mean."

"Who'd know better?"

"We wasted a chance." Rodgers could not bring himself to tell her about his quasi-epiphany. "*Tempus fugit*, Gisela, and you literally don't give a fuck."

"Yesterday you did Lorenzo Hart. This morning it's AMWA, Andrew Marvell With Attitude." She left the window to stand before a wall calendar bearing the legend *Raiffeisenbank Wettringen — Insingen — Oestheim* and a color photo of a small stream with a church in the meadow beyond it. Then she turned to him, to sing in a delicate, whispery voice:

> My crabby valen-tine,
> Lewd, grabby valen-tine,
> You poison love, like an asp.
> Your mind is gutter-bound,
> A lurid battle-ground,
> So watch me glissade, through your grasp.
> Are you a thwarted Good Old Boy?
> Is your life de-void of joy?
> When I see straight through your ploys,
> Do you ga-a-asp?
> Please lose that glare for me,
> That come-on stare for me,
> Change, venal valen-tine—

"Knock it off, Gisela."

"*—change!*" she defiantly sang. Then, quietly: "Each day is heart-felt, and strange."

"Cripes. Help yourself to a Grammy."

"At least I composed mine in this shower this morning, not over the span of a dozen grubby seductions."

"Take a star in heaven along with your Grammy."

"I'm more than this body, Rodgers. Even stones and metal have souls. How can *we* fail to have them?"

Along with fresh shorts, Gisela wore a light blue blouse with smocking at the bodice: no God-squad tee. Today, she intended to witness via lecture, not billboard. Her argument would probably run forever if he replied.

They ate in a tiny room off Frau Glocke's kitchen: yogurt, boiled eggs, ham, apple juice, butter, et cetera. Silence, save for the purrs of a huge tabby on an upholstered chair.

Rodgers raised his spoon over the orange-tinted crater of his egg. "Why'd you say metal has a soul? *Metal?* Jeez, that one came all the way from the Land of Mu."

Gisela brightened, not, he suspected, because he had broken the purr-scored silence, but because she thought his question a good one. And she had planted its seed.

"Do you know *A Christmas Carol*?"

"By Dickens? Everyone knows *A Christmas Carol*." (Although here in mid-August not many folks in Bavaria had Scrooge or Bob Cratchet on their minds.)

"Do you remember the first scene in which a ghost appears?"

"The ghost of Christmas Past?"

"No. Marley's ghost enters first, to tell Scrooge of the coming of the three Christmas spirits."

"So?"

"Marley comes wrapped in—surrounded by—*chains*. Those chains tells us that metal wrought to a specific purpose has a spiritual dimension. How else could Marley have carried them with him from the Other Side?"

How did a rational person reply to such tommyrot?

Rodgers ate a spoonful of egg. Gisela smiled as if she had just kicked the decisive shot past his bamboozled goalie.

"*A Christmas Carol* is a *story*, Gisela; *only a story*."

She shrugged, and stopped smiling. "Everything's a story, Rodgers. Everything."

Rodgers slowly crosses the Hauptbahnstrasse to the Hotel Hilleprandt, his suitcase seeming to contain bricks or forged chain links. He rings the side-door buzzer, next to a movie theater showing the "Sommerhit" *To Die For*, which he registers in English even though the posters on the alley wall proclaim it in German. The buzzer sounds, echoing, in the bowels of the locked hotel, but also in the little house behind it.

Seven years ago, he recalls, the film playing next door was *The Adventures of Baron Munchausen*, and the owner spoke to him through the speaker unit, switching to thick Prussian-flavored English when he realized he had an American on the hook—during which transaction, Gisela hovered in the Bahnhof giftshop, not wanting to play the Mrs. Hart role again, but hoping to sneak in after Rodgers once darkness fell.

Because a short in the speaker lopped whole phrases from their conversation, Christoph Hilleprandt, the owner, emerged from the house in back to negotiate face to face: 42 DMs for a single, with breakfast and an in-room shower included. Rodgers accepted, held out his hand for a key.

Hilleprandt, a friendly badger of a man, commenced to talk about a recent U.S. Supreme Court ruling allowing flag-burning as a social protest. How did this happen? Americans loved their flag more than the citizens of any other country loved theirs. A German, on the other hand, could not even raise his flag in most circumstances because of leftover qualms about runaway nationalism, und a fear of offending the veak. Vould President Bush push for a constitutional amendment outlawing flag-burning? Hilleprandt hoped so. He admired Americans' patriotism and, to prove it, waved a small imaginary flag.

"U.S.A., U.S.A., U.S.A.," he said amiably.

"Ja, ja," Rodgers said loudly, unconsciously imitating the man. "You haff zpoken a vel-kum troot."

"Americans haff mo-rality. Americans haff mo-rality de vay Germans *vunce* did, you know."

"Ja, ja," Rodgers said. "I know, I know."

"Americans do not trow avay *aul* der cloats to bade in de sea. Dey vurship Gott. 'Vun nay-shun, unter Gott' goes de pledge dey make, ja? Dey fights fur utter peoples, peoples veaker dan dey, peoples hongry und oppresst."

Rodgers, still hoping to make it into the hotel, ja-ja'd Hilleprandt's flattering pro-Americanism, nodding agreement but seeking escape. Their discussion merely got longer, stretching like well-chewed gum.

Gisela manifested. She spoke German, introduced herself as Frau Hart, explained how tired she and Rodgers were; in short, won Hilleprandt over and rescued her "husband." Hilleprandt gave them keys and apologized garrulously for his garrulity. He liked to talk, he liked Americans, and talking to Americans was a blissful conjoining of pleasures. With some difficulty, but with courteous resolution, he salaamed them a good day and retreated back to his house.

Rodgers kissed Gisela on the cheek, husband to wife.

"Thanks, gal. Clever going. I don't even begrudge the extra forty-two marks a night it'll cost."

At the door where Hilleprandt had ambushed and detained him, Rodgers recalls that Gisela shook her head and lost all color, as if someone had pulled a plug on her heel and drained the melanin from her flesh. But she climbed the stairs behind him, and they spent four nights in Detmold, a somewhat ordinary town near the Teutoburger Wald, even if for many centuries the capital of the former principality of Lippe.

Today Rodgers, suitcase aside, feels stripped, as nude as a new-hatched cowbird. Why has he come? He can hardly expect Christoph Hilleprandt to jump for joy, much less wax eloquent again over the patriotism and/or altruistic unselfishness of Americans. In fact, Rodgers identifies with the instigator of the "Lippische Shutze," the hapless bumbling local, who, in a moldy old conflict with the French, set out to scout the enemy and their revetments and triggered, literally, a fusillade that strewed him in scarlet collops across the "battlefield." Even as he presses the buzzer, Rodgers fears that he has activated a Lippische Shutze of his own . . .

A female voice asks in German what he wants.

"Ein Zimmer," leaning into the speaker, again doubting his own sanity. "Do you still have rooms?"

The woman switches to English: "Of course. One?"

"Yes, ma'am, one. On the third floor, a room overlooking Herr Hilleprandt's house."

"I must check to see if someone has already that room."

Even if no one does, Rodgers knows that the owner will deny it to him. If the owner sees him.

"Could I talk to Herr Hilleprandt?" he asks, thinking to flee if the woman says yes.

"If you mean Christoph," the woman says, "no, you cannot. Three years ago he died."

"Forgive me. I'm sorry."

"Did *you* give him his zick heart? Did *you* make him drink seven whisky-and-zodas a day?"

"I'm sure I didn't."

"Then you have nothing to zay zorry *about*."

A kind but erronious assumption, Rodgers thinks. He stays quiet. Later, Bruni Hilleprandt, Christoph's daughter, comes out and gives Rodgers the key to the room that he and Gisela shared that summer before the wall came down . . .

After posing with Frau Glocke for a photograph in front of a totem-pole-like sign declaring "Ferien auf dem 'Bruhlhof'" ("Vacation on the 'Farm'"), Rodgers and Gisela left Insingen and hitchhiked down the Romantische Strasse to Dinkelsbuhl, Nordlingen, and, with great good luck, given the distance, into the Bavarian Alps with a young opera-bawling truck driver, who dropped them in the resort town of Fussen.

In Fussen, they spent the night in a second-floor room of the Hotel Sonne. They spent it chastely, although on Gisela's rather than Rodgers's insistence, and the next morning visited King Ludwig II's Neuschwanstein Castle. Over subsequent days, mildly kvetching, playing creatively light-hearted games of look-how-much-more-thoughtful-of-you-I-am-than-you-are-of-me and gotcher-goat-again-didn't-I?, they contrived to see Munich (although they stayed in a smoky Gasthaus in Furstenfeldbruck and bounced the rails into the city); the concentration camp at Dachau; Ingolstadt; and Bamberg, where they took a boat ride on the Regnitz and ate some shamefully bad Mexican food.

Rodgers had feared that Dachau would spell the end for them; that the bare graveled expanse of the compound, and the ovens (even if allegedly unused at this camp), and the stylized Picassoesque agony of the figures in the wrought-iron sculpture memorializing the victims of Nazi persecution—that all these sights would deform, even sever, their relationship, especially since one hostile question agitated like a Wobbly to burst from his lips: *Tell me, gal, how could God inflict such cruelty on his peoples?"* But he refrained from posing it, and neither of them said much of anything, rain falling lightly as they walked from the camp museum past the foundations of the razed barracks to the mute chapels at the compound's far end. Silence—tacit complicity in the need to clamp their tongues—spared them the petty trauma of a breakup.

Later, in a guesthouse in Tutschengereuth, west of Bamberg, they set aside their memories of Dachau; the return of the sun and their nearness to a myriad sunflowers buoyed them. These yellow clock-faces reflected back the brightness so that Rodgers half believed the ambient fields a vast disco, their sunflowers shucking and rattling in the stir of passing vehicles.

After a night of live jazz in Ingolstadt, a lazy drift past flower-festooned balconies in Bamberg, and their discovery of these sun-flowers, life had reasserted its primacy, and Rodgers had hopes again: Gisela, too, he believed.

"Detmold." Rodgers tapped a Europcar map they had filched from one of their rides between Eichstatt and Weissenburg.

"Of all the beautiful and historic cities in Germany, you want to go to *Detmold?"*

"Sure. Why not?" Rodgers said, innocently baffled.

"It's like a Parisian crossing the Atlantic to see Peoria."

"Peoria's okay, and Detmold's near the Teutoburger Wald. It has this fifty-meter-tall statue of Arminius, the Cherusci chief who whupped up on the Romans. We can go biking."

Gisela let him persuade her. She also let Rodgers buy her a navy-blue tee with a quilted sunflower on it and slipped away to put the shirt on. As they left the guesthouse, the smiling owner bade them Godspeed.

They hiked. Before reaching the highway to Schweinfurt, though, Rodgers detected a change in Gisela's behavior. So far never a tease or a coquette, she took his hand. Tingling from fingertips to cock, he

walked with her past another sprawling sunflower field. She tugged
at him. He yielded. Gisela stopped, let him bump her, took his ear-
lobe into her mouth and sucked on it until Rodgers, seeing no other
soul around, tried to kiss her. She skipped away, glancing back occasionally like a soft-porn wanton.

"What gives?" Rodgers called.

"Maybe *I* do."

"For God's sake, Gisela!"

She returned, took his hand again, led him down an access row
to a sunflower glade where no one from the highway could see
them, then bestowed on him the kiss that a moment ago she had
denied. The kiss deepened and protracted.

"And for mine," smearing her lips away, warming the inside of
his ear.

"If this is double-dealing jive . . ."

She unbuckled his shorts, yanked his shirt up and over his chest,
asked him to strip completely. He figured she wanted him naked so
that she could grab his clothes, beat a scornful retreat, and mock
him up and down the Steigerwald, maybe all of Germany. He
grabbed his belt, thrust his shirt back down.

"I mean this," Gisela said. "Let me show you." She freed him, the
eager part of him that he'd begun to think a traitor, and used her
mouth, at first clumsily but then with an evolving getting-into-it
earnestness, to show him.

When, gripping her shoulders, he climaxed, she recoiled, turning
her head to spit and scour away with a finger the salt heat of his
seed. This experience—Gisela had to regard it as literally distasteful
and hugely degrading—would surely put an end to her out-of-
character limit-testing. Rodgers fought to rearrange himself and zip
back up.

"Don't," he heard Gisela say. She had mastered her disgust and
pivoted back toward him. Her face shone with a combination of
bewilderment and triumph. "Didn't that tell you something? Didn't
it prove my . . . ?"

Her voice trailed off. Rodgers had no idea what word she'd
meant. Not *love*, evidently.

"Please," touching his flank, "I want to see you naked."

Apparently she did. And she had already proved . . . well, the
unlikeliness of her stealing his clothes and abandoning him out
here like a rut-driven bumpkin. Uneasy in spite of his lust—isn't
this what he'd wanted ever since jabbing her with his pen in the
crime museum?—he dropped his backpack, skinned out of his
shirt, slid down his boxers along with his shorts, and, still partly
erect, stepped clear of the pile.

Gisela stood, walked away a few feet, and faced him again, her pupils dilating visibly even in the sunlight. "Get rid of your sandals, too."

He resisted the impulse to cover his crotch with his hands, and, balancing first on one foot and then the other, removed his sandals. *Now* would she dive for his clothes and bolt?

"Lie down. On your back."

"Give me something in trade, Gisela."

"I thought I'd already done that."

"You've taken whatever's going on here to a new level."

She considered this, then stepped out of her hiking shorts and underwear as he had done. Rodgers, gratified, knelt, put his hands on the earth, and stretched out on his back, the sun spotlighting him mercilessly.

Gisela went to Rodgers, straddled his waist, smoothed his hair, and kissed him, shallowly then tenderly then greedily, each kiss at once a taste and a repast. He responded. If she shot or stabbed him now, like an Islamic martyr he would soar straight to Paradise. Entering her, he had already entered it, and now she was touring him around.

"Take off your shirt," he begged into the hollow of her throat. "Gisela . . ."

"*No,*" not unkindly, not belligerently, attending wholly to Rodgers and the rhythms of their union. He did not mind her "no" because, when she reared above him, the tee's quilted sunflower radiated down almost as gaudily as the sun itself, but more hypnotically. He came, fell back, and knew, as he slipped out and away, that their interlude had ended. Gisela kissed him on the nose, softly. "Again," she said.

"I'm sexed out. It'll take me an hour or so to get back, maybe more. Sorry."

She smiled down, accepting him and not yet rejecting herself . . .

Rodgers climbs the stairs of the Hotel Hilleprandt. Each floor—there are only three above the first—has a landing with locked French doors that open into a shallow alcove from which three rooms debouch. On the stairward side of each landing, two more rooms face each other before the French doors, so that Herr Hilleprandt's successors—maybe Bruni runs the whole show now—have only seventeen units total, the ground level offering only two more rooms because the kitchen and dining area take up so much of its plan.

Why this obsession with layout? Rodgers, climbing, knows that he focuses on physical aspects to avoid thinking about either Gisela or his obscure purpose in returning. He can't. On the top floor, the fourth or the third depending on whether you count as a European

or an American, he unlocks the door to the left of the French doors
and bangs his way in. Chifforobe, bed, chest-of-drawers, portable
TV, and a strip of a bathroom overlooking the old theater . . .

He turns around and sees Gisela sitting on the bed. Not a ghost:
a memory-image. She wears the navy sunflower tee that she wore
hitchhiking from Tutschengereuth to Detmold; that she insisted on
wearing in that sunflower cove. Once upstairs from their powwow
with Hilleprandt, Gisela sat where this image sits and chastised him
for making fun of the poor man.

"Making fun of him?" Rodgers says the words he said then.

You took on his accent and inflections, Gisela says. You mocked
him shamefully.

"No. I couldn't have."

Yes. How often do you ordinarily say, *Ja, Ja,* or, *You haff zpoken a
vel-kum troot*?

"Cripes, I did say those things, didn't I?"

Loudly. As if you didn't think he'd understand unless you
shouted.

"Incredible. That's how fools talk to deaf people."

I heard you even in the Bahnhof. A good thing. You might still
be out there if I hadn't come over.

"I just wanted to get on his wavelength."

He probably thinks you took him for an idiot. He's not, you
know.

"'U.S.A., U.S.A., U.S.A.,' waving a make-believe flag."

That doesn't prove he's an idiot, only that he truly wanted to
make you feel welcome.

"Vel-kum."

You self-involved asshole! Gisela's memory-image bites her lip,
melts like sun-chased fog.

Rodgers understands that, then and now, her anger over his ludicrous impersonation of Hilleprandt had less to do with her compas-
sion for the owner and her disgust with him than with her
ambivalence about their sunflower-field carnality. She began it, she
enjoyed it, and now (then) she was second-guessing both her out-
of-character debauch and her delight in it. And her concern for
Hilleprandt? A red herring. (Given his bulk and pro-Americanism,
call it a tricolored flounder.)

With the departure of Gisela's memory-image the room seems
very empty. Rodgers sets his suitcase down—he has held it, a har-
rowing drag on his shoulder socket, ever since entering—and lists
toward the watercloset, not to urinate but to examine the shower
stall.

There. There it is. He opens its door and leans in. The spigot drips,
but a mildewed rubber mat pretty much absorbs the potential noise

from every drop. Rodgers checks the stall for Gisela spoor. Some reddish brown flecks on the tiles at ankle height could qualify, but the odds actually favor their turning out to be either mud or cockroach shit. He leans back out, shuts the pebble-glass door, clings to it in rue and nausea.

At first she clung to him, frolicked at his side. No one stopped to pick them up. Out of a piece of shirtboard from his backpack and a grease pencil, he made a sign reading DETMOLD!!! and flashed it at every vehicle whooshing past. He told her that if *she* held it out their chances of catching a ride would improve big-time. She held it out.

A long-faced hipster with short gray hair in a dilapidated Bentley approached. This auto had its steering wheel on the right side, in British fashion, so that when he pulled to the shoulder and said, "Get in"—in English, yet—they could speak to him without circling the bonnet. In fact, he flung open the right rear door for them. Gisela scooted in, Rodgers behind her, and off the Bentley leapt, Rodgers growing more and more antsy as, on one strip of two-lane, the graying hipster passed three farm vehicles even though he had to lean across his seat to look for oncoming traffic while steering with his right hand and making farty lip noises. Gisela ignored both his driving and the crude mouth music.

"And you kids are?" cutting in ahead of an onrushing truck whose horn dopplered away scarily.

Rodgers introduced Gisela and himself.

"Love your names, just as I love to see young people get together." He hummed "The Lady Is a Tramp," only a very small improvement over his bogus flatulence.

"And *your* name?" Rodgers leaning forward.

"Call me Ian Scuffling."

Rodgers noted the form of this reply and called him nothing at all. "You going to Detmold?"

"If you kids want, me'n this baby'll take you there."

Gisela seized Rodgers's arm, endured Scuffling's humming, watched the passing landscape. Then she looked at or through Rodgers and said, "'Is this a dagger which I see before me, / The handle toward my hand?'"

"What?"

"More proof. More proof that metal has soul."

"Another damn story, Gisela. Besides, it's 'A dagger of the mind.' Macbeth confesses as much."

"Can you trust Macbeth?" the hipster asked, then resumed humming "The Lady Is a Tramp." But he got them back to the highway and drove them madly up it to Fulda and Kassel and then up another highway to Bad Herrcutt and the Paderborn crossover to Horn and Detmold.

"Where to, kids?"

"The Hauptbahnhoff," for Rodgers had read in a guide of the hotels across from it.

Scuffling wheeled them through Detmold to the train depot, where they climbed out, told him good-bye, and stood watching as a pack of female riders in helmets and colorful cycling gear went pedaling by in an exhilarating eggbeater blur. Rodgers admired their energy, their style, their legginess.

In the hotel room, after the argument about his "mocking" Hilleprandt, he promised to apologize as soon as he could and never to commit such apery again. Gisela, her skin as white as candle wax, kissed Rodgers on the nose, begrudgingly forgiving him, then rolled over and drew her knees up to her chest.

"Don't go back to a guilt-driven celibacy, Gisela. You've already walked through that door."

Like a roly-poly, she made herself smaller, tighter, harder to uncoil. Rodgers, despite never having known this tactic to work before, stripped naked—the second time that day—and went around the bed so that Gisela could see him.

"Open your eyes," he coaxed. "Open 'em now, Gisela."

She opened her eyes and looked at him. Then reached out and pulled him to her by the warm ready-to-hold piton that he had provided. This time their climb lasted strenuous minutes, maybe as many as sixty, and Rodgers had the sense that Gisela, her lip-bitten silence aside, attained several modest summits in a row before he let go and they kicked down in a scalding avalanche. At the bottom, they rested entangled all night.

In the morning, they rented bicycles at a shop called Zweirad-Neuwohner on Krummestrasse: two Alassio Herculeses with wrapped handlebars and carryracks on their rear fenders. They biked to the Hermanns Denkmal, the towering statue of Arminius, and picnicked. The next day they rode to Adlerwarte Berlebeck and saw the eagles fly; and returned to visit the Westfalisches Freilichtmuseum, striding like modest Gullivers through quaint mockups of dozens of area villages. On their third full day, they mounted a morning shopping trip to Lemgo, where they ate at a McDonald's knockoff on a cobblestone thoroughfare clogged with foot traffic.

That evening, Gisela refused him, and he took the refusal as evidence of her weariness, not as a reversion to puritanical guilt. He shrugged and went out onto the landing to smoke a clandestine cigarette and to consider again how he wanted this dalliance, or romance, or accidental divertimento, to evolve. *If* he wanted it to evolve.

His business for Lindroth Pharmaceuticals had concluded nearly

two weeks ago, and he couldn't expect to sustain this make-do vacation—Germans always said "holiday"—much beyond the weekend.
If Gisela had agreed to sneak into the hotel every night, and to let
him smuggle breakfast items upstairs to her from the continental
smorgasbord, he would have saved enough to prolong the adventure
a little, but his fiancée in San Diego, State Senator and Mrs. Joaquin
Zabala's daughter Reina, had probably long since started puzzling
about the length of this trip and his infrequent calls . . .

Rodgers heard a cuffing—a bumping—a faint ratcheting—in the
stairwell and stood. Someone cursed. The curse echoed. Rodgers
went down the stairs two at a time and intercepted the imprecator
between the second and third floors, a young woman whom he
recognized as Ilse Obexer, one of seven female cyclists sharing
rooms in the Hilleprandt. He and Gisela had met them at breakfasts
downstairs; had even run into them out and about during excur-
sions. Fraulein Obexer had eyed Rodgers openly, lecherously, so
that once Gisela had even unjustly rebuked him for "encouraging
the flooze."

Lean in white-and-burgundy cycling clothes, Ilse braced her
machine in the landing's crook. "Usually, I can do this," she lamented
in English, "but tonight—" tossing her helmeted head as if she wanted
amber tresses to fly out from under it; they didn't, but Rodgers could
still see them, curled wetly about her ears, stuck to her tawny nape
with the sequined mucilage of her sweat.

"Don't you have a cable? There's a rack outside you could padlock your bike to."

"I *bought* this machine. I like it safely in my room."

"All right. Let me help." Rodgers helped her wrestle the bicycle—
an expensive one, much nicer than the old Alassios he and Gisela
had rented—to her third-floor lodgings, which this evening, owing
to her roommate's decision to spend the night in Bielefeld, she had
all to herself. Rodgers nodded, carried the bicycle into her room,
and did not come out again for another two hours.

Gisela stirred when he returned, but just that. Relieved, he fell
asleep and slept hard. In the morning he awoke to find Gisela straddling him, as in the sunflower field, but now with a different intent.
She had lifted his hand to her nostrils; finger by finger, she sniffed
it, rotating it, inhaling and surmising. She saw him watching her
but did not stop. When he tried to yank his hand away, she tightened her grip and flung it aside herself. Then she bent to his neck,
face, and hair and subjected each in turn to the same nosy scrutiny.
He knew that she knew, and a cavity opened within him, a pit into
which fear and a bilious cold joy poured.

"You—" she began.

"Gisela, I love you."

"You love it when I sin with you. Get out. Out of this bed. Out of this room."

"And go where?"

"To your slut. To Rothenburg-ob-der-Tauber. To hell!"

With puzzled annoyance, Ilse Obexer opened her door. With a kind of sour exultation, she let him in. He stayed with her the rest of that night and went boldly with her to breakfast in the dining room. Gisela did not appear. Other guests glanced occasionally at Rodgers and Ilse with mild—very mild, perhaps even ceremonious—disapproval.

Later that afternoon, finally uneasy, Rodgers went upstairs to try to entice Gisela out to dinner with him. He heard water drumming in the shower stall, clattering in ill-piped bursts. He used his key, let himself in, and found her at the bottom of the stall, an inch of crimson water lapping her porcelain-white feet, legs, and haunches.

Those fast-acting coagulants of hers didn't work this time, he thought helplessly.

"My God!" he cried aloud. *"Gisela!"*

Eventually, Christoph Hilleprandt, the police, and three suit-wearing Detmolders trudged upstairs to appraise the scene and to declare the death a suicide.

Rodgers perches on the bed where Gisela's memory-image sat, but she does not remanifest, either in that cognitive guise or as honest-to-God ghost. Why, after seven years, has he come back? What does he want to happen? He still can't say yet, but sometimes, in the midst of drought or barren wasteland, one feels summoned, and it seems to him that Detmold, the Peoria of Nordrhein-Westfalen, has summoned him: Detmold, or this hotel, or the dead Gisela—

We all get off on torture, she'd hinted once. *Even torturing ourselves . . .*

He hears noise in the Bahnhofstrasse, in Sedanstrasse, in Hermannstrasse, even over on Paulinstrasse, the town's foremost vehicle-friendly thoroughfare. A parade? He can't see the Bahnhof from this back-corner room, but, in the bathroom, with the window canted out, he can see a series of furniture-bearing floats moving toward town, bands of uniformed high-school kids among these floats, and some men in schmaltzy lederhosen and peaked caps herding sheep or pigs. Drummers rap out a cadence on the edges of their snares, children run beside the surging animals, teams of colorful cyclists glide past the bands, and rock music grinds from speakers somewhere in the heart of the city, probably the pedestrian Schlossplatz.

A festival or fair, Rodgers decides. Maybe a Fasching or carnival? An ale tasting? A Beidermeier potlatch, during which people heap up and set fire to rocking chairs, bookcases, coffee tables, and other flawed pieces from their furniture makers. A local variant of Cuxhaven's annual Shweinheldfest? Who knows?

Rodgers returns to bed, assumes the lotus position atop it. The noise outside does not abate, but he has seen all of this festival he cares to. It will probably interfere with his discovery of whatever Gisela wants him to discover. Twilight gathers and deepens, but this dissonant parade—or carnival—or potlatch—or footloose wassail—or movable and fulsomely moving Teutonic feast—continues to crash and ramble until dark. Then Rodgers hears the revelry, foot traffic, and competing music styles at a distance, filtered through cobblestone alleys, curbside trees, the outstretched arms and gaping mouths of bibblers and carousers.

Then, from the asphalt lot between the hotel and the house out back, a commotion—below and quite near.

Clattery shoes, excited human cries, mewling bleats.

Rodgers resents these sounds, which penetrate his trance and prod him off the bed, over to the back window, through whose blinds, peering down, he sees a young goat, a frightened kid, flee-ing several casque-wearing men wielding sticks, metal pipes, billy-clubs.

The kid, finding itself in a cramped blind, brakes, turns, and gal-lops toward a hole in its pursuers' line. They close ranks. The kid skids, scrambles, regains its feet, and, after backing away a few steps, trots forward to head-butt one of the men in leather jerkins and visored helms.

Security lights at the house corners illuminate the show, an expressionist set at the bottom of a night-filled reservoir, so that when the butted man stumbles and his companions swing their weapons in his defense, Rodgers not only hears but sees the result, the sickening Technicolor bludgeoning of the goat, which staggers back like a clueless club fighter and rolls onto its flank, its legs stick-ing out and then folding like a broken poker table's.

The men, still bashing it, hurrah.

Christ, says Rodgers, turning aside, realizing as he does that he has witnessed—either by chance or at somebody's glib instigation—an enacted parable.

Pfau.

The obviousness of the symbolism disgusts him. Did they have to *kill* that poor bleating kid? Do these jolly folks have no shame?

When he returns to the window later, the men have dragged the goat corpse out of the lot and faded into the merrymaking near the Schlossplatz. Rodgers can still see urine and blood across the asphalt, though—in fantails and smears—along with a casque, three clubs, and a slick of spermy-looking vomit. He closes the slats and flings himself at his bed.

Darkness cradles him.

He awakens—has he slept?—to the complaints of the hotel's plumbing and the clattering of a shower. These noises issue from the bathroom. He sits up, deliciously aghast, almost smug in his growing fear. The watercocks in the showerstall creak, shutting off the flow. Pipes bang like shunted boxcars. A pebble-glass door glances off a wall of tile with a stinging *crack!* A naked foot touches down.

"Gisela?" Rodgers straining toward these sounds.

The bathroom door nudges outward, and Gisela comes around it, naked. At least he supposes that this apparition (*not* a memory-image; *not* the product of a drunken fantod) is Gisela, for although he recognizes her breasts, belly, and legs, this faintly luminous figure totters under a Shame Mask, a bearded goat's head, with oval slits for eyes and a long flat tongue of iron lolling like a scroll of its caught-out paramours. Gisela lists beneath this mask.

And girdling her, like an upside-down and oddly unfinished birdcage, a padlocked chastity belt. She can sidle in it, but it and her Shame Mask shimmer with a static pearlescence, like television snow.

Gisela gasps—even in her ghostliness, she hurts—and puts out her hand. Her fingers flicker between energy states, sometimes over Here, sometimes over There: where life goes *when* life goes. Rodgers, dining on his own fear, knows better than to take what she extends. Taking would disrupt his continuity, scrambling him out of Being. Gisela moans, seeking apology or some thrifty squalid acknowledgment.

Rodgers says, "*You* did this—tortured yourself to suicide."

Yessssss. She, asinine revenant, buys his rebuke; totters toward him another step.

"You *should* wear a Shame Mask, but *not* a goat's head for screwing your crabby valentine here."

Noooooo? sidling toward him like an arthritic dancer in a sleazy slow-motion ballet.

"No, Gisela. The swollen tin head of a pop-eyed fool. The mask of a cowardly self-killer."

Eazzzzz-y, Gisela slurring, *for you to saaay.*

"Stop. Stop right there!" Rodgers has no clue what she has planned, or if she can do anything at all, but how can he fear this iron-freighted grotesquerie, this ludicrous burlesque of both woman and ghost?

Gisela stops. He can see not only the bright lateral cuts on her wrists, but the punctures that he visited on her belly and throat with his pen, tiny points that healed within a week of their infliction.

"You're no ghost," Rodgers says, "but a lamial creature who for seven years has fed on my living memories of Detmold."

Aaaah. A sigh of acquiescence? Of bitter mockery?

"Tonight I exorcise you, Gisela. Tonight I send you to the naked zero out of which we all blundered and to which we should all happily go back." He lays an index finger across the other and lifts this sign to her as taunt and ward.

She breaks the padlock holding up the chastity belt, steps gracefully out of it. Then throws it. In passing Rodgers, one of its edges tears his shoulder. Gisela has no pity for him. She breaks off the Shame Mask's lolling tongue and cracks open the helm itself. She yanks her head from this monstrosity and flings it, too, at Rodgers, missing him as he rolls backward off the bed. When he scoots under it to the other side and reaches out to grip her wavery ankles, he grips . . . air, memory, the deceit of her manifestation.

Wet splotches discolor the floor, but Gisela has gone. He can find nothing but his cut to prove to anyone that she pelted him with soulful facsimiles of items from the Mittelalterliches Kriminalmuseum . . .

How could Rodgers possibly sleep? He paces. Hums snatches of Lorenzo Hart's "My Funny Valentine." Checks out the shower for Gisela spoor. Avoids lying down.

Probably he dreamt the episode, sustaining the cut on his shoulder tumbling from bed.

Morning comes tardily. Rodgers trips down the stairs to the landing between the third and second floors. Halts. Hears a cuffing—a bumping—a faint ratcheting—above him. Looks up to see Gisela, this time in biking gear, positioning her clumsy Alassio Hercules on the topmost stair so that she can ride it hard down upon him.

The hairs on Rodgers's nape lift in a tingling fan. Where can he go? Down. Quickly.

Gisela begins her descent before he does. Looking up, he sees a silver fender, the wrapped handlebars, a sprocket blur, Gisela's clear but not necessarily vengeful eyes, her bicycle a plunging mechanical warhorse.

Rodgers puts a hand to the wall, receives a spin-imparting blow, feels the bumpety-bumping Alassio career past him on the switchback, and, thus whirled, topples all the way to the next floor, finishing with a head crack that finishes everything but his last volitionless sprawl.

Gisela, meanwhile, continues to freewheel downward . . .

Johnny's So Long at the Fair

Nancy Kress

Every young man someday faces the problem of cutting his mother's apron strings, but as the compelling study of obsession and Unearthly Love that follows demonstrates, *some* of them may have a harder time doing this than *others* . . .

Born in Buffalo, New York, Nancy Kress now lives in Brockport, New York. She began selling her elegant and incisive stories in the mid-seventies, and has since become a frequent contributor to *Asimov's Science Fiction*, *The Magazine of Fantasy and Science Fiction*, *Omni*, and elsewhere. Her books include the novels *The Prince of Morning Bells*, *The Golden Grove*, *The White Pipes*, *An Alien Light*, and *Brain Rose*; the collection *Trinity and Other Stories*; the novel version of her Hugo and Nebula-winning story, *Beggars in Spain*; and a sequel, *Beggars and Choosers*. Her most recent books include a new collection, *The Aliens of Earth*, and a new novel, *Oaths and Miracles*. She has also won a Nebula Award for her story "Out of All Them Bright Stars."

JOHNNY'S SO LONG AT THE FAIR

Most people cannot bear very much truth.

My son disappears into the crowd beyond the fairground gates. He thinks I don't know where he goes, pushing his way through the giggling teenagers and stout farm wives, the slightly drunken over-weight suburbanites and their sticky-fingered children cranky with the long day. It is dusk. The fair lights come on, one attraction at a time, the roller coaster first. Then the midway, with its French-fry stands and beer tent and cheap games. And finally the Ferris wheel, a large revolving circle of blue bulbs, although not as large as it might be. This is not a very big fair. The one my son visited last week was much larger.

No lights come on in the exhibition halls. They have closed for the day.

My son heads for the Tunnel of Love. He has never had much imagination. But oh, how beautiful he is! Far more beautiful than his father, the lying son of a bitch. My son and I never speak of his father. There is no need. I have my son in the father's stead, and the gain is all mine. Tall, wide-shouldered, with the bluest eyes in all the world.

I have made sure of that.

He steps around a dropped ice cream cone, gives right of way to a smiling, weary family. Young women turn to look as he passes, the seats of their tight jeans shifting with their motion. My son never returns the looks. He makes for the Tunnel of Love with the single-mindedness of a tomcat in heat.

I follow more slowly. There's no hurry.

I always know where he goes.

She's behind me, someplace. I can feel it. It doesn't matter. Once I'm inside the fairground, there's never anything she can do.

It's the only place she doesn't control us.

I decide to try the Tunnel of Love. Last time Cathy was there. But the fair before that, I found her in a dark grove of trees behind the beer tent. I don't ever know where she'll be, or how strongly she'll be there. But I take what I can get, and I'll look for her all night if I have to.

Today at work, in the warehouse where my mother got me my job, I dreamed all day about Cathy. I didn't get much work done. But I'll catch up tomorrow and anyhow there's nobody to notice. I'm the only one in the warehouse, not counting the computerized forklifts and conveyor belts. I control them. I sit at my computer high above the warehouse floor where I can see everything. I don't ever see any other human beings.

My mother likes it that way.

Then quit the job, Cathy said to me, last fair. She doesn't understand. I can't quit. If I try to walk out of that building, the heaviness comes on me. If I try to write a letter quitting the company, the heaviness comes on me. If I try to stay in bed in the morning, and not go to work, I can't do it. My legs lift me from the bed. My arms dress me. The only time I can get free is just after sunset, and only if I go to a fairground. Any fairground. I take trains, buses, hitch rides. My mother follows me in her car. There isn't anything I can do about that.

Cathy doesn't understand. But she doesn't have to. She only has to be there.

I walk faster toward the Tunnel of Love.

My son stands in line to buy a ticket. Six people stand in front of him, and he fidgets with impatience. Another part of him is impatient, too. I can see it, even from this distance, the sweet masculine bulge.

His father was the same way. He could never get enough of me. And it was all natural, in the first years—that was the best part. I laid no compulsion on him. He *wanted* me, of himself, and when those blue, blue eyes darkened with sexual excitement, I was the happiest woman alive. I was. It was not my fault that it ended. Men are like that. They are insatiable for you for a while, and then they want someone else. For variety. He did what his nature led him to do, and so did I.

Children are different. Children cannot decide to unmake your motherhood. My son is mine forever.

I don't count this business of the fairgrounds. It's not important. A young man's fancy, a delusion. The girl is not real. My son is young. He needs his physical delusions, at least for now.

The man and woman in front of him in line step into their mechanical boat. It glides into the gaudily painted tunnel. My son steps alone into the next boat. The carnie running the ride gives him a funny look—alone in the Tunnel of Love?—but my son doesn't notice. He's too intent. The silly unseaworthy craft lurches forward in its four inches of dirty water and disappears into the tunnel.

I walk around to where the passengers will eventually exit the ride.

      *   *   *

Cathy?

I think it. There's no need for spoken speech between us. We always understand each other.

For a few minutes, nothing happens, and my gut tightens up. But then I *feel* her, on the wood boat seat beside me, in the dark. At first just her right hand, real light on my shoulder. Then her body, sweet and warm against my side.

Cathy!

Hello, Johnny.

She moves closer. I can smell her, that spicy Cathy-smell. She laughs a little, and I know she's as happy and excited as me. I put my arms around her and pull her close. Her hair, long and curly, brushes my cheek, exciting me more. I cup my hand around her breast.

We get so little time! The Tunnel of Love lasts only seven minutes, at most fairs. It's better when Cathy comes to me behind a beer tent, or by the dark fence where the midway trucks park. But I'll take her wherever, and whenever, she can come.

Her left hand moves to my belt. I can't stand it anymore. Eagerly, I help her undo the buckle.

While I wait for my son, I watch the people around me at the fair. Those that are here, and a few that are not.

A tired mother buying hot dogs for her two kids. She probably wants to go home, but if she gets them the hot dogs, she won't have to bother cooking dinner when she gets there. Striding past her is a carnie, carrying a toolbox. Some ride somewhere is malfunctioning. On the other side of the midway, four teenagers rush up to a balloon-pop, laughing about who will shoot at the balloons first. Then I see that there are only three teenagers. The other one isn't there. He shimmers faintly at the edges, but a better giveaway are his clothes: wide pants worn not with a baggy tee but with a narrow-collared, button-down shirt and saddle shoes. Fifties, maybe even forties. In all decades, people have died at fairgrounds. And fairgrounds are natural refuges for people on the edge of existence, including the existence of death. At fairgrounds, it's easy to linger halfway between illusion and reality.

I really should have remembered all that fifteen years ago, when my son's father died. If I had remembered, his death would not have happened at a fairground. But I was young myself, although not as young as my son is now. One must forgive the young their inexperience. So often they have no idea where their own best interests lie.

My son emerges from the Tunnel of Love, his belt still unbuck-led, his zipper slightly open. Tch, tch. A woman glances at him in disgust. My son doesn't notice; he starts to walk very fast down the midway, and disappears around the corner of the last booth, the Ring-A-Ding Toss.

I follow, remembering his father's blue eyes.

Cathy has to still be here, someplace! We only got six minutes together, maybe even just five . . . She *has* to still be here! My best bet is to walk the fence, and hope she's waiting for me someplace there in the dark.

I see my mother standing in the middle of the midway, and, for a minute, I'm really scared. She'll put the heaviness on my legs again, on my arms and my back, so that I can't move except in the way she wants me to . . . but no. Not at a fairground. It's the only place she can't put the heaviness on me, and then only if I get there just after sunset. I used to think that was because fairs are so much fun. So dif-ferent from her horrible world of getting up, going to work, coming home, eating dinner together, watching TV sitting close together on the sofa but not too close because after all she's my *mother*, night after night, the endless stupid boring shows I can't escape from because she puts the heaviness on me, so I have to sit there with her hand sometimes just fondling my hair or patting my thigh or stroking my shoulder like she owns it . . . Night after night . . .

I used to think she couldn't put the heaviness on me at a fair-ground because a fairground is fun and cool and easy and every-thing else she is not. So I'd go there whenever I could, to escape her, getting out of the house in the little time just after sunset. Then I found Cathy.

I swerve sharply off the midway, toward the fence, where it's dark and things are different and my mother can't follow too close. Where Cathy might be.

My son was the most beautiful infant in our town. Everyone said so. I was living naturally then, like the others. Why not? I was still pretty, my husband loved me, even though I was so much older than he, and I had the most wonderful baby imaginable.

But the baby was still nothing to what the man would become. Look at him, rushing off in the darkness like that! Look at his strong back, the movement of his narrow hips, the way his fists clench at his sides, as men do when they're angry or determined . . . and he is mine. I am his mother. I made his body in my own, and it is mine.

His father's hands clenched like that, hanging on to the sides of the falling Ferris wheel. Unreal things, Ferris wheels—or, more accurately, half real. The view is actual enough, and the swaying car. But the motion and the giddy sense of danger are unreal—on a Ferris wheel you are in fact going nowhere, only in circles. And there is no danger, ordinarily. You mustn't count the one-in-a-million accident, the inexplicable time when a heaviness comes on the machinery and it doesn't function right. My husband's hands clutched the side of the car and he cried out his single descending syllable: Noooooooooooo! But it wasn't his hands that I was after. It was his eyes, those blue blue eyes that had looked at another woman, who sat close beside him as he fell. I don't know if her hands clutched anything, or if she felt the unnatural slow heaviness of her fall. I didn't care about her. Only him, and his lying cheating blue blue eyes, that when he hit ground were pierced through by the twisted metal wreckage of the one car that had torn loose and fallen through the dusk.

It was a very high Ferris wheel.

But somehow that one act created another twist in the illusionary unreality that fairs always are, and so my son can come here, and do what he does. Or maybe it isn't that at all. Maybe it's genetic, as the scientists locked in their own strange reality tell us. He is, after all, my son.

Mine.

No man has touched me since his father died. No man ever will. I live only for my son, as devoted mothers always have.

I find Cathy clear at the far end of the fairground, where the rides and attractions and food stands run out. There's a fence to separate the butt-end of the midway from some other buildings. The buildings look out of place here: dark, solid, plain. Cathy leans against the fence, as solid herself as I've ever seen her, in her long blue dress and clumsy shoes. She holds out her arms and I rush into them.

Johnny! Oh, Johnny . . .

Her dress is real thin material, and it's cool out after sundown, but Cathy feels warm and soft. She always does, no matter what the weather. I kiss her, and kiss her again. Slowly we sink into the rough grass. I lift the blue dress, and she's solid beneath it, hardly shimmery at all, and when I slide into her she gives a little gasp and holds me tighter, and I don't see the grass or the midway or the dark low buildings or anything except her.

But later, lying close together on the ground, I can't stop looking at those buildings. And Cathy looks, too. She lies heavy in my arms.

What are they, Johnny? Those buildings?

I don't know.

Then she's heavier still; her weight almost crushes me. Or maybe it's my own weight. God, no, not here, *she* can't reach me here, not at *fairgrounds* . . .

A figure moves toward us from the midway.

At first I think it's my mother. But the figure is too big, too powerful. My mother is little, shrunken and battered and old . . . The figure is a man. Cathy shrieks and covers her naked thighs with her blue dress. The powerful man stands over us, quiet, and I see that he isn't looking at us at all, not even at Cathy. He's looking beyond us, at the dark buildings on the other side of the fence.

I make my way through the midway crowds and clutter, not hurrying. There's no point. The fair will close for the night soon enough, and everyone will be sent back where they belong, including my son. Meanwhile, I walk slowly—my back is bothering me again—toward the front gate, watching the whole sad spectacle make itself disappear.

The man in the French-fry stand empties his vat of grease on the ground, while his daughter wearily cleans and fills the catsup dispensers, thinning the catsup with water.

The girls from the strip-show straggle from the back of the tent, dressed for the first time tonight, but with thick makeup still caking their faces. Most are nearly middle-aged. None are very pretty.

The woman running Luck o' the Irish switches off the lights in her booth, turning her illegally weighted shamrocks from emerald to dull olive.

A carnie hurries past, carrying his toolbox. But this time I see him clearly, as I did not outside the Tunnel of Love. I see his dated haircut, his excited expression, his clear air of dramatic disaster. I see the shimmer around him. I recognize him, and suddenly I know exactly where he's rushing to: a bad accident at the Ferris wheel, a fatal accident he will be too late to do anything about.

It's the first time, in all the long summer my son has gone to fairs, that I have seen anyone from *that* fair.

I try to run, but I'm old and stiff and can only manage a fast walk. Oh, that bodies wear out! I was young and beautiful and my husband desired me, and now I cannot run to claim him, although he is and always will be mine. My son, my son . . .

He's somewhere along this fence, with his illusions. I plunge off the midway and grope my way along the wire, searching in the darkness.

If I am too late, I swear I will find a way to put his eyes out yet again.

*   *   *

"Who are you?" I say to the figure. He doesn't answer, and then I get mad. The pervert, just wanting to watch while Cathy and me . . . I get to my feet and pull her up with me. If he wants a fight, tough shit. He's not going to get it, unless he tries to touch Cathy. If he dares to touch her . . . But he's three inches taller than I am, and maybe twenty pounds heavier.

Come on, Cathy.

No.

It's not Cathy's thoughts. It's *his*. He moves closer, and puts a hand on my arm, and the minute he does, I see the faint shimmer around him, and I stop stone-dead still.

No.

"Who *are* you?" I yell.

But it's like he can't say anything else. He shakes his head, and I see his eyes. Only they aren't there, just empty sockets, creepy as hell. He points to the low buildings. Cathy's warm hand tightens on mine.

Johnny—he wants us to go there.

Why? They're closed.

The man points hard. His whole body leans into pointing. Then he suddenly spins around, and by the dim light from the Tilt-A-Whirl I see my mother coming toward us across the dark grass.

The man throws up his arms to cover the place where his eyes should be. Then he falls forward—a weird, slow-motion fall, like he's terrified of the little drop to the grass, and I hear him in my head: *Noooooooooooooooo* . . . By the time his body hits ground, it's disappeared.

I grab at the fence and start climbing. I don't think about it, I just do it, pulling Cathy after me. I hear her dress tear on the fence, but I don't stop. The fence is only about six feet high, and isn't topped with any spikes or anything. I get over it and turn to help Cathy, and I see that it wasn't the fence that tore her blue dress, it was my mother, who's got hold of the thin material in one hand and Cathy's long hair in the other. My mother pulls viciously, and I climb back up on the fence and kick her in the face. She screams and falls backward, and I yank Cathy so hard her left breast scrapes on the wire, and Cathy screams, too. Blood smears my hand. I pull harder, and Cathy's over the fence, gasping and naked and bleeding. Her shoes are gone. I run, dragging her with me.

Johnny . . .

Come on!

She can hardly move, but I make her keep going. The buildings are pulling me now . . . No, that's not right. Something is *pushing* me toward them, from behind. Somehow, without words, I know it's the blind shimmery man that my mother made disappear.

We reach the first of the buildings and collapse against them, panting hard. The air smells bad. Cathy starts to cry. I take her in my arms and hold her.

"It's all right, Cathy. It's all right, love. We're here now."

"Oh, Johnny, I was . . . so scared!"

The words aren't in my head. I hear them with my ears. And Cathy is all the way solid in my arms, no shimmer at all, a cold shivering body sobbing naked against me, more real than anything else in the whole world.

He accomplished it! The lying son of a bitch actually *accomplished* it, the first real chance he got . . . Why does he hate me so much? All I did was love him, marry him, birth a son by him!

I lie on the ground where I fell when my son kicked me. My jaw is broken, I think, although there is surprisingly little pain. I need help: a doctor, an ambulance. I need my *son*.

Who has escaped, although he probably doesn't know it. Escaped into the exhibition buildings. Homemade jams and jellies. Pickled beets. Quilts, patiently sewn by hand over months and months. Prize pigs and heifers and sheep, the result of years of mundane, earthy, *real* tasks. Feeding, cleaning, sewing, cooking, growing . . . things that have as little to do with the pathetic illusions of the midway as with the tawdry flickering of TV. Gardening, measuring, making, preserving, feeding. What is in the exhibition halls of a fair are the only real things in it.

I had always been so glad that my son came to the fairgrounds at dusk, when the exhibition halls had already closed! I had counted on it. And now . . .

The pain comes, then, but not in my jaw. My son, my son . . . I forgive you. You didn't know what you were doing. And you are mine. My blood, my bone, my flesh. *Mine.*

"Ma'am? My God, ma'am, are you all right? Hey, Jack, over here, a lady's hurt!"

I can't bear for these men to touch me. But I will have to bear it, at least until they've set my broken jaw. No longer than that. No man *should* touch me except my son.

The air smells bad because there are pigs inside this building. It must be where the farmers show off their . . . whatever they show off. I never cared a rat's ass about all this stuff. Only . . . Cathy can talk to me here, right out loud. She can get chilled. She can bleed. Here, we are the same.

I throw my body against the door and pretty soon the hinges give way. I'm strong. Inside, I turn on a single light. It's pigs, all right. On the closest wall, a covered tunnel leads to another building. In the dim light, I see jars of food.

I find clean water, and wash the blood off Cathy. The gash on her breast isn't deep. I give her my jacket, until I can find something better. Then I make us a bed of clean straw and switch off the light.

After a while, I get up and set the door so it isn't obvious that the hinges were broken.

Cathy cuddles in the straw beside me, warm now, and eager. My hands explore her. I whisper, "In the morning, Cathy, we'll leave before these buildings open. We can buy food—I've got money with me." She nods. I think hard, trying to plan.

We can do it. I know we can. And when the fair moves on, we'll go *with* it. Until we find another. And another. All with pigs and jellies and stuff.

I whisper, "We'll stay in these buildings as much as possible, because here you're . . ."

"I'm Cathy," she says simply, and reaches for my belt buckle.

For the first time in my life, I believe that my mother doesn't know where I am.

My son is in the exhibition hall, behind the pigs. I know that, even though I lie in the back of a speeding ambulance. Damn him! But the fair is over Saturday, and I will be out of the hospital well before that. It won't be as easy for him to do as my son thinks that it will. He is so young. Too young to know that she and her reality will never possess him, because *I* already do. For better or worse, in sickness and health, body and soul, until the day he dies. No matter what any man thinks, there is nothing stronger in him than the reality his mother has put there.

But I won't ever tell him that, in so many words. Most people cannot bear very much truth. We who love them must keep the truth from them.

I do.

Abelard's Kiss
Madeleine E. Robins

Here's a disturbing and seductive story that demonstrates that sometimes it's the same way with sex as it is with drugs: the first taste is free. The rest, you have to *pay* for—one way or the other.

Madeleine E. Robins is a frequent contributor to *The Magazine of Fantasy and Science Fiction* and has also sold to markets such as *Asimov's Science Fiction, Invitation to Camelot,* and *Christmas Magic.* She is the author of five Regency Romances and is currently at work on a science fiction novel, *City On Fire.* She works as an editor for Acclaim Comics and lives in New York City.

ABELARD'S KISS

Beatrice's lover was made of lip. She wouldn't say more, just smiled, delicately tracing the edge of her glass with one finger. Susannah, more than anyone else there, knew Beatrice's theatricality, her beautifully detailed gestures. Susannah, more than anyone else there, knew that to give way to her curiosity was to give way to Beatrice.

Still, "Lip, Beatrice?" she murmured, trying to sound wry and doubtful.

"Uh huh." Beatrice's smile broadened and shone on Susannah; she finished her wine and turned to get more.

Was she the only one in Renata's living room who had heard Beatrice? Susannah wondered. Or did the others take the casual statement as an example, either of Beatrice's extravagance or of her hyperbole. No one but Susannah seemed particularly interested. And beside the delicious, disturbing image of Beatrice's lover there was only one thought in Susannah's mind: not to show Beatrice that she was intrigued. Captivated. Hooked again, like the old days.

"Wanna see something?" Beatrice would whisper. They were sammies then, refugee kids at a Samaritan school after the Big Everything, the disaster of '19 which had wiped out so much of New York City. "It'll cost you a halfie." And Susannah had found the half-dollar coin hidden in her pocket and given it to Beatrice, and been permitted to view the dead cat or the page torn from an old porn magazine or, once, the body of a bum who had frozen to death outside the school the night before.

"Wanna see something?" Beatrice would whisper. And every time, every damned time she fell for it.

Even now, twenty-five years later. The most Susannah had learned to do was look indifferent so that the others at the party—friends of Renata's, who was a sammie too—wouldn't notice her fascination.

Later, when the party was breaking up, Beatrice offered Sue a ride back to Manhattan by way of Tamerlane. "I have to stop home, anyway. Come in, I'll give you some real coffee."

Susannah opened her mouth to say No, and was unsurprised to hear herself say Yes. Old habit, old captivations. She followed Beatrice up to the copter on Renata's roof.

"I've named it Abelard," Beatrice said as she fastened her seat belt.

"Why not Dante?" Susannah asked, trying to play the game.

"Too obvious." Beatrice smiled, a whiteness glittering in the dusk. She flicked a row of switches and the copter hummed to life. In the fading daylight and the green glow of the instrument panel, Beatrice looked unearthly, vivid and perfect, her long fingers manipulating the toggles and dials expertly.

"Besides," she added once they were up in the air. "Abelard sounds sexier." It certainly did the way Beatrice said it, a sigh rolled along the tongue.

For ten minutes Susannah fought the temptation to ask, "Where did it come from?" Finally, unasked, Beatrice said, "I had him made for me. One of the bioengineering places squeezed my order in between batches of interferon or something. I understand it isn't hard to do. Just expensive." Beatrice lingered on the word. "A parent tissue, a little fuddling with DNA, program in some instincts . . ." Her voice was an elegant drawl, only her smile in the near-darkness was lewd. "There's only one in the world, and it's mine."

"Beatie—" Susannah murmured.

"I know you'll keep this a secret, love. It's not breaking the law, but . . . bending it a little."

Susannah stared into the deepening gloom. Below them scavenger boats fished scrap metal from the Long Island Sound; to the right in the distance the squat buildings of the rebuilt South Bronx Hospice glittered silently. After their hungry, grubby childhood, Susannah had continued on to college, gone to work, built up a small independence for herself. Grubbed for money, Beatrice said, and shook her head. *Her* path had been very different. Beatrice had worked only as long as it took to find, and marry, Felix Ferrar-Giroux, one of the mysteriously wealthy men who had emerged after the Everything. He took her home to Tamerlane, a huge house on the Sound that unfolded like a tesseract, disclosing rooms where none could logically be, and there Beatrice learned to spend his money. He encouraged her extravagances as if he were feeding a rare bird. No impulse too wild, no whim too expensive. Including, it appeared, this new extravagance.

I will keep my mouth shut, Susannah thought grimly. I will look at her new toy—despite herself a flush of warmth spread through her at the thought—and then I will go home.

At Tamerlane they were met at the door by a superior-looking manservant who took Susannah's three-year-old cloth coat with as much ceremony as he did Beatrice's fur. Beatrice led Sue to a small den and poured wine for them both.

"You must relax, Susah! You take everything so seriously. There, drink that. Why *are* you so edgy?"

"I'm not edgy, but I have work at home I need to get through tonight."

"Susah, you can't let work rule your life," Beatrice said irritably.

"I don't let it rule my life, Beatrice—"

"What else rules your life, then? You haven't had a lover since whatsisname walked out—"

"Greg," Susannah whispered.

Beatrice made no sign of hearing. "You *won't* enjoy yourself, you act like you haven't earned the right. That's the difference between us: you think you haven't *earned* anything. I *know* I've earned every-thing I can lay my hands on. We survived, Susah. We're alive. We don't owe anyone anything. *I* don't, anyway." Beatrice raked her hair back from her broad forehead with one hand and looked up at the ceiling. "Why do I bother? Come on, love. Let's go meet Abelard."

They went down a string of corridors, stopping just as Susannah began to get seriously lost. The room Beatrice led Sue into was almost empty, uncarpeted, dimly lit, painted a shining white. The floor was a parquet pattern, doubtless of real wood. There was a clean soft smell to the air, like talc or running water; two lush throw rugs and a futon in the corner; a fern hanging in a ceramic pot. Nothing stirred.

Beatrice crossed the room. "Shut the door behind you, Susah." Then she went through a door at the far side of the room. Susannah had a moment to look around curiously, breathe the sweet air, wait for revelation.

"Come on, precious. Come on sweetie-pie." Beatrice stood in the doorway a moment to assure herself of Susannah's attention before she reentered the room. Something moist and gibbous squirmed uneasily into the room behind her, moving by throwing its weight forward, falling and rolling over until it "stood" again. It was ovoid, dull red, strangely plastic, with a faint sheen that gave no impres-sion of sliminess. *Ugh*, Susannah thought, but was unable to take her eyes away as the thing rolled after Beatrice like a puppy after its master, struggling with that sidling somersault to keep up with Beatrice's elegant long stride.

"Abelard." Beatrice stopped in the center of the room, one palm extended to present the thing to Susannah. With the other hand she reached caressingly down to it and it responded, stretching upward in an effort to reach her circling finger. At last they touched, and the thing grew round her finger, nursed it. For the first time in all the years she had known Beatrice, Susannah saw her entirely capti-vated, not thinking of the next moment or the next, caught entirely in the present, all attention focused in that one finger.

The mood was contagious. Susannah's faint revulsion at her first sight of the thing dissipated. She felt a warmth and sweet laziness born of the fragrant humidity of the room and the unsettlingly erotic sight of the creature suckling Beatrice's manicured finger. She sighed quietly in the stillness.

"Do you want to touch him?" Beatrice's voice sounded abnormally loud.

Susannah tried to make her murmured Yes seem casual. She stepped near, reached out a finger and touched, tentatively, at the side of the lover. "Abelard?" she murmured. The thing did not move toward her, but it did not move away, either. Sue pushed her finger a little harder. The surface of the lover was warm, firmer than she had expected. Like lip. It gave slightly, then closed around her fingertip and nursed at it, tasted it. Susannah felt a string of electric pulses ripple up her spine; the flesh surrounding hers was damp and warm and faintly pulsing.

"I thought you'd like him," Beatrice said smugly. At the sound of her voice Abelard released its grip on Susannah's finger, dropped away and shrank back, its rolling weight carrying it toward Beatrice. "Hello, Pet," Beatrice crooned. "Is devoted to Beatie, isn't it? Is got Beatie under its skin, hasn't it?" She ran a caressing palm flat along one side of Abelard's top while Susannah, shivering in the warm air, tried to regain her composure. Then, abruptly, Beatrice pulled away from the lover and turned to the door. "Come on, Susah."

Susannah followed, trying to ignore the tremor that lingered in her arms and breasts and knees, making walking a shaky, uncertain chore. From the doorway she took one backward look and saw Abelard, shrunken and forlorn, abandoned in the center of the room.

"Potter will move it back to the tank later." Beatrice waved a vague hand in the direction of the room as they moved up the hall.

"Tank?"

"It spends most of its time in a nutrient bath. Or something. I told the people at Bioform I didn't want to know particulars, they're so unromantic. Potter takes care of him. *It*. Now, I promised you real coffee, didn't I?"

Susannah had forgotten about the work she had waiting in Manhattan. She followed Beatrice mutely back to the sitting room where a lavish meal, with the promised coffee, had been laid out. Through the meal and the copter ride into the city, where Beatrice landed on the roof of Susannah's building in violation of any number of ordinances, through the rest of the evening and the next day, Susannah was haunted by the memory, the teasing sensation of that warm flesh suckling at her finger. Which was just what Beatrice wanted, she told herself scornfully. An audience, someone to want what she has.

Which is just what Susannah wanted.

Sue saw Beatrice irregularly, now and then at Renata's house in Connecticut, sometimes at a restaurant in the city for lunch. With her usual perversity Beatrice did not mention Abelard, but sometimes in the midst of talking she would break off in midsentence and smile deliciously into space for a moment, then start theatrically. "What was I saying?" Sue believed these lapses were contrived for her benefit, but that didn't diminish their power. She was grimly certain that Beatrice understood that all too well, and was grimly determined to show herself unmoved.

Other than lunches with Beatrice, parties or weekends at Renata's, or her occasional work-related social duties, Susannah didn't seek out contacts, friends, lovers. Her last man had decamped more than a year before, in a shower of mutual accusation and disappointment, and Susannah couldn't nerve herself to try again, even approach trying again. Too messy, certain to fail, just not worth it, she said to Renata when she asked about Susannah's love life. To Beatrice she said she was too busy to think about sex, let alone love. She was not quite busy enough to forget the unsettling image of Beatrice's lover, nor the ghost sensation of the thing sucking on her own finger, even after months had gone by.

One day, several months after the visit to Tamerlane, Beatrice called her at work, arranged to meet for lunch. She bubbled and enthused, every word was an event, and by the time she put the phone down Susannah knew that Beatrice had some new extravagance and needed an audience. Needed *her*. She made arrangements to take an extra hour for lunch; her superiors looked kindly on her lunches with Beatrice Ferrar-Giroux.

They met at a small restaurant in the rehabilitated section of the east Fifties. The place had not yet been discovered by anyone but Beatrice, who would relentlessly drag it into fashion and then tire of it. Today she was dressed like a wealthy gypsy, scarves and beads and skirts layered around her so that she looked half buried in bright fabric. Her hair was in dark ringlets this time. She looked beautiful, elegant, radiantly pleased with herself and the world, and Susannah immediately loathed her own blue suit, which that morning had seemed fashionable and attractive, and her simply dressed dark hair.

"Susannah!" Beatrice rose and enveloped Susannah in a spicy, overwhelming embrace full of foreign enthusiasms and endearments. Susannah returned it carefully, fearful of disturbing Beatrice's artful disarray.

Before the first drink had arrived Beatrice was launched on an epic, a saga of her life since they had last met. By the time the second drink and the faux salmon appeared Beatrice had arrived at the

crux of her story. A new lover, a man. He was beautiful, he was
bright and shining, incredibly sensual, a gypsy, a madman. He had
been, until Beatrice discovered him, a gardener at Tamerlane.

"Who's doing the garden now?" Sue asked dryly. Beatrice blinked,
laughed, and went on. By the time the consommé arrived Beatrice
had descended from flowery abstracts to coarse particulars. Susannah
listened in silence.

It was not until the waiter served the veal and poured more wine
that Susannah could get a word in edgewise. "What's going to happen to Abelard?"

Beatrice looked at her blankly for a moment. Then, "Oh, God,
that's right. I hadn't even thought. Well, after all, Susah, it's only a
blob, isn't it? I'll have to tell Potter to take it back to Bioform."

Beatrice was paying for the meal; it was not often that Susannah
could afford real meat, let alone cheese and fruit and wine this
good. She ate every bite. It tasted like dust. Over coffee she asked,
"What will Bioform do with him?"

It took Beatrice a moment to understand what Susannah was
talking about.

"Put it back in the vat or something, I suppose. Recycle the ingre-
dients. Something. Really, Susannah," Beatrice drawled. "It was
only a toy."

She wasn't expected to care, Susannah knew. She was supposed
to change fascinations as Beatrice did, just one step behind. She
shook her head and changed the subject back to Beatrice's new
lover.

When they were putting on their coats, Beatrice regarded Susannah
with the old look: satisfaction wanting to flaunt itself. "Susah, you must
come meet him. When can you come out to Tamerlane?"

She faltered, thinking of the work on her desk, the reports in her
briefcase waiting to be taken home. Then Susannah surprised herself. "Tonight. I can come tonight, after work." And do what? Fight
free of the place with Abelard tucked under one arm? Ridiculous.
Still, "Tonight," she said.

"I won't say good-bye, then," Beatrice said. "I'll pick you up at
six!" She smiled again, suddenly irresistible and childlike. "Ooo,
Susah, wait 'til you see!" And then was gone.

Flying out to Tamerlane, Susannah let Beatrice's chatter wash
over her like warm, scented water. Potter waited at the door to
receive their coats and lead them to a different small den. Susannah
wondered briefly if Beatrice had a suite of rooms for each lover she
took: row on row of white rooms with the smell of running water
and one green vine in a white ceramic pot. She settled herself in a
deep soft chair and sipped wine, thinking. A young man, very tall
and muscular, with a face of masculine prettiness and a slow,

assured walk, joined them. Susannah noted that he was as besotted with Beatrice as she was with him.

"Susannah, this is John." Beatrice pulled the young man down to sit beside her on the sofa; their fingers found occasions to touch, and the air between them rippled as though superheated. Susannah looked away uncomfortably, embarrassed. When Potter announced a call for Beatrice the lovers rose together and left the room. Potter looked at Susannah as if she were part of some vulgar conspiracy, then he too left. Susannah could hear Beatrice's soft murmuring from the antechamber, the click of the phoneset replaced in its cradle, but neither Beatrice nor John returned. She thought she heard more murmurings, the soft sighing of silk against skin and skin against skin. Her face warmed as she realized that Beatrice meant her to hear, wanted her to hear. *Probably thought it was a great gift to her poor friend Susah*, she thought in disgust.

She rose and left the room. If anyone stopped her, she would say she was looking for the lavatory. No one stopped her. It took her three tries to find the right corridor, the right door. When she entered the room she found it empty; the futon and white rugs had been rolled up and piled on one side, the vine trailed unwatered from its dusty pot. The air was still and musty. She walked across the bare floor and opened the door to the inner room carefully, afraid she might startle the creature.

It was flattened, submerged in a shallow plastiglass tank that brimmed with viscous pink fluid. It looked like photographs Susannah had seen of human hearts prepared for transplant; there was something lonely and pathetic about it. *Ugh*, she thought. *How could anyone*—but Susannah thought she knew how. She stood very still, just inside the room, listening to her own pulse and breathing, watching the faint pulse of the lover in its tank. She was only aware that Potter had entered the room behind her when he cleared his throat.

"I was only looking—" she began.

Potter regarded her steadily and said nothing.

"I mean, it's horrible, just putting the poor thing back in some sort of vat, as if it were clay or something. I mean—" she faltered. "When does he—it—go?"

Potter smiled thinly. "When Madame remembers to instruct me."

Susannah nodded, still staring at Abelard in the tank. "I just mean, well, it was made deliberately. It seems so awful to just destroy it. It must feel something . . ."

"You want it," Potter stated baldly.

"It should be *saved*," Susannah corrected. She kept her gaze fixed on the lover. "We can't just let Beatrice throw it out. It's alive. It just seems . . ." she faded off. The only sound in the room was a faint hiss and bubble from the tank.

Then, "We might arrange something," Potter said. He closed the door behind them, shutting them into the humid, medicinal-smelling room with the creature. "Something could be arranged," he repeated. Susannah looked at him as he told her what.

They negotiated. As Potter made his offer and Susannah her counteroffer, she thought of the warm sucking at her finger, the firm plastic surface of the lover. Her breath came faster as she calculated her slender resources, the money she had saved for years, hoping to buy an apartment larger than her cramped two-room. She thought of little economies she could make, freelance work, extra income.

When she left the white suite Susannah and Potter had come to an agreement.

All the way back to Manhattan, riding with Beatrice in the copter, Susannah was aware of a new sensation, a smugness Beatrice herself would have recognized. She had taken something from Beatrice, and Beatie would never know it. It would be her own.

Susannah spent her lunch hour at the bank the next day, transferring money to the account Potter had named. As she wrote the figures out Susannah had a brassy taste in her mouth, a moment of cautionary fear: *What am I doing?* Then sanity was overwhelmed by the rising image, the image she had lived with for months now, of the lover at her fingertip, nursing gently. Susannah signed the bank chit recklessly and went back to work.

Potter was early. When the security guard at her building door called up for clearance Susannah was still eating dinner. She looked quickly around her apartment, a painfully neat room on which she had lavished all her energy, choosing fabrics and art that would create a sense of space and graciousness. Except for the dark wood folding table on which her dinner sat half-eaten, the apartment was in order. She went to the door to wait.

"Good evening, Miss." Potter might have been opening the door at Tamerlane for her, rather than she for him.

"Good evening," Susannah replied seriously.

It took only a few minutes to move the shrouded cart across the room, slide the tank as gently as possible onto the floor, unstack the cans of nutrient fluid that Potter had brought along. "Part of the accouterments," he told her. Then he looked around the apartment once, shook his head as if his worst fears had been confirmed.

"Well, Miss," he said at the door. "I hope it gives you great . . . pleasure."

Susannah blushed. "I'm just trying—" she began. Gave that up. "Good night, Potter."

"I certainly hope so, Miss."

When he was gone, Susannah turned back to the apartment,

seeing the drying track of fluid dribbled from the tank and the shifting sprawl of Abelard against the plastiglass walls. The tank and
cans of fluid took up a space about a meter square, displacing an
armchair she had stored away in the basement. Her heart beat so
strongly she felt the pulse under her jaw. Susannah walked toward
the tank. The pink fluid on the floor smeared greasily under her
foot. But when she reached out a hand and touched the lover its
surface was not greasy, scarcely even damp. At her touch, Abelard
slowly stirred, enveloping her fingertip with warm, firm flesh, just
as she remembered.

Susannah drew away. Some ritual was demanded. The lover sank
down into its tank again while she cleared the dishes and started a
bath. She soaked for a long time in water as hot as it ever got in her
building, then toweled herself dry. When she could think of no further reason to delay, she set about her seduction.

First there was the clumsy process of getting Abelard out of the
tank. The lover did not reach for her as it did to Beatrice, nor follow
the sound of her murmurs, her heat and scent. But when touched
it did respond, reaching upward to her. After a moment Susannah
figured out how to use its weight to move it, letting the lover over-
balance and roll forward over the beveled lip of the tank wall. Even
so, Susannah had to pull with both hands, palms flat against the
malleable flesh, until the creature was wholly out of the tank.
Susannah stared at her palms, which tingled from the contact.

Abelard waited, unmoving. Tentatively Susannah reached out
again and touched it, stroking the warm surface. The flesh of the
lover kissed her hand, rising to follow the line of her arm, nibbling
tenderly at the soft skin of the inner elbow. Susannah sighed,
shifted from kneeling to sitting, pushed gently at Abelard's surface
with her free hand until it was enveloped in soft, suckling tissue.
The lover was warm like the touch of breath against her skin. Seen
closely, its surface was a dusty rose, lined, porous and unappealing;
after a moment Susannah closed her eyes. Then there was only the
touch, the slow sliding pressure on her arms, a kissing of flesh on
flesh.

In the still of the room there was the faint singing of her breath and
nothing else. She floated from touch to touch at the lover's whim;
there was nothing to do but be there, be touched. No responsibility for
the lover's pleasure, no necessity for talk or reassurance. Just her own
sensations, intoxicating. Abelard swarmed over her, nuzzling and kissing, rocking her gently in the first orgasm, clinging warmly.

Gradually the stroking at her throat, her breasts, her inner thighs
and labia became more insistent, probing. The lover seemed to
absorb the energy of her arousal, feeding on it. Susannah was once
distantly aware of how strange it was to have no one to hold on to,

no shoulders or buttocks to knead. When she stroked the lover its skin kissed back, another sensation, distracting, and after a moment or two she let her hands fall to her sides.

The lover went on stroking, probing, kissing, shape-changing. Susannah grew tired, overexcited, and raw. Her languor turned into heavy-limbed paralysis: it was impossible even to shudder away from the ceaseless warm caress that went on and on. At last, dizzy to fainting, Susannah rolled away from the lover, shivering in the sudden uncovered cool of the room. She lay for a long time, boneless, flushed and exhausted against the pillows. When she turned over she saw Abelard, vaguely forlorn, returned to its squat ovoid shape. She knew she should put it back in its tank again—how long since she had coaxed it out?—but it was still difficult to move.

Finally she did rise from the floor, pulling on a robe, to attend to the lover, urging it back toward the tank and, at the last, pushing it over the shallow rim again into the nutrient bath. At the first touch of her hands the creature began its slow kissing again. Susannah felt as if every cell in her body was electrified by sensory memory; after the quick shove it took to up-end Abelard into the tank, she pulled away, panting again, waiting for the electric charge to dissipate. Foggy with surfeit she sank back to the floor. After a while she drifted to sleep where she lay.

At work the next day Susannah was tired and stiff. She found herself drifting into daydreams, her eyelids suddenly heavy and her mouth pursed in a soft "o" as if by surprise. Pressing her legs together she could summon up a flush of physical memory that was momentarily incapacitating. She felt a little drunk; she smiled often. At the stroke of five she cleared her desk and left.

Somehow she expected her apartment to be changed, tinted pink or filled with musky scent, something exotic. It was the same: two small rooms, her careful decorating scheme knocked awry by the tank in the corner. Susannah allowed herself a brief glance at the lover, then committed herself to ritual: dinner, small chores, a bath, all prolonging the expectation. Finally, when she could not distract herself further, she took Abelard from the tank.

It was as it had been the night before: soft caressing flesh, ripplings of sensation, her body bathed in warm kisses. Even when the pleasure began to mix with pain she could not stop, convinced by her body that the final sensation, the perfect sensation, was only a moment away. When languor gave over to exhaustion, sensation which broke itself, pleasure which hurt too much to bear, Susannah rolled away, shaking, listening to her heart pound in the silence of the room.

In the next few days Susannah developed dark patches under

her eyes, and a staccato way of talking. It was impossible for her to be in the apartment and not eventually succumb to the lover's allure. Beatrice called and Susannah said guiltily that she had no time for lunch. Renata called and Susannah pleaded a head cold. At home it piqued her that Abelard still had to be coaxed to her. She remembered the way the creature had yearned toward Beatrice's hand, her voice. What had Beatrice said? That it was programmed to respond to her physical chemistry. In time, Susannah thought, the lover would learn *her* chemistry, respond to her, not Beatrice.

Abelard had been in her apartment for a week when Susannah noticed a callus, a small rough patch on its surface. When she touched the patch the lover responded instantly, sucking gently at her finger.

"No, sweetie," she murmured absently. Concerned, she checked the nutrient fluid, but it was the same clear, uncontaminated pink it was supposed to be. For a moment Susannah entertained thoughts of sexually transmitted diseases, explanations to doctors. "This is ridiculous," she chided the creature. "There is nothing wrong with you." Still, when she took him from the tank that evening she made sure the leathery patch was turned away from her.

The next night the patch seemed larger.

Beatrice called again, insisting upon lunch. They met, embraced, and Beatrice was launched into her narrative before they had taken their seats. This time, though, there was a difference. After a few minutes, Beatrice broke off and stared curiously at Susannah.

"All right, what is it?" she asked.

Susannah trembled. "What is what?"

"Susah, you're off in Neverland somewhere, you haven't heard a thing I've said. It must be something. You've met a man! Tell me."

"I haven't met a man." Susannah was enjoying herself.

"All right, a woman, then. *Tell.*"

"I haven't met anyone, Beatrice. I spend my nights quietly at home." Susannah smiled seraphically. Beatrice's frown was petulant.

"Well, don't tell me." Her bad humor lasted another few minutes and then was forgotten as she launched into gossip about her gardener-lover at Tamerlane, about Felix and their parties. By the end of lunch she had talked herself into charity with Susannah again: "You must come out to Tamerlane soon. I'll even find a gardener for you."

Susannah smiled politely. They embraced again and she turned away. Behind her she felt Beatrice watching curiously, for once in all their lives the puzzled one.

That night as the lover churned over her body Susannah was suddenly aware of the complete silence, the lack of another breath contrapuntal to hers, no words, no noise at all. Later, when she rolled Abelard back into the tank, she found two new leathery patches, and the first was definitely larger, and cracking faintly. Before she left for work the next morning Susannah examined the lover. It seemed shrunken to her, slightly withered. This time she opened two cans of nutrient and recklessly dumped them into the tank. As her hand grazed the lover it nestled sluggishly. Poor thing, she thought. Up close in the light of day it was really kind of awful looking.

She was late at work, haranguing with a customer in Zurich over duty compensation; when she got home she had only enough energy to wash her face and fall into bed with a curious sense of relief. She did not remember to check Abelard for further sores then or in the morning. All day she was conscious of an edginess; that night, for the first time, she did not bother with her rituals but pulled off her clothes and tumbled the lover out of its tank as soon as she arrived home. She did not really look at it until later, afterward. The firm, pliant skin was scaly and withered, as if the creature itself had shrunk inside its flesh. The first of the calluses was cracked and oozing faintly. Susannah hurriedly pushed the lover into the tank and went to shower the touch of it from her. She did feel some brief compunction, and dropped more fluid into the already brimming tank before she went to sleep.

The lover was dull brown by morning and the fluid in the tank was contaminated with small particles. Susannah was horrified, thinking of the touch of that thing on her body only hours before.

When she got home the lover was dead.

Susannah knew it the moment she opened the door; there was no smell, but a sense of presence in the apartment was abruptly not there. Abelard floated in the tank, shriveled and dark, strands of peeling skin suspended in the murky fluid that surrounded it. Susannah wanted to close and lock the door to her apartment and disappear.

It took her a while to think what to do. Finally Susannah dragged the lover out of the tank and wrapped it in an old towel. Its withered form was surprisingly light and much smaller than it had been alive. Clutching the bundle tightly to her chest, she carried it down seven flights to the garbage room in the basement. Then she pushed it away from her violently, heaving the creature and the towel into a trashcan. The sight of the gray-brown husk half hidden by terry cloth in the bottom of the can was the final straw. Susannah fled, weeping, back to her apartment. It was some time before she thought to empty the tank of its tainted nutrient and bring it, and the remaining cans of fluid, down to the basement.

Then Susannah went into some kind of mourning, reducing her already small world to a simple loop of work and sleep. She lost weight, the former tidiness of her apartment declined into dusty clutter. She saw no one outside of work. The thought of people dismayed her. Friends called, Beatrice and Renata, an old boyfriend back in town, a man from work. Susannah left the phone off the hook and fell asleep each night to the rhythmic whine of the signal. Daily she watched what she was doing to herself and was appalled, but inertia overweighed everything and nothing changed.

At last Renata got through to her. A party at her place in Connecticut, Susannah would have to come, someone would certainly give her a lift out. Of all the people she had known from the Samaritan school, emphatic, generous Renata was the one Susannah liked best, feared least, and was most likely to ignore. But today Renata used her most persuasive voice and best blandishments. Perhaps, Susannah thought, it was time to go out.

Renata was delighted. "Wonderful, wonderful! Listen, Beatie's coming, I'll tell her to give you a ride out. Wonderful! Wear something nice, sweetie. There will be some lovely men."

Men. Susannah was not ready to consider the idea. And of all the people in the world, Beatrice was the last one with whom she wanted to ride out to Connecticut. She thought of calling back and canceling, but the habit of inaction was just too strong. It was easier, finally, to just go.

Beatrice was chattering before Susannah had closed the door of the copter: how had she been, where had she been, why all the mystery? "You look marvelous, Susah, so thin! But you just dropped out of sight. I was right, wasn't I? You had a new lover? My God, love, it's been months since I've seen you."

Susannah agreed that it had been months, and stared stolidly down at the forest of spires below them, the slowly reemerging Manhattan skyscape.

"I should have tried harder to get hold of you, I know." Beatrice went on, expertly guiding the copter east over the Sound. "We've been all at sixes and sevens out at the house, even poor Felix had to get tangled up in it. Can you imagine? We had to fire Potter."

Susannah felt a hollowness in her stomach, as if the copter had suddenly made a two-hundred-foot drop. "Fire Potter? Why?"

"God, Susah, he'd been taking advantage—they all do, it's expected, up to a point. But Potter overstepped the bounds." Beatrice's long eyebrows arched in amusement. "Do you know, he actually took it upon himself to throw out my little toy? You know, that thing I had made—"

"Abelard," Susannah whispered.

"God, *Abelard*. What a memory you have. Felix was convinced that Potter had sold the poor little thing on the black market, but I can't imagine anyone buying it."

Susannah stared straight ahead. What did Beatrice know? Was this one of her dreadful teasing games?

"I mean, there wouldn't have been any point," Beatrice continued.

She's waiting, Susannah thought, for me to pick up my cues. "Why not?" she asked.

"It couldn't have been used by anyone but me, love. Not for long, anyway. It was made for me. Touching anyone else that way would have poisoned it, like an allergy. Potter knew that, the Bioform people told him, for heaven's sake. He knew there was no point in anyone buying it. Unless he sold it as food, and that's too revolting a thought even—"

Susannah leaned against the door of the copter, wishing it would open and drop her into the water five hundred feet below. Beatrice went on and on and on. Susannah didn't listen. She was concentrating on not throwing up as the copter dipped and canted in the early evening breeze. In her mind she played over the picture of the lover, of Abelard, draped in her bathroom towel and discarded in the trash.

Renata was waiting for them, chivvied them into her small house, already packed with people. "Susannah, sweetie, you look like death. You were airsick, weren't you? Beatie, you fly that damned thing like a maniac. Go take off that dreadful fur and find yourself a drink." She pulled Susannah into a bathroom.

"Really, Susie, are you all right? Do you want to talk?" Her arm around Susannah's shoulders, Renata sat them both down on the side of the tub. Distantly Susannah felt the warmth and weight of Renata's arm around her. "Susie?"

Susannah shook her head, afraid to speak. Finally she managed, "Fighting off a bug or something. I'll be okay. Thank you."

Renata squeezed her again, then stood up. "All right, Susie. You don't have to tell me what it is, but fix yourself up and come out as soon as you can, will you? This is a party, love. You're here to . . . to part." She smiled with pleasure at her own silliness, kissed Susannah's cheek and left her.

Susannah stared around the blue and white lavatory, at the embroidered hand towels and sculpted soap. Here to part. With what? With Beatrice? Maybe, after all these years. Maybe. With Abelard? Another wave of deep nausea: she had killed Beatrice's lover, she had been deadly, the damned thing had died giving her pleasure.

She looked at herself in the mirror. Her face was pasty white; she splashed on icy water until some color returned to her face, then pushed at her hair until it fell a little more softly about her face, so that some of the stricken look diminished to mere fragility. Come out as soon as you can, Renata had said.

She thought of the lover, of the cool silence in her apartment, the safety of it. Then, with sudden warmth, she wanted caring, the human clamor that filled Renata's hallway, the sticky, confusing, demanding, and personal world outside the bathroom door. Friendships. Chaos. Love. It was time to go out. As she opened the door she thought she felt something warm at the nape of her neck. A brush of memory like Abelard's kiss.

THE MAP TO THE HOMES OF THE STARS

THE STARS

Andy Duncan

Here's another evocative story by new writer Andy Duncan, whose "Saved" appears elsewhere in this anthology. In this one, he demonstrates that even if you closely and carefully follow a map, you're never sure just exactly where you'll end *up* . . .

THE MAP TO THE HOMES OF THE STARS

Last night, I heard it again. About eleven, I stood at the kitchen counter, slathered peanut butter onto a stale, cool slice of refriger-ated raisin bread, and scanned months-old letters to the editor in an A section pulled at random from the overflow around the recycling bin. "Reader decries tobacco evils." "Economy sound, says NC banker." The little headlines give the otherwise routine letters such urgency, like telegraphed messages from some war-torn front where issues are being decided, where news is happening. "Arts funding called necessary." As I chewed my sandwich, I turned one-handed to the movie listings, just to reassure myself that everything I had skipped in the spring wasn't worth the trouble anyway, and then I heard a slowly approaching car.

We don't get much traffic on my street, a residential loop in a quiet neighborhood, and so even we single guys who don't have kids in the yard unconsciously register the sounds of each passing vehicle. But this was the fifth night in a row, and so I set down my sandwich and listened.

Tom used to identify each passing car, just for practice.

"Fairlane."

"Crown Victoria."

"Super Beetle."

This was back home, when we were as bored as two seventeen year olds could be.

"Even *I* can tell a Super Beetle," I said. I slugged my Mountain Dew and lowered the bottle to look with admiration at the neon-green foam.

Tom frowned, picked up his feet, and rotated on the bench of the picnic table so that his back was to Highway 1.

Without thinking, I said, "Mind, you'll get splinters." I heard my mother speaking, and winced.

Now Tom looked straight ahead at the middle-school basketball court, where Cathy and her friends, but mostly Cathy (who barely knew us, but whose house was fourth on our daily route), were playing a pick-up game, laughing and sweating and raking their long hair back from their foreheads. As each car passed behind him, he continued the litany.

"Jeep."

"Ford pickup."

"Charger."

I didn't know enough to catch him in an error, of course, but I have no doubt that he was right on the money, every time. I never learned cars; I learned other things, that year and the next fifteen years, to my surprise and exhilaration and shame, but I never learned cars, and so I am ill-equipped to stand in my kitchen and identify a car driving slowly past at eleven o' clock at night.

Not even when, about five minutes later, it gives me another chance, drives past again in the other direction, as if it had gotten as far as the next cul-de-sac, and turned around.

It passes so slowly that I am sure it is about to turn into someone's driveway, someone's, mine, but it hasn't, for five nights now it hasn't. I couldn't tell you if I had to precisely what make of car it is.

I could guess, though.

Maybe tonight, if, when, it passes by, I'll go to the front door and pull back the narrow dusty curtain that never gets pulled back except for Jehovah's Witnesses, and see for myself what make of car it is. See if I recognize it. But all I did last night, and the four nights before, was stand at my kitchen counter, fingertips black with old news, jaws Peter-Panned shut (for I am a creature of habit), stare unseeing at the piled-up sink, and trace in my head every long-gone stop on the map to the homes of the stars.

Even when all we had were bicycles, Tom and I spent most of our time together riding around town. We rode from convenience store to convenience store, Slim Jims in our pockets and folded comic books stuffed into the waistbands of our jeans. We never rode side by side or single file but in loopy serpentine patterns, roughly parallel, that weaved among trees and parked cars and water sprinklers. We had earnest and serious conversations that lasted for hours and were entirely shouted from bike to bike, never less than ten feet. Our paths intersected with hair-raising frequency, but we never ran into each other. At suppertime, we never actually said good-bye, but veered off in different directions, continuing to holler at each other, one more joke that had to be told, one more snappy comeback to make, until the other voice had faded in the distance, and we realized we were riding alone, and talking to ourselves. I remember nothing of what we said to each other all those long afternoons, but I remember the rush of the wind past my ears, and the shirttail of my red jersey snapping behind me like a hound, and the slab of sidewalk that a big tree root thrust up beneath me in the last block before home, so that I could steer around it at the last second and feel terribly skillful, or use it as a launching ramp and stand up on the pedals and hang there, suspended, invincible, until the pavement caught up with my tires again.

Then we were sixteen and got our licenses. Tom's bicycle went into the corner of his room, festooned with clothes that weren't quite ready to wash yet; mine was hung on nails inside the garage, in a place of honor beside my older sister's red wagon and my late Uncle Clyde's homemade bamboo fishing poles. Tom had been studying *Consumer Reports* and *Car & Driver* and prowling dealerships for months, and, with his father's help, he bought a used '78 Firebird, bright red exterior, black leather upholstery, cassette stereo, and a host of tire and engine features that Tom could rattle off like an auctioneer but that I never quite could remember afterward. Being a fan of old gangster movies, Tom called it his "getaway car." Tom and his dad got a great deal, because the getaway car had a dent in the side and its headlights were slightly cockeyed. "Makes it unique," Tom said. "We'll get those fixed right up," his dad said, and, of course, they never did. I inherited the car my father had driven on his mail route for years, a beige '72 Volkswagen Beetle that was missing its front passenger seat. My father had removed it so that he'd have an open place to put his mail. Now, like so many of my family's other theoretical belongings, the seat was "out there in the garage," a phrase to which my father invariably would add, "somewhere."

We always took Tom's car; Tom always drove.

We went to a lot of movies in Columbia and sometimes went on real trips, following the church van to Lake Junaluska or to Six Flags and enjoying a freedom of movement unique in the Methodist Youth Fellowship. But mostly we rode around town, looking—and *only* looking—at girls. We found out where they lived, and drove past their houses every day, hoping they might be outside, hoping to get a glimpse of them, but paying tribute in any case to all they had added to what we fancied as our dried-up and wasted and miserable lives.

"We need music," Tom said. "Take the wheel, will you, Jack?"

I reached across and steered while he turned and rummaged among the tapes in the backseat. I knew it was the closest I ever would come to driving Tom's car.

"In Hollywood," I said, "people on street corners sell maps to the stars' homes. Tourists buy the maps and drive around, hoping to see Clint Eastwood mowing his lawn, or something." I had never been to Hollywood, but I had learned about these maps the night before on *PM Magazine*.

"What do you want? You want Stones? You want Beatles? You want Aerosmith? What?"

"Mostly they just see high walls," I said, "and locked gates." I was proud to have detected this irony alone.

"We should go there," Tom said. "Just take off driving one day and *go*."

"Intersection coming up."

"Red light?"

"Green."

Tom continued to rummage. "Our map," he said, "exists only in our heads."

"That's where the girls exist, too," I said.

"Oh, no," Tom said, turning back around and taking the wheel just in time to drive through the intersection. "They're out there. Maybe not in this dink-ass town, but somewhere. They're real. We'll just never know them. That's all."

I had nothing to add to that, but I fully agreed with him. I had concluded, way back at thirteen, that I was doomed to a monastic life, and I rather wished I were Catholic so that I could take full advantage of it. Monastic Methodists had nowhere to go; they just got gray and pudgy, and lived with their mothers. Tom pushed a tape into the deck; it snapped shut like a trap, and the speakers began to throb.

Lisa lived in a huge Tudor house of gray stone across the street from the fifteenth fairway. To our knowledge, she did not play golf, but she was a runner, and on a fortunate evening we could meet her three or four times on the slow easy curves of Country Club Drive. She had a long stride and a steady rhythm and never looked winded, though she did maintain a look of thoughtful concentration and always seemed focused on the patch of asphalt just a few feet ahead, as if it were pacing her. At intersections, she jogged in place, looking around at the world in surprise, and was likely to smile and throw up a hand if we made so bold as to wave.

Tom especially admired Lisa because she took such good care of her car, a plum-colored late-model Corvette that she washed and waxed in her driveway every Saturday afternoon, beginning about one o'clock. For hours, she catered to her car's needs, stroking and rubbing it with hand towels and soft brushes, soaping and then rinsing, so that successive gentle tides foamed down the hood. Eventually, Lisa seemed to be lying face to face with herself across the gleaming purple hood, her palm pressed to the other Lisa's palm, hands moving together in lazy circles like the halfhearted sparring of lovers in August.

Crystal's house was low and brick, with a patio that stretched its whole length. From March through October, for hours each day,

Crystal lay on this patio, working on her tan—"laying out," she would have called it. She must have tanned successive interior layers of her skin, because even in winter she was a dusky Amazonian bronze, a hue that matched her auburn hair, but made her white teeth a constant surprise. Frequent debates as we passed Crystal's house: Which bikini was best, the white or the yellow? Which position was best, face up or face down? What about the bottles and jars that crowded the dainty wrought-iron table at her elbow? Did those hold mere store-bought lotions, or were they brimful of Crystal's private skin-care recipes, gathered from donors willing and unwilling by the dark of the moon? Tom swore that once, when we drove past, he clearly saw amid the Coppertone jumble a half stick of butter and a bottle of Wesson oil.

Gabrielle lived out on the edge of town, technically within the city limits but really in the country, in a big old crossroads farmhouse with a deep porch mostly hidden by lattices of honeysuckle and wisteria. She lived with her grandparents, who couldn't get around so good anymore, and so usually it was Gabrielle who climbed the tall ladder and raked out the gutters, cleared the pecan limbs off the roof of the porch, scraped the shutters, and then painted them. She had long black hair that stretched nearly to the ragged hem of her denim shorts. She didn't tie her hair back when she worked, no matter how hot the day, and she was tall even without the ladder.

Natalie lived in a three-story wooden house with cardboard in two windows and with thickets of metal roosters and lightning rods up top. At school, she wore ancient black ankle-length dresses in all weathers, walked with her head down, and spoke to no one, not even when called upon in class, so that the teachers finally gave up. Her hair was an impenetrable mop that covered her face almost entirely. But she always smiled a tiny secret smile, and her chin beneath was sharp and delicate, and when she scampered down the hall, hugging the lockers, her skirts whispered generations of old chants and endearments. Natalie never came outside at all.

Cynthia's was the first house on the tour. Only two blocks from Tom's, it sat on the brink of a small and suspect pond, one that was about fifty feet across at its widest. No visible stream fed this pond or emptied it, and birds, swimmers, and fishes all shunned it. The pond was a failure as a pond, but a marginal success as an investment, an "extra" that made a half-dozen nondescript brick ranch houses cost a bit more than their landlocked neighbors. Cynthia's house was distinguished by a big swingset that sat in the middle of the treeless yard. It was a swaybacked metal A-frame scavenged from the primary school. In all weathers, day and night, since her family moved to town when she was six, Cynthia could be found out there, swinging. The older she got, the higher she swung, the more reckless and joyful her sparkle and grin. When she was sixteen, tanned legs pumping in the afternoon sun, she regularly swung so high that the chains went slack for a half second at the top of the arc before she dropped.

"Zero gee," Tom said as we drove slowly past. Tom and I didn't swing anymore, ourselves; it made us nauseated.

Once a year, Cynthia actually came out to the car to say hi. Each Christmas, the people who lived on the pond, flush with their wise investment, expressed their communal pride with a brilliant lighting display. For weeks, everyone in town drove slowly, dutifully, and repeatedly around the pond and over its single bridge to see the thousands of white firefly lights that the people of the pond draped along porches and bushes and balustrades, and stretched across wire frames to approximate Grinches and Magi. The reflection on the water was striking, undisturbed as it was by current or life. For hours each night, a single line of cars crept bumper-to-bumper across the bridge, past Santa-clad residents who handed out candy canes and filled a wicker basket with donations for the needy and for the electric company. Painted on a weatherbeaten sandwich board at the foot of the bridge was a bright red cursive dismissal: "Thank You / Merry Christmas / Speed Limit 25."

At least once a night, Tom and I drove through this display, hoping to catch Cynthia on Santa duty. At least once a year, we got lucky.

"Hey there, little boys, want some candy?" She dropped a shimmering fistful into Tom's lap. "No, listen, take them, Dad said when I gave them all out I could come inside. I'm freezing my ass off out here. Oh, hi, Jack. So, where you guys headed?"

"Noplace," we said together.

She walked alongside Tom's Firebird, tugging down her beard to scratch her cheek. "Damn thing must be made of fiberglass. Hey, check out the Thompsons' house. Doesn't that second reindeer look just like he's humping Rudolf? I don't know *what* they were *thinking*. No? Well, it's clear as day from my room. Maybe I've just looked at it too long. When is Christmas, anyway? You guys don't know what it's like, all these goddamn lights, you can see them with your eyes closed. I've been sleeping over at Cheryl's where it's dark. Well, I reckon if I go past the end of the bridge, the trolls will get me. Yeah, right, big laugh there. See you later." Then, ducking her head in again: "You, too, Jack."

With the smoothness of practice, Tom and I snicked our mirrors into place (his the driver's side, mine the overhead) so that we could watch Cynthia's freezing ass walk away. Her Santa pants were baggy and sexless, but we watched until the four-wheel drive behind us honked and flashed its deer lights. By the time we drove down to the traffic circle and made the loop and got back in line again, Cynthia's place had been taken by her neighbor, Mr. Thompson.

"Merry Christmas, Tom, Jack," he said. "Y'all's names came up at choir practice the other day. We'd love to have you young fellas join us in the handbells. It's fun and you don't have to sing and it's a real ministry, too." He apologized for having run out of candy canes, and instead gave us a couple of three-by-five comic books about Hell.

Tina's house always made us feel especially sophisticated, especially daring.

"Can you imagine?" Tom asked. "Can you imagine, just for a moment, what our parents would do?"

"No," I said, shaking my head. "No, I can't imagine."

"I think you should try. I think we both should try to envision this. That way we'll be prepared for anything in life, anything at all."

I cranked down the windowpane until it balked. "I don't even want to think about it," I said. I pressed the pane outward until it was back on track, then I lowered it the rest of the way.

"Oh, but you've *been* thinking about it, haven't you? You're the one that found out where she lived. You're the one that kept wanting me to drive past her house."

"It's the quickest route between Laura's and Kathleen's, that's all," I said. "But if it's such a terrible hardship, then you can go around the world instead, for all I care. You're the driver, I'm just sitting here."

He fidgeted, legs wide, left hand drumming the windowsill, fingertips of his right hand barely nudging the steering wheel. "Don't get me wrong, I think she's a babe. But this neighborhood, I don't know, it makes me nervous. I feel like everybody we pass is looking at us."

"Do what you like. I'm just sitting here," I said. I craned to see Tina's house as we drove around the corner.

Tina lived in what our parents and our friends and every other white person we knew, when they were feeling especially liberal, broad-minded, and genteel, called the "colored" part of town. Tina's yard was colored all right: bright yellows, reds, oranges, and purples, bursting from a dozen flowerbeds. As so often when she wasn't at cheerleading practice, Tina knelt in the garden, a huge old beribboned hat—her grandmother's, maybe?—shading her striking, angular face. Her shoulders tightened, loosened, tightened again as she pressed something into place. Without moving her hands, she looked up at us as we passed. She smiled widely, and her lips mouthed the word "Hey."

Once we were around the corner, Tom gunned the engine.

"Uh-uh, no sir, hang it *up*," Tom said. "Not in my family, not in this town. Thousands of miles away, maybe. That might work. Oh, but then they'd want *photos*, wouldn't they? Damn. The other week, all my aunts were sitting around the kitchen table, complaining about their daughters-in-law. My son's wife is snotty, my son's wife is lazy, they aren't good mothers, they aren't treating our boys right, and so on and so on. Just giving 'em down the country, you know?"

"Uh-huh. I hear you."

"And I finally spoke up and said, 'Well, I know I'm never going to introduce y'all to any wife of *mine*, 'cause y'all sure won't like *her*, either.'"

"What'd they say to that?"

"They all laughed, and Aunt Leda said, 'Tom, don't you worry, 'cause you're the only boy in the family that's got any sense. We know we'll like *any* girl you pick out.' And then Aunt Emily added, 'Long as she isn't a black 'un!' And they all nodded—I mean, they were serious!"

After a long pause, he added, half to himself, "It's not as if I'm bringing *anybody* home, anyway—black or white or lavender."

"You bring me home with you sometimes," I said.

"Yeah, and they don't like *you* either," he said, and immediately cut me a wide-eyed look of mock horror that made me laugh out loud. "I'm kidding. You know they like you."

"Families always like me," I said. "Mamas especially. It's the daughters themselves that aren't real interested. And a mama's approval is the kiss of death. At this moment, I bet you, mamas all over town are saying, 'What about that nice boy *Jack*? He's so respectful, he goes to church, he makes such good grades,' and don't you know that makes those gals so hot they can't stand it."

Tom laughed and laughed.

"Oh, Jack!" I gasped. "Oh, Jack, your SAT score is so—so *big*!"

"Maybe you should forget the girls and date the *mamas*," Tom said. "You know, eliminate the middleman. Go right to the source."

"Eewww, that's crude." I clawed at the door as if trying to get out. "Help! Help! I'm in the clutches of a crude man!"

"Suppose Kathleen's home from Florida yet?"

"I dunno. Let's go see."

"Now, you aren't starting to boss me around, are you?"

"I'm just sitting here."

He poked me repeatedly with his finger, making me giggle and twist around on the seat. "'Cause I'll just put you out by the side of the road, you start bossing me."

"I'm not!" I gasped. "Quit! Uncle! Uncle! I'm not!"

"Well, all right, then."

On September 17, 1981, we turned the corner at the library and headed toward the high school, past the tennis courts. The setting sun made everything golden. Over the engine, we heard doubled and redoubled the muted grunts and soft swats and scuffs of impact: ball on racket, shoe on clay. The various players on the adjoining courts moved with such choreography that I felt a pang to join them.

"Is tennis anything like badminton?" I asked. "I used to be okay at badminton. My father and I would play it over the back fence, and the dogs would go wild."

"It's more expensive," Tom said. "Look, there she is. Right on time."

Anna, her back to us, was up ahead, walking slowly toward the parking lot on the sidewalk nearest me. Her racket was on one shoulder, a towel around her neck. Her skirt swayed as if she were walking much faster.

As we passed, I heard a strange sound: a single Road Runner beep. In the side mirror, tiny retreating Anna raised her free hand and waved. I turned to stare at Tom, who looked straight ahead.

"The *horn*?" I asked. "You honked the horn?"

"Well, *you* waved," he said. "I saw you."

I yanked my arm inside. The windblown hairs on my forearm tingled. "I wasn't waving. I was holding up my hand to feel the breeze."

"She waved at *you*."

"Well, I didn't wave at *her*," I said. "She waved because *you* honked."

"Okay," he said, turning into the parking lot. "She waved at both of us, then."

"She waved at *you*. I don't care, it doesn't matter. But she definitely waved at you."

"Are we fighting?" he asked. He reentered the street, turned back the way we had come. Anna was near, walking toward us.

"'Course we're not fighting. Are you going to honk at her again?"

"Are you going to wave at her again?"

Anna looked behind her for traffic, stepped off the sidewalk, and darted across the street, into our lane, racket lifted like an Olympic torch.

"Look out!"

"What the hell?"

Tom hit the brakes. The passenger seat slid forward on its track, and my knees slammed the dash. Dozens of cassettes on the back-seat cascaded onto the floor. Only a foot or two in front of the stopped car stood Anna, arms folded, one hip thrust out. She regarded us without expression, blew a large pink bubble that reached her nose and then collapsed back into her mouth.

"Hi, guys," she said.

Tom opened his door and stood, one foot on the pavement. "For crying out loud, Anna, are you okay? We could've killed you!"

"I was trying to flag you down," she said.

"What? Why?" Tom asked. "What for? Something wrong with the car?" I saw him swivel, and I knew that, out of sight, he was glancing toward the tires, the hood, the tailpipe.

"Nothing's wrong with the car, Tom," she said, chewing with half her mouth, arms still folded. "It's a really neat car. Whenever I see it, I think, 'Damn, Tom must take mighty good care of that car.' I get a *lot* of chances to think that, Tom, 'cause every day you guys drive by my house at least twice, and whenever I leave tennis practice, you drive past me, and turn around in the lot, and drive past me *again*, and every time you do that, I think, 'He takes mighty damn good care of that goddamn car just to drive past me all the fucking time.'"

Someone behind us honked and pulled around. A pickup truck driver, who threw us a bird.

"Do you ever *stop*? No. Say hi at school? Either of you? No. *Call* me? Shit." She shifted her weight to the other hip, unfolded her arms, whipped the towel from around her neck and swatted the hood with it. "So all I want to know is, just what's the *deal*? Tom? Jack? I see you in there, Jack, you can't hide. What's up, Jack? You tell me. Your chauffeur's catching flies out here."

Looking up at Anna, even though I half expected at any moment to be arrested for perversion or struck from behind by a truck or beaten to death with a tennis racket, purple waffle patterns scarring my corpse, I realized that I had never felt such crazed exhilaration, not even that night on Bates Hill, when Tom passed a hundred and twenty. My knees didn't even hurt anymore. The moment I realized this, naturally, the feeling of exhilaration began to ebb, and so before I lost my resolve, I slowly stuck my head out the window, smiled what I hoped was a smile, and called out: "Can we give you a lift, Anna?"

A station wagon swung past us with a honk. Anna looked at me, at Tom, at me again. She plucked her gum from her mouth, tossed it, looked down at the pavement and then up and then down again, much younger and almost shy. In a small voice, she said: "Yeah." She cleared her throat. "Yeah. Yes. That's . . . that's nice of you. Thank you."

I let her have my seat, of course. I got in the back, atop a shifting pile of cassettes and books and plastic boxes of lug nuts, but right behind her, close enough to smell her: not sweat, exactly, but salt and earth, like the smell of the beach before the tide comes in.

"Where to?" Tom asked.

"California," she said, and laughed, hands across her face. "Damn, Anna," she asked, "where did *that* come from? Oh, I don't know. Where are y'all going? I mean, wherever. Whenever. Let's just *go*, okay? Let's just . . . go."

We talked: School. Movies. Bands. Homework. Everything. Nothing. What else? Drove around. For hours.

Her ponytail was short but full, a single blond twist that she gathered up in one hand and lifted as she tilted her head forward. I thought she was looking at something on the floor, and I wondered for a second whether I had tracked something in.

"Jack?" she asked, head still forward. No one outside my family had made my name a question before. "Would you be a sweetie and rub my neck?"

The hum of tires, the zing of crickets, the shrill stream of air flowing through the crack that the passenger window never quite closed.

"Ma'am?"

"My neck. It's all stove up and tight from tennis. Would you rub the kinks out for me?"

"Sure," I said, too loudly and too quickly. My hands moved as slowly as in a nightmare. Twice I thought I had them nearly to her neck when I realized I was merely rehearsing the action in my head, so that I had it all to do over again. Tom shifted gears, slowed into a turn, sped up, shifted gears again, and I still hadn't touched her. My forearms were lifted; my hands were outstretched, palms down; my fingers were trembling. I must have looked like a mesmerist. You are sleepy, very sleepy. Which movie was it where the person in the front seat knew nothing about the clutching hands in the back? I could picture the driver's face as the hands crept closer: Christopher Lee, maybe? No: Donald Pleasence?

"Jack," she said. "Are you still awake back there?"

The car went into another turn, and I heard a soft murmur of complaint from the tires. Tom was speeding up.

My fingertips brushed the back of her neck. I yanked them back, then moved them forward again. This time, I held them there, barely touching. Her neck so smooth, so hot, slightly—damp? And what's *this*? Little hairs! Hairs as soft as a baby's head! No one ever had told me there would be hairs . . .

"You'll have to rub harder than *that*, Jack." Still holding her hair aloft with her right hand, she reached up with her left and pressed my fingers into her neck. "Like that. Right—*there*. And there. Feel how tight that is?" She rotated her hand over mine, and trapped between her damp palm and her searing neck I did feel something both supple and taut. "Oooh, yeah, like that." She pulled her hand away, and I kept up the motions. "Oh, that feels good . . ."

The sun was truly down by now, and lighted houses scudded past. Those distinctive dormer windows—wasn't that Lisa's house? And, in the next block, wasn't that Kim's driveway?

We were following the route. We were passing all the homes of the stars.

Tom said nothing, but drove faster and faster. I kept rubbing, pressing, kneading, not having the faintest idea what I was doing but following the lead of Anna's sighs and murmurs. "Yeah, my shoulder there . . . oh, this is wonderful. You'll have to stop this in about three hours, you know."

After about five minutes or ten or twenty, without looking up, she raised her left index finger and stabbed the dashboard. A tape came on. I don't remember which tape it was. I do remember that it played through both sides, and started over.

Tom was speeding. Each screeching turn threw us off balance. Where were the cops? Where was all the other traffic? We passed Jane's house, Tina's house. Streetlights strobed the car like an electrical storm. We passed Cynthia's house—hadn't we already? Beneath my hands, Anna's shoulders braced and rolled and braced again. I held on. My arms ached. Past the corner of my eye flashed a stop sign. My fingers kept working. Tom wrenched up the volume on the stereo. The bass line throbbed into my neck and shoulder blades, as if the car were reciprocating.

Gravel churned beneath us. "Damn," Tom muttered, and yanked the wheel, fighting to stay on the road. Anna snapped her head up, looked at him. I saw her profile against the radio dial.

"I want to drive," she said.

Tom put on the brakes, too swiftly. Atop a surging flood of gravel, the car jolted and shuddered to a standstill off the side of the road. The doors flew open, and both Tom and Anna leaped out. My exhilaration long gone, my arms aching, I felt trapped, suffocating. I snatched up the seat latch, levered forward the passenger seat, and stepped humpbacked and out of balance into the surprisingly cool night air. Over there was the Episcopal church, over there the Amoco station. We were only a few blocks from my house. My right hand stung; I had torn a nail on the seat latch. I slung it back and forth as Tom stepped around the car. Anna was already in the driver's seat.

"You want to sit in front?" Tom sounded hoarse.

"No," I said. "No, thanks. Listen, I think I'll, uh, I think I'll just call it a night. I'm nearly home anyway. I can, uh, I can walk from here. Y'know? It's not far. I can walk from here." I called out to Anna, leaning down and looking in: "I can walk from here." Her face was unreadable, but her eyes gleamed.

"Huh?" Tom said. It was like a grunt. He cleared his throat. "What do you mean, *walk*? It's early yet."

The car was still running. The exhaust blew over me in a cloud, made me dizzy. "No, really, you guys go on. I'm serious. I'll be fine. Go on, really. I'll see you later on."

"We could drop you off," Tom said. He spoke politely but awkwardly, as if we had never met. "Let's do that. We'll drop you off in your yard."

Anna revved the motor. It was too dark to see Tom's expression as he looked at her. Her fingers moved across the lighted instrument panel, pulled out the switch that started the emergency flashers, *ka-chink ka-chink ka-chink*, pushed it back again. "Cool," she said.

"I'll see you later," I said. "Okay? See you, Anna. Call me tomorrow," I said to Tom.

"Okay," he said. "I'll call you tomorrow."

"Okay," I said, not looking back. I waved a ridiculous cavalier wave, and stuck my hands in my pockets, trying to look nonchalant as I stumbled along the crumbling asphalt shoulder in the dark.

Behind me, two doors slammed. I heard the car lurching back onto the highway, gravel spewing, and I heard it make a U-turn, away from town and toward the west, toward the lake, toward the woods. As the engine gunned, my shoulders twitched and I ducked my head, because I expected the screech of gears, but all I heard was steady and swift acceleration, first into second, then into third, as the Firebird sped away, into fourth, and then it was just me, walking.

They never came back.

Tom's parents got a couple of letters, a few postcards. California. They shared them with Anna's parents, but no one else. "Tom wants everyone to know they're doing fine," that's all his mom and dad would say. But they didn't look reassured. Miss Sara down at the paper, who always professed to know a lot more than she wrote up in her column, told my father that she hadn't seen the mail herself, mind you, but she had *heard* from people who should *know* that the letters were strange, rambling things, not one *bit* like Tom, and the cards had postmarks that were simply, somehow, *wrong*. But who could predict, Miss Sara added, *when* postcards might arrive, or in *what* order. Why, sometimes they sit in the post office for *years*, and sometimes they never show up at *all*. Criminal, Miss Sara mourned, criminal.

Anna's parents got no mail at all.

I never did, either, except maybe one thing. I don't know that you could call it *mail*. No stamps, no postmark, no handwriting. It wasn't even in the mailbox. But it felt like mail to me.

It was lying on my front porch one morning—this was years later, not long after I got my own place, thought I was settled. At first I thought it was the paper, but no, as usual the paper was spiked down deep in the hedge. This was lying faceup and foursquare on the welcome mat. It was one of those Hollywood maps, showing where the stars can be found.

I spread it across the kitchen table and anchored it with the sugar bowl and a couple of iron owl-shaped trivets, because it was stiff and new and didn't want to lie flat. You know how maps are. It was bright white paper, and mighty thick, too. I didn't know they made maps so thick anymore. I ran my index finger over sharp paper ridges and down straight paper canyons and looked for anyone I knew. No, Clint Eastwood wasn't there. Nor was anyone else whose movies I ever had seen at the mall. A lot of the names I just didn't recognize, but some I knew from cable, from the nostalgia channels.

I was pretty sure most of them were dead.

I searched the index for Tom's name, for Anna's. I didn't see them. I felt relieved. Sort of.

"California," I said aloud. Once it had been four jaunty syllables, up and down and up and down, a kid on a bicycle, going noplace. California. Now it was a series of low and urgent blasts, someone leaning on the horn, saying, come on, saying, hurry up, saying, you're not too late, not yet, not *yet*. California.

It's nearly eleven. I stand in the cool rush of the refrigerator door, forgetting what I came for, and strain to hear. The train is passing, a bit late, over behind the campus. My windows are open, so the air conditioning is pouring out into the yard and fat bugs are smacking themselves against the screen, but this way I can hear everything clearly. The rattle as my neighbor hauls down the garage door, secures everything for the night. On the other side, another neighbor trundles a trash can out to the curb, then plods back. I am standing at the kitchen counter now. Behind me, the refrigerator door is swinging shut, or close enough. I hear a car coming.

The same car.

I move to the living room, to the front door. I part the curtain. The car is coming closer, but even more slowly than before. Nearly stopping. It must be in first gear by now. There was always that slight rattle, just within the threshold of hearing, when you put it in first gear. Yes. And the slightly cockeyed headlights, yes, and the dent in the side. I can't clearly see the interior even under the streetlight but it looks like two people in the front.

Two people? Or just one?

And then it's on the other side of the neighbor's hedge, and gone, but I still can hear the engine, and I know that it's going to turn, and come back.

My hand is on the doorknob. The map is in my pocket. The night air is surprisingly cool. I flip on the porch light as I step out, and I stand illuminated in a cloud of tiny beating wings, waiting for them to come back, come back and see me standing here, waiting, waiting, oh my God how long I've been waiting, I want to walk out there and stand in front of the car and make it stop, really I do, but I can't, I can't move, I'm trapped here, trapped in this place, trapped in this time, don't drive past again, I'm here, I'm ready, I wasn't then but now I am, really I am, please, please stop. Present or past, alive or dead, what does it matter, what did it ever matter? Please. Stop.

Please.

SILENT LOVE
Esther M. Friesner

Esther M. Friesner's first sale was to *Isaac Asimov's Science Fiction Magazine* in 1982; she's subsequently become a regular contributor there, as well as selling frequently to markets such as *The Magazine of Fantasy and Science Fiction*, *Amazing*, *Pulphouse*, and elsewhere. In the years since 1982, she's also become one of the most prolific of modern fantasists, with more than twenty novels in print, and has established herself as one of the funniest writers to enter the field in some while. Her many novels include *Mustapha and His Wise Dog*, *Elf Defense*, *Druid's Blood*, *Sphinxes Wild*, *Here Be Demons*, *Demon Blues*, *Hooray for Hellywood*, *Broadway Banshee*, *Ragnarok and Roll*, *Majyk by Accident*, *Majyk by Hook or Crook*, *Majyk by Design*, *Wishing Season*, and *The Water King's Daughter*. Her most recent books include *The Sherwood Game*, *Child of the Eagle*, and *The Psalms of Herod*. She lives with her family in Madison, Connecticut.

Freisner is best known for her Funny Stuff, of course, but in recent years, in another sharp change of pace, she has also been writing haunting, somber, and powerful stories such as "All Vows," "A Birthday," and "Death and the Librarian," which won her a Nebula Award in 1996. In the sleek, bleak, and merciless story that follows, definitely *not* one of her funny ones, she shows us that it's always a grave mistake to confuse the shadow and the substance, the image of the thing portrayed with the Thing Itself . . .

Silent Love

The house where she had lived was up for sale, and he had money. No one expected him to spend it at all, let alone on that great white elephant of a place. But it had been *her* house, and he had always been hers. The only thing was, he didn't know it until it was too late.

Four years at Harvard hadn't done Edward Claypool much harm, beyond a few bursts of youthful indiscretion in New York on certain weekends, but that had been with companions. When the madcap twenties spread their spangled wings over the cities, he saw only the steady trickle of ticker tape between his fingers. Left to his own devices, he invariably reverted to the same stolid, sparkless existence that had allowed generations of Claypool men to hold fast to their capital over the years and even through the Great War. He lacked imagination, which was all to the good, given that his chosen career was finance. Imagination spawned the sort of plungers that would be the ruination of the Market, or so his father always said.

Edward's life did not seem to be much the worse for this dearth of fancy's impracticalities. Each day he showed a round, bland, smooth, almost parboiled face to the other men in the office, took his commands from Father, and went forth to invest his clients' money with neither fanfare nor delight. Mornings he rode his horse in the Park, the noon hour was sacred to a brief, brisk walk in the environs of the Stock Exchange, and evenings called for either a meeting with old schoolchums at the Club or duty to be done at any of a number of social events at which his presence was considered *de rigeur* by Mother. He squired damsels in froths of white organdy through the Season, steered them deftly around the ballroom floor at the Ritz or the Plaza or the Biltmore, got them bootleg liquor to drink should they request or require it, and took his moonlight liberties with the same lukewarm detachment that characterized his style of doing business. After all, he knew that when he did choose to marry, it would be only another of the series of prudent investments that had formed the pattern of his life.

Buying her house was in no way prudent. He didn't know what possessed him. He could not for the life of him say how he'd come to allow the garrulous real estate agent—slick hair, cheap celluloid collar, poorly ironed cuffs, and toadying deference—to call upon him at home. Had he made a call arranging this? He must have. Had he been drunk at the time? Not according to the calendar. It was April; the last time he had overdone the gin to the point of aching amnesia was at the Harvard-Yale game, and then only because it was what was expected of him.

"It's a charming little place out on the Island," the agent was saying, having made himself quite at home in Edward's club chair. A cigarette was poised in the V of his fingers, unlit, a pointer he used to advantage on an invisible chalkboard. There was something disturbingly effeminate about the man's gestures, and there clung to him an aroma of violet-scented toilet water used with far too liberal a hand. Edward pursed his lips in mild distaste and dreamed of opening every window in the place once he had banished this man.

He didn't banish him, of course. He heard the fellow describe at length the property in question, using all the usual laudatory terms of his profession, then heard himself inform the man that he would be pleased to see it next Sunday. They could motor out together— using his car, of course. He would call for the agent at about five, after he was done with Sunday dinner at his parents' apartment off Fifth Avenue. It would be no trouble, no trouble at all.

Afterward, Edward spent the remainder of his evening drinking heavily from a bottle of fine old brandy that his father had given him in honor of his graduation, Prohibition be damned. In wine there was supposed to be truth, but the hard truth remained that Edward Claypool had no imagination, and therefor simply could *not* begin to imagine why he had agreed to see the property.

"*L'Hirondelle*?" Edward's mother repeated the name of the property in question. Her French pronunciation was perfectly Parisian, her disdain perfectly English, her lack of familiarity with the name of the famed North Shore estate much less than perfectly American. "'The Swallow,' what a charming name to give a home, how lovely, though I don't suppose there really *are* any swallows within miles of the place." She cut another bite of rare beef and chewed industriously.

"You're not actually thinking of living there," Edward's father stated, helping himself to more of Mary's excellent mashed potatoes. He too was ignorant of any histories connected with his son's intended purchase. It all came from reading the wrong newspapers. "You're a bachelor. Move to a larger apartment, if your money's burning a hole in your pocket. Buy a yacht. Invest in racehorses. But to purchase a house of that size—! People will call it a mindless extravagance. Your professional reputation will suffer. I forbid it." Mr. Claypool was convinced that his son was still of an age where the paternal veto retained any power beyond temporary irritation.

"I'm not *buying* anything," Edward gritted, toying with the remains of his Yorkshire pudding. Sunday dinner with his parents was a form of Purgatory in which even he, a bone-bred Episcopalian, could believe devoutly. Fortunately, his time in durance was abbreviated not by Masses said for the repose of his soul, but by the everadvancing hands of the boule clock on the dining-room mantelpiece. "I'm only going to *look* at it."

"Then it's a waste of time even if it's not a waste of money."

"I have my own resources," Edward asserted in an uncharacteristic access of spunk.

"Don't you take that tone with me, you puppy. You never worked a day in your life for those precious 'resources' of yours."

"He's right, you know," Mrs. Claypool spoke up. "My father didn't set up your trust fund so that you could go and squander—"

"Mother, I'm not about to squander anything."

"Don't interrupt your mother," Mr. Claypool directed.

"Thank you, dear," Mrs. Claypool said before returning her attention to their only child. "As I was saying, Edward, my father did not—"

"If you're off to market to buy mansions by the dozen, try taking just the money you've earned for *yourself!*" Mr. Claypool stabbed at his son's shirtfront with the Sheffield blade he used to carve the Sunday roast. Desolations of stainless white Irish linen lay between the knife's point and Edward's chest, but the younger man winced as if he felt the prick of fine steel in the flesh. "You *might* be able to make the down payment on a bungalow."

"It's not all that big, it's not really a mansion, it's just a good, large house such as I know I will need one of these days when I *do* marry, and in any case, I am only *looking*," Edward finished with some small ferocity.

"You sound as if you've already looked at this place, if you know all that much about it," his father said.

Edward lowered his eyes to the few scraps of food and smears of gravy left on his plate. "The real estate agent told me. I'll be seeing it for the first time this evening."

"Evening, is it?" His father snorted. "A fine time of day to go gathering impressions of an investment property. How can you hope to see any of the flaws? This entire affair smells to high heaven. Was this your idea, or have you fallen into the hands of a flimflam man? Have you lit on your head recently? Why *this* house, of all houses? Why *now*, of all times?"

"It *is* rather unexpected, Edward, dear," his mother murmured, discreetly signaling Joan to begin clearing away. "This one particular property . . ."

It was at that moment that he remembered. As he sat there, still staring down at his dinner plate, he glimpsed the maid's slim, white hand as it glided in to remove the dish, a soft, silver shape darting out of shadows. A tiny ghost, a living hand, and yet a haunt that laid hold of his memory and drew it back to where this madness had begun.

He had been in his office reviewing his accounts when his secretary had announced a caller. He knew the man, one of his most satisfied clients, a Mr. Caleb Peterson. Mr. Peterson was master of a fortune too recently acquired to be quite reputable in the better circles, yet this apparently didn't trouble him in the least. He simply kept on adding to its bulk—with Edward's aid and counsel—and never bothered himself about social climbing. He entertained show-girls, frequented speakeasies, and read the tabloids. He had one tucked under his arm then, as a matter of fact, and after his brief, comradely conference with Edward, he forgot it on the edge of the desk.

Edward had picked it up, leafed through the pages idly, and tossed it into the wastepaper basket without a second thought. Second thoughts came later, ghosting before his eyes in lines of crisp, black type, and the silvery smear of a dark-eyed face in an old, old publicity photograph. That was how he had come to call about the house, because he had read in Mr. Peterson's paper that it was for sale; because *she* was dead. The eyes swam up out of the blinding whiteness of the empty tablecloth before him and smiled.

So you still remember.

"I'm interested in this particular house because it's out near the Selkirk place," he lied, inspired. "You remember old 'Lemons' Selkirk, don't you? One class behind me, has a law practice in New Haven, I took his sister Rose to the Winter Dance my junior year." He blathered on at some length in this same vein, doling out commonplaces until his parents lost all interest in the matter of *L'Hirondelle*.

It was a serviceable ploy. Edward's father grumbled. "Rose Selkirk, eh? It strikes me there are simpler ways of courting a young lady than by pretending an interest in real estate, but, well, suit yourself." He turned the conversation to politics.

After dessert and coffee, Edward excused himself and went to keep the appointment he'd made with the disquieting real estate agent. Although he had offered to telephone the man before departing his parents' apartment for their rendezvous, the fellow had insisted that no such courtesy was needful. Mr. Claypool had suggested five as the hour of their meeting, five let it be. And if Mr. Claypool were detained, the agent would wait. The house would surely also be waiting.

It was quite dark by the time they reached the place. The roads out to that part of the Island were little more than dirt tracks that still showed the print of many hooves, both horseshoe-shod and cloven. "She liked her privacy," was what the agent said. "She told me that Hollywood's no better than a small town, really, with everyone knowing everyone else's business. That was what she'd left Iowa to *escape*, after all."

Edward said nothing. He kept his eyes on the road. There were too many eyes slivering the darkness with their stares of gold and glimmering green, too many small, hard minds intent on only prey. He thought his heart would shatter from such excess of terrible beauty. Beauty shines brightest, burns hardest, in the dark. Beside him, the agent was nattering on, mouse-tooth words nibbling away at the beautiful stillness. Edward said nothing to him at all, but Edward wanted to shout him mute.

She should have stayed in the cities, he thought, feeling the wheel becoming slick under his fingers. The night was cool, wisps of early lilac blossom casting their scented lures across the gulfs of air. Still, his plump palms were sweating. *The cities were her proper place, all silver and black. She'd never have been noticed there. A leopard hunts best where it's best hidden, where its pelt's the same dappled gold as the grass. You'd think she'd have at least as much sense as a cat.*

"We're almost there," the agent was saying, and true to his word, they were. A hard left off the main road, a long, straight course up an avenue of oak trees, and then pale moonlight on the lawns of *L'Hirondelle*.

He bought it, of course. There had never been any question that he would not, once he'd stepped across the marble threshold and looked up the grand staircase that seemed to trace the curve of a drowsing woman's hip and thigh. The electricity was still on—she had not died so long ago, the power company bills were paid up—and by the crystal-twinkling light of the great chandelier, he saw her.

The shock of color slammed into his eyes. He had worshipped her in tones of gray and silver, black and white, but this was nothing like the publicity photographs taken at the studio's command while she lived. This was a portrait in oils, done at her commission, in all the vibrant shades of life. She had been pleased to pose for it in the costume from one of her most famous movies, in the role of Semiramis, the legendary queen of Babylon. She stood at the gateway to her private kingdom, guarding the entry to all mysteries and splendors, beauty her only sword. Gold and gems shot rays of brilliance from the diadem nestled in her knee-length tumble of auburn hair, silks and silver netting draped her body from breast to thigh, though one leg was glimpsed naked to the hip and beyond, skin bared clear up to the little gem-girt waist. One hard, round breast showed itself ensnared in the shimmering net cloak, the nipple a smear of crushed roses.

"Wasn't she *divine*?" The little real estate agent was in ecstasies.

He clasped his hands together like a maiden pleading for her virginity at the villain's feet. "They billed her as 'The Woman All Men Desire.'" Just saying that made him giggle. Then abruptly, all business: "The asking price includes all furnishings currently on the property."

Edward swallowed hard and said, "I'll sign."

There really was nothing his parents could do about it except fume and call him seven kinds of fool whenever they saw him. His mother chose to do this obliquely, forever asking him if he was quite well, paying him more mind since his wild extravagance over the house than in all the years since she'd birthed him and handed over his care to Mary and Joan and the schools. He ignored them and their intrusive chatter. He banished them into the outer realm where noises and tumults and all the assaulting harshness of the world's clamor must abide.

Silence. Enclosed by his office's dark oak-paneled walls, he had had some small taste of it. In the stone-scented fastness of the library at Harvard, he had courted it. In the times spent in the solitude of his room at school, when his comrades and playmates and tormentors had gone elsewhere with their noisy business, he had savored fleeting tastes of it. Now it was his. He had purchased its kingdom and its guardian. She would understand.

"*L'Hirondelle*?" said "Lemons" Selkirk over oysters at the club. "That was that movie star's old place, wasn't it? Gosh, you should've heard Father having kittens all over the house when he heard *she'd* bought into the neighborhood! As far as he was concerned, it was the same as having a boatload of refugees from Sodom and Gomorrah pitch up on our dock. Not that she ever did anything particularly sinful while she lived there—too busy out in Hollywood most times to do more than have a little flying visit, here and gone. No orgies, no scandals—not at *L'Hirondelle*, anyway—no streams and streams of the vulgar rich—meaning anyone with more money than Father, money that they actually earned instead of getting from a dead man's hand—not even one chance for the old man to fly into a righteous rage and summon the local constabulary with a complaint of music played too loud." He chuckled, beefsteak face twinkling, an overfed pixie on a toot. "I think maybe that was what irked him most of all."

Edward said nothing. He squeezed a little lemon over the slick flesh of an oyster and watched the living creature writhe ever so slightly at the burning touch of the juice. He tilted the shell to his lips and swallowed the oyster whole.

"Lemons" Selkirk leaned across the table. "I suppose this makes you one of the landed gentry. Must've cost you a pretty penny. It's not one of the largest estates out our way, but still—I understand the debts she left behind were enormous. No heirs, but still a slew of creditors to be paid. Mother says you probably sold off some of the furnishings to cover your outlay. Mother thinks highly of you, you know."

Edward said nothing. He sipped a dry white wine and faced the possibility that he didn't want any more oysters, though better than half a dozen of them lay awaiting his pleasure on the plate. The waiter in his crimson jacket hovered near in blessed silence, ready to glide in and correct any faults found in the meal. Edward folded his napkin and laid it on the table beside his plate, a wordless signal that all was well, that it was his appetite to blame and not the oysters.

"Lemons" had no such problem with a sluggish appetite, neither for food nor for chatter. He devoured his portion of bluepoints avidly, hardly missing a breath as he jabbered away about things that neither interested nor concerned his host. Edward watched his old schoolchum calmly, and just as calmly pictured him dead. A shovelful of earth in the face was what it would take to silence "Lemons" Selkirk sufficiently.

The invitation to the Harvard Club had not been Edward's idea. Mother had received a call from Mrs. Selkirk, saying that business was bringing her Lawrence into the city and wouldn't it be a good idea if the boys got together. Really, it was so inspiring to see how hard young Edward was working these days. Hardly a soul of his old acquaintance heard from him at all. So Mother had relayed the conversation, handing it over to him at Sunday dinner all wrapped up in her carefully veiled command that he contact Lawrence, "Lemons," call him by whatever hideous nickname he liked, only he *must* see him.

"Why don't you invite him to your house?" Edward's mother concluded.

No. That was impossible. The thought of "Lemons" and his raucous, braying laughter admitted to the voiceless splendors of the kingdom . . . no. It would be rape. It would be desecration.

"I'm going to be busy," he'd offered. He might as well have flung a mouse into the maw of a hungry lion.

"Well then, seeing as how you're always out there on the weekends, how you never seem to have any time to visit your own parents these days, perhaps we ought to *all* motor out there, pay a call on the Selkirks, and then visit you. We wouldn't stay long, if *that's* what you're afraid of." She gave him one of the old, cold, condescending looks that had always poured out oceans of pity and contempt over any of his childhood shortcomings. Her thin mouth drew itself up small, only awaiting his next inevitable failure to tweak into a smile of low expectations justified.

If he objected to this, he would fail utterly in the duty of a Good

Son. He had already stumbled from that height when he bought the house, fallen farther away with every Sunday that he spent away from the parental dinner table, but he lacked the spine to turn his back on it entirely.

So he'd agreed to meet "Lemons" in the city, and to endure this extended outrage to his ears, and to pretend he was having a good time.

Dinner at the club wasn't the end of it, of course; not by a long shot. "Lemons" was now living in New Haven, if you could call that living. Blue laws snapped at his heels at every turn, sharp-fanged hydra-heads of the old, *passé* Puritan morality. Before he had to slink back into the spirit-sapping dullness of his daily life, he intended to get out and *live*.

That meant "speaks" and nightclubs, Harlem dives where the jazz was sleek and the cigarette smoke blued the air. It meant wild taxi rides up and down the avenues, familiar faces from the old Harvard days hailed across dance floors, parties brimming with brazen fellowship, loud and frantic festive groups that formed and scattered and reformed themselves according to the whim of the celebrants. Everyone knew "Lemons" and almost everyone knew Edward too, though he soon grew weary of hearing them tell him that they hadn't seen him on the town for so long that they'd thought he was dead.

At last, the party ended when "Lemons" sat down on the rim of the fountain in front of the Plaza Hotel and informed one of the stone turtles that he was incapable of going another step. Then he keeled over on the pavement, snoring. Edward knelt beside him, shaking him by the lapels of his dinner jacket. The evening was warm for May, and it smelled of cheap gasoline fumes and carriage horse droppings, the burgeoning green of Central Park, and the medicinal stab of gin on Selkirk's breath. Edward called out for help, but neither he nor the policeman who came running to answer his summons could discover anything like a hotel key on the happily snoring drunk's person. "Lemons" had made no more mention of where he was staying while in the city than to remark that he'd had to look afield since the Harvard Club was booked up. The fellow was in no condition to be accepted as a guest at any of the reputable hotels in town, and if he awoke in a fleabag there would be trouble about it afterward. "Lemons" himself would view it as a joke, but he was never one to keep jokes to himself. He'd tell his mother, who most definitely would *not* see the humor in the situation. She in turn would take care to pass the tale on to Mrs. Claypool, and then—

There was only one thing left to be done.

The taxi ride out to the Selkirk estate on Long Island was long, unpleasant, and expensive. Edward had plenty of time in which to curse his luck at leisure. His original plan—that failing a hotel room, he would drag "Lemons" back to his own city *pied-à-terre* and sling the sodden lawyer onto the divan—was shattered when he stepped from the taxi and realized that while his wallet was still with him, his keys must be somewhere in the gutter near the Plaza Hotel, most likely cast there when he'd tugged out his handkerchief to dab blood from the forehead scrape "Lemons" had earned himself when he keeled over.

It was past four in the morning and Edward lived in a respectable building. Some of his parents' oldest friends lived there as well. If he roused anyone to let him in, in company of so thoroughly gone a drunk as good old "Lemons," it would be noted. Word got around. Word would get back. He would have to listen to Father's lectures and bear with Mother's tidy scorn. Penance might be set at five Sunday dinners in succession, at the very least, five weekends cut short of all their sweetness by this . . . unpleasantness. He could kill "Lemons" gladly, and with a singing heart.

Instead, he took him home.

After a number of bad turns and unplanned diversions from the right way, the cab pulled up in front of the Selkirk home in the first glow of dawn. "Lemons" was deadweight on Edward's shoulder, making little, idiotic gurgling sounds. His fine patent leather dancing shoes scraped themselves a dull matte black on the gravel of his parents' drive.

Edward managed to haul him to the foot of the steps leading up to the front door. He was just contemplating whether it would be better to shift to the fireman's carry or simply prop "Lemons" against one of the stone bannisters and ring for a servant to take over the care and freightage of the Selkirk son-and-heir, when he heard footsteps behind him.

He turned in time to hear a gasp and to see a dainty young woman, clad in an old-fashioned riding habit, standing with her hands pressed to her mouth and her cheeks aflame. "Oh, Larry, you *fool*!" she cried, and stamped one small, booted foot.

Edward stared, his mouth dry and sour. "Rose?" It was the longest conversation he would have with her for almost half an hour. Rose Selkirk, no longer the giddy schoolgirl of Edward's junior year, rushed up the steps to the house and summoned forth the servants, slicing the air with her riding crop and snapping out orders like a Prussian field marshall. Edward lingered beside "Lemons" until four able-bodied men on the Selkirk payroll came trotting out to whisk the snoring lawyer away to his own bed.

"—brother of *mine*," Rose muttered as she stood overseeing the entire operation from the shelter of the Greek Revival portico. She said quite a bit more as well, all of it forceful without being

unladylike. Rose Selkirk had grown up, grown into full womanhood without having grown coarse or vulgar. She was at heart
that rarity of the Jazz Age, an old-fashioned girl. Her hair, the
color of late autumn sunsets, was untouched by the popular
mania for bobbed, boyish cuts. If freed from its restraining tor-
toiseshell pins, it would cascade well below her waist. In the
shadows between the fluted columns, her luminous eyes looked
almost black. Edward stared.

He came to call often, after that. The Selkirks approved. Rose was
at first bemused, then flattered, then sensibly in love. True, Edward
had escorted her to the Winter Dance those several years ago, but it
had been done in the manner of a business arrangement, a pairing
that could not compromise either one of them. She could not have
been in more reliable, less romantically inclined hands if she had
attended on the arm of her own brother.

All that had changed. There was a change in Edward. It was
nothing his parents or the Selkirks could put a finger on when they
saw the young couple together in public. There, as ever, Edward
was the model of phlegmatic propriety. Rose knew better. When he
came to call on her at her parents' home on the Island and the two
of them were left alone in the little parlor, she was devoured by the
change. It touched his eyes first, a slow warmth that came up
behind the hungry stare he fixed on her, a burgeoning heat that
built itself into a sudden blaze. When she first saw that look, she
was afraid, so frightened that she would have cried out for someone—Mother, Father, the servants, anyone at all—to come save her,
and to hell with how foolish she might seem for it after. But before
she could open her mouth, he covered it with his and poured her
full of fire.

What came after that was done with perfect consent, swiftly,
silently, without preamble or excuse. She did not tell him no. She
could not. Who could hear her ask or order anything at all over the
roar of a world ablaze? Even the fleeting thought of what would
happen were her parents to peep into the room was reduced to ash
in the heart of the flames.

They were married very soon, in a small and private ceremony.
The haste of the arrangements might have been called indecent in
some quarters, but Rose had a solid reputation, and her parents
were monied enough for the whispers to be assigned to envious
hearts, not suspicions. Everyone knew that June was the month for
brides, even if this was a courtship that had not properly begun
until early May.

The happy couple would honeymoon abroad. The trunks were
packed, the tickets safe in hand, the ship set to sail for Southhampton
the very day after the wedding. A bridal suite was taken at the Plaza

for the intervening night, and there the newlyweds were conveyed as soon as they might decently leave the intimate reception.

As soon as they were in their room, the bellboy dispatched with tip in hand, Rose seated herself on the edge of the great bed. Radiant in her pale blue traveling clothes, keen with anticipation, she tossed aside her white gloves and sprawled back across the mattress.

"Oh!" she gasped with delight, little shining nails digging into the spread. "It smells of lavender, Edward!" Her hair made a stain like old blood against the duvet.

Edward looked down at his bride, his eyes blinking in time with the sudden flutter of his heart. The walls melted and ran, all the room swirling around him. "Ex—excuse me," he stammered, and stumbled into the bathroom, slamming the door behind him.

He stood at the sink, his fingers trying to gouge holes in the basin's porcelain rim, acid creeping up his throat. A trickle of water swirled down the drain, the sight of it setting his head spinning. He was a man awaking from a dream, but no dream of his own mind's making. One moment he had been in a taxicab with his old schoolmate, "Lemons" Selkirk, and the next he was here, in this room, with that woman on the bed. Who *was* she? His head throbbed, a pain that became the sound of a great bass drum beating back the beautiful silence.

Hush, my love. The trickling water spun a thin strand of words against the throbbing in his head. *Who she is doesn't matter, so long as she is ours to hold.*

He raised his eyes from the basin and saw her face gazing back at him from behind the icy surface of the mirror, a smoky mask of white and black against a plane of purest silver. This was her true kingdom, cleansed of the strident clash of color, framed by the virginity of holy silence. Every time she came to him was like a new bridal night, all times the first time.

But it isn't enough, is it, what I gave you, what I must always give? The eyes of night and crystal behind the mirror met his eyes and held them fast in the spell cast by the chattering reels unspooling the film in the darkness. *I know, I know. Fickle, you human flesh, inconstant, gasping in astonished delight over the dreams I poured my life away to bring you. Each day before the lens, the camera stole another breath of my humanity, the lights burned me away, until only the image was left behind.*

Edward raised one hand to the looking glass, reaching for the face behind the thin transparency. "I love you," he whispered very softly, so that Rose could never hope to hear. "I always loved you."

The black lips never moved, but the black eyes pierced him with the same merciless, imperious look that Semiramis gave her most helpless, most enamored slave before a gesture of her slim white hand bid her guardsmen cast him to his death. *Do not lie to me. We who live on among illusions know the truth. We love an image, but we need the flesh.*

"No." She was turning her face from him, fading back into the mirror's depths. The vision flickered, a reel run in reverse, a mockery of that first night that he'd spent in *L'Hirondelle*. The lights were all out, only a lick of moonlight lying across the carpet, and he in her bed, remembering the boy-years he'd spent in a different darkness, watching her on the screens of a dozen moving picture palaces. How he'd loved her! First with the grateful love of a child who finds a secret door to let him escape from a father who will never find him good enough, a mother who will never really care, sullen servants on whom he is wished yet who never wished for him. And one day, gratitude was gone. She is no longer his escape, but his Grail, his goal, the ember of a boy's awakening needs, the image of all he truly longed to hold, to taste, to take for his own.

That first night, lying in her bed, wrapped in the lingering scent her skin had burned into the pillows, he closed his eyes and breathed deep, pretending to himself that now, at last, she was his.

Something thin and sleek and cool slid across his cheek. He opened his eyes to moonlight, moonshadow. Something rustled in the shadows, a footfall lighter than a breath sounded beyond the bedroom door. And then, out of the darkness, the shimmering white and smoke and silver apparition that was she.

He held his hands before his face and saw the silver netting fall over them, exposing the moon-white curve of her breast, the ashen smear of the bared nipple. Her hair had fallen over him in a stormcloud, its captive lightnings darting from her eyes. In all that portion of her life that she had fed into the camera's ever-hungry maw, she had never needed words. He had opened his mouth to cry out, in fear or in desire, and found his voice swallowed up entirely by the awful, the beautiful silence.

Now this.

"Come back." The words were scarcely louder than the breath it took to bear them. "I don't know what I was thinking, what possessed me. She looked so much like you, it was almost as if you were telling me to. . . !"

Words . . . The image in the glass drifted farther away, a deathmask drawn by a child's hand, a sketch abandoned in the rain, lines of ink that blurred and seeped away. *Don't you think I've heard them all before? I am past promises and vows, excuses and pleas for forgiveness. Do you think you're the first to betray me? At least now I can be the one to leave.*

"No!" He smashed his fists against the bathroom mirror and it shattered into dreams.

"Edward?" Rose was at the bathroom door, her little hands pounding frantically. He let her in, only in hopes of stopping that hideous row, but then she began to jabber at him. Why had he been in there so long, what had he been doing, why was the mirror smashed, why were his hands starred with blood, why had he been crying?

Rose, tractable Rose. Old-fashioned girls might rail against drunken brothers brought ignominiously home in the wee hours of the morning, but they never dreamed of questioning their lawful husbands. He told her it was an accident, and she believed him. He said he had a surprise for her, and she went without a word.

He drove the car himself out to the Island. He filled the time with charming explanations of how deeply he despised the impersonal surroundings of hotel rooms. When he handed her out of the car and up the steps, she must have thought how gallant he was. When he swept her up in his arms and across the threshold, she must have dreamed herself the most fortunate of brides. Then he set her on her feet on the cold marble floor and slipped away into the dark, and what she must have thought of that would remain a mystery.

"Rose."

She startled like a ghost caught by cockcrow at the sound of her own name. "Edward, where are you? Why don't you turn on the lights? Edward?"

He stepped out of the darkness, his arms laden. A spill of silk and silver netting fell to the floor between them. When she balked at what he wanted, he ripped her pale blue traveling suit into rags as he tore it from her body and made her put them on.

She whimpered like a dog as he dragged her up the stairs. Here was no grand queen of ancient Babylon, only poor little Rose Selkirk, helpless in a madman's house. She stumbled many times in the dark; Edward yanked her to her feet and down the hall.

There were scented candles burning in the room, a ring of flickering golden light around the bed, a bank of dancing flames before the portrait on the facing wall. He paused beneath the painting and gazed up at it with a holy rapture saintly nuns might long to feel, possessed by Christ.

"Do you see, my darling?" he cried at the painted face, jubilant. "*This* is why I made her my wife: to bring her here, to you, for *you*! No more captivity, my own! A body, young and living, the perfect mansion to hold your spirit close to me forever. Isn't that what you want? Come. Come and *take* her."

Rose gasped, then kicked bare feet against her husband's trousered legs. He subdued her struggles with almost insolent ease. "You'll be happy, Rose," he told her, the way one might address a child. "She died too young—I don't know how, the papers didn't say—with so much love still trapped within her, so much passion! What we share, she and I, is the real ghost, only a phantom of what we *should* have. She tells me that I need the flesh, but *she's* the one who—" He twitched his head to one side, harking to a voice only he could hear. "Yes," he said, all joyful obedience. "Yes."

But Rose said no. Rose screamed. Edward calmly balled his beefy hand into a fist and creased her jaw, so that she sagged unconscious in his arms. He laid her limp body on the bed, and doffed his own clothes with the solemn purpose of a virgin knight preparing for his vigil. In the golden candlelight, he lay down beside her and whispered to the silence, "Come."

The candles flickered as if battered by a vagrant breath of storm. The gauzy curtains at the windows flung their winding sheets into the room. The portrait that he had caused to be moved from the height of the grand staircase to the privacy of the bedchamber looked down, the painted eyes drinking in the life of the flames, the richly colored flesh paling into the silvered image he had first loved on the moving picture screen.

She stepped out of her portrait, sandaled feet hissing over the carpet. Edward thought he heard a crackling sound in her wake, and the whisper a snake's belly makes over stone. She was not smiling. Her face was rigid in the same expression of beauty and mastery that a hundred frames of film and more had frozen for the ages. Her lips never moved, but in his skull Edward felt more than heard her tell him: *No*.

No, she said, and again, *No*. The force of it was a fist stronger than the one he'd used on Rose. Its power knocked him from the bed, sent him pitching to the floor in an awkward, pathetic mass of naked pink limbs. He scrambled up the bedside again, gaping in shock at his divinity.

"What's wrong?" he panted. "Isn't this what you want? Isn't this what you need? Come back, my dearest, come back into the world and be with me!"

Her laughter made the candles dance, though her face remained the same. *I would sooner die*. Another tinny peal that made his skin turn clammy. *And I did*.

The hissing was louder, its rising clamor drawing Edward's eyes. He stared at the floor at her feet. Long and sleek, flat and shining, the strips of film coiled themselves around her ankles, darted out, shrank away, then slid across the carpet toward the trembling man.

Here is what you loved. Here is what you thought you knew, what you dreamed you could ever own. The film slipped forward, a cool, hideous bite against his leg. He tried to creep away, but he too was frozen in a single frame of time. He could only watch as the strips uncoiled themselves from around her body and snaked around his own. They twined higher with each breath he took, wrapping his calves, his thighs, binding down the rebel flesh that even now was rising, longing for her, wanting—

He clawed at the film before it could enmesh his arms, and threw himself toward her, crying out for reasons, begging for mercy, claiming love. His voice shattered the sacred silence of the kingdom, profaned the noiseless perfection that had held him her captive. The outraged breath of his shout sparked new life into the candleflames. They leaped up and caught hold of the shimmering strips of black and white and silver tangling his body, and where they caught hold, they set teeth that blazed.

He shrieked as the fire enveloped him, trying to rise to his feet, crashing down as his hair caught alight. In despair, he rolled himself over and over on the rug until at last the fires were gone. It was too late. He could no longer tell which curled and blackened strips were his extinguished bonds and which the remnants of his skin. His breath bubbled up liquid in his lungs, thick with blood, his eyesight all but extinguished.

And yet, it was enough for him to see her. She still remained as all her films would keep her, the icon of dead beauty, the idol of silent love. The candles all were gone; she glimmered with starlight. He watched as she drifted near the bed where Rose still lay, costumed in her image.

Rose . . . Was it his own thought or hers? He didn't know. He only saw how her icy seeming changed then, saw the gloating look come into her eyes as she hovered above the living girl's form, saw how desire softened the inky contours of her mouth. *Beautiful Rose, so like her, so like my lost darling. I sent her away when they found out, the studio men. They said we didn't dare, that I couldn't have her. Not while I lived, no. Not then, if I valued my career, they said. How would it look if anyone knew that the woman all men desired had desires of her own and those— What was one more illusion? But I am beyond all illusions now.*

Silver and white, black and gray covered the body on the bed. *And if she died first, deliberately flying from the loneliness of life without me, I thought I'd find her waiting when I followed. To live without her was hell enough. To die without her . . . Two suicides, we would be certain to meet again, we must!* A sigh shivered over the bed. *That too was an illusion. As she is too, this little offering you've brought, only the illusion of my desire, only the image . . . No matter.*

The silks shrouding Rose's skin slid to the floor in a pool of light and shadow, the silver netting holding her breasts melting away like mist touched by the sun. The living girl shifted against the satin coverlet, her hands rising up to hold emptiness close, her lips parting in the first murmur of delight. Triumphant laughter broke from the shadows.

Sometimes the image is enough. Hollow words tinkled like an old movie house piano inside Edward's skull, and then there was only silence.

Brody Loved the Masai Woman

Ian McDonald

British author Ian McDonald is an ambitious and daring writer with a wide range and an impressive amount of talent. His first story was published in 1982, and since then he has appeared with some frequency in *Interzone*, *Asimov's Science Fiction*, *New Worlds*, *Zenith*, *Other Edens*, *Amazing*, and elsewhere. He was nominated for the John W. Campbell Award in 1985, and in 1989 he won the *Locus* "Best First Novel" Award for *Desolation Road*. He won the Philip K. Dick Award in 1992 for his novel *King of Morning, Queen of Day*. His other books include the novels *Out on Blue Six* and *Hearts, Hands and Voices*, and two collections of his short fiction, *Empire Dreams* and *Speaking in Tongues*. His most recent books include the well-received *Evolution's Shore*, as well as several graphic novels, and he is at work on another new novel, tentatively entitled *Necroville*. Born in Manchester, England, in 1960, McDonald has spent most of his life in Northern Ireland and now lives and works in Belfast.

In the icy, elegant, and scary story that follows, he shows us that some encounters with Unearthly Love may prove to be deadly—and that some of them may be *worth* it.

Brody Loved the Masai Woman

In half a century a man inevitably draws a mantle of legend about him. Indeed, for a white man in Africa, it is almost mandatory. No matter that you have planned for yourself a peaceful retirement observing the passing world in all its exponential craziness from the cool of your verandah, punctuated by the occasional pause for contemplation of the ocean on the reef; rest assured that your legends, more so than your sins, will find you out. Among a people whose major form of recreation is gossip—ever the way with expatriate communities, which is why you will not find *me* down in those discreet bars and cafés far away from the tourist circuit—the yearning for a quiet life is no excuse: if you have no legends, they are more than content to make them up for you. With or without your consent.

Not that I am complaining; if it so happens that a few of those legends find their way into Berlitz, so much the better for the Inn, even if I must endlessly recount them at my table on the verandah to fat, peeling German *haufraus* in ghastly peach-melba micro-dresses, or barely post-teen share-brokers smelling of wetsuit and Piz Buin who cannot wait for the Old Fart to stop his Endless Rambling so they can tell everyone about the Really Important Things they do. If they think they are buying a piece of Real Africa—a thing I grow less and less certain exists as the years pass, or that, if it does exist, cannot be found in the pages of any Kuoni World-Wide Klub-Afrika brochure—I am content to please. The first rule of hospitality: the pleasure of one's guests. At my prices, they deserve it. The truth, as ever, is less glamorous.

I did not kill the leopard with my bare hands. I found him rooting around the back among the bins and, after promptly soiling my vestments (one thing the Great White Hunters never tell you is that Big Game is Big—bloody Big), blew the bugger to glory with the old Mauser that hangs up behind the bar now. The old Syrian taxidermist down in the Old Port most successfully patched up the bullet hole, and a legend was born.

I did not single-handedly drag Ernest Hemingway out of the bar, along the jetty, and throw him into the harbor. Certainly, he was grossly drunk, utterly obnoxious, and quite astonishingly boring, but it was Jack Patience, the then District Commissioner who, when the bum threatened me with violence if I did not serve him another whiskey-soda, had his faithful askaris handcuff the slob to the big baobab until he dried out. I subsequently read every word the man ever wrote and was disappointed to find the episode sadly omitted.

I was not held hostage while the Inn was taken over by the crew of a German U-Boat and used like some kind of submariner's Port-Royal until Kapitan Goestler and his merry crew were sent to the bottom of the Gulf of Aden by Sunderlands operating out of Oman. During the War I played host to Dr. Schrenk, an Ophthalmic Missionary for the Lutheran Church, who was placed under my custody mainly to protect him from people who might think he was a spy, which he almost certainly was not. Dr. Schrenk was a man of such angelic ingenuousness that had he indeed been a spy, he would have had "Occupation: Spy" written in his passport.

The one legend that has never found its way into Berlitz is the best of the lot, but you will not find me telling it to the tourists over G & quinine in the cocktail hour. You can never do the true ones justice.

As Hamid, my *maitre d'* back in those days in '38, would have said, "Necessity, she is the great mother of strange bedfellows." If only he had mixed his cocktails as well. There never was a stranger bedfellow than Angus Brody. Now, there was a man fitted by nature to bear the mantle of "legend." And legend was what he became—though not, I would think, in any way he could have imagined.

Under any other circumstances, in any other country, Brody and I would not even have crossed courses, much less become business partners. If the genteel Dr. Schrenk would have traveled the world under the title "spy," then Brody's passport would have had entered under "occupation" the word "cad," which might have been invented for the man. He was the only son of some decaying clan of Anglo-Irish nobility, and had been sent down from Cambridge on a conspiracy of such complexity that no matter how often he explained it—which he did, frequently, and with much relish—I still could not unravel it. He had been a radio-navigator on the big Imperial flying-boats from Southampton down to the Cape until, after a by-all-accounts-memorable disagreement with his Captain—they were an autocratic bunch of Blighs, those Imperial Captains—he walked out and left them high and dry on Lake Baringo until a replacement could be flown out from Khartoum. Immediately thereafter he took Lord Delamere and his Happy Valley bunch for a truly obscene sum in cards and, with a fine instinct for survival, fled to the coast before they closed ranks and arranged some small but mortal hunting accident for him.

I first met Brody the day he took delivery of a brand-new

Grumann Goose seaplane. Of course, it was memorable. Woken
from my siesta by an ungodly roar of engines, I was hailed by this
red-haired figure clad only in khaki shorts and flying goggles looming from the cockpit of a seaplane and asking would I mind awfully
grabbing hold of the end of this rope, he'd been tootling up and
down between those bloody dhows for the best part of an hour now
trying to find somewhere to tie up. The seaplane mail service he ran
up and down the coast was, on paper, perhaps the most spectacularly flagrant enterprise since the Tower of Babel, yet he still found
himself with enough of a surplus to sink into some West Country
bumpkin's daft notion of an Inn on the north mainland of Mombasa.

Money stuck to Brody like shit to a blanket. He spent profligately,
he earned even more prodigiously. When I proposed we name the
Inn after its major partner he said, "For God's sake don't. I have no
desire to be associated with it when the damn thing starts to make
pots of money." Which of course it did; far more than even he could
absorb with his gloriously unprofitable airline. In those last couple
of years before the War it became quite the fashionable thing to do;
pop down on the overnighter from Nairobi, spend a day or two
acclimatizing at Hedley's Inn, and then fly up to Malindi, Lamu, and
points north with Brody Marine Airways.

Once the Inn was firmly established as *the* place to swill your
Gordon's of an afternoon, I found myself propelled from the anonymity
of an impecunious English teacher at the Foreign Nationals' School
through the ivory doors of Coast Society, which suddenly opened
before me. Truth be told—and tonight we tell the truth, the whole
truth, the dark truths, the painful truths—I suspect that I rode into the
consular parties and dickie-bow and stiff-little-finger cocktail receptions
on Brody's coattails. Though it was my name on the shingle, it seemed
to be the one they could never quite remember. A salutary experience
was overhearing some plump—no, we are to tell the truth, so the truth
shall be told: *fat*—heiress asking her equally fat companion just who
was that one? . . . yes, that one standing there? . . . the little mousey,
schoolmastery one?

Brody of course was as attractive to women as to the pound ster-
ling. All credit to him, he always felt it meet, right, and his bounden
duty when at the center of some circle of bedazzled admirers to
summon me to join him with an imperious wave of the hand—
"Ladies, you really must meet my very good friend Mr. Neville
Hedley"—before gravitating toward the champagne, leaving me trying vainly to keep hold of the reins of social nicety as, one by one,
the dainty things made their apologies with ill-concealed boredom
and slipped away.

Perhaps if I had not gone to the coming-out party at the
Henderson place, it might never have happened. But then again,

this is Africa, where what will happen will happen. Here, God's ways are not easily frustrated by human free will. I would have declined but for the prospect of an evening behind an empty bar with only the enigmatic silences and occasional surreal pronouncements of Hamid for amusement. Not even a frock flown in from London could disguise *La Bella* Henderson's inherent lumpishness as she fluttered and twittered through her social *debut*, striking paroxysms of embarrassment into all with whom she came into contact. The horse riding; that is what I blame. Some kind of transfer of atoms takes place through the saddle between arse and ass.

"How about we quietly tip our champagne into the pot palms and vanish into the night?" I suggested. "We could be in Zanzibar by midnight. The smell of cloves on the wind from the shore, the soft caress of white surf on the reef, muted saxophones under the banyan trees . . ."

Brody was staring with the pietistic fervor of a contemporary Catholic saint at the door where a small, toadlike gentleman in a preposterous evening cloak and hat like a collapsing stovepipe was handing gloves and cane to the houseboy.

"My God, what kind of creature is that?"

"Sergio Schiavoni, the Italian Honorary Consul. I'm surprised you haven't met him before. Loves to scandalize. Something to do with being virtually socially ostracized over the Abyssinian affair."

"No no no, not him, not that tedious little tit. I know him. That. With him."

By any standards, she was quite staggering. As she drew the hood of her gown away from her face I will swear to this day that a gasp ran through the Henderson's ballroom, a thing I have only ever thought to be a writer's literary fancy. Sergio Schiavoni's Mr. Toad features were creased in unabashed smugness.

Somali, perhaps, or Galla. Masai even. She wore her Nilo-Hamitic poise and nobility with the sensuous grace that a panther wears its pelt. Her skin was of that texture that you know you must touch to feel if it is as powdery smooth as you imagine it; Earth-colored, the red ochre Earth of Africa: it will not be so bad, you think, to be buried in the earth if it is like her. She was dressed in white silk, Italian silk; a sheer, clinging sheath of fabric that amplified her essential *primality* into something almost godlike.

After the lightning, the thunder. As the rumbles and grumbles followed in the wake of the shock—*too much, too far, far too far this time, that damn Eyetie has gone too far this time, I tell you, bringing a black, look at Hettie, she's distraught, quite distraught, the dear thing*—a light gleamed in Brody's eye, a look of steely resolve I had not seen in him before.

"Mind this." He thrust his cocktail glass into my safekeeping.

"I've got to talk to her. I will die if I do not talk to her." He moved through the mutterers and nodders like an elegant snake while I attempted to console Hettie Henderson, spectacularly eclipsed and weeping long mascara tears down the front of her London party frock.

"Masai, actually."

If the Empire Upon Which the Sun Never Sets has a soft under-belly; it is the Slump; that half hour, forty-five minutes in early after-noon during which luncheon presses heavily on the duodenum, inducing a most un-English torpor and lassitude. Should it be let slip to assorted fuzzie-wuzzies, mahdis, dervishes, wallahs, and sepoys that around two-thirty, three o'clock the way to Buckingham Palace lies flung wide, belts slackened, collars undone, waistcoats unbut-toned, we would be swept from the face of the earth between Gin and Its and afternoon tea.

"I know. Lake Natron Masai, to be precise."

We sat in wicker chairs at a wicker table with a bottle of Bushmills, watching the white triangles of the dhows set out upon the trade winds for Arabia and India. A tramp steamer lay long and ugly and incongruous in the offing.

"What's more," I said, "I also know that she's a Mission widow." The primly dressed doctrinally sound missionaries have it all wrong. The universe is not monotheistic. The universe is governed by an essential dualism that balances evil with good and good with evil. Africans are born understanding this. We call it African Fatalism; they call it common sense. Why, even the *wazungu* missionaries prove it every time they morally blackmail some young Masai *moran* into taking a dip in the river: oh yes, you may sing with the saints and the saved, but it is Written that a man shall leave his par-ents and cleave to a woman and only unto her. Meaning, one woman only. Meaning, Solomon and his six hundred wives notwithstanding, no true washed-in-the-blood Christian can enjoy polygamy. Meaning, on the principle of last in, first out, you, you, and *you* are divorced and *you* will be my one and only.

It is not even that easy in Islam.

And so the poor cows end up drifting into the towns and petty prostitution or witchcraft or semi-slavery on some smug Gikuyu's shamba or a shadowy existence as concubines to fat, balding Great White Hunters, riddled with halitosis and impotent with gin and masturbation. Because sure as when an elephant shits it shits, no Masai worth his cattle is going to take a used wife; one careful owner.

"Story is some railway surveyor found her half-dead by the side of the Lake Magadi Branch line, took pity on her, and brought her down to Mombasa. He already had a Giriama woman but he kept her anyway—a little taste for the exotic, never suspected in the Uganda railway employee. Anyway, before long the Giriama woman is accusing this Masai of being a vampire—you know, one of those women who turn in the dead of night into leopards, or spiders, and do whatever scary things it is vampire leopards or spiders do. Superstitious people, the Giriama, almost as bad as ex-pats—they may have Allah on their side but they still have to say a prayer every time they turn on the tap or flush the toilet in case the *djinn* that lives down the *choo* drags them to perdition. The upshot is the Masai woman ups and leaves, the surveyor and his Giriama are posted to Eldoret, and the next thing we know Schiavoni is parading around all the best places to be seen with her on his arm. Took her back to Italy, you know. Met *Il Duce*."

"How the hell did you find this out, Hedley?" Brody poured two gushing measures from the banks of the far river Bush.

"People tell me things. You may find it hard to believe, but they do. It's because I stay quiet long enough to listen to them."

"Pretty much squares with what I learned from her. Didn't know about the Giriama bit." He studied the five fingers' worth in the tumbler. "Well Nev, here's cheers: up the King and down the queers." He threw down the liquid in one swift, golden motion. "I am going to have her, you know."

"It will be over Schiavoni's dead body."

"That can be arranged."

He was gone three days, up coast on a mail run and engaging in what he cautiously referred to as his "shameful secret," which seemed to involve Amharic coffin ornaments and forged bills of lading from Mogadishu. On his return, I had news.

"It seems Allah smiles favorably upon you. Your wish is to be granted."

"How now, *petit* Neville?"

"Schiavoni is sick."

He actually grinned, the rogue.

"Nothing trivial, I hope."

"Dr. Coupar's bluffing and blowing but he doesn't have a clue. Word is they might as well measure the poor bastard now."

"Italy's adversity is Ireland's opportunity."

"You appall me."

Schiavoni was dead within a month. Dr. Coupar, chief consultant of the big mission hospital across the pontoon bridge and a regular at the Inn, where I kept a bottle of sacramental single malt under the bar for his personal abuse (savvy Hamid? you no-good Muslim, there are more ways than one of marking a bottle), attributed the cause of death to Tropical Pneumonic Fever, which he, and we, and everyone in the ex-pat community with the possible exception of equine-arsed Hettie Henderson, knew meant Sweet F.A.

"Place'll be a lot quieter without him." The nearest the dour Coupar ever came to a eulogy.

"When's the funeral?" Only when you have known Angus Brody at the constant close range our partnership entailed can you distinguish the malevolent gleam in his smile of opportunism from a trick of dentistry. To the practiced eye, it is the exact shape and color of an Arab riyal.

Such a pity we never get to laugh at our own funerals. Schiavoni would have been delighted. As he lay in state hoping for a few fond farewells and perhaps forgivenesses from those he had so magnificently affronted, one of the bearers accidentally kicked out a trestle and sent Sergio tumbling from his coffin, smirking mordantly, to fall at the feet of the dowager Lady Amehurst who never quite recovered and was shipped back to Cheshunt on the first passing P & O. Then the Archbishop of Afars and Issas, apparently an old University friend, turned up in full arch-episcopal purple and was stoned by the local tenement children who later claimed he was an *afrit* but in all probability had heard of his reputation as a celebrated pederast. Then, as Schiavoni, at last eternally reunited with his box, was lowered into the earth, a sudden squall blowing up from God knows where reduced the dignified ensemble to a fleeing shambles of sagging feathers, dripping parasols, and drenched mourning suits.

"Tremendous fun," declared Brody. "I wish I'd known the chap better now. You noticed her, of course."

I had to admit that I had not. Brody waved in the direction of the Holy Ghost Church. A patch of darkness detached itself from the general shade beneath the trees that surrounded the tin-roofed church and moved away, as if ashamed to have been caught privy to some complex, secret white ritual.

"Excuse me, old son, if I dash, but the lady seems to be in need of a chaperone."

"For God's sake, the man isn't even cold yet."

"I know. Dreadful, aren't I?"

And off he went, loping across the still-wet grass with that silly, affected half run they only teach at public schools.

For Brody to absent himself for a week at a time was quite characteristic. Ten days was nothing unusual. When a fortnight passed without his breezing in and skimming his hat in the general direction of

Hamid I became concerned, but not unduly. When three weeks passed and the Goose was still tied up at her landing stage, I put the word out.

The very next evening, as I was preparing for the cocktail hour rush across the Nyali bridge—a flotilla of Baby Austins crunching to a halt on Hamid's neatly raked gravel—in he sauntered, fresh as the proverbial daisy. Damnably nonchalant, insufferably Brody. He slipped in behind the bar and helped himself to a brace of Guinness Exports.

"Really, Neville, there was no need to have your Baker Street Irregulars out after me. We're not married, you know."

"Where the hell were you?" Though I knew, and Brody knew that I knew, and I was angry at myself and angry at him and angry at all the subtle, feminine little psychological intrigues that such knowledge forced us to play with each other. He had been out and about. With her. All over town, into every club and restaurant that would admit them, making scenes at those that would not, up to Nairobi, down to Dar, showing her off everywhere and to everyone. And now, last of all, he had brought her home to show me. It was that that angered me most.

She was casually dressed, European style, in a sleeveless collared blouse and wide-legged cotton lounging pants. The heeled sandals seemed uncomfortable and confining to her, as though she had been born to go barefoot upon the earth. But neither casual nor formal, European nor African, dress could add to nor detract from her. She commanded attention, drew every eye in the room to her and would not release them.

"Isn't she a stunner, Nev?" His matey slap on the back felt heavy and treacherous as a wooden cross. He tossed her a Guinness bottle; with one swift, elegant pounce she caught it and uncapped it with her teeth. "My God, look at that! What can you say, Nev? What can you say?" He beckoned her over. She moved like the long rains. "N'Delé, Neville Hedley; Nev, N'Delé. Actually, Nev," (he leaned across the bar in best ham conspiratorial fashion) "I have a bit of a favor to ask you."

You can always tell the big ones. They are always "little." Or "a bit."

"Seems, old chap, that what with Schiavoni kicking the bucket, passing on, buying the farm, and going to join the choir invisible we have a bit of an accommodation problem. In that the house, old chap, has now passed into the hands of some aged Aunt, the erstwhile Terror of Salerno, and latterly Djibouti, who has made it manifestly clear in a broadside of truly blistering telegrams that under no circumstances, no circumstances, Nev, my son, will she tolerate the presence of *that woman* on the premises. So, Nev, old comrade, we find ourselves with a little bit of, shall we say, a housing crisis?

Which could be speedily and satisfactorily resolved by the simple application of the words *'Yes, Brody, I'd be delighted'* to the request *'Might N'Delé and I move into the Inn for a while?'* Old chap? Nev, old comrade? Nev, you've gone uncharacteristically quiet, even for you."

Quiet, Brody, old bean? You could hear the ice melting in the glasses. Every head was attentively turned elsewhere in that grotesquely stilted *me? listening?* attitude.

"No, Brody, I would not be delighted."

And the long bar room of Hedley's Inn came to life again.

He wheedled. He pleaded. He bantered and charmed and fawned. He blustered. He blew. He threatened, he bribed. Through it all I kept shaking my head and saying "No, Brody, no, not this time," and the Masai woman sat on the edge of a glass-topped bamboo table and took long, luxurious swigs from her triple-X Guinness.

As with everything to do with Brody, his departure from the Inn was spectacular. He could make an exit, I'll give him that. He lifted a heavy glass ashtray from the bar and hurled it with all his considerable strength (he had bowled for Cambridge, he claimed) into the bottles racked behind the bar.

It was not racism. Nothing as simple as that great late Twentieth Century panacea that always seems to be leveled at the white race and no other. I did not mind if Brody humped his Masai woman six times a night and crowed like a cock from the balcony each time. I did mind him doing it under my roof, in my rooms, at my bar; I did mind seeing my regular patrons that I had built up over the months drifting away one by one, with polite, but final apologies, to someplace with a more conducive atmosphere, you know, with a better class of clientele. You know.

It was a simple business decision.

The hell it was. Now I must come to the heart of my honesty. Half a century of life as a bachelor gay (cannot even say that anymore: no piracy on the high seas as dreadful as the piracy of the words on your lips) gives one a certain perspective, if not exactly breadth of vision, upon one's own self—one has little else to do than contemplate and cultivate the inner man when one *gets on*—and I know now that what really prompted me to say "no" was jealousy. Good Old Testament green-eyed bugger-you jealousy.

One thing. I remembered it after he had gone, she following three steps behind, a subtle, masklike smile on her face. One does remember things, afterward, one replays those painful scenes in the mind trying to make them come out right after all. But they never do. I remembered that throughout our conversation, Brody had picked incessantly at a long, narrow scab on his left forearm. Picked and picked and picked until it bled.

Of course it was the talk of the city. Damned perversity—just when I did not care if I never saw that freckled, grinning, *Boy's-Own-Paper* face again, I was bombarded by daily itineraries of their goings and doings, recorded and reported in such microscope detail that I could have retraced every step they took from the hotel where Brody rented a suite to the café where they took breakfast to Mackinnons market where the Masai woman bought the food she prepared so lovingly for her Brody. Biltong, papaya, and beer; I even had detailed breakdowns of their daily menu whispered to me across the bar.

All things pass. But by the time I was filled with repentance and remorse (and, truth be told, fed up to the back teeth with tedious old farts creaking in their wicker chairs all day and mumbling for whiskey-soda and longing for a bit of Brodian mirth and japes)— they were gone. Malindi, Lamu; or south, Pemba, Zanzibar. Rumors circulated that the Grumann Goose had been sighted as far down-coast as Isla da Moçambique.

It is not an illusion. It is true. Time is speeding up. For everyone, not just for old fascists like me. Three months is like an evening gone, as the hymn says; then, it was like a thousand ages. Three months, fed on nothing more substantial than rumors. I was upcountry when the telegram came, some safari with the Earl of Rutland—more an excuse for an epic piss-up than any serious shooting; if an elephant had blundered into our tents we would not even have been capable of hitting it. Hamid was waiting for me at the compound gate, driven by concern into hitherto unheard of unintelligibilities.

The telegram was eloquent enough. While attempting a takeoff run from Pemba to meet up with a safari group at lake Eyasi, Brody had lost control and crashed the Grumann. I later heard he had plowed straight through a fleet of fishing boats—not killing anyone purely by Anglo-Irish luck—hit a jetty and ripped off a float and the tail section. He was alive—more Celtic luck—and relatively uninjured, but on medical recommendation had been flown up on the first Imperial to Mombasa. The telegram was dated five days previous. I knew the schedule of the Imperials like the Lord's Prayer.

"Hamid, where is he?"

"The CMS Hospital, Mr. Hedley." I have never permitted Hamid any of the *bwana m'kuba* nonsense. "Ludwig Krapf Ward. I have taken the diabolical liberty of summoning a taxicab."

Pity he never could mix cocktails worth a damn.

Coupar was waiting for me at the inquiries desk. Prim Protestant missionary nurses from Halifax and Pontypridd rustled hither-thither, in crisply starched white linen.

"God, he's not dead is he?" What else could one's reaction be, on being greeted by the Chief Consultant.

"A little less free with the Fourth Commandment, Hedley. This is a Mission Hospital. Brody? Dead? Not a chance. However, he is a very sick man."

"The crash. But I'd heard he'd sustained only minor injuries."

"Mostly cuts and bruises. He walked away from it, up the beach, into the village, found a Catholic mission, and asked the sisters if they could contact his insurance broker for him. Then he collapsed. The sisters took one look at him and flew him up here.

"He seems to be suffering from some kind of pernicious anemia of a kind quite unfamiliar to the sisters, and, I must confess, to me." He looked at me askance in that parsimonious, Scots-covenanting way that does not apportion blame, but does not exonerate either. "Has he been in any fights recently?"

"Apart from ours? No. Brody has no shame. He is impossible to insult. He would walk away from any potentially violent situation."

"I was hoping you wouldn't say that. It's just that he has a number of scars, old lesions that do not seem to have been caused by the crash. A large number, in fact. Both forearms are very heavily scarred, calves likewise; upper arms and thighs are more lightly marked. Some are several months old, others barely scabbed over. If I did not know better, I would say they were knife wounds."

While we had been talking, Coupar had been leading me along the gloss-painted, antiseptic-perfumed corridors and stairs to the small private ward where Brody was being kept.

"See if you can get anything out of him" were Coupar's parting words to me as he opened the door and showed me in.

Someone, perhaps Brody himself, had filled the room with flowers, more as a defense against the all-pervasive and deeply dreadful smell of *hospital* than to cheer the room, which was brilliantly lit by a large latticed window with a splendid view of Port Tudor and the North Mainland. The sea was that pure ultramarine you only find in tropical waters, which seems deep and blue enough to invite you to drown there.

"If you open the window and hang out with one hand, you can see the old place," said Angus Brody. "So I'm told. Haven't been able to try it yet. Good of you to come, Nev. Got anything to drink?"

The brilliance of the room only emphasized the more his ghastliness. He was a ghost of himself. Gaunt. Drained. Exhausted and devoured. Skin a tight-stretched translucent drumskin behind which the life but barely beat. He sat propped up against pillows like a disconsolate marionette, dressed in smoking jacket and old Harrovian tie.

"Best bloody view in Mombasa. Pity you have to be here to enjoy it."

She sat at his side on a tall, straight-backed chair, like carved ebony, perfect, absolute, moving only to light cigarettes for her Brody. She did not even acknowledge my arrival. Her expressionless face remained fixed on Brody, like an icon, as she slipped the cigarettes between her lips, drew flame.

"Seem to have had a bit of a prang, as the saying goes. In fact, I would go so far as to say, a bona fide, *wizard* prang. Be a long time before I can look my insurers in the face again. Sure you've got nothing to drink?"

"Sorry."

"And you running a pub. N'Delé, love, do us a favor. Slip out the back way so Coupar doesn't see you down to the Falfarino and get me a bottle of Bush on the account?"

She looked from him to me and I saw suspicion flicker in her eyes. It is like a widening of the pupils, the look of suspicion, just wide enough for you to be able to see a little into the soul. When she was gone Brody seemed to relax. It was a painful relaxing, like a bag of bones settling onto the earth, but he seemed at ease.

"Coupar told you?"

"About what?"

"About my membership in a bizarre Thuggee self-mutilation cult? He's right, you know, but for all the wrong reasons, hah hah you bloody little Scot."

He drew up the sleeves of his smoking jacket. Both forearms were a raw, cross-hatched mess of scars, scabs, and still-oozing wounds.

"God Almighty, Brody . . ."

"She was right, you see."

"Who was right?"

"The Giriama woman."

I thought for a moment that he had succumbed to some malarial ranting madness, then remembered. Our conversation, at the table, over the bottle, in the Slump. "The railway surveyor's Giriama."

"Well done, Neville. The one who drove N'Delé out because she maintained she was a vampire." He lit a cigarette. It seemed a relief to him. The ashtray was full to overflowing. "She was right. All along. She is a vampire.

"Oh, none of that swirling capes and turning into bats and aversion to sunlight and garlic, not even changing into a leopard or spider at the full of the moon. Nothing remotely Bram Stokerian about it. She's a real vampire. A true vampire. She is a creature that feeds on blood.

"It's their way, you see. It's always been their way, the Masai. Blood and milk. From the cattle, usually. They'll open an artery in the leg or the neck, run off a quart or so—the cow can spare it—mix it in a gourd with milk and drink it freshly curdled.

"It's in the Old Testament, isn't it? I've been looking it up in the Gideon. Everything is in the Old Testament; here all human vice and wickedness are writ. The blood ye shall not touch, it is sacred to me, for in the blood is the life and the life is mine, saith Jehovah. Or words to that effect."

He exhaled slowly, luxuriously into the bright, flower-filled room. The scars on his forearms were livid.

"They were a nomadic people, the Jews, when the Ten Commandments were handed down to them. Like the Masai. Jehovah was right. The life is in the blood. Life, for her. She can't live without it. I don't understand the biology, maybe Coupar could give some explanation about cells and hemoglobin and vitamins and that stuff; all I know is that if she does not have blood, she will die.

"When she first suggested it, I must confess, I was horrified. Terrified. Something totally outside my experience, totally outside my imagining; dammit man, all I wanted was a little bit of snatch, not to have my wrists slit. Even though it seemed like the vilest perversion imaginable to me, I did not hate her. Can you understand that, Nev? I could not hate her. I love her—I think it is her nature that it is impossible for men not to love her—but I did refuse her. And she faded. Faded, Nev. Day by day, she faded before my sight. She grew listless, irritable, sensitive to the light. She was prone to bouts of dizziness, to fainting, vomiting up blood. What could I do? What else could I do? No hell worse, Neville, than being caught between two hells."

His fingers traced a pale, puckered laceration almost invisible beneath the festering slashes of new wounds.

"It was there she opened me that first time, that first night, with the edge of her Masai knife. In the end, I could not refuse her. But Neville, I learned a terrible thing that first time, that night in Schiavoni's house, in Schiavoni's room with the plaster cherubs on the ceiling, in Schiavoni's bed, something about myself. Neville, I have never known a love as deep, as thrilling, as totally consuming, as lying there in the hot, sweating dark having my blood lovingly, adoringly sucked from my veins."

"Christ, Brody!"

"She's here, Nev."

But I did not hear anything.

"You'll have to go. You must go. No, I know what you're thinking. I wouldn't even dream of leaving her. I love her. She loves me, after her fashion. Blood seals the bond. She needs me in a way no one else has ever needed me; for once in my goddam spendthrift useless life, I am important to someone."

The door opened. The Masai woman entered with a bottle wrapped in a copy of the *Times* several months out of date. She flickered her eyes toward me, studied me suspiciously. It was the most regard I had ever received from her.

"Nev's just leaving, darling. Pour us one, would you?"

One of the manifold curses of age is that imagination becomes too easily confused with memory. In my mind I see still the glitter concealed within the curve of the fingers of her right hand—but is it imagination, or the real, bright gleam of the knife's edge?

The Viking funeral was Jack Patience the D-C's idea. He was a Manxman, the Norse blood ran thick and frothing in his veins—and anyway, we had been drinking. When you drink, and reminisce, when you sit on the verandah with a bottle and a few friends and the moon rising out of the distant edge of the monsoon, when you commemorate all the many infuriations and excesses and eccentricities and dazzling triumphs of a life like Angus Brody's, you pass beyond mere drunkenness into a clear-sighted, rational insanity where a notion as mad as the hero's farewell seems utterly reasonable, even desirable.

"What did the cause of death read?" I asked Coupar as the edge of dawn lit the oceanward horizon. "Tropical Pneumonic Fever?"

"A pneumonic fever caused by unknown infection. Did he ever tell you, Hedley? What the hell caused those scars? What the woman had to do with it?"

I shook my head. We were all—myself, Jack Patience, Coupar, and the mechanics who had had the Grumann towed up from Pemba by dhow—too drunk to see what a bad lie it was.

"I don't know. I'd like to say I'd never seen anything like it before, but I had," Coupar said.

"Schiavoni," I murmured into my glass, but no one heard.

Coupar signed the release forms that morning—the prim Protestant nurses regarded him queerly, sniffing as they rustled past—and we had Scobie the Harbor Master tow the seaplane out beyond the reef. It was a nightmarish voyage; with the exception of Scobie we were all dreadfully hungover. One of the mechanics set the engines to idle, the other liberally soused the plane with fuel. Scobie's Harbor Commission launch kept a respectful station as the Grumann headed east, toward China across the ocean. Jack Patience assumed the mantle of responsibility. He was the best shot of any of us, but what with the tossing boat and the brilliant noonday sun and our general malaise, it took him three attempts before he hit the Grumann with a flare from the Very pistol. As flames engulfed the speeding seaplane, he pronounced the epitaph: "Fare thee well, Angus Brody, we salute you."

We bobbed on the tossing sea, watching, each much occupied with our own thoughts. Then a bright blossom of flame lit the ocean, and seconds later the thump of an explosion shook the boat and we all thought it was the bloody best funeral we had ever been to.

So that is the legend: the legend of the man who died from the love of the Masai woman. But legend is not life. Life goes on beyond the end of the story. Life is not conveniently tied to literary devices and contrivances. Despite Coupar's suspicions, which he carried with him until he died a few years back, I never told a living soul the secret of the Masai woman. She disappeared soon after Brody's death; the fool had left her a colossal whack of his fortune, but all the money in the world, for her, would not have balanced a single drop of blood. The remainder passed to me, with it I was able to expand the Inn into a small hotel and restaurant. Brody was right, it did make pots of money. Flying in the face of all economic trends, it still does.

I never saw the Masai woman again. Rumors of her still abound up and down the east coast, from Cairo to the Cape, though by now she must be very old, unless, like the vampires of legend, she possesses eternal youth and beauty; doubtless she has found new prey for her appetites. But I do not think she does it callously, I believe she did love Brody, as best she could; and that each man she takes, she loves as deeply, and truly. The blood is the bond, the sign and seal of the covenant of souls.

Why did Brody die? Why did Schiavoni die? The Masai are careful of their herds, they count their wealth in cattle; they would not bleed one of their cows to death.

The answer lies, I think, with the new, powerful mythologies by which we explain the world. We know so much more now. We have our own, unique Twentieth Century legends: physics, biology, biochemistry.

It is said that we very seldom invent a new sin. Also true, I think, is that we very seldom invent a new plague. They have all been waiting for us since man first walked in the valley of Olduvai. Some we defeat: the more blatant, immediate ones, the ones that once ravaged entire populations, and the old ones, the slow ones; but the subtle ones move up to take their place. New plagues, old plagues. I read an article in a magazine recently. It was by a French scientist. He said that it has always been with us. All those laws handed down from Sinai on the morality of sex were to keep it out of the household of the Chosen. It kills primarily by sex, but also by blood. I see the photographs of today's victims in the newspapers and my mind is cast back inescapably to Brody, pale and luminous in his bed in the bright room. The only difference is half a century.

Those nightly subjections to the tender knife, the slow, sensuous swallowing down of his blood, must have weakened him until he had no resistance. Then it swept through him and within two months killed him.

Rationalizations. Explanations. Mythologies. Legends. We do not like to think that there are such things as monsters prowling the edges of our comfortable human societies. When we banish them with our incantations—physical, chemical, biological, psychological—are we any different from the Giriama woman who mutters a prayer to the *djinn* in the toilet and sees the beast in a beautiful woman?

No new plagues.

No new sins.

No new truths?

How I wish I could take comfort from that.

ANOTHER COUNTRY
K. D. WENTWORTH

One of the most popular aphorisms of our times is that, when faced with temptation, you should "Just Say No." As the hair-raiser that follows proves, though, sometimes that's easier said than *done* . . .

New writer K. D. Wentworth has made sales to *The Magazine of Fantasy and Science Fiction, Tomorrow, Aboriginal Science Fiction, Return to the Twilight Zone*, and *Ellery Queen's Mystery Magazine*, among other markets. She is the author of the novels *The Imperium Game* and *Moonspeaker*. Coming up is a new novel, *House of Moons*. She lives in Tulsa, Oklahoma.

ANOTHER COUNTRY

> But that was in another country;
> And besides, the wench is dead.

—Christoper Marlowe, *The Jew of Malta*

Paula huddles against his spine, her spare flesh molded to his, seeking his warmth in the bedroom's air-conditioned dimness. Anthony lies on his side, one arm pillowed under his head. Beyond the bedroom window, the moon's chill sliver drifts among stars spattered like paint across some vast canvas. He feels Michelle out there; she always comes to him on steamy summer nights like this. That final moment, the terrible crack of the gun's report, the shattering impact of the bullet, all seem to be forgiven and his part forgotten.

He eases away from the dark red spill of Paula's hair over the pillows and pulls on jeans before he pads down the carpeted hall. Hesitating outside the girls' bedrooms, he listens. Their breathing is soft, even, oblivious, their faces pale and remote in the darkness. He feels a surge of tenderness as Stephanie, his oldest, turns over and mumbles in her sleep, but then the old hollowness spurs him on. He slips into the kitchen and eases back the dead bolt. The bricks are cool against his bare feet as he walks across the patio. The sultry air is warm and sweet with honeysuckle. Crickets shrill thin-edged courting songs that admit nothing of the coming winter which will freeze the life from their bodies. He pauses, then sees the glint of a star-kissed outline under the smooth-limbed mimosa tree.

Tony! Michelle opens her slim arms, oval face framed in the same night-dark straight hair, still and forever fourteen.

As always, he knows this is wrong. He should go back in the house and pull sensible, sane Paula into his arms, but on nights like this, not even her familiar loving touch can fill the terrible void that threatens to consume him.

You bad boy, if we don't leave soon, we'll miss the first dance. Michelle's whisper tickles inside his head.

He shudders. His toes curl against the wiry blades of grass. "It's late—and I have to get up early. I have a big meeting tomorrow."

Come on, Tony. Please. Her teeth are a blaze of ivory, her eyes pearls.

She wears the same simple A-line minidress and white sandals from the night they sneaked down into the basement and made love for the first time. She cocks her head and peers out from under her dark fall of bangs, mysterious and grown-up, young and vulnerable.

Aching with the need to touch her, he wonders what she would have done with her life—nurse, astronaut, mother, junkie, divorcee, president? Would they have married and fought like territorial jungle cats, or parted to say disinterested hellos at high school reunions over stale chocolate cake? He'll never know. Michelle has become part of him in a way she could never have achieved otherwise. She stands between him and his future, his friends, his family, anchoring him back to that one fateful moment when he could have done any of a thousand things differently, and so lived in a bearable future.

She extends her hand. Even in the darkness, her red nails shine. *Sit with me.*

He wants to say no, but he never does. Her skin is cool fire against his palm, smoother than glass. His larger fingers cradle her slim delicate ones. Easing down into the grass, he leans back against the comforting solidity of the tree trunk. She presses her yielding body against his side. Her dress rides up and her soft white thighs gleam in the dark. He slides his hand up that marvelous expanse of young skin. Her breath flutters against his neck, cool, scented with mimosa flowers.

After he married Paula, Michelle came less and less frequently, as though what was between them was gradually running down like a clock he had forgotten to wind, but for some reason, this summer she has been out here almost every night. He watches the house over the smooth dark curve of her head as she presses against him and his body responds. If Paula wakes, she'll reach for him in the darkness, and then in the morning they'll argue again about where he's been.

With his other hand, Anthony absently strokes Michelle's hair, still the rich dark brown of fine walnut, not threaded with silver like his. She reminds him now more of his own daughters than of a girlfriend. He thinks of the first time he mentioned her name to Paula, sitting on the riverbank, watching the moonlight ripple on black water. "Such a shame," she had said. "She was so young and pretty. She had so much to live for." She took his hand between both of hers, and her dark eyes pierced him through, as though some part of her understood at least a little about guilt and loss and unending despair.

The mosquitoes whine; the breeze strengthens and rustles through the mimosa's feathery leaves. He watches the velvet sky as the stars wheel slowly above, until his back stiffens and his legs have gone to sleep and he can't put it off any longer. "I have to go."

Not yet! She turns her face up; her fresh young lips brush his.

He feels the same stirrings of pity/lust/sorrow she always arouses in him. He could take her out here in the dew-drenched grass. They've done it before, a hundred times, a thousand, but it is always the same empty coupling, with no sense of climax or release, the inexperienced fumbling of that first and last night, repeated infinitely.

"It's almost morning." He heaves onto his feet and walks toward the black outline of the three bedroom brick house. She tugs at his arm, her fingers as insubstantial as cobwebs, but he can't look back, or he'll never have the strength to go, and it's even worse when Paula wakes to find him out here.

Her weeping follows him through the darkness. *Don't leave me!* she cries.

As if he ever could.

"You look like—" Paula's eyes flicker across the breakfast table toward ten-year-old Cassie, dark-haired like him, and thirteen-year-old red-headed Stephanie "—hell."

Anthony keeps his gaze on the white bowl of cereal in front of him. "I couldn't sleep last night."

"Most people find it easier to sleep in bed than in the backyard with the bugs." His wife's tone is caustic.

He glances up and winces at the depth of the anger line between her brows. Paula never used to refer to his nocturnal forays in front of the girls. The rules are changing, and he feels even more adrift than usual.

"You'll have to paint your own chigger bites this time." Paula says.

Stephanie giggles, then covers her mouth, still self-conscious about her new braces. Just crossed into puberty, her breasts are firming up, her waist tucking in. She has a certain coltish grace, but most of the time has no idea what to do with it. He sees a glimmer of bright promise in her, like an uncut emerald peering from beneath sheltering granite.

He crunches a mouthful of grainy cereal. "I was thinking about the presentation for Hinchlow Electric today."

"You ought to be able to do those things in your sleep by now." Paula's dark liquid eyes bore into him. "In fact, I think you should take a few days off. Mom's sixtieth birthday is next week. Let's go up to Winfield and stay at Aunt Sally's for the party."

A thin trickle of dread runs down his spine. "I— You know I can't get off in the summer."

"Harvey takes off in the summer." She positions her spoon beside her bowl on the vinyl flowered tablecloth with exaggerated care. "And Ed, and George."

"That's—why." Anthony's hand trembles as he stirs his coffee. "Someone has to stay behind and run things. I'm junior to everyone else. You take the girls and go. I'm sure your mother will understand."

"Can we, Mom?" Cassie's honey-brown eyes gleam with anticipation. At ten, she still likes visiting cousins and grandparents.

Stephanie leans back in her chair and drags her fingers back through the thick red waves of her newly permed hair. "Well, *I* can't go. I have a date with Bobby for the rec center dance."

"There will be a lot of other dances, but Grandma will only be sixty this one time." Paula's lips compress into a thin bloodless line.

Stephanie's eyes brim with bright, unshed tears. She stares at Anthony in a mute appeal for backup, then wads her paper napkin and jerks away from the table.

Paula watches her retreat down the hall to her bedroom. Her fingers drum on the table. "Maybe we should stay."

"No," he hears himself say, "your mother is expecting you. I don't want you to disappoint her."

The next two nights pass by, quiet and undisturbed. Refreshed by the unbroken sleep, Anthony signs the sentimental birthday card Paula lays before him, nods his approval of the lacy white blouse. Before he leaves for work, he carries the suitcases out to the green Ford station wagon and heaves them into the back. Cassie hugs him hard, but Stephanie averts her face and slides across the backseat, refusing to kiss him good-bye. The July sun beats down on the back of his neck as he clicks her door shut.

Paula waits for him by the front steps where the bees are buzzing in and out of the morning glories. She shreds one of the velvety blue blossoms between her restless fingers. "I suppose, as always, you won't tell me what's wrong."

Anthony shifts his weight uneasily. A drop of sweat rolls down his neck.

"You'd think by now, I'd be used to it." Her honest face with its overbold nose stares at him frankly. "I realized, when we got married, that there were parts of you I would never know, parts hurt too badly. No one can go through what you did and be the same, but, Anthony, it's been over twenty years."

"Look," he says, sliding his hands into his pockets, "I'm sorry. I've just had a lot on my mind."

She wipes a tear out of the corner of her eye, but her expression is fierce. "The girls deserve a father who exists in the same universe with their braces and dances and boyfriends." She snaps open her purse and fishes for her keys. "If things aren't a whole hell of a lot better by the time we get back, you'll have to move out."

He glances aside at the car. Cassie grins from the front seat and waves.

"Join AA, or sign up for counseling, or come out of the closet, or—" Tears spill down her pale cheeks. She hugs her arms around her chest and looks away. "Hell, I don't know what to tell you. Just admit whatever it *is*, so we can deal with it, even if it's another god-damned woman! I can't take not knowing anymore."

He nods, his throat too constricted to say anything. Her fingertips graze his cheek, then she drops into the driver's seat. A moment later, the tires sigh against the hot pavement as the station wagon turns the corner.

That night, he shuffles papers at the office until the cleaning crew chases him out, then can't bear the thought of eating alone in the silent, empty house. He stops for a hamburger and fries on the way home and carries his dinner out to the picnic table on his patio. The air is as warm and thick as the syrup used to be on his mother's pancakes. Michelle surrounds him in the dusk, her blue eyes ringed with black mascara, lipstick red as berries. Cool fingers touch the back of his neck. He jerks to his feet.

She laughs, low and throaty, wispy. Her flowery perfume circles his neck like a noose. He reaches for her numbly, but she glides away into the yard. He follows, wondering—did he desire her like this before? They were so young then, fumbling, unsure. Now, when his body knows the way, she teases as though she is the one who has matured.

Her dark hair flies as she swirls through the grass, dancing to some melody only she can hear. He sinks to his knees. "Michelle . . ." He wets his lips and forces the words out. "I can't live like this anymore."

I love you, Tony. Her face is sweet and sad.

"This isn't doing either of us any good." He feels wetness on his cheeks. "I keep getting older. My wife needs me, and my girls . . ."

She touches his face with frosty fingertips. He catches her wrist and presses his lips to the chill skin, then jerks to his feet, appalled at himself. He dumps the rest of his dinner and retreats inside to his bedroom. His heart pounds as he stretches out on the bedspread, presses his face to the pillow that still smells of the no-nonsense freshness of Paula's lemon-scented cologne.

He remembers that long-ago hot summer night, when his folks had gone to a dinner at the lodge. He and Michelle had been dating since the month before school was out. The world seemed wider when he looked into her creamy face; his shoulders felt broader. Full of plans and anticipation, he picked her up an hour before the dance and took her back to his house.

"Come down and look at our new pool table," he said, pulling her by the hand through the entrance hall. She raised a slim black eyebrow, but let him guide her past his mother's china knickknacks to the basement steps.

It was quiet down there, cool and secluded. The pool table was a sea of green amidst the clutter of Christmas decorations, old magazines, his dad's gun-cleaning bench, and a sagging couch. Michelle picked up a polished wooden cue and leaned over the green felt to shoot. Her minidress rode up in the back, exposing her sleek thighs and the bottom curve of one cheek. The multicolored balls clicked and spun crazily, but missed every pocket. She laughed. "I'd have to practice a million years to be any good at this."

He took her in his arms, feeling daring, smoothed her hair back from her eyes, breathing in the clean flowery scent of her newly washed hair. "Wouldn't you rather practice this?"

She turned her face up and closed her eyes. Even now, Anthony can taste the sweet innocence of that kiss, which continued until they were breathing the same air, until their clothes were like a vise and he couldn't contain himself anymore. Ripping at buttons, they collapsed on the old couch and lost themselves in the amazing flash-fire sensuality of naked skin against skin, fumbling and gasping, and then suddenly it was over, without any sense of satisfaction. He collapsed on her porcelain-white chest, spread-eagled across her body, aching, still wanting and having no idea what to do next.

Michelle laughed self-consciously and pushed him off, fumbling her dress back down. Her cheeks were red in the dimness as she turned away, and he could barely pull on his own clothes for the shaking of his hands. She slipped on her shoes and looked up over the sofa. "Hey, what's this for?" She pulled his dad's target pistol out of the rack and the point swung to him. "You guys expecting burglars or something?"

"Be careful with that!" Alarmed, Anthony jerked the pistol out of her hands and cracked his elbow on the rim of the pool table. The gun bucked in his hand—thundered toward the wall. For a fraction of a second, he was relieved it wasn't pointing at either one of them, then he heard the ping of a ricochet and a fleshy red flower bloomed in the middle of Michelle's forehead.

The expression on her face as she collapsed to the cluttered floor wasn't fear or anger, just disbelief. He felt it mirrored on his own. She was only fourteen. This wasn't supposed to happen.

He does not remember his parents coming home later that night, or the ambulance, or the funeral, and very little about the next few months, only the intense gnawing emptiness that pervaded his every thought, making it impossible to get on with the business of living. Life took on the quality of watching television; he heard what was said, saw what happened, but none of it involved him. Sometimes, when he turned around, just for a second the world would appear normal, then the red would come, everywhere he looked, the ground, his shoes, the sky, his parents' faces, all a deep, abiding, soul-wrenching red. He had nothing left but emptiness and loss, a vast aching void where his life had been.

His parents sent him to a succession of doctors and counselors, a private school they couldn't afford. Then one night, when he was huddled outside in the sheltering darkness, wishing his father hadn't gotten rid of the gun, so that he could use it on himself, Michelle came to him in the moonlight, smiling with that familiar crooked front tooth.

He almost passed out, but when she appeared again the next night, it was easier. She was just *there*, that was all, not angry or vengeful, just lonely. The nights with her made it possible for him to start thinking again, to reconnect. He finished school, began to date, eventually meeting Paula down at the Speedway Café where she worked as a waitress.

He turns over in bed and stares up at the ceiling. He would never have looked at a girl like Paula before the shooting. She is reserved and thin, with large-knuckled hands and fierce eyes, but strength shines through her plain, well-scrubbed exterior. When he lies within the circle of her arms, he knows without a doubt that *she* could have taken the gun from Michelle without it going off. She is smart and competent, and as long as he's known her, she's never given up on anything she wanted. Until now.

The next night, and then the next, he closes the curtains, locks the doors, and turns on every television and radio in the house. He paces from kitchen to bedroom to living room, staring at the tiny moving figures as though they were saying things that really mattered, things that could order a person's life and give it meaning, but, concentrate though he might, the TV people are nothing more than ants scurrying around some vast disturbed anthill, methodical and mindless.

Even without looking, he feels Michelle outside. He closes his eyes and sees her out under the starlight, an enchanting child of glass. The blood beats in his temples to a rhythm that has nothing to do with Girl Scouts and station wagons and school dances. He rocks back and forth in his easy chair, willing her to vanish. Sweat mats his hair and glues his shirt to his back.

He can hear her fingers tap the windowpane, feel her baffled gaze, sweet and sorrowful. "Paula," he whispers to himself. "I want Paula. I want my wife and my girls."

By the third morning, his head aches; his knees are drawn up to his chest in a fetal knot. He fumbles for the phone to call in sick, then sinks back exhausted, as though some essential element of blood and bone has leached away in the night and left him ready to fall apart.

He drifts into a restless sleep off and on throughout the day, but wakes each time with a start as though someone had leaned over him and whispered his name.

At dusk, he gets up, feeling worse than ever. His hands shake as he opens the pantry. He pours a can of chicken noodle soup into a pan, then stares at the noodles curled like long white worms. Nothing is right—nothing will ever be right again. He can't stand it another minute.

He turns away and jerks open the kitchen door. The warm night air rushes in, cool against his overheated face. A silvery shape glides out of the shadows.

"No!" He backs into the kitchen. Goose bumps march up his arms. He is bathed in sweat and his knees threaten to give way.

Her empty hand rises like a beacon. Every cell in his body cries out for the balm of her touch. He shudders and steps forward.

She waits for him, humming "Ticket to Ride," a mournful melody played at the last dance they attended. He remembers the tingle of her warm body in his arms, the magnolia scent of her perfume as they slow-danced in their socks on the slippery gym floor. Over the song, he hears the click of a cue striking billiard balls, then the deafening report of a gun. He collapses to his knees on the rough patio bricks, clutching his hands over his ears.

Dance with me, Tony. She looks so sad and afraid, he finds himself reaching out to her. They come together in the darkness, her small cool hands lost inside his. Inside his head, the familiar litany runs, *his fault, he should have been more careful, his fault—*

The back door opens, bathing the patio in yellow light. He feels the glare of it on the back of his head.

"Anthony?" Paula asks. "Is that you?"

He can't breathe as Michelle fades to glitter in his arms, disappears.

Paula's shoes clatter across the patio, then whisper through the grass. "What are you doing out here?" She touches his cheek and looks at her wet fingertips. "Stephanie was so miserable that I came back early so she could go to her dance."

"Stephanie?" He rubs his eyes with the back of his sleeve. The night seems empty, drained. "Where is she?"

"Inside—getting dressed. The dance starts in half an hour." She studies him with narrowed eyes. "What in the hell is it that you *do* out here in the middle of the backyard in the dark, Anthony? I'd really like to know."

"Stephanie's so young." The words escape his throat in a harsh whisper. "So . . . naive."

"She has a good head on her shoulders, and Bobby is a nice boy. They're only meeting at a dance, not running off to Las Vegas, for Christ's sake."

He shakes his head, not wanting to look in her eyes. "It's just that things—happen sometimes."

"You mean guns." Paula's voice is flat.

His hands knot together.

"It was an *accident*." Her nails dig into his arm. "You *know* that."

He looks down into her face, so strong, so pure in its certainty.

She swallows hard. "Come inside and let me get you some supper. You look terrible."

He catches a glint of starlight under the mimosa tree in the back and his heart leaps. "No, I—can't."

She follows his gaze into the darkness. "Who is it?"

"No—no one." He forces the words through clenched teeth.

Paula steps out of the circle of light into the darkness. "Come out where I can see you!"

Anthony's ears roar. "Paula, please—"

She shakes his hand off her arm. "Goddammit, I'm sick of all this pussyfooting around! Show yourself!"

Michelle glides out from under the tree, little more than an outline that reflects the stars. Paula stares, her body stiff and unbelieving.

"This has nothing to do with you," Anthony manages to say. "Go inside and help Stephanie get ready."

"My God, it's *her*, isn't it?" She sways, shakes her head. "It has everything to do with me! If she were another woman, then I could fight for you, or even if it were a man—but she's not *real*, Anthony!"

"I—" He sees Michelle smile and hold her hand out to him. "She needs me. I'm all she has now."

"Bullshit!" Paula shoves him backward. "*She* needs *you?* She's *dead,* Anthony! She doesn't need anything here, or anyone!"

He takes her arm. "But—"

Paula shakes him off, then steps in front of him and faces Michelle, legs braced, hands on her hips. "Why are you still here? Why haven't you gone on—to heaven, or the light, or your next life, or whatever it is that's out there waiting for you?"

Michelle cocks her head, as though listening to something. *He needs me.*

"No!" Anthony struggles back onto his feet.

"That's it, isn't it?" Paula's mouth compresses. "As long as you still have your little teenybopper princess like this, she's not really dead, right? You can pretend it never happened."

He stares past her at Michelle's composed, star-outlined face.

"Come on, Anthony. You've been to enough shrinks by now; you know what this is. It's been over twenty years, but you're still in denial."

"Mom?" Stephanie calls from the back door. "It's time to go."

Paula's hand grasps his chin, forces him to meet her dark eyes. "It wasn't your fault. Forgive yourself. Hell, forgive *her*, and get on with your life!"

Michelle hums "Ticket to Ride" again, soft and sweet, the theme song of his blasted youth. Her smile is moonlight and diamonds.

"Mom, Dad, come on!" Stephanie shades her eyes and stares out into the darkness. She wears a new dress of form-fitting black spangled with rhinestones. "I'm going to be late if we don't leave right now."

Michelle glides between them and the house, her arms upraised, her willowy figure silhouetted against the yellow light. The haunting refrain of the song tears at him as she sings of the lover who no longer cares. Stephanie shakes her head, baffled, and for a moment, he sees Michelle's calm white face superimposed on hers. He shudders—what must Michelle's father have thought when he saw her shattered face at the morgue in the early hours of the next morning? How had he borne it?

Stephanie walks into the yard, then stops, staring at the insubstantial dancer. "What—who is that?"

Paula darts around Michelle's glistening form and takes her daughter by the shoulders. "We'd better hurry. Have you got your purse?"

The girl twists out of her grip, unable to take her eyes off the combination of starlight and shadow in the middle of the yard. "Daddy?" Her face is fearful.

Paula turns to the glasslike girl. "Go away. Leave us alone!"

Tony . . . Michelle holds her hand out. *Come and dance with me.*

"I—" His jaws clench. "I don't need you. You have to go!"

Michelle smiles thinly. Her eyes narrow, and she suddenly seems older, her face sharp and reflective as he's never seen her before. Her eyes glitter with the hard coolness of stars.

He gathers his daughter into his arms and pulls her face to his chest. He watches Michelle over the top of her head. "You have to go now." Inside his head, the shot cracks again, then whines away from the wall. His arms tighten around Stephanie's shoulders.

I'll never leave you, Tony.

A few feet away, moths flutter around the yellow rectangle of the open kitchen door. He closes his eyes and then hustles Paula and Stephanie into the house. They stare at him with accusing eyes, but he feels lighter, almost free. He told her to go, and Michelle understood. It's going to be all right.

Later, after picking Stephanie up at the dance, he and Paula lie in their bed, spooned against each other, his arms around her angular shoulders. Paula sleeps, her eyes darting restlessly beneath closed lids while he watches by the light of the clock radio's red digits. This is the only thing that's real, he tells himself. Michelle is gone for good, and it's time. He doesn't need her anymore. He needs his real life and now he has it, once and for all.

Stephanie sleeps safely in her own bed, after having "a blast" at the dance. Cassie is still in Winfield with her grandparents. Paula lies in the sheltering circle of his arms. He can breathe again, can think about tomorrow, even envision having grandchildren some-day. For the first time since his childhood died in that basement, he feels the future stretching out before him. Life will go on.

A face appears in the doorway to his bedroom, peeking in. He recognizes Stephanie and sits up, careful not to wake Paula. "What's wrong, baby?" he whispers. "Can't you sleep?"

Her eyes shine blue in the dimness and her hand traces the graceful line of her throat. *"I love you, Tony."*

His heart stutters. "W-what?"

She smiles wistfully and he can see, just for a second, the super-imposition of a familiar crooked front tooth over his daughter's braces. *"You bad boy, come on! We're going to miss the dance if we don't leave soon."*

He jerks out of bed, his throat so tight, he can barely breathe. "Stephanie, what are you talking about?"

"We'll always be together. You know that." She holds out a hand to him and comes closer. He sees now that she's naked. Her small breasts rise like pale moons and the dark red thatch of hair between her legs reminds him of another country he has visited many times before. Blood thunders through his head.

"Let's go to the tree," she murmurs. The touch of her fingers is ice-fire, yet also all-too-human flesh, as she draws him down the hall and into the shadowy recesses of the kitchen. His skin tries to crawl off his protesting bones. *"We can be alone there. I remember how much you like that."*

When they open the outside door, the torrid humidity strikes his face like a wall, and there is not the least breath of wind. He takes this willowy child, who both is, and is not, his daughter, in his arms, and buries his face in her fragrant sweep of hair. His hands wander down her back, explore the baby-smooth flanks, the sweet sensual curves, all the wild innocence of that country beyond. Arousal burns through him and he understands. This is the way it must be. Now and forever.

Michelle always comes to him on steamy summer nights like this.

NEVERMORE
Ian R. MacLeod

British writer Ian R. MacLeod has been one of the hottest new writers of the nineties to date, and, as the decade progresses, his work continues to grow in power and deepen in maturity. MacLeod has published a slew of strong stories in the first years of the nineties in *Interzone, Asimov's Science Fiction, Weird Tales, Amazing,* and *The Magazine of Fantasy and Science Fiction,* among other markets. Several of these stories made the cut for one or another of the various "Best of the Year" anthologies; in 1990, in fact, he appeared in three different "Best of the Year" anthologies with three different stories, certainly a rare distinction. He has just sold his first novel, *The Great Wheel,* and is at work on another. Upcoming is his first short story collection. MacLeod lives with his wife and young daughter in the West Midlands of England.

Here, in a stylish and compelling look at a decadent modern world that *ought* to be Utopia, he proves once again that Art—like Passion—is in the eye of the beholder.

Nevermore

Now that he couldn't afford to buy enough reality, Gustav had no option but to paint what he saw in his dreams. With no sketchpad to bring back, no palette or cursor, his head rolling up from the pillow and his mouth dry and his jaw aching from the booze he'd drunk the evening before—which was the cheapest means he'd yet found of getting to sleep—he was left with just that one chance, and a few trailing wisps of something that might once have been beautiful before he had to face the void of the day.

It hadn't started like this, but he could see by now that this was how it had probably ended. Representational art had had its heyday, and for a while he'd been feted like the bright new talent he'd once been sure he was. And big lumpy actuality that you could smell and taste and get under your fingernails would probably come back into style again—long after it had ceased to matter to him.

So that was it. Load upon load of self-pity falling down upon him this morning from the damp-stained ceiling. What *had* he been dreaming? Something—surely something. Otherwise, being here and being Gustav wouldn't come as this big a jolt. He should've got more used to it than this by now . . . Gustav scratched himself, and discovered that he also had an erection, which was another sign—hadn't he read once, somewhere?—that you'd been dreaming dreams of the old-fashioned kind, unsimulated, unaided. A sign, anyway, of a kind of biological optimism. The hope that there might just be a hope.

Arthritic, cro-magnon, he wandered out from his bed. Knobbled legs, knobbled veins, knobbled toes. He still missed the habit of fiddling with the controls of his window in the pockmarked far wall, changing the perspectives and the light in the dim hope that he might stumble across something better. The sun and the moon were blazing down over Paris from their respective quadrants, pouring like mercury through the nanosmog. He pressed his hand to the glass, feeling the watery wheeze of the crack that now snaked across it. Five stories up in these scrawny empty tenements, and a long, long way down. He laid his forehead against its coolness as the sour thought that he might try to paint this scene speeded through him. He'd finished at least twenty paintings of foreal Paris; all reality engines and cabled ruins in gray, black, and white. Probably done, oh, at least several hundred studies in ink-wash, pencil, charcoal. No one would ever buy them, and for once they were right. The things were passionless, ugly—he pitied the potentially lovely canvases he'd ruined to make them. He pulled back from the window and looked down at himself. His erection had faded from sight beneath his belly.

Gustav shuffled through food wrappers and scrunched-up bits of cartridge paper. Leaning drifts of canvas frames turned their backs from him toward the walls, whispering on breaths of turpentine of things that might once have been. But that was okay, because he didn't have any paint right now. Maybe later, he'd get the daft feeling that, today, something might work out, and he'd sell himself for a few credits in some stupid trick or other—what had it been last time; painting roses red dressed as a playing card?—and the supply ducts would bear him a few precious tubes of oils. And a few hours after that he'd be—but what was that noise?

A thin white droning like a plastic insect. In fact, it had been there all along—had probably woken him at this ridiculous hour—but had seemed so much a part of everything else that he hadn't noticed. Gustav looked around, tilting his head until his better ear located the source. He slid a sticky avalanche of canvas board and cotton paper off an old chair, and burrowed in the cushions until his hand closed on a telephone. He'd only kept the thing because it was so cheap that the phone company hadn't bothered to disconnect the line when he'd stopped paying. That was, if the telephone company still existed. The telephone was chipped from the time he'd thrown it across the room after his last conversation with his agent. But he touched the activate pad anyway, not expecting anything more than a blip in the system, white machine noise.

"Gustav, you're still *there*, are you?"

He stared at the mouthpiece. It was his dead ex-wife Elanore's voice.

"What do you want?"

"Don't be like that, Gus. Well, *I* won't be anyway. Time's passed, you know, things have changed."

"Sure, and you're going to tell me next that you—"

"—Yes, would like to meet up. We're arranging this party. I ran into Marcel in Venice—he's currently Doge there, you know—and we got talking about old times and all the old gang. And so we decided we were due for a reunion. You've been one of the hardest ones to find, Gus. And then I remembered that old tenement . . . "

"Like you say, I'm still here."

"Still painting?"

"Of *course* I'm still painting! It's what I do."

"That's great. Well—sorry to give you so little time, but the whole

thing's fixed for this evening. You won't *believe* what everyone's up
to now! But then, I suppose you've seen Francine across the sky."

"Look, I'm not sure that I—"

"—And we're going for Paris, 1890. Should be right up your
street. I've splashed out on all-senses. And the food and the drink'll
be foreal. So you'll come, won't you? The past is the past, and I've
honestly forgotten about much of it since I passed on. Put it into con-
text, anyway. I really don't bear a grudge. So you *will* come?
Remember how it was, Gus? Just smile for me the way you used to.
And remember . . ."

Of course he remembered. But he still didn't know what the hell to
expect that evening as he waited—too early, despite the fact that
he'd done his best to be pointedly late—in the virtual glow of a
pavement café off the Rue St-Jacques beneath a sky fuzzy with Van
Gogh stars.

Searching the daubed figures strolling along the cobbles, Gustav
spotted Elanore coming long before she saw him. He raised a hand,
and she came over, sitting down on a wobbly chair at the uneven
swirl of the table. Doing his best to maintain a grumpy pause, Gustav
called the waiter for wine, and raised his glass to her with trembling
fingers. He swallowed it all down. Just as she'd promised, the stuff
was foreal.

Elanore smiled at him. And Elanore looked beautiful. Elanore
was dressed for the era in a long dress of pure ultramarine. Her red
hair was bunched up beneath a narrow-brimmed hat adorned with
flowers.

"It's about now," she said, "that you tell me I haven't changed."

"And you tell me that I *have*."

She nodded. "But it's true. Although you haven't changed *that*
much, Gus. You've aged, but you're still one of the most . . . solid
people I know."

Elanore offered him a Disc Bleu. He took it, although he hadn't
smoked in years and she'd always complained that the things were
bad for him when she was alive. Elanore's skin felt cool and dry in
the moment that their hands touched, and the taste of the smoke as
it shimmered amid the brush strokes was just as it had always been.
Music drifted out from the blaze of the bar where dark figures
writhed as if in flames. Any moment now, he knew, she'd try to say
something vaguely conciliatory, and she'd interrupt as he attempted
to do the same.

He gestured around at the daubs and smears of the other empty
tables. He said, "I thought I was going to be late . . ." The underside
of the canopy that stretched across the pavement blazed. How poor

old Vincent had loved his cadmiums and chromes! And never sold one single fucking painting in his entire life.

"What—what I told you was true," Elanore said, stumbling slightly over these little words, sounding almost un-Elanore-like for a moment; nearly uneasy. "I mean, about Marcel in Venice and Francine across the sky. And, yes, we *did* talk about a reunion. But you know how these things are. Time's precious, and, at the end of the day it's been so long that these things really do take a lot of nerve. So it didn't come off. It was just a few promises that no one really imagined they'd keep. But I thought—well, I thought that it would be nice to see *you* anyway. At least one more time."

"So all of this is just for me. *Jesus*, Elanore, I knew you were rich, but . . ."

"Don't be like that, Gustav. I'm not trying to impress you or depress you or whatever. It was just the way it came out."

He poured more of the wine, wondering as he did so exactly what trick it was that allowed them to share it.

"So, you're still painting?"

"Yep."

"I haven't seen much of your work about."

"I do it for private clients," Gustav said. "Mostly."

He glared at Elanore, daring her to challenge his statement. Of course, if he really *was* painting and selling, he'd have some credit. And if he had *credit*, he wouldn't be living in that dreadful tenement she'd tracked him down to. He'd have paid for all the necessary treatments to stop himself becoming the frail old man he so nearly was. *I can help, you know,* Gustav could hear Elanore saying because he'd heard her say it so many times before. *I don't need all this wealth. So let me give you just a little help. Give me that chance . . .* But what she actually *said* was even worse.

"Are you recording yourself, Gus?" Elanore asked. "Do you have a librarian?"

Now, he thought, now is the time to walk out. Pull this whole thing down and go back into the street—the foreal street. And forget.

"Did you know," he said instead, "that the word reality once actually *meant* foreal—not the projections and the simulations, but proper actuality. But then along came *virtual* reality, and of course, when the *next* generation of products was developed, the illusion was so much better that you could walk right into it instead of having to put on goggles and a suit. So they had to think of an improved phrase, a super-word for the purposes of marketing. And someone must have said, *Why don't we just call it reality?*"

"You don't have to be hurtful, Gus. There's no rule written down that says we can't get on."

"I thought that that was exactly the problem. It's in my head, and it was probably there in yours before you died. Now it's . . ." He'd have said more. But he was suddenly, stupidly, near to tears.

"What exactly *are* you doing these days, Gus?" she asked as he cleared his throat and pretended it was the wine that he'd choked on. "What are you painting at the moment?"

"I'm working on a series," he was surprised to hear himself saying. "It's a sort of a journey-piece. A sequence of paintings which begin here in Paris and then . . ." He swallowed. ". . . Bright, dark colors . . ." A nerve began to leap beside his eye. Something seemed to touch him, but was too faint to be heard or felt or seen.

"Sounds good, Gus," Elanore said, leaning toward him across the table. And Elanore smelled of Elanore, the way she always did. Her pale skin was freckled from the sunlight of whatever warm and virtual place she was living. Across her cheeks and her upper lip, threaded gold, lay the down that he'd brushed so many times with the tips of his fingers. "I can tell from that look in your eyes that you're into a really good phase . . ."

After that, things went better. They shared a second bottle of *vin ordinaire*. They made a little mountain of the butts of her Disc Bleu in the ashtray. This ghost—she really *was* like Elanore. Gustav didn't even object to her taking his hand across the table. There was a kind of abandon in all of this—new ideas mixed with old memories. And he understood more clearly now what Van Gogh had meant about this café being a place where you could ruin yourself, or go mad, or commit a crime.

The few other diners faded. The virtual waiters, their aprons a single assured gray-white stroke of the palette knife, started to tip the chairs against the tables. The aromas of the Left Bank's ever-unreliable sewers began to override those of cigarettes and people and horse dung and wine. At least, Gustav thought, *that* was still foreal . . .

"I suppose quite a lot of the others have died by now," Gustav said. "All that facile gang you seem to so fondly remember."

"People still change, you know. Just because we've passed on, doesn't mean we can't *change*."

By now, he was in a mellow enough mood just to nod at that. And how have *you* changed, Elanore? he wondered. After so long, what flicker of the electrons made you decide to come to me now?

"You're obviously doing well."

"I am . . ." She nodded, as if the idea surprised her. "I mean, I didn't expect—"

"—And you look—"

"—And *you*, Gus, what I said about you being—"

"—That project of mine—"

"—I know, I—"

They stopped and gazed at each other. Then they both smiled, and the moment seemed to hold, warm and frozen, as if from a scene within a painting. It was almost . . .

"Well . . ." Elanore broke the illusion first as she began to fumble in the small sequined purse she had on her lap. Eventually, she produced a handkerchief and blew delicately on her nose. Gustav tried not to grind his teeth—although this was *exactly* the kind of affectation he detested about ghosts. He guessed, anyway, from the changed look on her face, that she knew what he was thinking. "I suppose that's it, then, isn't it, Gus? We've met—we've spent the evening together without arguing. Almost like old times."

"Nothing will ever be like old times."

"No . . ." Her eyes glinted, and he thought for a moment that she was going to become angry—goaded at last into something like the Elanore of old. But she just smiled. "Nothing ever will be like old times. That's the problem, isn't it? Nothing ever was, or ever will be . . ."

Elanore clipped her purse shut again. Elanore stood up. Gustav saw her hesitate as she considered bending down to kiss him farewell, then decide that he would just regard that as another affront, another slap in the face.

Elanore turned and walked away from Gustav, fading into the chiaroscuro swirls of lamplight and gray.

Elanore, as if Gustav needed reminding, had been alive when he'd first met her. In fact, he'd never known anyone who was *more* so. Of course, the age difference between them was always huge—she'd already been past a hundred by then, and he was barely forty—but they'd agreed on that first day that they met, and on many days after, that there was a corner in time around which the old eventually turned to rejoin the young.

In another age, and although she always laughingly denied it, Gustav always suspected that Elanore would have had her sagging breasts implanted with silicone, the wrinkles stretched back from her face, her heart replaced by a throbbing steel simulacrum. But she was lucky enough to exist at a time when effective anti-aging treatments were finally available. As a post-centarian, wise and rich and moderately, pleasantly, famous, Elanore was probably more fresh and beautiful than she'd been at any other era in her life. Gustav had met her at a party beside a Russian lake—guests wandering amid dunes of snow. Foreal had been a fashionable option then; although for Gustav, the grounds of this pillared ice-crystalled palace that Catherine the Great's Scottish favorite Charles Cameron had built seemed far too gorgeous to be entirely true. But it *was* true—foreal,

actual, concrete, genuine, unvirtual—and such knowledge was what
had driven him then. That, and the huge impossibility of ever really
managing to convey any of it as a painter. That, and the absolute certainty that he would *try*.

Elanore had wandered up to him from the forest dusk dressed in
seal furs. The shock of her beauty had been like all the rubbish he'd
heard other artists talk about and thus so detested. And he'd been a
stammering wreck, but somehow that hadn't mattered. There had
been—and here again the words became stupid, meaningless—a
dazed physicality between them from that first moment that was so
intense it was spiritual.

Elanore told Gustav that she'd seen and admired the series of trip-
tychs he'd just finished working on. They were painted directly onto
slabs of wood, and depicted totemistic figures in dense blocks of color.
The critics had generally dammed them with faint praise—had talked
of Cubism and Mondrian—and were somehow unable to recognize
Gustav's obvious and grateful debt to Gauguin's Tahitian paintings.
But Elanore had seen and understood those bright muddy colors.
And, yes, she'd dabbled a little in painting herself—just enough to
know that truly creative acts were probably beyond her . . .

Elanore wore her red hair short in those days. And there were
freckles, then as always, scattered across the bridge of her nose. She
showed the tips of her teeth when she smiled, and he was conscious
of her lips and her tongue. He could smell, faint within the clouds of
breath that entwined them, her womanly scent.

A small black cat threaded its way between them as they talked, then,
barely breaking the crust of the snow, leaped up onto a bough of the
nearest pine and crouched there, watching them with emerald eyes.

"That's Metzengerstein," Elanore said, her own even greener
eyes flickering across Gustav's face, but never ceasing to regard him.
"He's my librarian."

When they made love later on in the agate pavilion's frozen
glow, and as the smoke of their breath and their sweat clouded the
winter twilight, all the disparate elements of Gustav's world finally
seemed to join. He carved Elanore's breasts with his fingers and
tongue, and painted her with her juices, and plunged into her sweet
depths, and came, finally, finally, and quite deliciously, as her fingers slid around and he in turn was parted and entered by her.

Swimming back up from that, soaked with Elanore, exhausted,
but his cock amazingly still half-stiff and rising, Gustav became conscious of the black cat that all this time had been threading its way
between them. Its tail now curled against his thigh, corrugating his
scrotum. Its claws gently kneaded his belly.

Elanore had laughed and picked Metzengerstein up, purring herself
as she laid the creature between her breasts.

Gustav understood. Then or later, there was never any need for her to say more. After all, even Elanore couldn't live forever—and she needed a librarian with her to record her thoughts and actions if she was ever to pass on. For all its myriad complexities, the human brain had evolved to last a single lifetime; after that, the memories and impressions eventually began to overflow, the data became corrupted. Yes, Gustav understood. He even came to like the way Metzengerstein followed Elanore around like a witch's familiar, and, yes, its soft sharp cajolings as they made love.

Did they call them ghosts then? Gustav couldn't remember. It was a word, anyway—like spic, or nigger—that you never used in front of them. When he and Elanore were married, when Gustav loved and painted and loved and painted her, when she gave him her life and her spirit and his own career somehow began to take off as he finally mastered the trick of getting some of the passion he felt down onto the lovely, awkward canvas, he always knew that part of the intensity between them came from the age gap, the difference, the inescapable fact that Elanore would soon have to die.

It finally happened, he remembered, when he was leaving Gauguin's tropic dreams and nightmares behind and toying with a more straightforwardly Impressionist phase. Elanore was modeling for him nude as Manet's *Olympia*. As a concession to practicalities and to the urgency that then always possessed him when he was painting, the black maidservant bearing the flowers in his lavish new studio on the Boulevard des Capucines was a projection, but the divan and all the hangings, the flowers, and the cat, of course— although by its programmed nature, Metzengerstein was incapable of looking quite as scared and scrawny as Manet's original—were all foreal.

"You know," Elanore said, not breaking pose, one hand toying with the hem of the shawl on which she was lying, the other laid negligently, possessively, without modesty, across her pubic triangle, "we really should reinvite Marcel over after all he's done for us lately."

"Marcel?" In honesty, Gustav was paying little attention to anything at that moment other than which shade to swirl into the boudoir darkness. He dabbed again onto his testing scrap. "Marcel's in San Francisco. We haven't seen him in months."

"Of course . . . Silly me."

He finally glanced up again, what could have been moments or minutes later, suddenly aware that a cold silence that had set in. Elanore, being Elanore, never forgot anything. Elanore was light and life. Now, all her *Olympia*-like poise was gone.

This wasn't like the decay and loss of function that affected the elderly in the days before recombinant drugs. Just like her heart and her limbs, Elanore's physical brain still functioned perfectly. But the effect was the same. Confusions and mistakes happened frequently after that, as if consciousness drained rapidly once the initial rent was made. For Elanore, with her exquisite dignity, her continued beauty, her companies and her investments and the contacts that she needed to maintain, the process of senility was particularly terrible. No one, least of all Gustav, argued against her decision to pass on.

Back where reality ended, it was past midnight and the moon was blazing down over the Left Bank's broken rooftops through the grayish brown nanosmog. And exactly where, Gustav wondered, glaring up at it through the still-humming gantries of the reality engine that had enclosed him and Elanore, is Francine across the sky? How much do you have to pay to get the right decoders in your optic nerves to see the stars entwined in some vast projection of her? How much of your life do you have to give away?

The mazy streets behind St-Michael were rotten and weed-grown in the bilious fog, the dulled moonlight. No one but Gustav seemed to live in the half-supported ruins of the Left Bank nowa-days. It was just a place for posing in and being seen—although in that respect, Gustav reflected, things really hadn't changed. To get back to his tenement, he had to cross the Boulevard St. Germain through a stream of buzzing robot cars that, no matter how he dodged them, still managed to avoid him. In the busier streets beyond, the big reality engines were still glowing. In fact, it was said that you could now go from one side of Paris to the other without having to step out into foreal. Gustav, as ever, did his best to do the opposite, although he knew that, even without any credit, he would still be freely admitted to the many realities on offer in these generous, carefree days. He scowled at the shining planes of the powerfields that stretched between the gantries like bubbles. Faintly from inside, coming at him from beyond the humming of the trans-formers that tamed and organized the droplets of nanosmog into shapes you could feel, odors you could smell, chairs you could sit on, he could hear words and laughter, music, the clink of glasses. He could even just make out the shapes of the living as they postured and chatted. It was obvious from the way that they were grouped that the living were outnumbered by the dead these days. Outside, in the dim streets, he passed figures like tumbling decahedrons who bore their own fields with them as they moved between realities. They were probably unaware of him as they drifted by, or perhaps saw him as some extra enhancement of whatever dream it was they were living. Flick, flick. Scheherazade's Baghdad. John Carter's Mars. It really didn't matter that you were still in Paris, although

Elanore, of course, had showed sensitivity in the place she had selected for their meeting.

Beyond the last of the reality engines, Gustav's own cheap unvirtual tenement loomed into view. He picked his way across the tarmac toward the faint neon of the foreal Spar store beside it. Inside, there were the usual gray slabs of packaging with tiny windows promising every possible delight. He wandered up the aisles and activated the homely presence of the woman who served the dozen or so anachronistic places that were still scattered around Paris. She smiled at him—a living ghost, really; but then, people seemed to prefer the illusion of the personal touch. Behind her, he noticed, was an antiquated cigarette machine. He ordered a packet of Disc Bleu, and palmed what were probably the last of his credits—which amounted to half a stick of charcoal or two squeezes' worth of Red Lake. It was a surprise to him, in fact, that he even had enough for these cigarettes.

Outside, ignoring the health warning that flashed briefly before his eyes, he lighted a Disc Bleu, put it to his lips, and deeply inhaled. A few moments later, he was in a nauseous sweat, doubled up and gasping.

Another bleak morning, timeless and gray. This ceiling, these walls. And Elanore . . . Elanore was dead. Gone.

Gustav belched on the wine he was sure that he'd drunk, and smelled the sickness and the smoke of that foreal Disc Bleu still clinging to him. But there was no trace of Elanore. Not a copper strand of hair on his shoulder or curled around his cock, not her scent riming his hands.

He closed his eyes and tried to picture a woman in a white chemise bathing in a river's shallows, two bearded men talking animatedly in a grassy space beneath the trees, and Elanore sitting naked close by, although she watches rather than joins in their conversation . . .

No. That wasn't it.

Somehow getting up, pissing cloudily into the appropriate receptacle, Gustav finally grunted in unsurprise when he noticed a virtual light flickering through the heaped and broken frames of his easels. Unlike the telephone, he was sure that the company had disconnected his terminal long ago. His head fizzing, his groin vaguely tumescent, some lost bit of the night nagging like a stray scrap of meat between his teeth, he gazed down into the spinning options that the screen offered.

It was Elanore's work, of course—or the ghost of entangled electrons that Elanore had become. Hey, presto!—Gustav was back on line; granted this shimmering link into the lands of the dead and the living. He saw that he even had positive credit, which explained why he'd been able to buy that packet of Disc Bleu. He'd have slammed his fist down into the thing if it would have done any good.

Instead, he scowled at his room, the huddled backs of the canvases, the drifts of discarded food and clothing, the heap of his bed, wondering if Elanore was watching him now, thrusting a spare few gigabytes into the sensors of some nano-insect that was hovering close beside him. Indeed, he half expected the thin partitions and dangling wires, all the mocking rubbish of his life, to shudder and change into snowy Russian parkland, a wooded glade, even Paris again, 1890. But none of that happened.

The positive credit light still glowed enticingly within the terminal. In the almost certain knowledge that he would regret it, but quite unable to stop himself, Gustav scrolled through the pathways that led him to the little-frequented section dealing with artist's foreal requisites. Keeping it simple—down to fresh brushes, and Lefranc and Bourgeois's extra-fine Flake White, Cadmium Yellow, Vermilion, Deep Madder, Cobalt Blue, and Emerald Green—and still waiting as the cost all of that clocked up for the familiar credit-expired sign to arrive, he closed the screen.

The materials arrived far quicker than he'd expected, disgorging themselves into a service alcove in the far corner with a *whoosh* like the wind. The supplier had even remembered to include the fresh bottles of turpentine he'd forgotten to order—he still had plenty of clean stretched canvases anyway. So here (the feel of the fat new tubes, the beautiful, haunting names of the colors, the faint stirring sounds that the brushes made when he tried to lift them) was everything he might possibly need.

Gustav was an artist.

The hours did funny things when Gustav was painting—or even thinking about painting. They ran fast or slow, passed by on a fairy breeze, or thickened and grew huge as megaliths, then joined up and began to dance lumberingly around him, stamping on every sensibility and hope.

Taking fierce drags of his last Disc Bleu, clouding his tenement's already filmy air, Gustav finally gave up scribbling on his pad and casting sidelong glances at the canvas as the blazing moon began to flood Paris with its own sickly version of evening. As he'd always known he'd probably end up doing, he then began to wander the dim edges of his room, tilting back and examining his old, unsold, and generally unfinished canvases. Especially in this light, and seen from upside down, the scenes of foreal Paris looked suitably wan.

There was so little to them, in fact, such a thinness and lack of color, that they could easily be re-used. But here in the tangled shadows of the furthest corner, filled with colors that seemed to pour into the air like a perfume, lay his early attempts at Symbolism and Impressionism . . . Amid those, he noticed something paler again. In fact, unfinished—but from an era when, as far as he could recall, he'd finished everything. He risked lifting the canvas out, and gazed at the outlines, the dabs of paint, the layers of wash. He recognized it now. It had been his attempt at Manet's *Olympia*.

After Elanore had said her good-byes to all her friends, she retreated into the white virtual corridors of a building near the Cimetière du Père Lachaise that might once have been called a hospital. There, as a final fail-safe, her mind was scanned and stored, the lineaments of her body were recorded. Gustav was the only person Elanore allowed to visit her during those last weeks; she was perhaps already too confused to understand what seeing her like this was doing to him. He'd sit amid the webs of sliver monitoring wires as she absently stroked Metzengerstein, and the cat's eyes, now far greener and brighter than hers, regarded him. She didn't seem to want to fight this loss of self. That was probably the thing that hurt him most. Elanore, the proper foreal Elanore, had always been searching for the next river to cross, the next challenge; it was probably the one characteristic that they had shared. But now she accepted death, this loss of Elanore, with nothing but resignation. *This is the way it is for all us*, Gustav remembered her saying in one of the last cogent periods before she forgot his name. *So many of our friends have passed on already. It's just a matter of joining them . . .*

Elanore never quite lost her beauty, but she became like a doll, a model of herself, and her eyes grew vacant as she sat silent or talked ramblingly. The freckles faded from her skin. Her mouth grew slack. She began to smell sour. There was no great fuss made when they finally turned her off, although Gustav still insisted that he be there. It was a relief, in fact, when Elanore's eyes finally closed and her heart stopped beating, when the hand he'd placed in his turned even more flaccid and cold. Metzengerstein gave Gustav one final glance before it twisted its way between the wires, leaped off the bed, and padded from the room, its tail raised. For a moment, Gustav considered grabbing the thing, slamming it down into a pulp of memory circuits and flesh and metal. But it had already been deprogrammed. Metzengerstein was just a shell; a comforter for Elanore in her last dim days. He never saw the creature again.

Just as the living Elanore had promised, her ghost only returned to Gustav after a decent interval. And she made no assumptions about their future at that first meeting on the neutral ground of a shorefront restaurant in virtual Balbec. She clearly understood how difficult all this was for him. It had been a windy day, he remembered, and the tablecloths flapped, the napkins threatened to take off, the lapel of the cream brocade jacket she was wearing kept lying across her throat until she pinned it back with a brooch. She told him that she still loved him, and that she hoped they would be able to stay together. A few days later, in a room in the same hotel overlooking the same windy beach, Elanore and Gustav made love for the first time since she had died.

The illusion, Gustav had to admit, then and later, was always perfect. And, as the dying Elanore had pointed out, they both already knew many ghosts. There was Marcel, for instance, and there was Jean, Gustav's own dealer and agent. It wasn't as if Elanore had even been left with any choice. In a virtual, ghostly daze himself, Gustav agreed that they should set up home together. They chose Brittany, because it was new to them—unloaded with memories—and the scenery was still often decent and visible enough to be worth painting.

Foreal was going out of style by then. For many years, the technologies of what was called reality had been flawless. But now, they became all-embracing. It was at about this time, Gustav supposed, although his memory once was again dim on this matter, that they set fire to the moon. The ever-bigger reality engines required huge amounts of power—and so it was that the robot ships set out, settled into orbit around the moon, and began to spray the surface with antimatter, spreading their wings like hands held out to a fire to absorb and then transmit back to earth the energies this iridescence gave. The power the moon now provided wasn't quite limitless, but it was near enough. With so much alternative joy and light available, the foreal world, much like a garden left untended, soon began to assume a look of neglect.

Ever considerate to his needs, Elanore chose and had refurbished a gabled clifftop mansion near Locronan, and ordered graceful and foreal furniture at huge extra expense. For a month or so, until the powerlines and transformers of the reality engines had been installed, Gustav and Elanore could communicate with each other only by screen. He did his best to tell himself that being unable to touch her was a kind of tease, and kept his thoughts away from such questions as where exactly Elanore was when she wasn't with him, and if she truly imagined she was the seamless continuation of the living Elanore that she claimed herself to be.

The house smelled of salt and old stone, and then of wet plaster and new carpets, and soon began to look as charming and eccentric as anything Elanore had organized in her life. As for the cost of all this forgotten craftsmanship, which, even in these generous times, was quite daunting, Elanore had discovered, like many of the ghosts who had gone before her, that her work—the dealing in stocks, ideas, and raw megawatts in which she specialized—was suddenly much easier. She could flit across the world, make deals based on long-term calculations that no living person could ever hope to understand.

Often, in the early days when Elanore finally reached the reality of their clifftop house in Brittany, Gustav would find himself gazing at her, trying to catch her unawares, or, in the nights when they made love with an obsessive frequency and passion, he would study her while she was sleeping. If she seemed distracted, he put it down to some deal she was cooking, a new antimatter trail across the Sea of Storms, perhaps, or a business meeting in Capetown. If she sighed and smiled in her dreams, he imagined her in the arms of some long-dead lover.

Of course, Elanore always denied such accusations. She even gave a good impression of being hurt. She was, she insisted, configured to ensure that she was always exactly where she appeared to be, except for brief times and in the gravest of emergencies. In the brain or on the net, human consciousness was a fragile thing—permanently in danger of dissolving. *I really* am *talking to you now, Gustav.* Otherwise, Elanore maintained, she would unravel, she would cease to be Elanore. As if, Gustav thought in generally silent rejoinder, she hadn't ceased to be Elanore already.

She'd changed, for a start. She was cooler, calmer, yet somehow more mercurial. The simple and everyday motions she made, like combing her hair or stirring coffee, began to look stiff and affected. Even her sexual preferences had changed. And passing over *was* different. Yes, she admitted that, even though she could feel the weight and presence of her own body just as she could feel his when he touched her. Once, as the desperation of their arguments increased, she even insisted in stabbing herself with a fork, just so that he might finally understand that she felt pain. But for Gustav, Elanore wasn't like the many other ghosts he'd met and readily accepted. They weren't *Elanore*. He'd never loved and painted *them*.

Gustav soon found that he couldn't paint Elanore now, either. He tried from sketches and from memory; once or twice he got her to pose. But it didn't work. He couldn't quite loose himself enough to forget what she was. They even tried to complete that *Olympia*, although the memory was painful for both of them. She posed for him as Manet's model, who in truth she did look a little like; the same model who'd posed for that odd scene by the river, *Déjeuner sur l'Herbe*. Now, of course, the cat as well as the black maid had to be a projection, although they did their best to make everything else the same. But there was something lost and wan about the painting as he tried to develop it. The nakedness of the woman on the canvas no longer gave off strength and knowledge and sexual assurance. She seemed pliant and helpless. Even the colors grew darker; it was like fighting something in a dream.

Elanore accepted Gustav's difficulties with what he sometimes found to be chillingly good grace. She was prepared to give him time. He could travel. She could develop new interests, burrow within the net as she'd always promised herself, and live in some entirely different place.

Gustav began to take long walks away from the house, along remote clifftop paths and across empty beaches, where he could be alone. The moon and the sun sometimes cast their silver ladders across the water. Soon, Gustav thought sourly, there'll be nowhere left to escape *to*. Or perhaps we will *all* pass on, and the gantries and the ugly virtual buildings that all look like the old Pompidou Centre will cease to be necessary; but for the glimmering of a few electrons, the world will revert to the way it was before people came. We can even extinguish the moon.

He also started to spend more time in the few parts of their rambling house that, largely because much of the stuff they wanted was handbuilt and took some time to order, Elanore hadn't yet had fitted out foreal. He interrogated the house's mainframe to discover the codes that would turn the reality engines off and on at will. In a room filled with tapestries, a long oak table, a vase of hydrangeas, pale curtains lifting slightly in the breeze, all it took was the correct gesture, a mere click of his fingers, and it would shudder and vanish, to be replaced by nothing but walls of mildewed plaster, the faint tingling sensation that came from the receding powerfield. There—then gone. Only the foreal view at the window remained the same. And now, click, and it all came *back* again. Even the fucking vase. The fucking flowers.

Elanore sought him out that day. Gustav heard her footsteps on the stairs, and knew that she'd pretend be puzzled as to why he wasn't working in his studio.

"*There* you are," she said, appearing a little breathless after her climb up the stairs. "I was thinking—"

Finally scratching the itch that he realized had been tickling him for some time, Gustav clicked his fingers. Elanore—and the whole room, the table, the flowers, the tapestries—flickered off.

He waited—several beats, he really didn't know how long. The wind still blew in through the window. The powerfield hummed faintly, waiting for its next command. He clicked his fingers. Elanore and the room took shape again.

"I thought you'd probably override that," he said. "I imagined you'd given yourself a higher priority than the furniture."

"I could if I wished," she said. "I didn't think I'd need to do such a thing."

"No. I mean, you can just go somewhere else, can't you? Some other room in this house. Some other place. Some other continent . . . "

"I keep telling you. It isn't like that."

"I know. Consciousness is fragile."

"And we're really not that different, Gus. I'm made of random droplets held in a force field—but what are *you*? Think about it. You're made of atoms, which are just quantum flickers in the foam of space, particles that aren't even particles at all . . ."

Gustav stared at her. He was remembering—he couldn't help it—that they'd made love the previous night. Just two different kinds of ghost; entwined, joining—he supposed that that was what she was saying. And what about my *cock*, Elanore, and all the stuff that gets emptied into you when we're fucking? What the hell do you do with *that*?

"Look, Gus, this isn't—"

"—And what do you dream at night, Elanore? What is it that you do when you pretend you're sleeping?"

She waved her arms in a furious gesture that Gustav almost recognized from the Elanore of old. "What the hell do you *think* I do, Gus? I *try* to be human. You think it's easy, do you, hanging on like this? You think I enjoy watching *you* flicker in and out?—which is basically what it's like for me every time you step outside these fields? Sometimes I just wish I . . ."

Elanore trailed off there, glaring at him with emerald eyes. Go on, Gustav felt himself urging her. *Say* it, you phantom, shade, wraith, ghost. Say you wish you'd simply died. But instead, she made some internal command of her own, and blanked the room—and vanished.

It was the start of the end of their relationship.

Many guests came to visit their house in the weeks after that, and Elanore and Gustav kept themselves busy in the company of the dead and the living. All the old crowd, all the old jokes. Gustav generally drank too much, and made his presence unwelcome with the female ghosts as he decided that once he'd fucked the nano-droplets in one configuration, he might as well try fucking them in another. What the hell was it, Gus wondered, that made the living so reluctant to give up the dead, and the dead to give up the living?

In the few hours that they did spend together and alone at that time, Elanore and Gustav made detailed plans to travel. The idea was that they (meaning Elanore, with all the credit she was accumulating) would commission a ship, a sailing ship, traditional in every respect apart from the fact that the sails would be huge power receptors driven directly by the moon, and the spars would be the frame of a reality engine. Together, they would get away from all of this, and sail across the foreal oceans, perhaps even as far as Tahiti. Admittedly, Gustav was intrigued by the idea of returning to the painter who by now seemed to be the initial wellspring of his creativity. He was certainly in a suitably grumpy and isolationist mood to head off, as the poverty-stricken and desperate Gauguin had once done, in search of inspiration in the South Seas; and ultimately to his death from the prolonged effects of syphilis. But they never actually discussed what Tahiti would be *like*. Of course, there would be no tourists there now—only eccentrics bothered to travel foreal these days. Gustav liked to think, in fact, that there would be none of the tall ugly buildings and the huge Coca-Cola signs that he'd once seen in an old photograph of Tahiti's main town of Papeete. There might—who knows?—not be any reality engines, even, squatting like spiders across the beaches and jungle. With the understandable way that the birth rate was now declining, there would be just a few natives left, living as they had once lived before Cook and Bligh and all the rest—even Gauguin with his art and his myths and his syphilis—had ruined it for them. That was how Gustav wanted to leave Tahiti.

Winter came to their clifftop house. The guests departed. The wind raised white crests across the ocean. Gustav developed a habit, which Elanore pretended not to notice, of turning the heating down; as if he needed chill and discomfort to make the place seem real. Tahiti, that ship of theirs, remained an impossibly long way off. There were no final showdowns—just this gradual drifting apart. Gustav gave up trying to make love to Elanore, just as he had given up trying to paint her. But they were friendly and cordial with each other. It seemed that neither of them wished to pollute the memory of something that had once been wonderful. Elanore was, Gustav knew, starting to become concerned about his failure to have his increasing signs of age treated, and his refusal to have a librarian; even his insistence on pursuing a career that seemed only to leave him depleted and damaged. But she never said anything.

They agreed to separate for a while. Elanore would head off to explore pure virtuality. Gustav would go back to foreal Paris and try to rediscover his art. And so, making promises they both knew they would never keep, Gustav and Elanore finally parted.

Gustav slid his unfinished *Olympia* back down amid the other canvases. He looked out of the window, and saw from the glow coming up through the gaps in the houses that the big reality engines were humming. The evening, or whatever other time and era it was, was in full swing.

A vague idea forming in his head, Gustav pulled on his coat and headed out from his tenement. As he walked down through the misty, smoggy streets, it almost began to feel like inspiration. Such was his absorption that he didn't even bother to avoid the shining bubbles of the reality engines. Paris, at the end of the day, still being Paris, the realities he passed through mostly consisted of one or another sort of café, but there were set amid dazzling souks, dank medieval alleys, yellow and seemingly watery places where swam strange creatures that he couldn't think to name. But his attention wasn't on it anyway.

The Musée D'Orsay was still kept in reasonably immaculate condition beside the faintly luminous and milky Seine. Outside and in, it was well lit, and a trembling barrier kept in the air that was necessary to preserve its contents until the time came when they were fashionable again. Inside, it even *smelled* like an art gallery, and Gustav's footsteps echoed on the polished floors, and the robot janitors greeted him; in every way, and despite all the years since he'd last visited, the place was the same.

Gustav walked briskly past the statues and the bronze casts, past Ingres's big, dead canvases of supposedly voluptuous nudes. Then Moreau, early Degas, Corot, Millet . . . Gustav did his best to ignore them all. For the fact was that Gustav hated art galleries—he was still, at least, a painter in that respect. Even in the years when he'd gone deliberately to such places, because he knew that they were good for his own development, he still liked to think of himself as a kind of burglar—get in, grab your ideas, get out again. Everything else, all the ahhs and the oohs, was for mere spectators . . .

He took the stairs to the upper floor. A cramp had worked its way beneath his diaphragm and his throat felt raw, but behind all of that there was this feeling, a tingling of power and magic and anger—a sense that perhaps . . .

Now that he was up amid the rooms and corridors of the great Impressionist works, he forced himself to slow down. The big gilt frames, the pompous marble, the names and dates of artists who had often died in anonymity, despair, disease, blindness, exile, near-starvation. Poor old Sisley's *Misty Morning*. Vincent Van Gogh in a self-portrait formed from deep, sensuous, three-dimensional oils. Genuinely great art was, Gustav thought, pretty depressing for would-be great artists. If it hadn't been for the invisible fields that were protecting these paintings, he would have considered ripping the things off the walls, destroying them.

His feet led him back to the Manets, that woman gazing out at him from *Dejéuner sur l'Herbe*, and then again from *Olympia*. She wasn't beautiful, didn't even look much like Elanore . . . But that wasn't the point. He drifted on past the clamoring canvases, wondering if the world had ever been this bright, this new, this wondrously chaotic. Eventually, he found himself face-to-face with the surprisingly few Gauguins that the Musée D'Orsay possessed. Those bright slabs of color, those mournful Tahitian natives, which were often painted on raw sacking because it was all Gauguin could get his hands on in the hot stench of his tropical hut. He became wildly fashionable after his death, of course; the idea of destitution on a faraway isle suddenly stuck everyone as romantic. But it was too late for Gauguin by then. And too late—as his hitherto worthless paintings were snapped up by Russians, Danes, Englishmen, Americans—for these stupid, habitually arrogant Parisians. Gauguin was often poor at dealing with his shapes, but he generally got away with it. And his sense of color was like no one else's. Gustav remembered vaguely now that there was a nude that Gauguin had painted as his own lopsided tribute to Manet's *Olympia*—had even pinned a photograph of it to the wall of his hut as he worked. But, like most of Gauguin's other really important paintings, it wasn't here at the Musée D'Orsay, this supposed epicenter of Impressionist and Symbolist art. Gustav shrugged and turned away. He hobbled slowly back down through the galley.

Outside, beneath the moonlight, amid the nanosmog and the buzzing of the powerfields, Gustav made his way once again through the realities. An English tea house circa 1930. A Guermantes salon. If they'd been foreal, he'd have sent the cups and the plates flying, bellowed in the self-satisfied faces of the dead and living. Then he stumbled into a scene he recognized from the Musée D'Orsay, one, in fact, that had once been as much a cultural icon as Madonna's tits or a Beatles tune. *Le Moulin de la Galette*. He was surprised and almost encouraged to see Renoir's Parisian figures in their Sunday-best clothing, dancing under the trees in the dappled sunlight, or chatting at the surrounding benches and tables. He stood and watched, nearly smiling. Glancing down, saw that he was dressed appropriately in a rough woollen navy suit. He studied the figures, admiring their animation, the clever and, yes, convincing way that, through some trick of reality, they were composed. . . . Then he realized that he recognized some of the faces, and that they had also recognized him. Before he could turn back, he was called to and beckoned over.

"Gustav," Marcel's ghost said, sliding an arm around him, smelling of male sweat and Pernod. "Grab a chair. Sit down. Long time no see, eh?"

Gustav shrugged and accepted the brimming tumbler of wine that was offered. If it was foreal—which he doubted—this and a few more of the same might help him sleep tonight. "I thought you were in Venice," he said. "As the Doge."

Marcel shrugged. There were breadcrumbs on his mustache. "That was *ages* ago. Where have you been, Gustav?"

"Just around the corner, actually."

"Not still *painting* are you?"

Gustav allowed that question to be lost in the music and the conversation's ebb and flow. He gulped his wine and looked around, expecting to see Elanore at any moment. So many of the others were here—it was almost like old times. There, even, was Francine, dancing with a top-hatted man—so she clearly wasn't across the sky. Gustav decided to ask the girl in the striped dress who was nearest to him if she'd seen Elanore. He realized as he spoke to her that her face was familiar to him, but he somehow couldn't recollect her name—even whether she was living or a ghost. She shook her head, and asked the woman who stood leaning behind her. But she, also, hadn't seen Elanore; not, at least, since the times when Marcel was in Venice and when Francine was across the sky. From there, the question rippled out across the square. But no one, it seemed, knew what had happened to Elanore.

Gustav stood up and made his way between the twirling dancers and the lantern-strung trees. His skin tingled as he stepped out of the reality, and the laughter and the music suddenly faded. Avoiding any other such encounters, he made his way back up the dim streets to his tenement.

There, back at home, the light from the setting moon was bright enough for him to make his way through the dim wreckage of his life without falling—and the terminal that Elanore's ghost had reactivated still gave off a virtual glow. Swaying, breathless, Gustav paged down into his accounts, and saw the huge sum—the kind of figure that he associated with astronomy, with the distance of the moon from the earth, the earth from the sun—that now appeared there. Then he passed back through the terminal's levels, and began to search for Elanore.

But Elanore wasn't there.

Gustav was painting. When he felt like this, he loved and hated the canvas in almost equal measures. The outside world, foreal or in reality, ceased to exist for him.

A woman, naked, languid, and with a dusky skin quite unlike Elanore's, is lying upon a couch, half-turned, her face cupped in her hand that lies upon the primrose pillow, her eyes gazing away from the onlooker at something far off. She seems beautiful but unerotic, vulnerable yet clearly available, and self-absorbed. Behind her— amid the twirls of bright yet gloomy decoration—lies a glimpse of stylized rocks under a strange sky, while two oddly disturbing figures are talking, and a dark bird perches on the lip of a balcony; perhaps a raven . . .

Although he detests plagiarism, and is working solely from memory, Gustav finds it hard to break away from Gauguin's nude on this canvas he is now painting. But he really isn't fighting that hard to do so, anyway. In this above all of Gauguin's great paintings, stripped of the crap and the despair and the self-justifying symbolism, Gauguin was simply *right*. So Gustav still keeps working, and the paint sometimes almost seems to want to obey him. He doesn't know or care at the moment what the thing will turn out like. If it's good, he might think of it as his tribute to Elanore; and if it isn't . . . Well, he knows that, once he's finished this painting, he will start another one. Right now, that's all that matters.

Elanore was right, Gustav decides, when she once said that he was entirely selfish, and would sacrifice everything—himself included—just so that he could continue to paint. She was eternally right and, in her own way, she too was always searching for the next challenge, the next river to cross. Of course, they should have made more of the time that they had together, but as Elanore's ghost admitted at that Van Gogh café when she finally came to say good-bye, nothing could ever quite be the same.

Gustav stepped back from his canvas and studied it, eyes halfclosed at first just to get the shape, then with a more appraising gaze. Yes, he told himself, and reminded himself to tell himself again later when he began to feel sick and miserable about it, this is a true work. This is worthwhile.

Then, and although there was much that he still had to do, and the oils were still wet, and he knew that he should rest the canvas, he swirled his brush in a blackish puddle of palette-mud and daubed the word NEVERMORE across the top, and stepped back again, wondering what to paint *next*.

PERMISSIONS

GARDNER DOZOIS has been honored with the Hugo
Award for Best Editor eight times and has twice received
the Nebula Award for his own short fiction. He is the editor
of *Isaac Asimov's Science Fiction Magazine* and lives in
Philadelphia, Pennsylvania.